Praise for Karen Marie Moning's
KISS OF THE HIGHLANDER

"Moning's snappy prose, quick wit, and charismatic
characters will enchant."
—*Publishers Weekly*

"Moning is quickly building a reputation for writing
poignant time travels with memorable characters. This
may be the first book I've read by her, but it certainly
won't be my last. She delivers compelling stories with
passionate characters readers will find enchanting."
—*The Oakland Press*

"RITA award–winning romance author Karen Marie
Moning pens another contender for that coveted award.
Kiss of the Highlander belongs on everyone's list of best
novels of the year." —*Romance Reviews Today*

"*Kiss of the Highlander* IS WONDERFUL. . . . Her
storytelling skills are impressive, her voice and pacing
dynamic, and her plot as tight as a cask of
good Scotch whisky."
—*The Contra Costa Times*

"If you enjoy a brisk-paced book, an ingenious plot,
good humor, and erotic love scenes, then you won't
want to miss *Kiss of the Highlander*."
—*Romance Fiction Forum*

"*Kiss of the Highlander* is a showstopper."
—*Rendezvous*

The
DARK
HIGHLANDER

KAREN MARIE MONING

A DELL BOOK

A Dell Book
Published by
Dell Publishing
a division of
Random House, Inc.
New York, New York

Copyright © 2002 by Karen Marie Moning
Cover art by Franco Accornero

Dell® is a registered trademark of Random House, Inc., and the colophon is a trademark of Random House, Inc.

ISBN: 0-440-23755-6

Manufactured in the United States of America

Published simultaneously in Canada

October 2002

10   9   8   7   6   5   4   3   2   1
OPM

*This one is for the women
who made it possible through their extraordinary
encouragement, support, and patience:
Deidre Knight, Wendy McCurdy,
and Nita Taublib—thank you!*

Time is the coin of your life.
It is the only coin you have,
and only you can determine how it will be spent,
Be careful lest you let other people spend it for you.

—CARL SANDBURG

FIRST PROLOGUE

In a place difficult for humans to find, a man, of sorts—
it amused him to go by the name of Adam Black among
mortals—approached a silk-canopied dais and knelt before his queen.

"My queen, The Compact is broken."

Aoibheal, queen of the Tuatha Dé Danaan, was silent
for a long time. When finally she turned to her consort,
her voice dripped ice. "Summon the council."

SECOND PROLOGUE

Thousands of years before the birth of Christ, there settled in Ireland a race called the Tuatha Dé Danaan who, over time, became known as the True Race, or the Fairy.

An advanced civilization from a faraway world, the Tuatha Dé Danaan educated some of the more promising humans they encountered in Druid ways. For a time, man and fairy shared the earth in peace, but sadly, bitter dissension arose between them, and the Tuatha Dé Danaan decided to move on. Legend claims they were driven "under the hills" into "fairy mounds." The truth is they never left our world, but hold their fantastic court in places difficult for humans to find.

After the Tuatha Dé Danaan left, the human Druids warred among themselves, splintering into factions. Thirteen of them turned to dark ways and—thanks to what the Tuatha Dé Danaan had taught them—nearly destroyed the earth.

The Tuatha Dé Danaan emerged from their hidden places and stopped the dark Druids moments before they succeeded in damaging the earth beyond repair. They stripped the Druids of their power, scattering them to the far corners of the earth. They punished the thirteen who'd turned dark by casting them into a place between dimensions, locking their immortal souls in an eternal prison.

The Tuatha Dé Danaan then selected a noble bloodline, the Keltar, to use the sacred knowledge to rebuild and nurture the land. Together, they negotiated The Compact: the treaty governing cohabitation of their races. The Keltar swore many oaths to the Tuatha Dé Danaan, first and foremost that they would never use the power of the standing stones—which give the man who knows the sacred formulas the ability to move through space and time—for personal gain or political ends. The Tuatha Dé Danaan pledged many things in return, first and foremost that they would never spill the lifeblood of a mortal. Both races have long abided by the pledges made that day.

Over the ensuing millennia, the MacKeltar journeyed to Scotland and settled in the Highlands above what is now called Inverness. Although most of their ancient history from the time of their involvement with the Tuatha Dé Danaan has melted into the mists of their distant past and been forgotten, and although there is no record of a Keltar encountering a Tuatha Dé Danaan since then, they have never strayed from their sworn purpose.

Pledged to serve the greater good of the world, no MacKeltar has ever broken his sacred oath. On the few occasions they have opened a gate to other times within the circle of stones, it has been for the noblest of reasons:

to protect the earth from great peril. An ancient legend holds that if a MacKeltar breaks his oath and uses the stones to travel through time for personal purposes, the myriad souls of the darkest Druids trapped in the in-between will claim him and make him the most evil, terrifyingly powerful Druid humankind has ever known.

In the late-fifteenth century, twin brothers Drustan and Dageus MacKeltar are born. As their ancestors before them, they protect the ancient lore, nurture the land, and guard the coveted secret of the standing stones.

Honorable men, without corruption, Dageus and Drustan serve faithfully.

Until one fateful night, in a moment of blinding grief, Dageus MacKeltar violates the sacred Compact.

When his brother Drustan is killed, Dageus enters the circle of stones and goes back in time to prevent Drustan's death. He succeeds, but between dimensions is taken by the souls of the evil Druids, who have not tasted or touched or smelled, not made love or danced or vied for power for nearly four thousand years.

Now Dageus MacKeltar is a man with one good conscience—and thirteen bad ones. Although he can hold his own for a while, his time is growing short.

The darkest Druid currently resides in the East 70s in Manhattan, and that is where our story begins.

· 1 ·

Dageus MacKeltar walked like a man and talked like a man, but in bed he was pure animal.

Criminal attorney Katherine O'Malley called a spade a spade, and the man was raw Sex with a capital S. Now that she'd slept with him, she was ruined for other men.

It wasn't just what he looked like, with his sculpted body, skin poured like gold velvet over steel, chiseled features, and silky black hair. Or that lazy, utterly arrogant smile that promised a woman paradise. And delivered. One hundred percent satisfaction guaranteed.

It wasn't even the exotic golden eyes fringed by thick black lashes beneath slanted brows.

It was what he did to her.

He was sex like she'd never had in her life, and Katherine had been having sex for seventeen years. She thought she'd seen it all. But when Dageus MacKeltar touched her, she came apart at the seams. Aloof, his every movement smoothly controlled, when he stripped off his clothing he stripped off every ounce of that rigid discipline and turned into an untamed barbarian. He fucked with the single-minded intensity of a man on death row, execution at dawn.

Just thinking about him made places low in her belly clench. Made her skin feel stretched too tight across her bones. Made her breath come short and sharp.

Now, standing in the anteroom outside the enameled French doors of his exquisite Manhattan penthouse overlooking Central Park that fit him like a second skin—starkly elegant, black, white, chrome, and hard—she felt intensely alive, every nerve wired. Drawing a deep breath, she turned the handle and pushed open the door.

It was never locked. As if he feared nothing forty-three floors above the flash and razor edges of the city. As if he'd seen the worst the Big Apple had to offer and found it all mildly amusing. As if the city might be big and bad, but he was bigger and badder.

She stepped inside, inhaling the rich scent of sandalwood and roses. Classical music spilled through the luxurious rooms—Mozart's *Requiem*—but she knew that later he might play Nine Inch Nails and stretch her naked body against the wall of windows that overlooked the Conservatory Water, driving into her until she screamed her release to the bright city lights below.

Sixty feet of coveted Fifth Avenue frontage in the East 70s—and she had no idea what he did for a living. Most of the time she wasn't certain she wanted to know.

She pushed the doors shut behind her and allowed the buttery-soft folds of her leather coat to spill to the floor, revealing black lace-topped thigh-highs, matching panties, and a sheer push-up bra that presented her full breasts to perfection. She caught a glimpse of her reflection in the darkened windows and smiled. At thirty-three, Katherine O'Malley looked good. She should look good, she thought, arching a brow, as much exercise as she'd been getting in his bed. Or on the floor. Sprawled across the leather sofa. In his black marble Jacuzzi . . .

A wave of lust made her dizzy, and she breathed deeply to slow her pounding heart. She felt insatiable around him. A time or two she'd briefly entertained the outrageous thought that he might not be human. That maybe he was some mythical sex god, perhaps Priapus beckoned by the needy inhabitants of the city that never slept. Or some creature of long-forgotten lore, a *Sidhe* that had the ability to heighten pleasure to extremes mortals weren't meant to taste.

"Katie-lass." His voice floated down from the top floor of the fifteen-room duplex, dark and rich, his Scottish accent making her think of peat smoke, ancient stones, and aged whisky.

Only Dageus MacKeltar could get away with calling Katherine O'Malley "Katie-lass."

As he descended the curving staircase and entered the thirty-foot living room with its vaulted ceilings, marble fireplace, and panoramic view of the park, she remained motionless, drinking him in. He wore black linen trousers, and she knew there would be nothing beneath them but the most perfect male body she'd ever seen. Her gaze drifted over his wide shoulders, down his hard chest and his rippling abs, lingering on the twin ropes of muscle that cut his lower stomach and disappeared into his pants, beckoning the eye to follow.

"Good enough to eat?" His golden eyes glittered as they raked her body. "Come." He extended his hand. "Lass, you take my breath away. Your wish is my command this eve. You have only to tell me."

His long midnight hair, so black it seemed as blue-black as his shadow beard in the amber glow of recessed lights, spilled over one muscled shoulder, falling to his waist, and she sucked in a quick breath. She knew the feel of it sweeping her bare breasts, abrading her nipples, falling lower, across her thighs as he brought her to peak after shuddering peak.

"As if I need to say anything. You know what I want before I know myself." She heard the edge in her voice, knew he heard it too. It unnerved her how well he understood her. Before she knew what she wanted, he was giving it to her.

It made him dangerously addictive.

He smiled, but it didn't quite reach his eyes. She wasn't certain she'd ever seen it reach his eyes. They never changed, merely observed and waited. Like a tiger's golden eyes, his were watchful yet aloof, amused yet detached. Hungry eyes. Predator eyes. More than once she'd wanted to ask what those tiger-eyes saw. What judgment they passed, what the hell he seemed to be waiting for, but in the bliss of his hard body against hers she forgot time and again, until she was back at work and it was too late to ask.

She'd been sleeping with him for two months, and knew no more about him now than the day she'd met him in Starbucks, across the street from O'Leary Banks and O'Malley, where she was a partner, thanks partly to her father, the senior O'Malley, and partly to her own ruthlessness. One look at the six foot four, darkly seductive man over the rim of her café au lait and she'd known she had to have him. It might have had something to do with the way he'd locked eyes with her as he'd lazily licked whipped cream off his mocha, making her imagine that sexy tongue doing far more intimate things. It might have had something to do with the pure sexual heat he gave off. She knew it had a great deal to do with the danger that rolled off him. Some days she wondered if she'd be defending him as one of her controversial high-profile clients in the months or years to come.

That same day they'd met, they'd rolled across his white Berber carpet, from fireplace to windows, wrestling silently for the supreme position, until she'd no longer cared how he'd taken her, so long as he had.

With a reputation for a razor-sharp tongue and the mind to back it up, she'd never once turned it on him. She had no idea how he maintained his lavish lifestyle, how he afforded his obscenely expensive collections of art and ancient weapons. She didn't know where he'd been born, or even when his birthday was.

At work, she'd mentally prepare her interrogatory, but inevitably the probing questions stalled on her tongue the moment she saw him. She, the merciless interrogator in a courtroom, tongue-tied in his bedroom. On occasion, tied in infinitely more pleasurable ways. The man was a true master of the erotic.

"Woolgatherin', lass? Or merely deciding how you want me?" he purred.

Katherine wet her lips. *How she wanted him?*

She *wanted* him out of her system. Kept hoping the next time she slept with him, the sex might not be so mind-blowing. The man was far too dangerous to get involved with emotionally. Just yesterday she'd lingered at Mass, praying that she would get over her addiction to him—*please, God, soon.* Yes, he heated her blood, but there was something about him that chilled her soul.

In the meantime—hopelessly fascinated as she was— she knew exactly how she would have him. A strong woman, she was aroused by the strength of a dominant man. She would end the night sprawled over his leather sofa. He would fist his hand in her long hair, drive into her from behind. He would bite the nape of her neck when she came.

She inhaled sharply, took one step forward, and he was on her, dragging her down to the thick carpet. Firm lips, sensual, with a hint of cruelty, closed over hers as he kissed her, golden eyes narrowing.

There was something about him that bordered on terrifying, she thought as he pinned her hands to the floor and rose over her, too beautiful, rife with dark secrets she suspected no woman should ever know—and it made the sex so much more exquisite, that fine edge of danger.

It was her last coherent thought for a long, long time.

🐾

Dageus MacKeltar braced his palms against the wall of windows and stared out into the night, his body separated from a plunge of forty-three stories by a pane of glass. The soft buzz of the television was nearly lost in the patter of rain against the windows. A few feet to his right, the sixty-inch screen was reflected in the glistening glass and David Boreanaz stalked broodingly, playing *Angel*, the tortured vampire with a soul. Dageus watched long enough to ascertain it was a repeat, then let his gaze drift back to the night.

The vampire always found at least partial resolution, and Dageus had begun to fear that for him, there would be none. Ever.

Besides, his problem was a little more complicated than Angel's. Angel's problem was a soul. Dageus's problem was a legion of them.

Raking a hand through his hair, he studied the city below. Manhattan: A mere twenty-two square miles. Inhabited by nearly two million people. Then there was the metropolis itself, with seven million people crammed into three hundred square miles.

It was a city of grotesque proportions to a sixteenth-century Highlander, the sheer immensity inconceivable. When he'd first arrived in New York City, he'd walked around the Empire State Building for hours. One hundred and two floors, ten million bricks, the interior thirty-seven million cubic feet, one thousand two hundred and fifty feet tall, it was struck by lightning an average of five hundred times per year.

What manner of man built such monstrosities? he'd wondered. Sheer insanity was what it was, the Highlander had marveled.

And a fine place to call home.

New York City had beckoned the darkness within him. He'd made his lair in the pulsing heart of it.

A man without clan, outcast, nomad, he'd doffed the sixteenth-century man like so much worn plaid and applied his formidable Druid intellect to assimilating the twenty-first century: the new language, the customs, the incredible technology. Though there were still many things he didn't understand—certain words and expressions utterly stumped him, and more often than not he thought in Gaelic, Latin, or Greek and had to hastily translate—he'd adapted at a remarkable rate.

A man who possessed the esoteric knowledge to open a gate through time, he'd *expected* five centuries to make the world a vastly different place. His understanding of Druid lore, sacred geometry, cosmology, and natural laws of what the twenty-first century called physics had made the wonders of the new world easier for him to fathom.

Not that he didn't frequently gawk. He did. Flying on a plane had fashed him greatly. The clever engineering and fabulous construction of Manhattan's bridges had kept him occupied for days.

The people, the masses of teeming people, bewildered

him. He suspected they always would. There was a part of the sixteenth-century Highlander he'd never be able to change. That part would forever miss wide-open expanses of starry sky, leagues and leagues of rolling hills, endless fields of heather, and blithesome and bonny Scots lasses.

He'd ventured to America because he'd hoped that journeying far from his beloved Scotland, from places of power such as the standing stones, might lessen the hold of the ancient evil inside him.

And it *had* affected them, though it had only slowed his descent into darkness, not stopped it. Day by day he continued to change . . . felt colder, less connected, less fettered by human emotion. More detached god, less man.

Except when he tooped—och, then he was alive. *Then* he felt. Then he was not adrift in a bottomless, dark, and violent sea with naught but a puny bit of driftwood to cling to. Making love to a woman staved off the darkness, replenished his essential humanity. Ever a man of immense appetites, he was now insatiable.

I'm no' entirely dark yet, he growled defiantly to the demons coiled within him. The ones who bided their time in silent certainty, their dark tide eroding him as steadily and surely as the ocean reshaped a rocky shore. He understood their tactics: True evil didn't aggressively assault, it lay coyly hushed and still . . . and seduced.

And it was there each day, clear evidence of their gains, in the little things he did without realizing he was doing them till after they were done. Seemingly harmless things like lighting the fire in his hearth with a wave of his hand and a whispered *teine,* or the opening of a door or blind with a soft murmur. The impatient summoning of one of their conveyances—a taxi—with a glance.

Wee things, mayhap, but he knew such things were far

from harmless. Knew that each time he used magic, he turned a shade darker, lost another piece of himself.

Each day was a battle to accomplish three things: use only what magic was absolutely necessary, despite the ever-growing temptation, toop hard and fast and frequently, and continue collecting and searching the tomes wherein might lie the answer to his all-consuming question.

Was there a way to get rid of the dark ones?

If not . . . well, if not . . .

He raked a hand through his hair and blew out a deep breath. Eyes narrowed, he watched the lights flickering beyond the park, while behind him, on the couch, the lass slept the dreamless sleep of the utterly exhausted. On the morrow, dark circles would mar the delicate hollows beneath her eyes, etching her features with beguiling fragility. His bed play took a toll on a woman.

Two nights past, Katie had wet her lips and oh-so-casually remarked that he seemed to be waiting for something.

He'd smiled and rolled her onto her stomach. Kissed her sweet, warm, and willing body from head to toe. Dragged his tongue over every inch, then taken her, ridden her, and when he'd finished with her she'd been crying with pleasure.

She'd either forgotten her question or had thought better of it. Katie O'Malley was not a fool. She knew there was more to him than she really wanted to know. She wanted him for sex, nothing more. Which was well and fine, because he was incapable of more.

I wait for my brother, lass, he hadn't said. *I wait for the day Drustan wearies of my refusal to return to Scotland. For the day his wife is not so pregnant that he fears to leave her side. For the day he finally acknowledges what he already knows in his heart, though he so desperately clings to my lies: that I am dark as the night sky, with but a few starlike flickers of light left within me.*

Och, aye, he was waiting for the day his twin brother would cross the ocean and come for him.

See him for the animal he was.

If he permitted that day to arrive, he knew one of them would die.

· 2 ·

Across the ocean in not Scotland but England, a land where Drustan MacKeltar had once erroneously claimed the Druids scarce possessed enough knowledge to weave a simple sleep spell, a hushed and urgent conversation was taking place.

"Have you made contact?"

"I dare not, Simon. The transformation is not yet complete."

"But it has been many months since the Draghar took him!"

"He is a Keltar. Though he cannot win, still he resists. It is the power that will corrupt him, and he refuses to use it."

A long silence. Then Simon said, "We have waited thousands of years for their return, as was promised us in the Prophecy. I weary of waiting. Push him. Give him reason to *need* the power. We will not lose the battle this time."

A quick nod. "I will take care of it."

"Be subtle, Giles. Do not yet alert him to our existence. When the time is right, I will do so. And should anything go wrong . . . well, you know what to do."

Another quick nod, an anticipatory smile, a flutter of cloth and his companion was gone, leaving him alone in the circle of stones beneath a fiery English dawn.

The man who'd given the order, Simon Barton-Drew, master of the Druid sect of the Draghar, leaned back against a mossy stone, absently stroking the winged-serpent tattoo on his neck, his gaze skimming the ancient monoliths. A tall, lean man with salt-and-pepper hair, a narrow foxlike face and restless gray eyes that missed nothing, he was honored that such an auspicious moment had come in his hour of rule. He'd been waiting thirty-two years for this moment, since the birth of his first son, which had coincided with the day he'd been initiated into the sect's inner sanctum. There were those like the Keltar, who served the Tuatha Dé Danaan, and there were those like himself, who served the Draghar. The Druid sect of the Draghar had kept the faith for thousands of years, handing the Prophecy down from one generation to the next: the promise of the return of their ancient leaders, the promise of the one who would lead them to glory. The one who would take back all the power the Tuatha Dé Danaan had stolen from them so long ago.

He smiled. How fitting that one of the Tuatha Dé's own cherished Keltar now held within him the power of the ancient Draghar—the league of thirteen most powerful Druids that had ever lived. How poetic that one of the Tuatha Dé's very own would finally destroy them.

And reclaim the Druids' rightful place in the world.

Not as the much maligned, tree-hugging, mistletoe-gathering fools they'd permitted the world to believe them to be.

But as rulers of mankind.

※

"You've *got* to be kidding me," Chloe Zanders snapped, raking her long curly hair from her face with both hands. "You want me to take the third Book of Manannán—and yes, I know it's only a reproduction of a portion of the original, but it's still priceless—to some man on the East Side who's probably going to eat *popcorn* while he paws through it? It's not as if he might actually read it. The parts that aren't in Latin are in old Gaelic." Fists at her waist, she glared up at her boss, one of several cocurators of the medieval collection housed in The Cloisters and The Met. "What does he want it for? Did he say?"

"I didn't ask," Tom replied, shrugging.

"Oh, that's just great. You didn't ask." Chloe shook her head disbelievingly. Though the copy her fingers currently rested delicately upon was not illuminated, and was a mere five centuries old—nearly a thousand years younger than the original texts that resided in the National Museum of Ireland—it was a sacred bit of history, demanding utmost reverence and respect.

Not to be toted about the city, entrusted to the hands of a stranger.

"How much did he donate?" she asked irritably. She knew a bribe of sorts must have changed hands. One didn't "check things out" of The Cloisters any more than one could stroll up to Trinity College and ask to borrow the Book of Kells.

"A jeweled fifteenth-century *skean dhu* and a priceless Damascus blade," Tom said, smiling beatifically. "The

Damascus dates to the Crusades. Both have been authenticated."

A delicate brow rose. Awe made short work of outrage. "Wow. Really?" A *skean dhu*! Her fingers curled in anticipation. "Do you have them already?" Antiquities; she loved them one and all, from the single rosary bead with the entire scene of The Passion carved on it, to the Unicorn Tapestries, to the splendid collection of medieval blades.

But she especially loved all things Scottish, as they reminded her of the grandfather who'd raised her. When her parents died in a car accident, Evan MacGregor swooped in and took the broken four-year-old to a new home in Kansas. Proud of his heritage, endowed with a passionate Scots temperament, he imbued her with his love for all things Celtic. It was a dream of hers to one day journey to Glengarry, to see the town in which he'd been born, to visit the church in which he'd wed Gran, to stroll the heathery moors beneath a silvery moon. She had her passport ready, waiting for that lovely stamp; she just had to save enough money.

It might take her another year or two, especially now with the cost of living in New York, but she would get there. And she couldn't wait. As a child she'd been lulled to sleep on countless nights by her grandfather's soft burr, as he'd woven fantastic tales of his homeland. When he died five years ago she'd been devastated. Sometimes, alone at night in The Cloisters, she found herself talking aloud to him, knowing that—though he would have hated city life even more than she did—he would have loved her choice of career. Preserving the artifacts and the old ways.

Her eyes narrowed as Tom's laughter shattered her reverie. He was chuckling over her swift transition from outrage to wonder. She caught herself and pasted a scowl on her face again. It wasn't hard. A stranger was going to be touching a priceless text. Unsupervised. Who knew what might happen to it?

"Yes, I have them already, Chloe. And I didn't ask your opinion of my methods. Your job is to manage the records—"

"Tom, I have my master's in ancient civilizations and speak as many languages as you do. You've always said my opinion counts. Does it or doesn't it?"

"Of course it counts, Chloe," Tom said, sobering swiftly. He removed his glasses and began polishing them with a tie that sported its usual accumulation of coffee stains and jelly-donut crumbs. "But if I hadn't agreed, he was going to donate the blades to the Royal Museum of Scotland. You know how stiff the competition is for quality artifacts. You understand the politics. The man is wealthy, he's generous, and he has quite a collection. We might be able to coax him to draw up some sort of bequest upon his death. If he wants a few days with a five-hundred-year-old text, one of the lesser-valued ones at that, he's going to get it."

"If he so much as gets *one* popcorn smudge on the pages, I'm going to kill him."

"Precisely why I coaxed you here to work for me, Chloe; you love these old things as much as I do. And I acquired two more treasures today, so be a dear and *deliver the text*."

Chloe snorted. Tom knew her too well. He'd been her professor of medieval history at the University of Kansas before he'd assumed a position as cocurator. A year ago he'd tracked her down where she'd been working at a depressing excuse for a museum in Kansas, and offered her a job. Though it had been hard to leave the home she'd grown up in, filled with so many memories, a chance to work at The Cloisters was not to be missed, no matter the extreme culture shock she'd suffered. New York was sleek and hungry and worldly, and in the sophisticated thick of it, the girl from rural Kansas felt hopelessly gauche.

"What, am I supposed to just walk outside with this thing tucked under my arm? With the Gaulish Ghost running around out there?" Lately there'd been a rash of thefts of Celtic manuscripts from private collections. The media had dubbed the thief the Gaulish Ghost because he stole only Celtic items and left no clues behind, appearing and disappearing like a wraith.

"Have Amelia package it up for you. My car's waiting out front. Bill has the man's name and address. He'll drive you there and circle the block while you run it up. And don't harass the man when you deliver it," he added.

Chloe rolled her eyes and sighed, but gently collected the text. As she was walking out, Thomas said, "When you get back I'll show you the blades, Chloe."

His tone was soothing but amused, and it pissed her off. He *knew* she would hurry back to see them. Knew she would overlook his spurious acquisition methods one more time.

"Bribery. Abject bribery," she muttered. "And it *won't* make me approve of what you do." But already she was aching to touch them. To run a finger down the cool metal, to dream of ancient times and ancient places.

Nurtured on Midwest values, an idealist to the core, Chloe Zanders had a weakness, and Tom knew it. Put something ancient in her hands and she was seduced.

And if it was ancient *and* Scottish? Sheesh, she was a goner.

Some days Dageus felt as ancient as the evil within him.

As he hailed a cab to take him to The Cloisters to pick

up a copy of one of the last tomes in New York that he needed to check, he didn't notice the fascinated glances women walking down the sidewalk turned his way. Didn't realize that, even in a metropolis that teemed with diversity, he stood out. It was nothing he said or did; to all appearances he was but another wealthy, sinfully gorgeous man. It was simply the essence of the man. The way he moved. His every gesture exuded power, something dark and . . . forbidden. He was sexual in a way that made women think of deeply repressed fantasies therapists and feminists alike would cringe to hear tell of.

But he realized none of that. His thoughts were far away, still mulling over the nonsense penned in the Book of Leinster.

Och, what he wouldn't give for his da's library.

In lieu of it, he'd been systematically obtaining what manuscripts still existed, exhausting his present possibilities before pursuing riskier ones. Risky, like setting foot on the isles of his ancestors again, a thing fast seeming inevitable.

Thinking of risk, he made a mental note to return some of the volumes he'd "borrowed" from private collections when bribes had failed. It wouldn't do to have them lying about too long.

He glanced up at the clock above the bank. Twelve forty-five. The cocurator of The Cloisters had assured him he would have the text delivered first thing that morn, but it hadn't arrived and Dageus was weary of waiting.

He needed information, *accurate* information about the Keltar's ancient benefactors, the Tuatha Dé Danaan, those "gods and not gods," as the Book of the Dun Cow called them. They were the ones who had originally imprisoned the dark Druids in the in-between, hence it followed that there was a way to reimprison them.

It was imperative he find that way.

As he eased into the cab—a torturous fit for a man of his height and breadth—his attention was caught by a lass who was stepping from a car at the curb in front of them.

She was different, and it was that difference that drew his eye. She had none of the city's polish and was all the lovelier for it. Refreshingly tousled, delightfully free of the artifice with which modern women enhanced their faces, she was a vision.

"Wait," he growled at the driver, watching her hungrily.

His every sense heightened painfully. His hands fisted as desire, never sated, flooded him.

Somewhere in her ancestry the lass had Scots blood. It was there in the curly waves of copper-and-blond hair that tumbled about a delicate face with a surprisingly strong jaw. It was there in the peaches-and-cream complexion and the huge aquamarine eyes—eyes that still regarded the world with wonder, he noticed with a faintly mocking smile. It was there in a fire that simmered just beneath the surface of her flawless skin. Wee, lusciously plump where it counted, with a trim waist and shapely legs hugged by a snug skirt, the lass was an exiled Highlander's dream.

He wet his lips and stared, making a noise deep in his throat that was more animal than human.

When she leaned back in through the open window of the car to say something to the driver, the back of her skirt rode up a few inches. He inhaled sharply, envisioning himself behind her. His entire body went tight with lust.

Christ, she was lovely. Lush curves that could make a dead man stir.

She leaned forward a smidgen, showing more of that sweet curve of the back of her thigh.

His mouth went ferociously dry.

No' for me, he warned himself, gritting his teeth and shifting to lessen the pressure on his suddenly, painfully hard cock. He took only experienced lasses to his bed. Lasses far older in both mind and body. Not reeking, as she did, of innocence. Of bright dreams and a bonny future.

Sleek and worldly, with jaded palates and cynical hearts—they were the ones a man could tumble and leave with a bauble in the morn, no worse for the wear.

She was the kind a man kept.

"Go," he murmured to the driver, forcing his gaze away.

⸙

Chloe tapped her foot impatiently, leaning against the wall beside the call-desk. The blasted man wasn't there. She'd been waiting fifteen minutes, hoping he might appear. A few moments ago she'd finally told Bill to go on without her, that she'd catch a cab back to The Cloisters and expense it to the department.

She drummed her fingers impatiently on the counter. She just wanted to deliver her parcel and go. The sooner she got rid of it, the sooner she could forget her part in the whole sordid affair.

It occurred to her that unless she could find an alternative, she was probably going to end up wasting the rest of her day. A man who lived in the East 70s in such affluence was a man accustomed to having others await his convenience.

Glancing about, she spied a possible alternative. Taking a deep breath and smoothing her suit, she tucked the parcel beneath her arm and strode briskly across the elegant grand foyer to the security desk. Two beefy men in crisp black-and-white uniforms snapped to attention as she approached.

When she'd first arrived in New York last year, she'd known instantly that she would never be in the same league with city women. Polished and chic, they were Mercedes and BMWs and Jaguars, and Chloe Zanders was a . . . Jeep, or maybe a Toyota Highlander on a good day. Her purse never matched her shoes—she was lucky if her *shoe* matched her shoe. Still, she believed in working with what one had, so she did her best to put a little feminine charm into her walk, praying she wouldn't break an ankle.

"I have a delivery for Mr. MacKeltar," she announced, curving her lips in what she hoped was a flirtatious smile, trying to soften them up enough that they'd let her go drop the blasted thing off where it would be a bit more secure. No way she was giving it to the pimply teen behind the call-desk. Nor to these beefy brutes.

Two leering gazes swept her from head to toe. "I'm sure you do, honey," the blond man drawled. He gave her another thorough look. "You're not his usual type though."

"Mr. MacKeltar gets *lots* of deliveries," his dark-haired companion smirked.

Oh, great. Just great. The man's a womanizer. Popcorn and God-only-knows what else on the pages. Grr.

But she supposed she should be thankful, she told herself a few minutes later, as she rode the elevator up to the forty-third floor. They'd let her go up to the penthouse level unescorted, which was astounding in a luxury East-Side property.

Leave it in his anteroom; it's secure enough, the blond had said, though his smarmy gaze had clearly said that he believed the real package was *her*, and he didn't expect to see her again for days, at least.

If Chloe had only known how true that was—that indeed he wouldn't be seeing her again for days—she'd *never* have gotten on that elevator.

⟡⟡⟡

Later, she would also reflect that if only the door hadn't been unlocked, she would have been fine. But when she arrived in Mr. MacKeltar's anteroom, which was overflowing with exotic fresh flowers and furnished with elegant chairs and magnificent rugs, all she'd been able to think was that Security might let some bimbo up, just as they had her, and said bimbo might tear a page out of the priceless text to wad up her chewing gum in, or something equally sacrilegious.

So, sighing, she smoothed her hair and tried one of the double doors.

It slid silently open on—heavens, were those gold-plated hinges? She caught sight of her gaping reflection in one. Some people had more money than sense. Just *one* of those stupid hinges would pay the rent on her tiny efficiency for months.

Shaking her head, she stepped inside and cleared her throat. "Hello?" she called, as it occurred to her that it might be unlocked because he'd left one of his apparently myriad women there.

"Hello, hello!" she called again.

Silence.

Luxury. Like she'd never seen.

She glanced about, and *still* might have been okay if she hadn't spotted the glorious Scottish claymore hanging above the fireplace in the living room. It drew her like a moth to the flame.

"Oh, you gorgeous, lovely, splendid little thing, you," she gushed, hurrying over to it, promising herself she was just going to place the text on the marble coffee table, take a quick glance, and leave.

Twenty minutes later, she was in the midst of a thorough exploration of his home, her heart hammering with nervousness, yet too enthralled to stop.

"How *dare* he leave his door unlocked?" she grumbled, frowning at a magnificent medieval broadsword. Casually propped against the wall in a corner. Ripe for the plucking. Though Chloe prided herself on sound morals, she suffered a shocking urge to tuck it beneath her arm and make a run for it.

The place was full of artifacts—all Celtic at that! Scottish weapons dating back to the fifteenth century, if she didn't miss her guess, and she rarely did, adorned a wall in his library. Priceless Scots regalia: sporran, badge, and brooches in mint condition lay beside a pile of ancient coins on a desk.

She touched, she examined, she shook her head disbelievingly.

Where previously she'd felt nothing but distaste for the man, she was growing fonder of him by the moment, shamelessly seduced by his excellent taste.

And growing more curious about him with each new discovery.

No photos, she noticed, glancing around the rooms. Not one. She'd love to know what the guy looked like.

Dageus MacKeltar. What a name.

Nothing against Zanders, Grandda had often said, *it's a fine name, but it's as easy to fall in love with a Scotsman as an Englishman, lass.* A weighty pause. A harumph. Then, inevitable as sunrise, *Easier, actually.*

She smiled, remembering how he'd endlessly encouraged her to get a "proper" last name for herself.

Her smile froze as she stepped into the bedroom.

Her desire to know what he looked like escalated into obsession territory.

His bedroom, his sinful, decadent bedroom, with the enormous hand-carved, curtained bed covered with silks and velvets, with the exquisitely tiled fireplace, the black marble Jacuzzi in which one might sit sipping champagne, gazing down over Manhattan through a wall of windows. Dozens of candles surrounded the tub. Two glasses had been carelessly knocked over on the Berber carpet.

His scent lingered in the room, scent of man and spice and virility.

Her heart pounded as the enormity of what she was doing occurred to her. She was snooping through a very wealthy man's penthouse, currently standing in the man's bedroom, for heaven's sake! In his very lair where he seduced his women.

And from the looks of things, he had seduction down to a fine art.

Virgin wool carpet, black velvet draping the monstrous bed, silk sheets beneath a sumptuous beaded velvet coverlet, ornate museum-worthy mirrors framed in silver and obsidian.

Despite the warning bells going off in her head, she couldn't seem to make herself leave. Mesmerized, she opened a closet, trailing her fingers over fine hand-tailored clothing, inhaling the subtle, undeniably sexual scent of the man. Exquisite Italian shoes and boots lined the floor.

She began conjuring a fantasy image of him.

He would be tall (she was *not* having short babies!) and handsome, with a nice body, though not too exceptional, and a husky burr. He would be intelligent, speak several languages, (so he could purr Gaelic love words in her ear), but not too polished, a little rough around the edges.

Forget to shave, things like that. He would be a little introverted and sweet. He would like short, curvy women whose noses were in books so much that they forgot to pluck their brows and comb their hair and put on makeup. Women whose shoes didn't always match.

As if, the voice of reason rudely popped her fantasy bubble. *The guy downstairs said you weren't his usual type. Now get out of here, Zanders.*

And it still might not have been too late, she *still* might have escaped had she not moved closer to that sinful bed, peeking curiously and with no small amount of fascination at the silky scarves knotted about bedposts the size of small tree trunks.

Corn-fed-Kansas Chloe was shocked. Never-gone-all-the-way-with-a-man Chloe was . . . suddenly breathing very shallowly, to say the least.

Shakily averting her gaze, and backing away on legs that wobbled, she nearly overlooked the corner of the book poking out from beneath his bed.

But Chloe never missed a book. An ancient one at that.

Moments later, skirt twisted around her hips, purse abandoned on a chair, suit jacket tossed on the floor, she'd dug out his stash: seven medieval volumes.

All of which had been recently reported stolen by various collectors.

Good God—she was in the lair of the nefarious Gaulish Ghost! And it was no wonder he had so many artifacts: He *stole* whatever he wanted.

On her hands and knees, rooting about beneath his bed for more evidence of his heinous crimes, Chloe Zanders' opinion of the man had taken a sharp turn for the worse. "Womanizing, *thieving* creep," she muttered under her breath. "Unbelievable."

Gingerly, with thumb and tip of forefinger, she flung a black lace thong out from under the bed. *Eww.* Condom wrapper. Condom wrapper. Condom wrapper. *Sheesh! How many people lived here?*

Magnum, the wrapper advertised smugly, *for the Extra-Large Man.*

Chloe blinked.

"I've no' yet tried it beneath the bed, lass," a deep Scots burr purred behind her, "but if 'tis your preference . . . and the rest of you is half as lovely as what I'm seeing . . . I might be persuaded to oblige."

Her heart stopped beating.

She froze, her brain stuttering over the fight or flight dilemma. At five foot three, fight wasn't the most promising option. Unfortunately, her brain failed to process the fact that she was still under the bed when it downloaded the surge of adrenaline necessary to flee, so she succeeded only in cracking the back of her head against the solid wood frame.

Woozy, seeing stars, she began to hiccup—a mortifying thing that *always* happened to her when she got nervous, as if simply being nervous weren't bad enough.

She didn't have to back out from under the bed to know she was in very, very deep shit.

· 3 ·

A strong hand clamped around her ankle, and Chloe let out a little scream.

She tried for a big scream, but an inconvenient hiccup turned it into an imploded screech that left her gasping.

Ruthlessly, he tugged her from beneath his bed.

Frantically, she grabbed her skirt with both hands, trying to keep it from bunching up around her waist as she slid inexorably backward. Last thing she wanted to do was make an appearance bare bottom first. Her panty line showed under this particular skirt (which was one reason she didn't wear it often, coupled with the fact that she'd gained a little weight and it was snug), so she'd worn hose with no panties. Not something she did frequently. Figured she'd have to do it today.

When she was clear of the bed, he dropped her ankle.

She lay on her tummy on the carpet, hiccuping and trying desperately to gather her wits.

He was behind her, she could *feel* him staring at her. In silence.

In terrible, awful, disconcerting silence.

Swallowing a hiccup, unable to summon the nerve to look behind her, she said brightly, in her breathiest ditz voice, *"Je ne parle pas anglais. Parlez-vous français?"* Then with a stilted French accent (pretending to be dumb in Latin seemed a bit far-fetched to her), "Maid Service!" Hiccup. "I clean zee bedroom, *oui?*" Hiccup.

Nothing. Still silence behind her.

She was going to have to look at him.

Gingerly rising to her hands and knees, she smoothed her skirt, pushed herself into a sitting position, then managed to stand on trembling legs. Still too distraught to face the man, she focused on an empty glass and plate atop a table beside the bed and, determined to convince him she was Maid Service, pointed at it, chirping, "Dirtee dish-es. *Vous aimez* I wash, *oui?*"

Hiccup.

Heavy, ponderous silence. A rustling sound. What *was* he doing?

Taking deep breaths, she slowly turned. And all the blood drained from her face. She noticed two things at once, one absolutely irrelevant, the other terribly significant: He was the most breathtakingly gorgeous man she'd ever seen in her life, and he was holding her purse in one hand, slipping the battery out of her cell phone with the other.

He dropped the battery on the floor and crushed it beneath his boot.

"M-M-Maid Service?" she squeaked, then lapsed into French again, too nervous to do more than babble her way through, amid hiccups, elementary weather conversation she'd learned in freshman French, but he wouldn't know that.

"Actually, it's *no'* raining, lass," he said dryly in English with a pronounced Scots burr. "Though admittedly 'tis one of the few moments it hasn't been in the past week."

Chloe's heart plummeted to her toes. Oh, blast it—she should have tried Greek!

"Chloe Zanders," he said, tossing her license at her. She was too stunned to catch it; it bounced off her and dropped to the floor.

Shit. Merde. Bloody hell.

"From The Cloisters. I met your employer a quarter hour past. He said you awaited me here. I would never have guessed he meant in my bed." Dangerous eyes. Mesmerizing eyes. They locked with hers and she couldn't look away.

"Under the bed," she babbled, abandoning her overblown French accent. "I was *under* the bed, not in it."

His sensual mouth curved with a hint of a smile. The mild amusement did not touch his eyes.

Oh, God, she thought, staring wide-eyed. Her life was quite probably in danger and all she could do was stare. The man was beautiful. Impossibly so. Terrifyingly so. She'd never seen a man like him before. He was her every darkest fantasy sprung to life. Scottish blood was stamped all over his chiseled features.

Clad in black trousers, black boots, a cream fisherman's sweater, and a buttery-soft leather coat, he had silky black-as-midnight hair that was pulled back at his nape from a savagely masculine face. Firm, sensual lips, the lower one much fuller than the upper, proud, aristocratic nose, dark, slanted brows, bone-structure a model would die for. A perfectly sculpted dusting of a beard shadowed his perfect jaw.

Six foot four, at least, she'd guess. Powerfully built. The grace of an animal.

The exotic golden eyes of a tiger.

She suddenly felt like so much fresh meat.

" 'Twould seem we have a wee bit of a problem, lass," he said with silky menace, stepping toward her.

Her hiccups vanished instantly. Sheer terror could do that. Better than a spoonful of sugar or a paper bag anytime.

"I have no idea what you're talking about," she lied through her teeth. "I just came to deliver the text and I'm so sorry I got distracted by all your lovely treasures, and I sincerely apologize for invading your home, but Tom is expecting me back, actually Bill is waiting just downstairs for me, and I don't see any problem." She gazed wide-eyed at him and concentrated on looking soft and stupid and feminine. "What problem?" Demure batting of the lashes. "There's no problem."

He said nothing, merely let his gaze drop to the stolen texts scattered around her feet amid thongs and condom wrappers.

She glanced down too. "Well, yes, you certainly do have an active love life," she murmured vacuously. "But I won't hold that against you." *Womanizer!*

The look he gave her made the fine hair on the nape of her neck stand on end. His gaze drifted meaningfully to the tomes again.

"Oh! You mean the books. So you like books," she said lightly. "No big." She shrugged.

Again he said nothing, merely held her with that intense golden gaze. God, the man was stunning! Made her feel like . . . like that Rene Russo in *The Thomas Crown Affair*—ready to throw in with the thief. Run off to exotic lands. Stroll about topless on a terrace overlooking the sea. Live beyond the law. Pet his artifacts when she wasn't petting him.

"Och, lass," he said, shaking his head, "I'm no' a fool, so doona insult me with lies. 'Tis plain to see you know precisely what they are. *And* whence they came," he added gently.

Gentle from him was dangerous. She knew it instinctively. Gentle from this man meant he was about to do something she really *really* wasn't going to like.

And he did.

Crowding her with his powerful body, he backed her toward the bed and gave her a light push that sent her sprawling backward across it.

With the grace of a tiger he followed her down, pinning her to the mattress beneath him.

"I swear," she babbled hastily, "I won't tell a soul. I don't care. It's okay with me if you have them. I have absolutely no desire to go to the police or anything like that. I don't even *like* the police. Police and me have never gotten along. They gave me a ticket once for going forty-eight in a forty-five zone; how could I possibly like them after that? It doesn't matter one *whit* to me if you steal half The Met's medieval collection, I mean, really, they have six thousand pieces, so who's going to notice a few missing? I am an *excellent* secret-keeper," she practically screeched. "I definitely, most assuredly, cross-my-heart-and-hope-to . . . er, will not breathe the teeniest word. Mum. Mum's the word. And you can take that to the—"

His lips took the rest of her words along with her breath.

Oh, yeah. Rene Russo here.

Those sensual lips closed over hers, brushing lightly, tasting. But not taking.

And for an absolutely insane moment, she wanted him to take. Wanted him to crush her mouth in a hard, starving, bruising kiss and help her find that red-hot button of love that had never once hit lukewarm. The man filled a woman's head with fantasies she would have *sworn* she didn't have. Her traitorous lips parted beneath his. Fear, she told herself, it was just that fear could translate swiftly into arousal. She'd heard about people facing certain death suddenly getting a sexual charge that just wouldn't quit.

So bizarrely, intensely aroused, she didn't even notice that he was knotting a scarf around her wrist, until he swept it tight, and it was too late and she was tied to his bed. His sinful, decadent bed. Moving with inhuman grace and suddenness, he deftly knotted her other wrist to the far post.

She opened her mouth to scream, but he caught it with one powerful hand. Lying atop her, staring dead into her eyes, he said quietly, carefully, enunciating each word, "If you scream, I will be forced to gag you. I prefer not to, lass. It bears considering that no one can hear you up here anyway. 'Tis your choice. What will it be?" He lifted his hand infinitesimally, just enough that he might hear her reply.

"D-don't hurt me," she whispered.

"I have no intention of hurting you, lass."

But you are, she was about to say, then realized with a flush that that hard thing digging into her hip was not a gun, but a magnum of another sort entirely.

He must have seen something in her eyes, because he raised himself slightly.

Which meant, she concluded with a huge flood of relief, that he wasn't going to rape her. A rapist would have shifted a few inches to the right, not raised his hips.

"I'm afraid I'm going to have to keep you for a time, lass. But you'll suffer no harm at my hands. Mind you, however, one scream, one loud noise, and you're gagged."

There was no mercy in his gaze. She knew he meant it. She could either be bound, or bound and gagged.

She shook her head, then nodded, befuddled by whether she was supposed to say yes or no. "Won't scream," she promised stiffly. *No one can hear you up here anyway.* God, that was probably true. On the penthouse level walls were thick, there was no one above, and the elite were given wide berth unless they requested something. She could probably scream her *head* off, and no one would come.

"There's a bonny lass," he said, lifting her head with a palm and slipping a plump pillow beneath it.

Then, in one swift, graceful move, he pushed away from the bed and stalked from the bedroom, closing the door behind him, leaving her alone, tied by silken scarves to the sinful bed of the Gaulish Ghost.

She was the kind a man kept.

Dageus cursed softly in five languages, recalling his earlier thought, palming himself roughly through his trews. It didn't help. Indeed, made it worse. Happy for any attention.

Scowling, he went to stand before the wall of windows, gazing sightlessly out over the city.

He'd handled that badly. He'd frightened her. But he'd not been able to offer her soothing words, for he'd had to get away from her, quickly, lest he give his blood what it had been howling for. Though he told himself he'd pressed his lips to hers only to distract her while he bound her, he'd kissed her because he'd needed to, because he'd quite simply not been able *not* to. It had been a brief, sweet taste without tongue, for had he crossed that barrier, he'd have been lost. Lying atop her had been sheer agony, feeling the darkness rustle and flex within him, knowing tooping her would drive it back. Feeling cold and hungry, trying desperately to be human and kind.

He'd gone to The Cloisters, pleased with how firmly he'd put all thoughts of the Scots lass from his mind. There, he'd discovered the parcel was en route to him, while he was en route to it. The cocurator had, with much fawning and gushing, assured him Chloe Zanders would be waiting for him, as someone named Bill had already returned, having left her at his address.

But the lass hadn't been downstairs and Security had, with much winking and grinning, told him that his "delivery" awaited him upstairs.

Not finding the woman from the museum in the anteroom, he'd glanced about the living room, then heard noises upstairs.

He'd loped swiftly up the stairs and walked into his bedroom, only to discover the loveliest pair of legs he'd ever seen, poking out from beneath his bed. Succulent thighs he wanted to nip with his teeth, slender ankles, pretty little feet clad in delicate high heels.

Beautiful feminine legs. Bed.

Those two things in close proximity had a tendency to divert all the blood from his brain.

The legs had looked alarmingly familiar and he'd assured himself he was imagining things.

Then he'd plucked her out by an ankle and confirmed the identity of the lass attached to those heavenly legs, and his blood had simmered to a boil.

Staring down at her shapely backside as she'd lain unmoving on her tummy, a legion of fantasies riding him hard, it had taken him several moments to realize what she was lying amid.

The "borrowed" books.

The last thing he needed was the twenty-first century's law enforcers hunting him down. He had much to do, and too little time in which to do it. He couldn't afford complications.

He wasn't ready to leave Manhattan just yet. There were two final texts he needed to check.

By Amergin—he'd nearly been done! A few days at most. He didn't need this! Why now?

He inhaled deeply, exhaled slowly. Repeated it several times.

He'd had no choice, he assured himself. He had been wise to immediately restrain her. For the next few days, until he finished, he was simply going to have to hold her captive.

Though he could use magic, a memory spell to make her forget what she'd seen, he wasn't willing to risk it. Not only were memory spells tricky and oft damaging things, taking more memory than intended, he used magic only if there was no human way to handle the situation. He knew what it cost him each time. Tiny spells to obtain the texts he needed were one thing.

Nay. No magic. The lass would have to endure a short time of comfortable captivity while he finished translating the final tomes, then he would leave, and release her somewhere along the way.

Along the way to where? his conscience demanded. *Do you finally accept that you're going to have to return?*

He sighed. The past few months had confirmed what he'd suspected; there were only two places he might find the information he needed: in Ireland's and Scotland's museums, or in the MacKeltar library.

And the MacKeltar library was by far the best bet.

He'd been avoiding it at all cost, for it was fraught with myriad and varied perils. Not only did the land of his ancestors make the darkness inside him stronger, he dreaded facing his twin brother. Admitting that he'd lied. Admitting what he was.

Arguing bitterly with his da, Silvan, seeing the anger and disappointment in his eyes had been bad enough, Dageus wasn't certain he'd ever be ready to face his twin brother—the brother who'd never broken a vow in his life.

Since the eve he'd broken his oath and turned dark, Dageus had not once worn the colors of his clan, though a scrap of well-worn Keltar plaid was tucked beneath his pillow. Some evenings, after he'd seen whichever woman it was into a cab (though he tooped many, he shared his bed with none), he would close his hand around it, shut his eyes and pretend he was in the Highlands again. A simple man, naught more.

All he wanted was to find a way to fix the problem, to get rid of the dark ones himself. Then he would regain his honor. *Then* he could proudly face his brother and reclaim his heritage.

If you wait much longer, that nagging voice warned, *you may no longer care to reclaim it. You may no longer even understand what it means.*

He forced his thoughts away from such an unpleasant bent, and they drifted with alarming intensity straight back to the lass tied to his bed. Tied vulnerably and helplessly to his bed.

Dangerous thought, that. Seemed all he ever had anymore were dangerous thoughts.

Raking a hand through his hair, he forced his attention to the text she'd left on the coffee table, refusing to dwell on the disconcerting fact that a part of him had taken one look at the lass in such proximity to his bed and said simply: *Mine.*

As if from the moment he'd seen her, that he would claim her had been as certain as the morrow's dawn.

Several hours later, Chloe's volatile emotions had run the gamut. She'd pretty much exhausted fear, plunged with effusive glee, for a time, into outrage at her captor, and was now thoroughly disgusted at herself for her impetuous curiosity.

Curious as a wee kitten, you are, but a cat has nine lives, Chloe, Grandda used to say. *You have but one. Beware where it leads you.*

You can say that again, she thought, listening intently to see if she could hear the thief moving around out there. His penthouse had one of those music systems that was piped into every room and, after an initial painfully loud blast of a bass-heavy song that sounded suspiciously like that Nine Inch Nail's song that had been banned from airplay a few years ago, he'd put on classical music. She'd been treated to a medley of violin concertos for the past few hours. If it was intended to soothe her, it was failing.

It didn't help that her nose itched and the only way she could scratch it was to bury her face in his pillows and bob her head.

She wondered how much time would have to pass before Bill and Tom would start to wonder where she'd gotten off to. Surely they would come looking for her, wouldn't they?

Not.

Though both would say, "but Chloe never deviates from routine," neither would question or accuse Dageus MacKeltar. After all, who in their right mind would believe the man anything but a wealthy art collector? If asked, her captor would simply say, "No, she dropped it off and left, and I have no idea where she went." And

Tom would believe, and no one would push, because men like Dageus MacKeltar weren't the kind one questioned or pushed. No one would ever imagine him a kidnapper and a thief. *She* was the only one who knew differently, and only because she'd gotten all foolishly infatuated with his artifacts and gone snooping through his bedroom.

No, although Tom might send Bill around this afternoon, or more likely tomorrow, asking when Chloe had left, it would end there. In a day or two, she imagined Tom would really start to worry, call her at home, stop by, even report her missing to the police, but there were oodles of unexplained disappearances in New York all the time.

Deep shit, indeed.

With a sigh, she puffed a ticklish strand of hair out of her face and did the nose-in-pillow thing again. He smelled good, the dirty rotten scoundrel. Womanizing, bullying, amoral, larcenous, vilest-of-the-vile, debaucher of innocent texts.

"Thief," she muttered with a little scowl.

She inhaled, then caught herself. She was not going to appreciate his scent. She was *not* going to appreciate a darned thing about him.

Sighing, she wriggled her way up the bed until she was leaning, in a mostly upright position, against the headboard.

She was tied to a strange man's bed. A criminal to boot.

"Chloe Zanders, you've got all kinds of problems," she murmured, testing the silken bonds for the hundredth time. A little play, no give. The man knew how to tie knots.

Why hadn't he hurt her? she wondered. And since he hadn't, just what did he plan to do with her? The facts were pretty simple and quite horrifying; she'd managed to stumble into the lair of an expert, slick, thoroughly top-notch thief. Not a petty thief or a bank robber, but a master thief who broke into impossible places and stole fabulous treasures.

This was not small-time stuff.

There weren't thousands riding on her silence, but *millions*.

She shivered. That dismal thought could send her straight into hysterics, or at the least, a potentially terminal bout of hiccups.

Desperate for a distraction, she wriggled as far to the edge of the bed as the bonds permitted, and peered down at the stolen texts.

She sighed longingly, aching to touch. Though not originals—any originals worth having were securely tucked away in the Royal Irish Academy or Trinity College Library—they were superb late-medieval copies. One of them had fallen open, revealing a lovely page of Irish majuscule script, the capital letters gloriously embellished with the intricate interlacing knotwork for which the Celts were renowned.

There was a copy of *Lebor Laignech* (the Book of Leinster), *Leborna hUidre* (the Book of the Dun Cow), *Lebor Gabála Érenn* (the Book of Invasions), and several lesser texts from the Mythological Cycle.

Fascinating. All of them about the earliest days of Éire, or Ireland. Full of tales of the Partholonians, the Nemedians, the Fir Bolg, the Tuatha Dé Danaan, and the Milesians. Rich in legend and magic, and endlessly disputed by scholars.

Why did he want them? Was he selling them to fund his fabulous lifestyle? Chloe knew there were private collectors who didn't give a damn where the item came from, so long as they could own it. There was always a market for stolen artifacts.

But, she puzzled, he had only Celtic artifacts. And she knew for a fact that most of the collections he'd raided for those texts boasted far more valuable items from many different cultures. Items he'd not taken.

Which meant, for whatever reason, that he was highly selective and not motivated solely by the value of the artifact.

She shook her head, befuddled. It didn't make any sense. What thief wasn't motivated by the value of the artifact? What thief stole a lesser-valued text and left dozens of more valuable items untouched once he'd gone to the trouble of breaching security? And *how* was he managing to breach security? The collections he'd robbed had some of the most sophisticated anti-theft systems in the world, requiring sheer genius to penetrate.

The door suddenly opened, and she scrunched hastily away from the edge of the bed, donning her most innocent expression.

"Are you hungry, lass?" he said in his deep burr, glancing around the partially opened door at her.

"Wh-what?" Chloe blinked. Not only was the dastardly man not killing her, he was going to feed her?

"Are you hungry? I was preparing food for myself and it occurred to me that mayhap you were hungry."

Chloe puzzled over that for a moment. Was she hungry? She was completely freaked out. She was going to have to use the bathroom soon. Her nose itched furiously and her skirt was getting all bunched up again.

And in the midst of it all, yes, she was hungry.

"Uh-huh," she said warily.

Only after he left did it occur to her that maybe that was how he was going to get rid of her—by poisoning her!

· 4 ·

Poached salmon, stovies and cullen skink. A salad tossed with nuts and cranberries. A plate of Scottish cheeses, shortbread and marmalade. Sparkling wine in Baccarat goblets.

Death by scrumptious Scots cuisine and fine crystal? "I thought I'd get a peanut butter sandwich or something," Chloe said warily.

Dageus placed the final dish on the bed and looked at her. His entire body tightened. Christ, she was fantasy come to life on his bed, sitting back against the headboard, her wrists tied to the posts. She was all soft curves, her skirt riding up her sweet thighs, teasing him with forbidden glimpses, a snug sweater hugging full, round breasts, hair tousled about her face, her eyes wide and stormy. He had no doubt that she was a maiden. Her response to his brief kiss had told him that much. He'd never had a lass like her in his bed. Not even in his own century, where proper lasses had given the Keltar brothers wide berth. Rumors about "those pagan sorcerers" had been abundant in the Highlands. Though experienced women, married women, and maids had eagerly sought their beds, even they'd eschewed more permanent ties.

They're drawn to danger, but of no mind to live with it, Drustan had once said with a bitter smile. *They like to stroke the beast's silky pelt, feel his power and wildness, but make no mistake, brother—they'll never, never trust the beast around children.*

Well, 'twas too late. She was with the beast whether she liked it or not.

If only she'd stayed on the street, she'd have been safe from him. He'd have left her alone.

He'd have done the honorable thing and erased her from his mind. And if by chance he'd encountered her again, he'd have turned coldly about and walked the other way.

But 'twas too late for honor. She hadn't stayed on the street like a good lass. She was here in his bed. And he was a man, and not an honorable one at that.

And when you leave her? the tatters of his honor hissed.

I'll leave her so weel pleasured she'll no' rue it. Some other bumbling fool would hurt her. I'll awaken her in ways she'll never forget. I'll give her fantasies that will heat her dreams for the rest of her life.

And that was the end of that argument, so far as he was concerned. He needed. The darkness in him grew wild without a woman. He no longer had the option of entertaining Katie, or any other women, in his home. But seduction, not conquest, was the main course on the table this eve. He would give her this night, mayhap the morrow, but anon, 'twould be conquest.

"So, um, are you going to untie me?"

With effort, he pried his gaze from her twisted skirt. She'd clamped her knees together anyway. *Wise lass,* he thought darkly, *but 'twill do you no good in the end.*

"You can't just keep me," she said frostily.

"But I can."

"People will be looking for me."

"But no' here. None will press me, you know that."

When he eased himself down on the bed facing her, she plastered herself back against the headboard.

"You'll come to no harm at my hands, lass. I give you my word."

She opened her mouth, then closed it, as if she'd thought better of it. Then she seemed to change her mind, shrugged, and said, "How can I believe that? I'm sitting in the middle of all this stolen stuff and you've tied me up. I can't help but worry about how you plan to deal with me. So, how do you?" When he didn't respond immediately, she added heatedly. "If you're going to kill me, I'm warning you right now—I'll haunt you till the end of your thieving days. I'll make your life a living hell. I'll make your legendary banshee seem demure and soft-spoken by comparison. You . . . you . . . you barbarian Visigoth," she spat.

"Och, and there's your Scots blood, lass," he said with a faint smile. "A fine bit o' temper too. Though Visigoth is a bit far-fetched, I'm hardly doing anything so epic as the sacking of Rome."

She scowled. "Lots of books were lost then too."

"I treat them with care. And you needn't fash yourself, lass. I will no' harm you. Naught will be done to you that you doona wish done. I may borrow a few tomes, but that's the extent of my crimes. I'll be leaving soon. When I do, I'll release you."

Chloe searched his face intently, thinking she didn't quite like that part about "naught will be done to you that you doona wish done." Just what did he mean by that? Still, his gaze was level. She couldn't imagine why he would bother lying. "I could almost believe you mean that," she finally said.

"I do, lass."

"Hmph," she said noncommittally. A pause, then, "So, why do you do it?" she asked, nodding her head in the direction of the stolen texts.

"Does it matter?"

"Well, it shouldn't, but it sort of does. You see, I know those collections you stole from. There were far more valuable relics in them."

"I seek certain information. I merely borrowed them. They will be returned when I leave."

"And the moon is made of cheese," she said dryly.

"They will, though you doona believe me."

"And all the other things you've stolen?"

"What other things?"

"All that Celtic stuff. The knives and swords and badges and coins and—"

"All of that is mine by right of birth."

She gave him a skeptical look.

" 'Tis."

Chloe snorted.

" 'Tis Keltar regalia. I am a Keltar."

Her gaze turned measuring. "Are you saying the only things you've actually stolen are the texts?"

"Borrowed. And aye."

"I don't know what to make of you," she said, shaking her head.

"What does your viscera"—nay, that wasn't quite the right word—"instinct tell you?"

She looked at him intently, so intently that it was intimate. He wondered if a lass had ever looked at him so piercingly before. As if trying to probe the depths of his soul, down to the blackest heart of it. How would she judge him, this innocent? Would she damn him as he'd damned himself?

After a few moments, she shrugged and the moment was lost.

"What kind of information are you looking for?"

" 'Tis a long story, lass," he evaded, with a mocking smile.

"If you let me go, I really won't tell anyone. I far prefer to stay alive than get all hung up on moral compunctions. That's always been a no-brainer for me."

"No-brainer," he repeated slowly. "Simple decision?"

Chloe blinked. "Yes." She peered at him. Between some of the words he used and the way he occasionally paused, as if mulling over a word or phrase, it occurred to her that perhaps English wasn't his native tongue. He'd understood French. Curious, testing him, she asked him—in Latin—if Gaelic was his first language.

He answered in Greek that it was.

Sheesh, the thief was not only gorgeous, he was multi-lingual! She was starting to feel treacherously like Rene Russo again. "You're actually *reading* these things, aren't you?" she said wonderingly. "Why?"

"I told you, lass, I'm looking for something."

"Well, if you tell me what, maybe I can help." The minute the words left her mouth, she was appalled. "I didn't mean that," she retracted the offer hastily. "I did *not* just offer to aid and abet a criminal."

"Curious lass, aren't you? I suspect it oft gets the best of you." He gestured toward the food. " 'Tis cooling. What would you like?"

"Anything you eat first," she said instantly.

A look of incredulity crossed his face. "Think you I would poison you?" he said indignantly.

When *he* said it, it sounded like a patently ridiculous

and perfectly paranoid thought. "Well," she said defensively; "how am I supposed to know?"

He gave her a chiding glance. Then, holding her gaze, he took a full bite from each plate.

"It might only kill in large doses," she countered.

Raising a brow, he took two more bites from each dish.

"My hands are tied. I can't eat."

He smiled then, a slow, sexy, shiver-inducing smile. "Och, but you can, lass," he purred, spearing a tender slice of salmon and raising it to her lips.

"You've got to be kidding me," she said flatly, clamping her lips shut. Oh, no, he wasn't going to harm her, he was just going to torture her, tease her, pretend he was being seductive, and watch Chloe Zanders turn into a stammering idiot while being hand-fed by the most incredibly gorgeous man this side of the Atlantic. No way. She wasn't going there.

"Open," he coaxed.

"I'm not hungry," she said mulishly.

"You are too."

"Am not."

"You will be on the morrow," he said, a faint smile playing about his sensual lips.

Chloe narrowed her eyes at him. "Why are you doing this?"

"There was a time, long ago in Scotland, when a man would select the finest from his trencher and feed his woman." His glittering golden gaze locked with hers. "Only after he'd sated her desires—fully and completely— did he sate his own."

Whuh. That comment went straight to her tummy, filling it with butterflies. Went straight to a few other parts, too, parts it was wiser not to think about. Not only was he a womanizer, he was smooth as silk. Stiffly, she gritted,

"We aren't in long-ago Scotland, I'm *not* your woman, and I'll *bet* she wasn't tied up."

He smiled at that and she noticed what had been bothering her about his smile then: Though he'd smiled several times, his amusement never seemed to reach his eyes. As if the man never quite dropped his guard. Never relaxed fully. Kept some part of himself locked away. Thief, kidnapper and seducer of women: What other secrets did he hide behind those cool eyes?

"Why do you fight me? Think you I might slay you with my fork?" he said lightly.

"I—"

Salmon in her mouth. Tricky thief. And it was good. Cooked to perfection. She swallowed hastily. "That wasn't fair."

"But was it good?"

She glared at him in stalwart silence.

"Life isn't always fair, lass, but that doesn't mean it can't still be sweet."

Disconcerted by his intense regard, Chloe decided it would be wiser to simply capitulate. God only knew what he might do if she didn't, and besides, she was hungry. She suspected she could argue with him until she was blue in the face and get nowhere. The man was going to feed her and that was that.

And frankly, when he was sitting there on the bed, all sinfully gorgeous and playful and pretending to be flirtatious . . . it was a little hard to resist, even though she knew it was just some kind of game to him. When she was seventy years old (assuming she survived unscathed), sitting in her rocking chair with great-grandkids trundling about, she could reflect upon the memory of the strange night the irresistible Gaulish Ghost had fed her bits of Scots dishes and sips of fine wine in his penthouse in Manhattan.

The brush of danger in the air, the incredible sensuality of the man, the bizarreness of her situation were all combining to make her feel a little reckless.

She'd not known she had it in her.

She was feeling . . . well . . . rather intrepid.

Hours later, Chloe lay in the dark, watching the fire sputter and spark, her mind racing over the events of the day, reaching no satisfying conclusions.

It had been, by far, the strangest day of her life.

Had someone told her that morning, when she'd tugged on her panty hose and suit, how this ordinary, chilly, drizzly Wednesday in March would unfold, she'd have laughed it off as pure nonsense.

Had someone told her she would finish the day tied to a sumptuous bed in a luxurious corner penthouse in custody of the Gaulish Ghost, watching a fire burn down to embers, well fed and sleepy, she'd have escorted that person to the nearest psychiatric ward.

She was frightened—oh, who was she kidding? Embarrassed though she was to admit it, she was every bit as fascinated as she was frightened.

Life had taken a decidedly loopy turn and she wasn't as upset about it as she suspected she probably should be. It was a little difficult to work oneself into a satisfying fit of fear-for-one's-life, when one's captor was such an intriguing, seductive man. A man who cooked a full Scots meal for his prisoner, built a fire for her, and played classical music. An intelligent, well-educated man.

A sinfully sexy man.

When not only hadn't one been harmed, one had been quite tantalizingly kissed.

And although she had no idea what tomorrow would bring, she was curious to find out. What could he be looking for? Was it possible he was no more than what he presented himself as? A wealthy man who needed certain information for some reason, who—if he couldn't obtain the texts he needed by legitimate means—stole them, intending to return them?

"Right. Color *me* stupid." Chloe rolled her eyes.

Still, throwing a wrench into the works, impairing her ability to neatly label him a thief, was the fact that he'd donated valuable, authenticated artifacts in exchange for the third Book of Manannán.

Why would the Gaulish Ghost do such a thing? The facts just weren't adding up to the profile of a cold-blooded mercenary. She was bursting with curiosity. She'd long suspected it might one day be her downfall and, indeed, it had landed her in quite a pickle.

After dinner, he'd untied her and escorted her to the bathroom adjoining the master suite (walking a bit too close for her comfort, making her painfully aware of two hundred-plus pounds of solid male muscle behind her). A few minutes and a knock later, he'd informed her he'd placed a shirt and sweats (he'd called them trews) outside the door.

She'd spent thirty minutes in the locked bathroom, first snooping for a convenient person-sized heating duct—the kind one frequently saw in the movies but never found in real life—then deliberating over whether writing an SOS message in lipstick on the window might accomplish anything. Other than him finding it and getting aggravated. She'd opted not. Not just yet anyway. No need to alert him to her intention to escape at the earliest opportunity.

She'd not felt brave enough to risk nudity and showering, even with the locked door, so she'd washed up a bit, then brushed her teeth with his toothbrush because there was no way she was *not* going to brush her teeth. She'd felt strange using it. She'd never used a man's toothbrush before. But after all, she'd rationalized, they'd eaten from the same fork. And she'd nearly had his tongue in her mouth. Honestly would have rather *liked* his tongue in her mouth, so long as she had a firm guarantee it would stop there. (She wasn't *about* to become the next pair of panties beneath his bed, not that she had any to leave.)

She drowned in his clothes, but at least when he'd retied her to the bed, she hadn't had to worry about her skirt riding up. The sweats were drawstring—the only saving grace—rolled up about ten times, the shirt fell to her knees. No panties was a bit disconcerting.

He'd tucked her beneath the coverlet. Tested the bonds. Lengthened them slightly so she might sleep more comfortably.

Then he'd stood at the edge of the bed a moment, gazing down at her with an unfathomable expression in his exotic golden eyes. Unnerved, she'd broken eye contact first and rolled—inasmuch as she was able—onto her side away from him.

Sheesh, she thought, blinking heavy-lidded, sleepy eyes. She smelled like him. It was all over her.

She was falling asleep. She couldn't believe it. In the midst of such dreadful, stressful circumstances, she was falling asleep.

Well, she told herself, she needed her sleep so her wits would be sharp tomorrow. Tomorrow she would escape.

He hadn't tried to kiss her again, was her final, slightly wistful, and utterly ridiculous thought before she drifted off.

Several hours later, too restless to sleep, Dageus was in the living room, listening to the rain pattering against the windows and poring over the Midhe Codex, a collection of mostly nonsensical myths and vague prophecies ("a massive muddling mess of medieval miscellany," one renowned scholar had called it, and Dageus was inclined to agree), when the phone rang. He glanced at it warily, but did not rise to answer it.

A long pause, a beep, then "Dageus, 'tis Drustan."

Silence.

"You know how I hate talking to machines. Dageus."

Long silence, a heavy sigh.

Dageus fisted his hands, unfisted them, then massaged his temples with the heels of his palms.

"Gwen's in the hospital—"

Dageus's head whipped toward the answering machine, he half-rose, but stopped.

"She had untimely contractions."

Worry in his twin brother's voice. It knifed straight to Dageus's heart. Gwen was six-and-a-half-months pregnant with twins. He held his breath, listening. He'd not sacrificed so much to bring his brother and his brother's wife together in the twenty-first century, only to have something happen to Gwen now.

"But she's fine now."

Dageus breathed again and sank back down to the sofa.

"The doctors said sometimes it happens in the last trimester, and so long as she doesn't have further contractions, they'll consider releasing her on the morrow."

A time filled with naught but the faint sound of his brother's breathing.

"Och . . . brother . . . come home." Pause. Softly, "Please."

Click.

· 5 ·

Dageus was perilously close to losing control.

"That means 'bridge,' not 'adjoining walkway,' " she was saying, peering over his shoulder and pointing at what he'd just scribbled in the notes he was taking. Some of her hair tumbled over his shoulder and spilled down his chest. It was all he could do not to slip his hand into it and tug her lips to his.

He should never have untied her this morn. But it wasn't as if she could escape him, and it bordered on barbaric to keep her tied to the bed. Besides, the mere thought of her tied to the bed was obsessing a dark part of his mind. Still, it was no better having her flitting about, examining everything, pestering him with incessant questions and comments.

Each time he looked at her, a silent growl rose in his

throat, scarce repressed hunger, need to touch her and taste her and—

"Doona be hanging over my shoulder, lass." Her scent was filling his nostrils, inciting a lustful stupor. Scent of lush woman and innocence. Christ, didn't she sense that he was dangerous? Mayhap not overtly, but in the way a mouse took one look at a cat and kept wisely to the shadowy corners of a room? Apparently not, for she chattered on.

"I'm just curious," she said peevishly. "And you're getting it wrong. That says, 'When the man from the mounts, high where the yellow eagles soar, takes the low . . . er, path or journey . . . on the bridge that cheats death'—how curious, the bridge that cheats death?—'the Draghar will return' Who are the Draghar? I've never heard of them. What is that? The Midhe Codex? I've never heard of that either. May I see it? Where did you get it?"

Dageus shook his head. She was irrepressible. "Sit lass, or I'll tie you up again."

She glared at him. "I'm only trying to be helpful—"

"And why is that? I'm a thief, remember? A barbarian Visigoth, as you put it."

She scowled. "You're right. I don't know what got into me." A long pause. Then, "It's just that I thought if you really *were* going to return them"—she gave him a searingly skeptical look—"the sooner you finished with them, the sooner they'd go back. So I'd be helping for a good cause." She nodded pertly, looking inordinately pleased with her rationalization.

He snorted and motioned her to sit down. 'Twas evident the lass was obsessed with antiquities and curious as the day was long. Her fingers actually curled absently whenever she looked at the Codex, as if she was aching to touch it.

He'd like to see her aching to touch him like that. Worldly women all but pushed him into bed. He'd never seduced an innocent before. He sensed she would resist. . . . The thought both amused and aroused him.

Huffily, she plunked down on the sofa opposite him, folded her arms and stared at him across piles of texts and notebooks on the marble coffee table between them. Lush lips pursed, one foot tapping.

One wee, bare delicate foot, with shell-pink toenails. Slender ankles peeking from his rolled-up sweats. Clad in one of his linen shirts, the sleeves pushed up to the elbows, which was also where the shoulders dropped to on her delicate frame, her hair mussed about her face, she was a vision. The fickle March sun had decided to shine for the moment, like as not, he thought, just so it could spill in the wall of windows behind her, and kiss her curly coppery-blond tresses.

Tresses he'd like to feel spilling over his thighs. While those lush pink lips . . .

"Eat your breakfast," he growled, turning back to the text.

She narrowed her eyes. "I already did. I'm going to lose my job, you know."

"What?"

"My job. I'm going to get fired if I don't show up for work. And then how will I live? I mean, assuming you really mean it about letting me go."

She gave him another haughty glare, then glanced toward the door for the dozenth time, and he knew she was wondering if she could make it to it before he stopped her. He wasn't worried. Even if she made it out the door, she'd never make it onto the elevator in time. He knew also that earlier, she'd stood behind him, her gaze drifting betwixt a heavy lamp and the back of his skull. She hadn't tried to bash him with it, wise lass.

Mayhap she'd seen his tense readiness, mayhap she'd decided his skull was too thick.

He inhaled deeply and released it slowly. If he didn't get her out of the room soon, he was going to leap the table betwixt them, pin her to the sofa, and have his way with her. And though he fully intended to, he needed to finish the Midhe Codex first. Discipline was a crucial part of controlling the evil within him. The first portion of the day was for work, the evening for seduction, the wee hours for more work. He'd been living that way for many moons. 'Twas imperative he keep things neatly compartmentalized, for he could too easily become a man consumed by indulging whatever momentary need or whim struck him. Only by rigidly maintaining his routines, never deviating, did he prove to himself that he was indeed in control.

The Draghar, he brooded. This was the third mention of them he'd encountered. The peculiar phrasing did seem to encompass his actions. The man from the mounts . . . the bridge that cheats death. But who or what were the Draghar? Were they mayhap some faction of the legendary Tuatha Dé Danaan? Would they return from their mythic hidden places to hunt him now that he'd broken his oath and violated The Compact?

The deeper he dug into tomes that neither he nor Drustan had previously spared a thought for, the more he realized that his clan had forgotten, even abandoned, much of their ancient history. The Keltar library was vast, and in his thirty-three years he'd scarce made a dent in it. There were texts no Keltar had bothered with for centuries, mayhap millennia. There was too much lore for a man to absorb in a single lifetime, and verily, there'd been no need to. Over the aeons, they'd grown careless and content, looking forward not behind. He supposed it was man's way to relinquish the past, to live in the now, unless suddenly the ancient past became critical.

Had they not forgotten so much, he might never have stood in the circle of stones, assuring himself there was no evil in the in-between awaiting him should he use the stones for personal motive. He might never have half-convinced himself that the Tuatha Dé Danaan, a vague race spoken of in vaguer terms, were but a myth, a fae-tale woven to prevent a Keltar from misusing his power. Not that he'd believed he had been abusing it. He'd not thought of his actions as serving personal motives. Well, not entirely, for was love not the greatest and most noble purpose of all?

She was *havering* away again.

How best to make her give him some peace?

A predatory smile curved his lips.

He looked up. Raised his eyes from the text and looked at her, deliberately letting all that he was thinking about doing to her—which was everything—show on his face, blaze in his gaze.

She sucked in a soft breath.

Head canted down, he looked at her from beneath his brows. It was the kind of look one warrior might give to another in challenge, or the kind of look a man gave a woman he intended to thoroughly plunder. Slowly, with lazy sensuality, he wet his lower lip. Dropped his gaze from hers, to her lips and back again.

Her eyes grew impossibly round and she swallowed.

He caught his full lower lip with his teeth and slowly released it, then smiled. It was not a smile meant to reassure. It was a smile that promised dark fantasies. Whether she wanted them or not.

"I'll just be in the study," she said faintly, hopping briskly from the sofa and practically running from the room.

Only after she'd left did he make that noise. A long, low growl of anticipation.

⟡

Chloe's heart was hammering furiously and she wasn't seeing a darned thing as she pretended to peer at the titles of the books on the shelves in his study.

Heavens, that look! Holy cow!

There he'd sat across from her, looking breathtakingly gorgeous in black from head to toe, his gorgeous midnight hair pulled back from his gorgeous face, essentially ignoring her, then he'd raised his eyes—but not his head—from the text and given her a look of . . . quintessential sexual heat.

No man had ever looked at Chloe Zanders like that. Like she was some kind of succulent dessert and he was coming off a week-long fast of bread and water.

And his lip—God, when he caught and released that sinfully full lower with his teeth, it made a girl just want to snack on it. For hours.

I do believe the man might be planning to seduce me, she thought wonderingly. Yes, she knew he was a womanizer, and yes, last night he'd seemed flirtatious, but she hadn't taken it seriously. She wasn't exactly the kind of woman that men like him fell all over themselves trying to get to. Chloe was pretty realistic about her looks; she wasn't tall, leggy, model material, that was for sure. Even the Security guys had said she wasn't his type.

But that look . . .

"He only did it to get you to leave, Zanders," she muttered to herself. "And it worked. You willy-nilly chicken, you."

She was on the verge of stomping back out there and calling his bluff; indeed, had moved back toward the door and was about to step out, when he made a sound.

A sound that made her shiver and close the door instead.

And lock it.

A hungry animal sound.

Leaning back against the door, Chloe took slow, deep breaths.

She was in way over her head. It was one thing to be held hostage by a criminal. To maybe fantasize about kisses. It was entirely another thing to be seduced by him. The dastardly man was both a thief and a kidnapper, and she dare not forget that.

She had to escape before it was too late. Before she was fabricating reasons, not merely to aid and abet the criminal, but to present him with her virginity on a silver platter.

❧

When Chloe crept from the study half an hour later, the arrogant man actually let her get all the way to the door before he bothered moving. Then he stood slowly, as if he had all the time in the world, and gave her a look of gentle reproof and disappointment.

As if *she* was doing something wrong.

Defiantly, Chloe brandished the short sword she'd pilfered from his wall collection, having decided it was best for her size, eighteen inches of razor-sharp steel. "I told you I won't tell anyone and I won't. But I can't stay here."

"Put down the blade, lass."

Chloe twisted the interior dead bolt.

The precise moment she tugged at the door, he lunged, and when it didn't open she was stunned, then realized that it hadn't been locked to begin with. Frantically, she scrabbled to turn it the other way, but his palm hit the door above her head and he crowded her with his body. Instinctively, she raised the sword and he stiffened, as the tip of it came to rest at his heart.

They stared at each other a long moment. Dimly, she realized his breath was coming as shallowly as hers.

"Do it, lass," he said coolly.

"What?"

"Kill me. I'm a thief. The evidence is here. You'll need but summon your police and show them that I am—or was—the Gaulish Ghost, that I held you captive. None will blame you for killing me to escape. 'Tis no more than any honest lass would do."

She gaped. Kill him? She didn't like hearing him speak about himself in the past tense. It put a cold, awful knot in her stomach.

"Do it," he insisted.

"I don't want to *kill* you. I just want to *leave*."

"Because I've treated you so badly?"

"Because you're holding me captive!"

"And it's been awful, has if no'?" he mocked lightly.

"Just step back," she hissed. When he deliberately pressed his body forward against the tip of the sword and she felt his skin give beneath the blade, she gasped. His lips curved in a chilling smile.

And she knew if she drew the blade back, it would gleam red with his blood. The awful knot was joined by nausea.

"Kill me or put down the sword," he said with deadly intensity. "Those are your options. Your only options."

Chloe searched his eyes, those glittering golden eyes. They seemed to be swirling with shadows, changing color, dimming from molten amber to burnt copper, but that wasn't possible. The moment was taut with danger, and she had the sudden bizarre feeling that something . . . *else* . . . was in the penthouse with them. Something ancient and very, very cold.

Or was it just the coldness in those eyes? She shook herself, scattering her absurd thoughts.

He was serious. He would make her kill him to leave.

She couldn't do it.

It wasn't even remotely possible. She didn't want Dageus MacKeltar dead. She didn't *ever* want him dead. Even if it meant he was out there, a rogue thief, beautiful as a fallen angel, breaking laws and stealing artifacts.

When she let the sword dip, his hand moved in a lightning-fast blur of motion. She screamed, dropping the sword as the silver flash of a blade arced up toward her face.

It sank into the door beside her ear.

"Look at it, lass," he ordered.

"Wh-what?"

"The dirk. 'Tis a fourteenth-century *skean dhu*."

She turned her head gingerly and peered at the blade protruding from the door, then glanced back at him. She was walled in by six feet plus of muscle and man, palms on either side of her head. A knife by her ear. He'd had it somewhere on his body all along. Could have used it on her at any moment. But hadn't.

"You like your artifacts, doona you, lass?"

She nodded.

"Take it."

Chloe blinked.

He dropped his hands suddenly and stepped back. "Go on, take it."

Eyeing him warily, Chloe tugged the blade from the door with a little grunt. It required both her hands to free it. "Oh," she breathed. Hilt studded with emeralds and rubies, it was exquisite. The finest blade she'd ever seen. "This must be worth a fortune! It's in mint condition. There's not even the teeniest nick on the blade! Tom would give anything for this."

So, she was afraid, might she.

" 'Tis my own. 'Tis the crest of the Keltar on the hilt. Now 'tis yours. For when you leave. Should you lose your job."

He turned around and stalked back to the sofa.

When he sat down and resumed working on the text, Chloe stood in stunned silence, her gaze drifting from him to the *skean dhu* and back again. Several times she opened her mouth to speak, then closed it.

His actions had just demonstrated, more persuasively than any words he might have used, that he'd meant it when he'd said he wouldn't hurt her. What words had he used last night? *Naught will be done to you that you doona wish done.*

She didn't find that quite as comforting as she might have, had her own wishes been a bit purer.

He'd just put an ancient Celtic artifact in her hands and called it hers.

Her fingers curled possessively around the hilt of the dagger. She should object strenuously. Or at least, protest politely. And she was going to, anytime now.

She waited. Anytime now.

Sighing dismally, she acknowledged that some things just weren't humanly possible—not even Martha Stewart could fold fitted sheets.

Oh, Grandda, why didn't you ever tell me Scotsmen were so fascinating? He knows just how to get to me.

She almost thought she heard Evan MacGregor's soft laughter. As if he'd answered her from somewhere beyond the stars, *You wouldn't be satisfied with less, Chloe. You've got your share of wild blood in you too.*

Did she? Was that why, lately, she'd been waking up in the middle of the night, full of energy that desperately needed an outlet? Why, despite how well her job was going (she knew she was going to be promoted soon), she'd been growing increasingly restless? For months now, a small but insistent voice inside her had been murmuring, "Is this all there is of my life?"

The Gaulish Ghost was offering her a bribe, a payoff of sorts. Be a "good lass" and leave with a prize. Her very own Celtic artifact.

In exchange for her silence and cooperation.

Chloe was having an ethical crisis.

Fortunately, it was brief.

She stooped to pick up the forgotten sword and return it to the study. "I could use some clothes that *fit*," she grumbled as she passed behind him.

Had his back not been to her, had she seen the smile that curved his lips, she would have shivered from head to toe.

༺ঔৣ৶

"Dageus, darling, I miss you, I need you. I'm *dying* without you." Pause. "Call me. It's Katherine."

The answering machine clicked off.

A moment later Dageus appeared. Their gazes collided as he turned down the volume on the answering machine.

"Dageus, darling," Chloe cooed, feeling inexplicably irritable. There she'd been, paging delicately through the Midhe Codex and feeling strangely content while he rattled about domestically in the kitchen, cooking for her, when Katherine had interrupted.

He flashed her an entirely-too-devastating smile and shrugged. "I'm a man, lass." Then went back to the kitchen.

Leaving Chloe to mutter beneath her breath. Just why she cared she had no idea. But it irritated her.

༺ঔৣ৶

"Were you born in Scotland?" Chloe asked later, pushing her plate back with a sigh. Another fabulous dinner: Aberdeen Angus steak with mushrooms in wine sauce, young red potatoes with chives, salad and crusty bread spread with honey-butter. And wine, though he was sipping Macallan, fine single-malt scotch.

"Aye. The Highlands. Near Inverness. And you?"

"Indianapolis. But my parents died when I was four, so I went to live in Kansas with my grandda."

"That must have been difficult."

It had been horrible. They'd refused to let her see her parents' bodies, which, though now she understood, at the time she hadn't. She'd thought someone had stolen them and wouldn't give them back. Hadn't believed they could just not *be* anymore. But eventually she'd healed. She knew it had shaped her in ways people with parents would never understand, but she'd been lucky. She'd had someone who'd rescued her, and Chloe believed one should always count one's blessings.

"Where's the Scots blood in you, lass?"

"My grandda. Evan MacGregor. Do you have family?"

A dark shadow flitted through his eyes, a brief flash of anguish, there and gone so quickly that she wasn't certain she hadn't imagined it.

"My mother and da are dead. I have a brother." He rose abruptly, gathering plates and taking them to the kitchen, leaving her to puzzle over what she thought she'd glimpsed. She was determined to pursue it, but when he returned, he distracted her by placing a glass of sparkling blood-red liquor in one hand and a cigar in the other.

Chloe blinked. "What is this?"

"The finest cigar money can buy and a glass of equally fine port."

"And just what do you think I'm going to do with it?"

"Enjoy." He flashed her a charming smile.

Chloe peered at the cigar curiously, rolling it in her fingers. She'd never smoked. Not anything. Had never wanted to. But if ever a moment was ripe to try new things, it was here and now, with a man who certainly wouldn't sit in judgment upon her, no matter what she might do. It was strangely freeing, she realized, being around a man like him.

"Doona fash yourself, you needn't inhale. 'Tis but the subtle combination of the port and pungent smoke on your tongue. Give it a try. If you doona like it, at least you'll know the next time someone offers you one."

He showed her how, preparing the cigar, coaxing her to puff it alight.

"I feel like I'm doing something bad." She sneezed.

Och, she had no idea how bad. A small thing, to get her to smoke a cigar and have port. Lasses loved to flirt with danger, with things they'd never tried before, no matter how good they were. Oft *because* of how good they were. And one wee taste of the forbidden, oft translated into hunger for other fruit. *Hunger, Chloe-lass,* he willed silently. *I'll sate any desire you have.* He could nearly taste her innocence on his tongue. Indeed, would, very soon.

"You've been doing something bad since the moment you met me, lass," he purred, meaning himself, but when she glanced askance, he provoked, "snooping about in my bedroom—"

"I only snooped in your bedroom because you had stolen artifacts in there—"

"And why were you in my bedroom in the first place?" he asked silkily.

She flushed. "Because I was, er . . . I got, er . . ." she sputtered.

"And I must confess, I've been wondering just what

you were doing near enough my bed to find those books. You must have been all but *in* it. Were you curious about me? About my bed? Mayhap about me in it?"

Her blush deepened. "I was just snooping, okay? But if I'd had any idea what I was going to find, I wouldn't have."

He smiled, a slow seductive smile, and Chloe caught her breath.

"Take a sip of port and let it lie upon your tongue a moment."

Chloe sipped.

"Now the cigar."

She puffed lightly. Sweet and smoky, a fascinating combination. Another sip, another puff. She laughed. She felt silly puffing on the fat cigar. She felt warm and alive. She turned her head to tell him what she thought, but he'd dropped beside her on the sofa and she ran into his lips.

Smack into that decadent, full, sinful mouth, and the minute they made contact, Chloe *sizzled*. Heat lanced through her from head to toe; a kind of wild heat she'd never felt before. A heat that she instinctively understood could burn her beyond recognition. He'd not smoked his cigar, and he tasted of malt, then his hot tongue slipped inside her mouth and her entire world upended. She scarcely noticed when he deftly slid the cigar and glass from her hands, depositing them elsewhere. He might have dropped them on the floor for all she cared.

"Chloe-lass. I need to taste you. Open more. *Give* me."

He buried his hands in her hair, kissing her, and suddenly it was utterly insignificant that he stole artifacts, that he'd taken her captive, that he lived outside the law. She cared only that his tongue was in her mouth, and how it made her feel. The world ceased to exist beyond that.

Slow, deep kisses, erotic nips with his teeth, his mouth

gliding, slipping and sliding over hers. He caught her lower lip and tugged lazily away, returned to catch it again, then slanted his mouth firmly over hers, plundering. He nibbled, he sucked, he consumed. The man didn't simply kiss, he made love to a woman's mouth, made it feel all hot and swollen and achy. Made her make funny noises and feel shaky all over. Made her feel like she might—

I'm dying without you. Call me. It's Katherine.

—totally lose herself and fall for him like countless women undoubtedly had. A woman he'd not called back. And unlike what she'd heard in the sophisticated purr of Katherine's voice, Chloe didn't possess the proper worldliness, the necessary defenses. If she were foolish enough to let him, the man would use her and discard her. And there'd be no one to blame but herself. It wasn't as if she didn't know, going in, what kind of man he was. Definitely the love-'em-and-leave-'em type. And how would she feel, knowing she'd been just another hit-and-run? Used, that was how.

"S-stop," she breathed.

He didn't. His hands dropped from her hair to her breasts, moving possessively over them, cupping and plumping. His thumbs glided over her nipples, and they peaked instantly. She felt like she was drowning. The man was too overwhelmingly male and sexual, and Chloe knew that she had to stop him, because in a few more moments, she wouldn't be able to remember why she should.

"Please," she cried. "Stop!"

He held her lower lip hostage for a long, erotic moment, then, with a ragged growl, he broke the kiss. He rested his forehead against hers, his breathing shallow and fast. When had it gotten so cold in the room? she wondered dimly. There must be a window open somewhere, letting in an icy breeze. She shivered. Her skin was hot, flushed from his passion, yet the fine hair all over her body had puckered into goose bumps.

"I won't hurt you," he said, his voice low and urgent.

Maybe not physically, she thought, *but there are other kinds of pain.* In twenty-four hours she'd become hopelessly infatuated with a thief. Mesmerized by a stranger who dripped "forbidden" and "secrets" and "criminal." She shook her head, straining to pull away from him. Accepting a bribe was one thing, losing herself was another. And she had no doubt that she could get lost in such a man. They simply weren't in the same league.

His hands went back up to her hair and he clutched tightly, his head down, and for a moment she thought he would refuse to let her go. Then he raised his head and looked at her, his gaze dark and intense.

"I want you, lass."

"You hardly even know me," she retorted shakily. She suspected that when Dageus MacKeltar told a woman he wanted her in such a voice, he didn't hear "no" often, if ever.

"I wanted you the moment I saw you on the street."

"On the street?" He'd seen her on the street? When? Where? The thought that he'd noticed her before they'd met in his bedroom made her feel breathless.

"You were arriving when I was leaving. I was in the cab behind you. I saw you and I—" he broke off abruptly.

"What?"

He smiled bitterly and traced the pad of his thumb over her lower lip, still swollen and damp from his kisses. "And I told myself a lass like you was no' for me."

"Why?"

The desire in his eyes ebbed, replaced by such a remote, empty expression that she felt it like a slap. He'd shut her out. Completely. She could feel it, and didn't like it one bit. Felt bereft.

He stood abruptly. "Come, lass, let's put you to bed." He smiled mockingly, another one of those that didn't reach his cool eyes. "Alone, if you insist."

"But why? Why would you think that?" It was terribly important to her to hear his answer.

He didn't answer her. Merely escorted her to the bathroom, offered her towels for a shower if she wished—which she was definitely too uncomfortable to do and refused, but washed up and brushed her teeth again—then motioned her toward the bed so he could tie her.

"*Must* you do this?" she protested as he knotted the first scarf.

"No' if I'm sleeping with you," was his cool reply.

She thrust her wrist at him.

"I know you're untouched, if 'tis what fashes you."

"And we both know *you're* not," she muttered irritably. *Mr. Multiple-Magnums-beneath-the-bed. How did he know she was a virgin? Was it stamped on her forehead? Were her kisses so inept?*

" 'Twas naught but practice for the day I might please you."

She shivered. Smooth, very smooth. "If you don't tie me, I promise I won't try to escape."

"Aye, you would."

"I give you my word."

With a graceful flick of his hand, he tossed one of the pillows from the bed.

Chloe didn't have to glance down to know what he'd just revealed: the *skean dhu* she'd wrapped earlier in a soft piece of plaid she'd found, then tucked beneath the pillow so she might cut herself free later. "I was keeping it safe. I didn't know where else to put it." She batted her lashes.

"No words of promise or even desire binds a woman. Bonds bind a woman." He scooped up both blade and plaid, crossed the room, and tucked them in a drawer.

She narrowed her eyes. "Who taught you that? Women? Sounds to me like maybe you pick the wrong ones. What are your criteria? Do you *have* any criteria?"

He shot her a dark look. "Aye. That they'll have me."

Blinking, she let him tie her. The man could have any woman.

There was a very dangerous moment when he fastened her second wrist. A long pregnant pause where they simply stared at each other. She wanted him, ached for him, and the intensity of it terrified her. She hardly knew the man, and what she did know about him was anything but reassuring.

As he closed the door he said over his shoulder, "Because you're a good lass." A heavy sigh. "And I'm no' a good man."

It took her a moment to understand what he was talking about. Then she realized he'd finally answered her question—why she was not for him.

·6·

I'm no' a good man.

'Twas the only real warning she would ever get from him on her sweet, inevitable fall from grace.

Dageus sipped his whisky and stared at her. That kiss, that one mere sip of a kiss still lay upon his tongue, honey-sweet, and no amount of whisky could wash it off. He'd scarce begun to taste her when she'd stopped him.

And stopping had damn near killed him. His tongue in her mouth, his hands in her hair, for a brief moment he'd been filled with icy rage, pure and black, something that refused to be denied. The ancient ones had stirred, demanding he sate his hunger. *Force her,* a dark voice had purred. *You can make her like it.*

He'd waged a dread battle against them, hence the carefulness with which he'd pulled away. That blackness was not him. Would not be him. He would not permit it. It could too easily consume him.

He knew he shouldn't be in the bedchamber. He wasn't in the best temper for many reasons, not the least of them that he'd used magic earlier, first on a brief visit to Security before she'd wakened, reminding them that they saw Chloe Zanders leave yestreen, and later when she'd tried to escape, a reflexive action, without thought. The interior dead bolt had been locked for a change, and she'd unlocked it, and he'd jammed it with a whispered word before she could open it.

Then, pressed close to her, with blades betwixt them and a bit of blood on his skin and the darkness rising, he'd made clear the cost of her escape: his life.

Wagering she'd back down swiftly.

A perverse part of him daring her to end his dishonor at the end of his own sword.

Either way, he'd have more peace.

She'd accepted his blade and stayed. She didn't ken the full significance of that. When a Druid offered his favored weapon, his *Selvar*, the one he wore against his skin, to a woman, he offered his protection. His guardianship. Forever.

And she'd taken it.

She was sleeping on her back, the only way she could, with her wrists restrained, though he'd left considerable play in the bonds. Her lovely breasts rose and fell with the gentle, slow breaths of deep slumber.

He should let her go.

And he knew he wasn't going to. He wanted Chloe Zanders in ways he'd never wanted a lass before. She made him feel like a sapling lad, wanting to impress her with masculine feats of prowess, protect her, sate her every desire, to be the focus of her shiny bright heart, so full of innocence. As if she might somehow wash him clean again.

She was curiosity and wonder; he was cynicism and despair. She was bursting with dreams; he was carved out and hollow inside. Her heart was young and true; his was iced with disillusion, scarce beating enough to keep him alive.

She was all he'd dreamed of once, long ago. The kind of lass to whom he'd have given binding Druid vows, pledged his life to forever. Smart, the woman spoke four languages that he knew of. Tenacious, determined, logical in a circuitous way. Real, believing in things. Protective of the old ways, that was evident each time she watched him turn a page. Twice she'd handed him a tissue to do it with when he'd forgotten, lest he get the oil of his skin on the precious pages.

And he could sense in her a woman that wanted to break out. A woman who'd lived a quiet life, a respectable life, but hungered for more. He could sense, with the unerring instincts of a sexual predator, that Chloe was wanton at heart. That the man she chose to grant liberties to, would be granted them unconditionally. Sexually aggressive, dominant to the bone, he recognized in her his perfect bedmate.

He was a man who could offer no promises, no assurances. A man with a terrible darkness growing inside him.

And all he could think was . . .

. . . when he took her, he would strip the clothing from her body, baring every inch of her to his immense hunger.

He would stretch himself atop her, forearms flush to the bed on either side of her head, pinning her long hair beneath his weight. He would kiss her . . .

He was kissing her and she was drowning in the heat and sensuality of the man. Her hands tied to the bedposts, her body naked, she was lying in his bed, on fire. His for the taking.

He didn't just kiss, he claimed ownership. Took her mouth with urgency, as if his life depended on his kissing her. Licked and nipped and tasted, sucking her lower lip, catching it with his teeth. His hands were on her breasts and her skin ached with need where he touched. He kissed her long and deep and slow, then kissed her hard and punishing and fast. . . .

. . . like fine china, delicate china, then he would punish her with hard kisses for being so perfect, for being everything he didn't deserve. For the wonder she still had, the wonder she made him remember once feeling.

Being a man, he would have to know that she needed him. So he would kiss every inch of her silken skin, dragging his tongue over the peaks of her nipples. Rasping them with his unshaven jaw, till they budded hard and tight for him, teeth nipping, then he would move those kisses to the sweet feminine heat between her legs, where he would taste that taut aching bud. Slow long strokes of his tongue there.

Ever-so-delicate nips.

Then more strong strokes, faster and faster until she writhed beneath him.

But still, she wouldn't be wild enough for him.

So he would slip his finger inside her. Find that spot, one of several special ones, that drove a woman wild. Feel her tighten convulsively around him. Feel her hunger. Then withdraw and taste her with his tongue again. Lapping. Lapping. Drowning in the sweet taste of her.

Then two fingers. Then his tongue. Until she . . .

"Please!" Chloe cried, arching her back, arching up and up, begging for his touch.

Dageus loomed above her, his hard body gilded by firelight, a sheen of sweat glistening on his skin.

"What do you want, Chloe?" His glittering gaze challenged

her, dared her to want, dared her to speak of those things she'd never said aloud. Secret fantasies she sheltered in her woman's heart. Fantasies she knew he'd be only too willing to fulfill; one and all.

"Please!" she cried, not knowing how to put it into words. "Everything!"

His nostrils flared and he inhaled sharply, and she suddenly wondered if she'd said something far more dangerous than she knew.

"Everything?" he purred. "Everything I might want? Everything I might dream of doing to you? Do you mean to gift me your innocence—without condition?"

A heartbeat passed, then two.

. . . would say that she needed him. Was willing to relinquish everything. He would turn his years of mastery—all those years he'd made heated love with a cold heart to women who'd wanted nothing from him but his body—to Chloe's lush curves, the backs of her knees, the inside of her thighs, laving every inch with his tongue. He would untie her, roll her onto her stomach. Stretch her hands above her head, catch them in one of his, nipping the nape of her neck. He would drag his tongue down her spine, lavishing attention on his favorite spot, the slender, delicate arch where a woman's back met her bottom, then kiss every inch of her sweet ass.

Kneeling above her, straddling her, he would nudge her soft curves with his hard cock. Feel her buck up and back . . .

"Dageus!" Chloe cried. He was behind her, hot and silky and hard against her bottom, and she felt so damned empty inside that it hurt.

"What, lass?"

"Make love to me," she gasped.

"Why?" He stretched flat atop her, skin to skin from her head to her toes, his palms to the backs of her hands, pressing them against the bed, letting her feel the full weight of him, making it hard for her to breathe. He nudged her thighs apart with his knee. He thrust his hips, pushing against her, but not inside her. Deliberately teasing her.

"I want you."

"Want is no' enough. You must feel like you can't breathe wi'out me inside you. Do you need me? No matter the cost? Though I've warned you I'm no' a good man?"

"Yes! God, yes!"

"Say it."

"I need you!"

"Say my name."

"Dageus!"

Chloe snapped awake with a violent start, sweating and breathing hard, and so intensely aroused that she hurt from head to toe. "Wh-what . . ." she trailed off, remembering the dream. *Oh, God,* she thought, appalled. Shaking her head, she suddenly realized she wasn't alone.

He was in the room with her.

Sitting not two feet away from her in a chair beside the bed, watching her with those glittering tiger-eyes.

Their gazes collided.

And she had the most awful feeling that he somehow knew. Knew that she'd been dreaming of him. In his smoldering gaze was a strange satisfaction.

A hot flush suffused her from head to toe. She glanced frantically down. Thank God, she was still fully clothed. It had been but a dream.

He couldn't *possibly* know.

She tugged the covers up to her chin. The air in the room was positively frigid.

"You sounded restless," he purred, his voice dark as the shadowy room. "I came to check on you and thought I'd sit nearby till you calmed."

"I'm calm now," she lied blatantly. Her heart was hammering and she turned away so she wouldn't betray something with her eyes.

She sneaked a quick peek at him. Beautiful man. Sitting half-gilded by the dying firelight. One side of his face golden, the other in shadows. She was nearly panting. Bit her lip to quiet herself.

"Then I should go?"

"You should go."

"You doona . . . *need* . . . anything, Chloe-lass?"

"Just for you to let me go," she said stiffly.

Never, Dageus thought, pulling the door firmly closed. When she'd wakened, he'd been stunned to realize that somehow his thoughts, the painfully intense seduction he'd been imagining, had crept into her dreams.

Power. There was power inside him and he dare not forget that. Somehow that power had made her share his fantasy.

A dangerous thing.

Apparently, he'd used magic yet again, without even realizing it.

A muscle leaped in his jaw. 'Twas getting damned hard to see where the ancient ones began and he ended.

He had work yet to do this eve, he reminded himself, shaking himself sharply, resisting the darkness that stretched and flexed within him. The darkness that tried to convince him he was a god, and aught he wished was his due.

Tugging on his boots and donning his coat, he cast a last glance in the direction of the bedchamber before he slipped from the penthouse. She was securely bound, would never know he was gone. It would be but for a few hours.

Before he left, he turned the thermostat up. It was cold in the penthouse.

· 7 ·

He had to use magic again, the *féth fiada,* the Druid spell that made the user difficult for the human eye to see, and by the time Dageus returned to the penthouse, he was too tightly strung to sleep. He'd not known such a spell existed before the dark ones had claimed him that fateful eve. Now their knowledge was *his* knowledge, and although he tried to pretend he was unaware of the full extent of the power within him, sometimes when he was doing something, he'd suddenly know a spell to make it easier, as if he'd known it all his life.

Some of the spells he now "simply knew" were horrific. The ancient ones within him had been judge, jury, and executioner on many occasions.

It was getting dangerous, he was growing more detached. Perched at the edge of the abyss, and the abyss was looking back, with feral, crimson eyes.

He needed. A woman's body, a woman's tender touch. A woman's desire to make him feel like a man not a beast.

He could go to Katherine; it wouldn't matter the hour. She would welcome him with open arms and he could lose himself in her, shove her ankles above her head, and drive himself into her until he felt human again.

He didn't want Katherine. He wanted the woman upstairs in his bed.

He could all too easily see himself taking the stairs three at a time, stripping as he went, stretching atop her helpless, tied form, teasing her until she was animal with need, until she begged him to take her. He knew he could make her give herself to him. Och, mayhap she'd not be willing at first, but he knew ways of touching that could drive a woman wild.

His breathing was ragged.

He was headed for the stairs, tugging his sweater over his head when he caught himself.

Deep breaths. Focus, Keltar.

If he went to her now, he would hurt her. He was too raw, too hungry. Gritting his teeth, he yanked his sweater back on and whirled about, stared sightlessly out the window for a time.

Two more times he caught himself heading up the stairs. Two more times he forced himself back down. He dropped to the floor and did push-ups until his body ran with sweat. Then crunches, and more push-ups. He recited bits of history, counted backward in Latin, then Greek, then in the more obscure, difficult languages.

Eventually, he regained control. Or as much control as he was going to get without sex.

She was going to shower today, he decided, suddenly chafed by her lack of faith in him, if he had to lock her in the bathroom all day.

As if he might break in on her when she was in the shower.

He'd just *proved* that he was in control. Verily, he was all about control where she was concerned. Had she any idea what he was battling, and how difficult it had been thus far—yet he'd prevailed—then she'd shower.

Ha. Then she'd, like as not, fling herself from my terrace forty-three floors up merely to escape me, he thought, getting up and propping one of the terrace doors slightly ajar.

He stared out over the quiet city—as quiet as Manhattan ever got, still humming, even at four in the morning. Fickle March weather, the clime had been fluctuating for days, rising and dropping as much as thirty degrees in a few hours. Now it was temperate again, but the light rain could well turn to snow by midmorn. Spring was trying to beat back winter and failing, rather mirroring his bleak internal landscape.

Blowing out a gusty breath, he sat down to immerse himself in the third Book of Manannán. This final tome, then he would go. Not on the morrow, but the next day. He'd done all he could here. He doubted what he wanted was in the tome anyway. There'd once been five Books of Manannán, but only three were extant. He'd already read the first two; they'd dealt with the legends of Ireland's gods before the arrival of the Tuatha Dé Danaan. This third volume continued the tales of the gods, and their encounters with the first wave of settlers to invade Ireland. As slowly as the historical timeline was moving, Dageus suspected the arrival of the race of creatures he was interested in would not be addressed until the fifth volume. Which no longer existed except mayhap in one place: the Keltar library.

Whether he liked it or not, he was going to have to go home. Face his brother so he could search the Keltar collection. He'd wasted many months trying to find a solution on his own, and time was running out. If he waited much longer . . . well, he dare not wait longer.

And what of the lass? his honor roused.

He was too weary to bother lying to himself.

Mine.

He would endeavor to seduce her with her own desires first, make it easier for her, but should she resist, one way or another, she was going with him.

Chloe stood in the hot spray of seven jetting shower heads—three on each side, one above—sighing with pleasure. She'd been feeling like the poster child for grunge. The door was locked and the chair Dageus had brought her to prop beneath the handle was propped snugly beneath the handle.

After dreaming about him and waking in the middle of the night to find him watching her with virtually the same look he'd worn in her dream, she'd hardly been able to meet his gaze when he'd untied her this morning. Just thinking about the dream made her feel flushed and shaky.

I'm no' a good man, he'd said. He was right. He wasn't. He was a man who lived by his own rules. He stole other people's personal property—though he insisted he was "borrowing" and, oddly, left more valuable items. He held her captive—though he cooked scrumptious meals and, frankly, she'd agreed to cooperate for a bribe. Criminal at worst, at best he existed on the fringes of civilized society.

Then again, since she'd accepted his bribe, she supposed she was on those fringes now too.

Still, she mused, a truly bad man wouldn't bother warning a woman that he wasn't a good man. A truly bad man wouldn't stop kissing a woman when she said stop.

What an enigma he was, and so strangely anachronistic! Though his penthouse was modern, his demeanor was distinctly old-world. His speech also was modern, yet he lapsed, at times, into an infrequent, curious formality, splashed with old Gaelic colloquialisms. There was something more to him than she was seeing. She could feel it dancing just at the edge of her comprehension, but no matter how hard she tried, she couldn't bring it into focus. And there was definitely something about his eyes . . .

She might not be as worldly as New York women, but she wasn't completely naïve; she could feel danger in him—a woman would have to be dead not to. It dripped from him as liberally as testosterone oozed from his pores. Still, he tempered it with discipline and restraint. He had her at his complete mercy, and he'd not taken advantage of it.

She shook her head. Maybe for him, she thought, as easily as women must fall for him, it was the chase he enjoyed most.

Well, she thought, bristling, he could chase all he wanted. She might be on the fringes, but that didn't mean she was just going to up and fall in bed with him, no matter how much she might secretly long to be initiated into the exotic, erotic, mysterious Dageus MacKeltar club. Salient word there being "club"—as in, with *lots* of members.

With that resolved, she shampooed her hair twice (she'd never gone without a shower for two days straight before) and stood under the pulsing spray until she felt squeaky clean. And then a bit longer. Those massaging shower heads were to die for.

Wrapping herself in a luxurious towel, she dislodged the chair and unlocked the door.

When she opened it, she gaped. Half her wardrobe

was piled neatly on the bed. She blinked. Yup, there it was. In tidy piles. Panties (uh-hmm, and *those* were staying firmly on her butt), bras, dresses, sweaters, jeans, a lacy little nightie, socks, boots, shoes, the works. They were stacked in "outfit" piles, she noted, bemused. He'd not just grabbed clothing, but had matched things together as if envisioning her wearing them.

He'd even brought some of her books, she noticed, wandering over to the bed.

Three *romance* novels, the dastardly man. Scottish romance novels. What had he done? Poked through all her stuff while he was there? Right on top was *The Highlander's Touch*, one of her favorite novels about an immortal Highlander.

She snorted. The man was incorrigible. Bringing her steamy, sexy things to read. As if she needed any help thinking steamy thoughts around him.

She could hear him downstairs, talking quietly on the phone. She could smell the scent of fresh-brewed coffee.

And though she knew she should be offended that he'd broken into her apartment and rummaged through her drawers, he'd put much thought into his selections, and she was oddly charmed.

※

He hardly spoke to her all day. He was in a downright brooding mood. Controlled and remote. Perfectly polite, perfectly disciplined. Utterly self-contained. His eyes were . . . strange again, and she wondered if maybe they took on varying hues under different lighting, like hazel sometimes went from greenish-blue to greenish-brown. Not amber, they were the dull shade of copper just before it blackened.

She'd perched on the counter and watched him cook breakfast—kippers, tatties, toast, and porridge with cream and blueberries—eyeing him while his back was to her. For the first time she'd noticed his hair. She'd known it was long; she hadn't realized how long because he wore it pulled back. But now that she was behind him, she could see that he'd folded it up several times before binding it in a leather wrap.

She decided it must fall to his waist when it was free. The thought of his sleek black hair sweeping his naked muscled back drove her crazy.

She wondered if he ever wore it down. It seemed so in keeping with his character that it would be long and wild, but meticulously restrained unless he chose to free it.

She tried to make small talk, but he didn't rise to any of the bait she cast. Fishing, trying to pick his brain, getting nothing but grunts and incoherent murmurs.

They sat together in silence for hours that afternoon, with Chloe delicately turning the pages of the Midhe Codex with tissues, and sneaking peeks at Dageus while he worked with the Book of Manannán, scribbling notes as he translated.

At five o'clock, she got up and turned the news on, wondering if there might be some small mention of her disappearance. As if, she thought wryly. One little girl gone missing in the wormy Big Apple? Both police and newscasters had better things to do.

He looked at her then, a hint of smugness playing about his lips.

She arched a questioning brow, but he said nothing. She listened absently while she read, then suddenly her attention was riveted to the screen.

"The Gaulish Ghost struck again last night, or so the police believe. Baffled might be the best way to describe New York's finest. At an unknown time, early this morning, all the artifacts previously stolen by the Gaulish Ghost were left at the front

desk of the police station. Once again, no one saw a thing, which makes one wonder just what our police . . ."

There was more, but Chloe didn't hear it.

She glanced down at the text she was holding. Then at him.

"I bartered for that one, lass."

"You really did it," she breathed, shaking her head. "When you went to my apartment for my things, you took them back. I don't believe it."

"I told you I was merely borrowing them."

She stared at him, utterly flummoxed. He'd done it. He'd returned them! A sudden thought occurred to her. One she didn't much care for. "That means you're leaving soon, doesn't it?"

He nodded, his expression unfathomable.

"Oh." She pretended a hasty fascination with her cuticles to conceal the disappointment that flooded her.

Hence she missed the cool, satisfied curve of his lips, a touch too feral to be called a smile.

❧

Outside Dageus MacKeltar's penthouse, on a sidewalk crammed with people rushing to escape the city at the end of the long work week, one man wove his way through the crowd and joined a second man. They moved discreetly aside, loitering near a newsstand. Though clad in expensive dark suits, with short hair and nondescript features, both were marked by unusual tattoos on their necks. The upper part of a winged serpent arced above crisp collar and tie.

"He's up there. With a woman," Giles said softly. He'd just come down from rented rooms in the building on the opposite corner, where he'd been watching through binoculars.

"The plan?" his companion, Trevor, inquired softly.

"We wait until he leaves; with luck he'll leave her there. Our orders are to get him on the run. Force him to rely upon magic to survive. Simon wants him back overseas."

"How?"

"We'll make him a fugitive. Hunted. The woman makes things simpler than I'd hoped. I'll slip in, take care of her, alert the police, anonymously of course, and make his penthouse the stage of a cold-blooded, gruesome murder. Set all the cops in the city after him. He'll be forced to use his powers to escape. Simon believes he won't permit himself to be imprisoned. Though if he were, that might work to our advantage as well. I've no doubt time in a federal prison would hasten the transformation."

Trevor nodded. "And I?"

"You wait here. Too risky for both of us to go up. He's not to know we exist yet. If anything goes awry, ring Simon immediately."

Trevor nodded again, and they drifted apart, to settle back and wait. They were patient men. They'd been waiting for this moment all their lives. They were the lucky ones, those born in the hour of the Prophecy's fruition.

To a man, they would die to see the Draghar live again.

A messenger from a travel agency arrived shortly before the small crew of people who delivered dinner from Jean Georges.

Chloe couldn't begin to imagine what something like that cost—didn't think Jean Georges delivered—but she suspected that when one had as much money as Dageus MacKeltar, virtually anything could be bought.

While they ate before the fire in the living room, he

continued working on the book that had initially landed her in this mess.

The envelope from the travel agency lay unopened on the table between them—a glaring reminder, chafing her.

Earlier, while he'd been in the kitchen, not quite brazen enough to tear open the envelope, she'd snooped instead through his notes—what she could read of them. It appeared that he was translating and copying every reference to the Tuatha Dé Danaan, the race that had allegedly arrived in one of several waves of Irish invasions. There were a few scribbled questions about the identity of the Draghar, and numerous notes about Druids. Between her major in ancient civilizations and Grandda's tales, Chloe was well versed in most of it. With the exception of the mysterious Draghar, it was nothing she'd not read about before.

Still, some of his notes were written in languages she couldn't translate. Or even identify, and that gave her a kind of queasy feeling. She knew a great deal about ancient languages, from Sumerian to present, and could usually target, at least, area and approximate era. But much of what he'd penned—in an elegant minuscule cursive worthy of any illuminated manuscript—defied her comprehension.

What on earth was he looking for? He certainly seemed to be a man on a mission, working on his task with intense focus.

With each new bit of information she gathered about him, she grew more intrigued. Not only was he strong, gorgeous, and wealthy, but he was unarguably brilliant. She'd never met anyone like him before.

"Why don't you just tell me?" she asked point-blank, gesturing at the book.

He raised his gaze and she felt the heat of it instantly. Throughout the day, when he hadn't been utterly ignoring her, the few times he'd looked at her, there'd been such blatant lust in his gaze that it was eroding every bit of common sense she possessed. The sheer force of his unguarded desire was more seductive than any aphrodisiac. No wonder so many women fell prey to his charm! He had a way of making a woman feel, with a mere glance, as if she were the most desirable woman in the world. How was a woman to stare into the face of such lust, and not feel lust in response?

He was leaving soon.

And he couldn't have made it more clear that he wanted to sleep with her.

Those two thoughts in swift conjunction were abjectly risky.

"Well?" she pressed irritably. Irritated with herself for being so weak and susceptible to him. Irritated with him for being so attractive. And he'd just *had* to go and return those texts, confounding her already confounded feelings about him. "What, already?"

He arched a dark brow, his gaze raking her in a way that made her feel as if a sudden sultry breeze had caressed her. "What if I told you, lass, that I seek a way to undo an ancient and deadly curse?"

She scoffed. He couldn't be serious. Curses weren't real. No more than the Tuatha Dé Danaan were real. Well, she amended, she'd never actually reached a firm conclusion about the Tuatha Dé or any of the "mythological" races said to have once inhabited Ireland. Scholars had dozens of arguments against their alleged existence.

Still . . . Grandda had believed.

A professor of mythology, he'd taught her that every myth or legend contained some reality and truth, however distorted it had grown over centuries of oral repetition by bards who'd adapted their recitations to the unique interests of their audiences, or scribes who'd heeded the dictums of their sponsors. The original content of uncounted manuscripts had been corrupted by shoddy translations and adaptations designed to reflect the political and religious clime of the day. Anyone who devoted time to a study of history eventually realized that historians had succeeded in gathering only a handful of sand from the vast, uncharted desert of the past, and it was impossible to vouchsafe the terrain of the Sahara from a few mere grains.

"Do you believe in this stuff?" she asked, waving a hand at the jumble of texts, curious to know his take on history. As smart as he was, it was certain to be interesting.

"Much of it, lass."

She narrowed her eyes. "Do you believe the Tuatha Dé Danaan really existed?"

His smile was bitter. "Och, aye, lass. There was a time when I didn't, but I do now."

Chloe frowned. He sounded resigned, like a man who'd been given incontrovertible proof. "What made you believe?"

He shrugged and made no reply.

"Well, then, what kind of curse?" she pressed. This was fascinating stuff, the kind that had led her to her choice of career. It was like talking with Grandda again, debating possibilities, opening her mind to new ones.

He looked away, stared into the fire.

"Aw, come on! You're leaving soon, what harm is there in telling me? Who would I tell?"

"What if I told you that 'tis *I* who am cursed?"

She glanced about at his opulent home. "I'd tell you a lot of people would like to be cursed like you."

"You'd never believe the truth." He flashed her another of those mocking smiles that didn't reach his eyes. She realized that she'd give a great deal to see him smile, actually smile and mean it.

"Try me."

It took him longer to respond this time, and when he did his gaze was filled with cynical amusement. "What if I told you, lass, that I'm a Druid from a time long past?"

Chloe gave him an exasperated look. "If you don't want to talk to me, all you have to do is tell me that. But don't try to shut me up with nonsense."

With a tight smile, he nodded once, as if he'd satisfied himself of something. "What if I told you that when you kiss me, lass, I doona feel cursed? That mayhap your kisses could save me. Would you?"

Chloe caught her breath. It was such a silly thing to say, as silly as his joke about being a Druid . . . but so hopelessly romantic. That her kisses could save a man!

"I thought not." His gaze dropped back to the text and the heat of it had been so intense she felt chilled by its absence.

She frowned. Feeling like the biggest coward, feeling strangely defiant. She glared at the infernal envelope from the travel agency. "*When* are you leaving?" she asked irritably.

"On the morrow's eve," he said, without looking at her.

Chloe gaped. So soon? Tomorrow her grand adventure would be over? Though only yesterday she'd tried to escape him, she felt oddly deflated by her encroaching freedom.

Freedom didn't seem so sweet when it meant never seeing him again. She knew all too well what would happen: He would disappear from her life, and she would return to her job at The Cloisters (Tom would never fire her—not for missing a few days of work—she'd think of some excuse), and each time she looked at a medieval artifact she would think of him. Late at night, when she awakened filled with that terrible restlessness, she would sit in the dark, holding her *skean dhu*, wondering the worst question of all: What might have been? She would never again be wined and dined in a luxury penthouse on Fifth Avenue. Never again be looked at in such a way. Her life would resume its usual stultifying cadence. How long before she would forget that she'd once felt intrepid? Felt so briefly and intensely alive?

"Will you be coming back to Manhattan?" she asked in a small voice.

"Nay."

"Never?"

"Never."

A soft sigh escaped her. She fidgeted with a curly strand of hair, spiraling it around a finger. "What kind of curse?"

"Would you try to aid me if I was?" He looked up again and she felt a tension in him she couldn't fathom. As if her reply was somehow critical.

"Yes," she admitted, "I probably would." And it was true. Though she didn't approve of Dageus MacKeltar's methods, though there was much about him she didn't understand, were he suffering, she wouldn't be able to refuse him.

"Despite what I've done to you?"

She shrugged. "You haven't exactly hurt me." And he'd given her a *skean dhu*. Would he really let her keep it?

She was about to ask him that when, with a swift flick of his wrist, he tossed the envelope from the travel agency at her. "Then come with me."

Chloe caught the envelope by one end, her heart skipping a beat. "Wh-what?" She blinked at him, thinking she must have heard him wrong.

He nodded. "Open it."

Frowning, Chloe opened the envelope. She smoothed

the papers wonderingly. Tickets to Scotland, for Dageus MacKeltar . . . and Chloe Zanders! Just seeing her name printed on the ticket gave her a little chill. Departing tomorrow night at seven o'clock from JFK. Arriving in London for a short layover, then on to Inverness. Within less than forty-eight hours she could be in Scotland!

If she dared.

She opened and closed her mouth several times.

Finally, "Oh, what *are* you?" she breathed disbelievingly. "The devil himself, come to tempt me?"

"Do I, lass? Do I tempt you?"

On just about every freaking level, she thought, but refused to give him the satisfaction of hearing that.

"I can't just up and travel to Scotland with some . . . some—" She broke off, sputtering.

"Thief?" he supplied lazily.

She snorted. "Okay, so you returned those things. So what? I hardly even know you!"

"Do you wish to? I'm leaving on the morrow. 'Tis now or never, lass." He waited, watching her. "Some chances come but once, Chloe, and swift are gone."

Chloe stared at him in silence, feeling utterly divided. Part of her was resolutely digging in her heels, ticking off on her fingers a thousand reasons why she absolutely could *not* do such a crazy, impulsive thing. Another part— a part that both horrified and intrigued her—was jumping up and down, shouting, "Say yes!" She had the sudden, strange desire to get up and go look at herself in the mirror, to see if she was changing outside as well as in.

Dare she do something so patently outrageous? Take such a chance? Put everything on the line and see what came of it?

On the other hand, dare she go back to her life the way it was? Go back to living in her tiny one-room plus bathroom-the-size-of-a-matchbox efficiency, making her solitary way to work each day, gaining solace only from playing with artifacts that would never be hers?

She'd tasted more, and—damn the man—now she wanted it.

What was the worst that could happen? If he had any intention of physically harming her, he could have done so long before now. The only real threat he posed was one *she* controlled: whether she would let him seduce her. Whether she would risk falling for a man who was, without question, an inveterate lone wolf and bad boy. A man who made no apologies and offered no comforting lies.

If she didn't fall for him, if she was a smart girl and kept her wits about her, pretty much the worst that could happen was that he might leave her stranded in Scotland. And that didn't strike her as completely unpalatable. If he did, she was confident that, with her waitressing experience in college, she could get a job in a pub over there. She could stay awhile, see her grandda's homeland, her trip over paid for. She would survive. She would more than survive. She might finally live.

What did she have here? Her job at The Cloisters. No social life to speak of. No family. She'd been alone for years now, ever since Grandda had died. In fact, more lonely than she'd cared to admit. A little lost and rootless, which she suspected accounted for her determination to visit Grandda's village, in hopes that she might find some remnants of roots there.

Here was her golden opportunity, coupled with the promise of an adventure she'd never forget, at the side of a man she already knew she'd never be able to forget.

Oh, God, Zanders, she thought, marveling, *you're talking yourself into this!*

What if he was leaving tomorrow and hadn't asked you to go with him? a tiny inner voice pressed. *What if he'd made it absolutely clear that he was leaving, and you would never see*

*him again? What would you have done with this last night
with him?*

Chloe inhaled sharply, shocked at herself.

Under those hypothetical circumstances, hypotheti-
cally, of course, she might have taken her one incredible
shot at a man like him, and let him take her to bed.
Learned what he had to teach her, eagerly allowed herself
to become the focus of all that smoldering promise of
sensual knowledge in his exotic eyes.

Looked at that way, going to Scotland with him didn't
seem quite so crazy.

He'd been watching her intently, and when she lifted
her wide-eyed gaze to his, he rose abruptly from the
couch opposite her and moved to stand before her. Impatiently, he pushed the coffee table aside and slipped to his
knees at her feet, wrapping his hands around her calves.
She felt the heat of his strong hands through her jeans.
His mere touch made her shiver.

"Come with me, lass." His voice was low and urgent.
"Think of your Scots blood. Doona you wish to stand on
the soil of your ancestors? Doona you wish to see the
heathery fields and moors? The mountains and the lochs?
I'm no' a man who oft makes promises, but I promise you
this"—he broke off, laughing softly as if at some private
joke—"I can show you a Scotland no other man could
ever show you."

"But my job—"

"To hell with your job. You speak the old languages.
Two of us can translate faster than one. I'll pay you to
help me."

"Really? How much?" Chloe blurted, then flushed, appalled by how quickly she'd asked.

He laughed again. And she knew that he knew he just
about had her.

"Select a piece—any piece—from my collection."

Her fingers curled covetously. He was the very devil; he had to be! He knew her price.

His voice dropped to an intimate purr. "Then choose two more. For one month of your time."

Her jaw dropped. Three artifacts, plus a trip to Scotland, for one month of her time? Was he *kidding*? She could sell any one of the artifacts upon her return to Manhattan (she made a mental note to choose one with which she could bear to part), go back to school, get her Ph.D. and work in any darned museum she wanted to! She could afford to take fabulous vacations, see the world. She—Chloe Zanders—could lead a glamorous, exciting life!

And all the devil ever wants in exchange, a small voice inside her purred caustically, *is a soul.*

She ignored it.

"Plus the *skean dhu*?" she clarified hastily.

"Aye."

"Why Inverness?" she asked breathlessly.

A shadow flitted across his gorgeous face. " 'Tis where my brother Drustan, and his wife live." He hesitated a moment, then added, "He collects texts as well."

And if she'd been wavering before, that clinched it for her. His brother and his wife; they would be seeing his family. How dangerous could a man be if he was taking her to his family? It wasn't as if they'd be alone together all the time. They'd be with his family. If she was clever, she'd be able to insulate herself from his seduction. And to spend a month with him! To get to know him, learn what made such a man tick. Who knew what might happen in a month? *And the prince fell in love with the peasant girl* . . .

Her heart was hammering.

"Say aye, lass. You want to, I see it in your eyes. Choose your pieces. We'll drop them off at your place before we leave."

"They'd never be safe in my apartment!" Even she knew how feeble that protest was.

"Then in one of those boxes. . . . One of those . . ." He glanced askance.

"Safety deposit boxes at a bank, you mean?"

"Aye, that's it, lass."

"And I get the key?" she pounced.

He nodded, the light of victory glittering in his predatory gaze. In a movie, the devil would wear just such a look before he said, "Sign here."

"Why are you doing this?" she breathed.

"I told you. I want you."

She shivered again. "Why?"

He shrugged. "Mayhap 'tis soul-alchemy. I doona ken. I doona care."

"I won't sleep with you, MacKeltar," she said suddenly. She didn't want him expecting that, needed it spelled out very carefully. If, at some point, she decided it was something she was willing to risk, that was one thing. But he needed to understand that it was not part of their bargain. Such things couldn't be bargained for. "Your artifacts purchase only my company as a translator. Not sex. That's not part of our deal."

"I doona wish it to be part of our 'deal.' "

"You think you can seduce me," she accused.

He caught his bottom lip with his teeth, released it slowly, and smiled. It was such an obvious thing, that gesture, Chloe thought irritably, deliberately designed to focus her attention on his lips. She saw through it, she did—but that didn't stop it from working every darned time he did it. From making her self-consciously moisten her own. Damn and double-damn, she thought, the man was good.

You're already seduced, Chloe-lass, Dageus thought, watching her, *'tis but a matter of accepting, a mere matter of time now.* She wanted him. 'Twas no one-sided heat. Theirs was a dangerous attraction that defied logic or reason. She was as helplessly fascinated by him as he was by her. Each knew they *should* walk away from the other: he, because he had no right to corrupt her; she, because on some level she sensed that something was wrong with him. But neither was able to resist the pull. Devil and Angel: he, seduced by her lightness; she, tempted by his darkness. Each drawn to what they lacked.

"Well, you won't succeed," she said stiffly, piqued by his smug masculinity.

"I trust you'll forgive a man for tryin', lass. A kiss to seal it?"

"I mean it," she pushed. "I'm not going to be just another one of your women."

"I doona see any other women around here, lass," he said coolly. "Do you?"

Chloe rolled her eyes.

"Have I asked anyone else to go to Scotland?"

"I said okay, all right? I'm just making sure you understand the terms."

"Och, I understand the terms," he said in a dangerously soft voice.

She thrust out her hand. "Then shake."

When he raised it to his lips and kissed it, Chloe felt suddenly light-headed.

The moment felt, well . . . positively momentous. As if she'd just made a decision that would forever alter her life, in ways she couldn't even begin to imagine. The Greeks had a word for such a moment. They called it *Kairos*—a moment of destiny.

Giddy with excitement, she rose and, with a connoisseur's eye and no mercy for the devil's wallet, began selecting her treasures.

· 8 ·

The man had never *really* tried to seduce her, Chloe decided the next morning when she raced down the steps and ran smack into him as he was stepping out of the first floor bathroom at the base of the stairs.

Seduction was this: one look at him in nothing but a towel.

Towering, two hundred pounds-plus of glistening golden skin poured over solid muscle, a sinfully small towel about his hips. Sculpted torso, rippling abs. A small cut marring his muscled chest, from their skirmish yesterday. A dark silky trail of hair disappearing beneath the soft white fabric.

Wet. Little beads of water shimmering on his skin. Thick black hair slicked back from his face, falling in a wet tangle to his waist.

And she knew that if she said the word, he would

stretch that incredible body full-length on top of her and—

Chloe made a little puffing noise, as if the air had been knocked out of her. "G'morning," she managed.

"*Madainn mhath,* lass," he purred his reply in Gaelic, steadying her by the elbows. "I trust you slept well without the bonds?"

He may not have tied her, but he'd slept outside her door. She'd heard him out there, moving about. "Yes," she said a bit breathlessly.

The man was just too beautiful for any woman's peace of mind.

He stared down at her a long moment. "We've much to do before we leave," he said, releasing her arms. "I'll be but a few moments getting dressed."

He skirted around her and went up the stairs. She turned, bemused, watching him with wide eyes. He hadn't even tried to kiss her, she thought, irritated with him that he hadn't, and irritated with herself for being irritated that he hadn't. Heavens, the man filled her with impossible duality. She was determined not to be seduced, yet she relished his seduction. It made her feel utterly feminine and alive.

Holy cow, she thought, watching him. With each step he ascended, the muscles in his legs flexed. Perfect calves, hard-as-rock thighs. Tight butt. Trim waist flaring to muscular shoulders. Absolutely ripped with muscle, he was powerful-looking in a lean, hungry way. Time seemed to spin out dreamily while she watched him.

"Oh!" she gasped suddenly, going rigid with shock.

Had he *really* done that?

God! How would she ever get that vision of him out of her mind?

At the top of the stairs the blasted man had dropped his towel!

As he was taking that last step. Legs slightly parted. Giving her the briefest glimpse of . . . *oh!*

She was still trying to breathe and not succeeding very well, when she heard a soft, husky and *very* smug laugh.

Shameless womanizer!

❦

Dageus left when Chloe got in the shower. It was either leave, or join her, and she was not yet ready to permit what he needed. Wiser not to imagine stepping into the shower behind her, taking her slippery, wet body in his arms, getting his hands on those magnificent bare breasts. He'd have her in Scotland anon, and there in his beloved land, he would claim her completely.

She would have let him kiss her, he'd seen it in the dilation of her eyes, in the softening of that lush petal-soft mouth.

But there was much to do before they left, and a skilled lover knew there were times when heightening a woman's anticipation was far more seductive than satisfying it. So, with a provocative bit of aloofness, he'd resisted the kisses he might have claimed and shown her instead what she was denying herself. What she could have if she but said the word. All of him, his insatiable desire, his need, his stamina, his determination to pleasure her as no other man could. Slave to her every carnal wish. He knew she'd seen the heavy weight of his testicles betwixt his legs and the thick head of his shaft below them as he'd taken the last step.

Best she get acquainted with his body now, in slow degrees.

He smiled, as the cab came to a dead stop in bumper-to-bumper traffic, recalling her soft, shocked little gasp. The knowledge that she had never been touched by another man inflamed him. He swallowed, his mouth dry with anticipation.

She'd given him a list of things she needed, and had told him her passport was in her jewelry box. She'd said aye. She'd agreed to come with him. He'd not liked the thought of having to coerce her.

He may not have yet seduced her into his bed, but he'd succeeded in seducing her into his life in countless other ways, each an invisible, silken knot, binding her to him as he lured her deeper into his world.

He was obsessed with her, as he'd never been with any other woman. He wanted to tell her more of his story. He'd been testing the waters last eve, feeling her out, trying to determine how much she might be able to take. He'd never once considered telling a woman aught about himself—particularly not one he hadn't yet bedded—but the possibility of a woman such as Chloe knowing what he was and choosing to be his woman anyway made the blood burn like fire in his veins. A part of him wanted to cram his reality down her throat, forcing her to accept him, with no excuses offered. A wiser part of him, the man he'd used to be, warned against such ruthlessness.

Slowly. He need employ utmost care and caution if he hoped to achieve his aim.

Late last eve, while watching her dither over which artifacts to choose, he'd realized with startling clarity, that it wasn't merely her body he wanted in his bed, he wanted *all* of her, given without reservation. He wanted it nigh as much as he wanted to be free of the evil within him, as if the two were somehow intertwined. And the animal in him sensed her killing weakness: Chloe was a lass who could be trapped by the man who won her heart. Netted and kept for life. His strategy was no longer simple seduction; he was vying for the core of her, her very lifeblood.

A woman such as she—entrust you with her heart? his honor mocked. *Have you lost your mind as well as your soul?*

"Haud yer wheesht," he growled softly.

The cab driver glanced at him in the rearview mirror. "Eh, what?"

"I wasn't talking to you."

And if you somehow manage to win her, what, then, will you do with her? his honor taunted. *Promise her a future?*

"Doona be trying to steal my now," Dageus gritted. " 'Tis all I own." And since her advent into his life, the now held more interest for him than it had in a long time. He was a man who'd succeeded at living since the eve he'd turned dark, only by doing it hour to hour.

Shrugging at the cabbie who was now watching him with blatant unease, he reached in his pocket, double-checking to be certain the list and her key were there.

The key wasn't. Thinking back, he realized he'd left it on the kitchen counter.

Though no one was more adept at breaking and entering than he, he did it only when necessary. And never in broad daylight.

He eyed the backed-up traffic impatiently. By the time the cab driver got them turned around in this mess, he could, like as not, be back at the penthouse on foot.

He shoved fare through the slot and stepped out into the rain.

Chloe shaved her legs with one of Dageus's razors (studiously ignoring the cheeky little voice that volunteered the wholly unsolicited opinion that a girl didn't need to shave when it was so cold out, unless she was planning to take her pants off for some reason), then stepped out of the shower and smoothed on lotion.

She moved into the bedroom, slipped into panties and

bra, then packed a few things in the luggage he'd set out for her while the lotion absorbed into her skin.

She was going to Scotland.

She couldn't believe it—how much her life had changed in just a few days. How much *she* seemed to be changing. In four days, to be exact. Four days ago she'd entered his penthouse, and today she was getting ready to fly across the ocean with him, with no idea what might come.

She shook her head, wondering if she'd completely lost her mind. She refused to ponder that thought too hard. When she thought about it, it seemed all wrong.

But it *felt* right.

She was going and that was that. She wasn't willing to let him walk out of her life this afternoon—forever. She was drawn to him as irresistibly as she was drawn to artifacts. Logic didn't have a damn thing to do with it.

Her mind raced over last-minute details and she decided she *had* to get word to Tom. He was probably already sick with worry and if he didn't hear from her for another month, he'd have the entire police department in an uproar. But she didn't want to talk to him on the phone, he would ask her too many questions; and the answers weren't completely convincing, even to her.

E-mail! That was it. She could shoot him a short note on the computer in the study.

She glanced at the clock. Dageus should be gone for at least an hour. She slipped into her jeans, tugged a T-shirt over her head, and hurried downstairs, wanting to get it out of the way immediately.

What would she say? What excuse could she possibly give him?

I met the Gaulish Ghost and he's not exactly a criminal. Actually, he's the sexiest, most intriguing, smartest man I've ever met and he's taking me to Scotland and he's paying me with

*ancient artifacts to help him translate texts because he thinks
he's somehow cursed.*

Yeah. Right. That coming from the woman who'd
endlessly berated Tom for his less than lily-white ethics.
Even if she told him the truth, he wouldn't believe it of
her. *She* didn't believe it of her.

She went into the study and was briefly sidetracked by
the artifacts scattered about. She would never get used to
such casual treatment of priceless relics. Scooping up a
handful of coins, she sorted through them. Two had
horses etched on them. Replacing the others on the desk,
she studied the two coins wonderingly. The ancient Con-
tinental Celts had etched horses on their coins. Horses
had been treasured creatures, symbolic of wealth and
freedom, meriting their own goddess, Epona, who'd
been commemorated in more surviving inscriptions and
statues than any other early goddess.

"Nah," she said, snorting. "There's no way they're that
old." They were in such mint condition that they looked
as if they'd been fashioned only a few years ago.

But then, she mused, all of his property did. Looked
new, that was. Impossibly new. New enough that she'd
entertained the possibility that they might be brilliant for-
geries. Very few artifacts survived the centuries in such
impeccable condition. Without the proper means to au-
thenticate them, she had to trust her judgment. And her
judgment said—impossible though it was to believe—his
artifacts were genuine.

A sudden image rose in her mind: Dageus, dressed in
full Scots tartan and regalia, his hair wild, war braids
plaited at his temples, swinging the claymore that hung
above the fireplace. The man exuded Celtic warrior, as if
he'd been transplanted in time.

"You are *such* a dreamer, Zanders," she chided herself.
Shaking her head to scatter her fanciful thoughts, she re-

placed the coins in their pile, and turned her attention back to the task at hand. She turned on the computer, and tapped her foot impatiently, waiting for it to boot up. While it whirred and hummed, she sidled out into the living room and eyed the answering machine, twirling a strand of curly wet hair around a finger. The phone had rung many times since he'd turned the volume down.

She peered at it. There were nine messages.

Her hand hovered over the play button for several indecisive moments. She wasn't proud of her proclivity to snoop, but figured as far as sins went, it wasn't chiseled in stone on the Top Ten. After all, a girl had a right to arm herself with all the knowledge she could, didn't she?

It would be naïve and foolish not to.

Her finger inched down toward the play button. Hesitated, and inched again. Just as she was about to press it, the phone rang loudly, startling a little screech out of her. Heart hammering, she skittered back into the study feeling weirdly caught and guilty.

Then, with an exasperated snort, she dashed right back out there and turned the volume up.

Katherine again. Sultry-voiced and purring. Ugh.

Scowling, Chloe turned it back down, deciding she'd really rather *not* hear them all. She didn't need anymore reminders that she was one of many.

A few moments later, she logged onto the Internet, signed into her Yahoo! account and typed swiftly:

Tom, my Aunt Irene (God forgive her, she didn't have one) *was taken suddenly ill and I had to leave immediately for Kansas. I'm so sorry I wasn't able to get in touch with you before, but she's in critical condition and I've been staying at the hospital. I'm not sure when I'll be back. It may be a few weeks or longer. I'll try to call you soon. Chloe.*

How neatly she lied, she thought wonderingly. She was smoking cigars, accepting bribes and lying. What was happening to her?

Dageus MacKeltar, that was what.

She reread it several times before hitting the send button. She was still staring at the "your message has been sent" message, feeling a little shaky about what she'd just done because it made it all seem so final, when she heard the door open and close.

He was back already!

She hit the shut down button, praying it would also disconnect the Internet. Though she had nothing to feel guilty about, she preferred to dodge a potential dispute. Especially after almost listening to his messages. God, he would have walked in and caught her doing it! How humiliating that would have been!

Taking a deep breath, she pasted an innocent expression on her face. "What are you doing back already?" she called as she strolled out of the study.

Then gasped, startled, and drew up short near the doorway to the kitchen.

A man, clad in a dark suit, was standing in the living room, glancing through the books on the coffee table. Of average height, wiry build, with short brown hair, he was well dressed and had a cultured air about him.

Apparently, she wasn't the only one who strolled at will into Dageus's unlocked penthouse. He really should start locking it, she thought. What if she'd still been in the shower, or had wandered downstairs in a towel to find a stranger there? It would have scared the bejeezus out of her.

The man turned at her gasp. "I'm sorry I startled you, ma'am," he apologized gently. "Might Dageus MacKeltar be about?"

British accent, she noted. And a funny tattoo on his

neck. Didn't seem quite in character with the rest of him. He didn't seem the tattoo sort.

"I didn't hear you knock," Chloe said. She didn't think he had. Maybe Dageus's friends didn't. "Are you a friend of his?"

"Yes. I'm Giles Jones," he said. "Is he in?"

"Not at the moment, but I'll be happy to tell him you stopped by." She peered at him, curiosity never dormant. Here was one of Dageus's friends. What might he tell her about him? "Are you a *close* friend of his?" she fished.

"Yes." He smiled. "And who might you be? I can't believe he's not mentioned such a lovely woman to me."

"Chloe Zanders."

"Ah, he has exquisite taste," Giles said softly.

She blushed. "Thank you."

"Where did he go? Will he be returning soon? Might I wait?"

"It'll probably be an hour or so. Can I give him a message for you?"

"An hour?" he echoed. "Are you certain? Perhaps I could wait; he might be back sooner." He glanced questioningly at her.

Chloe shook her head. "I'm afraid not, Mr. Jones. He went to get some things for me; we're leaving for Scotland later and—"

She broke off as the man's demeanor changed abruptly.

Gone was the disarming smile. Gone was the appreciative gaze.

Replaced by a cold, calculating expression. And—her brain seemed to resist processing this fact—there was suddenly, bewilderingly, a knife in his hand.

She shook her head sharply, unable to absorb the bizarre turn of events.

With a menacing smile, he moved toward her.

Still trying to get some dim grasp on the situation, she said stupidly. "You're n-not his f-friend." *Oh, gee, did the knife give it away, Zanders?* she snapped at herself silently. *Get a grip. Find a blasted weapon.* She inched slowly backward, into the kitchen, afraid to make a sudden move.

"Not yet," was the man's bizarre reply as he paced her.

"What do you want? If it's money, he has lots of money. Tons of money. And he'll happily give it to you. And there are artifacts," she babbled. She was almost there. Surely there was a knife lying on the counter somewhere. "Worth a fortune. I'll help you pack them up. There are oodles of things here you can take. I won't get in your way a bit. I promise, I'll just—"

"It's not money I'm after."

Oh, God. A dozen horrid scenarios, each worse than the last, flashed through her mind. He'd duped her into freely admitting that she was alone for an hour by pretending to know Dageus. How gullible she'd been! *You can take the girl out of Kansas, but you can't take Kansas out of the girl,* she thought, hysteria bubbling inside her.

"Oh, would you look at that! I've mistaken the time! He's due back any minute—"

A sharp bark of laughter. "Nice try."

When he lunged for her, she scrambled backward, adrenaline flooding her. Frantically, with hands made clumsy by fear, she snatched things off the counter and flung them at him. The thermal coffeepot bounced off his shoulder, spewing coffee everywhere; the butcher block hit him squarely in the chest. Flailing behind her, she grabbed one Baccarat goblet after another from the sink and flung them at his head. He ducked and dodged, and glass after glass exploded against the wall behind him, raining down on the floor.

He hissed with fury and kept coming.

Gasping for breath, dangerously close to hyperventilating, Chloe groped for more arsenal. A pot, a colander, some keys, a timer, a skillet, spice jars, more glasses. She needed a freaking weapon! In the midst of this damned museum, surely she could get her hands on one blasted knife! But her bare feet kept slipping in coffee as she tried to avoid both her assailant and the broken glass.

Afraid to take her eyes off him, she fumbled for a drawer behind her and felt frantically about: towels.

The next drawer: trash bags and Reynolds Wrap. She flung both boxes at him.

Glass crunching beneath his shoes, he advanced, backing her against the counter.

Wine bottle. Full. *Thank you, God.* She kept it behind her back and went motionless.

He did exactly what she'd hoped. Gave her the bum's rush, and she smashed the bottle down on his head with all her might, drenching them both with glass-spiked wine.

He grabbed her around the waist as he went down, taking her with him. She was no match for the wiry strength of the man as he wrestled her onto her back beneath him.

She caught a flash of silver perilously close to her face. She went limp for a moment, just long enough to make him wonder, then twisted and went for his groin with her knee and his eyes with her thumbs, whispering a silent thank-you to Jon Stanton in Kansas, who'd taught her "ten dirty tricks" when they'd dated in high school.

"Ow, you bloody *bitch!*" When he convulsed reflexively, Chloe pounded at him with her fists, scrabbling desperately to get out from beneath him.

His hand locked on her ankle. She grabbed a piece of glass, heedless of her numerous cuts and turned on him, hissing and spitting like a cat.

And when she slashed at his hand on her ankle, a fierce

triumph filled her. She may be on the floor, bloody and crying, but she was *not* going to die without one hell of a fight.

◈

Dageus stepped into the anteroom, wondering if Chloe might still be in the shower. He entertained a brief vision of her, gloriously nude and wet with all that lovely hair trailing down her back. Hand on the doorknob, he smiled, then flinched when he heard a crash, followed by cursing.

Pushing the door open, he gaped, incredulity and shock paralyzing him for a precious moment.

Chloe—dripping red liquid that his mind *refused* to accept might be blood—was standing in the living room, turned toward the kitchen, her back to him, clutching the claymore from above the fireplace with both hands, crying and hiccuping violently.

A man stepped out of the kitchen, his murderous gaze fixed on Chloe, a knife in his hand.

Neither of them registered his presence.

"Chloe-lass, back away," Dageus hissed. Instinctively, he used the Voice of Power, lacing the order with a spell of Druid compulsion, lest she be too frightened to move on her own.

The man startled and saw him then, his face registering shock and . . . something more, a thing Dageus couldn't quite define. An expression that made no sense to him. Recognition? Awe? The intruder's gaze darted to the door behind Dageus, then to the open doors leading to the rain-slicked terrace.

Snarling, Dageus began stalking. No need to rush, the man had no place to go. Chloe had responded to his command and backed away toward the fireplace, where she stood clutching the claymore tightly, white as a ghost.

She was still standing. That was a good sign. Surely the red stains couldn't *all* be blood.

"Are you all right, lass?" Dageus kept his gaze fixed on the intruder. Power was roiling inside him. Ancient power, power that was not his, power that was untrustworthy and bloodthirsty, goading him to destroy the man using archaic, forbidden curses. To make him die a slow and horrific death for daring to touch his woman.

Fisting his hands, Dageus struggled to close his mind to it. He was a man, not an ancient evil. More than man enough to handle this himself. He knew—though he knew not how he knew—that should he use the dark power within him to kill, it would seal his doom.

Hiccup. "Uh-huh, I think so." More sobs.

"You son of a bitch. You hurt my woman," Dageus growled, moving inexorably forward, backing the man out onto the terrace. Forty-three floors above the street.

The intruder glanced over his shoulder at the low stone wall encircling the terrace, as if gauging the distance, then back at Dageus again.

What he did next was so strange and unexpected that Dageus failed to react in time to stop him.

His eyes blazing with fanatic zeal, the man bowed his head. "May I serve the Draghar with my death, as I failed with my life."

Dageus was still trying to process the fact that he'd said "the Draghar" when the man spun about, leaped up onto the wall, and took a swan dive into forty-three floors of nothingness.

· 9 ·

"What *is* that stuff?" Chloe asked, wincing.

"Easy, lass. 'Tis but a salve that will speed the healing." Dageus smoothed it on her myriad cuts, murmuring healing spells in an ancient tongue she'd not know. A language so long dead that the scholars of her century had no name for it. The sticky red on her clothing had been wine not blood. She'd come away remarkably unscathed, all considered, with cuts on her hands and feet, a few scratches on her arms, but no debilitating injury.

"That does feel better," she exclaimed.

He glanced at her, forcing himself to look in her eyes, not at the lush, delectable curves scarce concealed by her delicate, lacy bra and panties. After the man had jumped, Dageus had stripped Chloe more roughly than he'd intended, frantic to know the extent of her wounds. Now she sat beside him on the sofa, facing him, her wee feet in his lap as he tended them.

"Here, lass." He snatched the cashmere throw from the back of the sofa and draped it around her shoulders, pulling it snugly about her so it covered her from neck to ankles. She blinked slowly, as if only now realizing her state of undress, and he knew her mind was still numb from her ordeal.

He forced his attention back to her feet. The healing spells were pushing him ever nearer the limits of his control. He'd used too much magic in the past few days. He needed a long space of time with no spells to recover.

Or her.

The longest he'd ever gone without a woman, since the eve he'd turned dark, was a sennight. At the end of it, he'd been up on that terrace wall himself. Clutching a bottle of whisky, dancing a Scots reel atop the slippery stones in the midst of an ice storm, letting fate choose which side he fell off first.

"He lied to me," she said, raking her hair, still damp from the shower, back from her face with a bandaged hand. "He said he was a friend of yours and I told him you wouldn't be back for an hour." Her eyes widened. "Why *did* you come back?"

"I forgot the key, lass."

"Oh, God," she breathed, looking panicked all over again. "What if you hadn't?"

"But I did. You're safe now." *Never again will I permit danger to touch you.*

"You didn't know him, did you? I mean, he just said that to find out how long you'd be gone, right?"

"Nay, lass, I'd never seen the man before." That much was true. " 'Tis as you thought, he lied to find out when I'd be returning, how long you'd be alone. He may have gotten my name anywhere. The mail call, the phone book." He wasn't listed in either of those places. But she didn't need to know that.

"Why would Security let him up?"

Dageus shrugged. "I'm sure they didn't. There are ways to circumvent Security," he evaded, scanning the damage resultant from the attack. He needed to tidy the kitchen before the police inevitably came to question the occupants on his side of the building. Fortunately, there were twenty-eight terraces below his, down to the fourteenth level, and the police would, he knew, in that wide berth the rich were ceded in any century, leave the penthouse level for last.

His mind raced over details: eradicate all sign of a tussle, pack up the last two tomes, stop at her place for her passport, take her artifacts to the bank, get them to the airport. He was glad they were leaving today. He'd dragged her into something even he didn't understand, and only he could protect her.

And he would protect her. She was keeper of his *Selvar*. His life was now her shield.

May I serve the Draghar . . . the man had said.

It made no sense to him. He'd been so startled to hear those words on the man's lips that he'd stared blankly. He was furious with himself because, had he moved or spoken more quickly, he could have forced answers from the man. Apparently, someone knew more about his problem than he himself did. How? Who could *possibly* know what he'd gotten himself into? Not even Drustan knew for certain! Who the blethering hell were the Draghar? And in what fashion had the man been serving them?

If they were, as he'd considered earlier, some part of the Tuatha Dé Danaan, and if they had indeed decided to hunt him down, why harm an innocent woman? And if they were the allegedly immortal race, why send a mortal to do their bidding? There was no question the man had been mortal. Dageus had seen him. He'd landed on a car, or rather, merged with the car.

While he'd cleansed Chloe's wounds, he'd quizzed her thoroughly about the intruder, in part to keep her talking so she wouldn't go into shock. The man had identified himself to her as Giles Jones, though Dageus suffered no illusions 'twas his real name. The man had recognized him somehow. He might not have known Giles Jones, but Giles Jones had known him. How long had the man been watching him? Spying on him. Waiting for a moment to strike.

A sudden fear for his brother and Gwen gripped him. If he was being watched, was Drustan also? What curse had he brought down upon himself and his clan?

He shook his head, sorting through dozens of questions for which he had no answers. Thinking was of no avail. Action was necessary now. He needed to get things tidied up, get them out of the country, then he could concentrate on discovering who the Draghar were.

He finished with the last cut and glanced up at her. She was watching him in silence, her eyes huge, but the color was slowly returning to her face.

"Forgive me, lass. I should have been here to protect you," he apologized gravely. " 'Twill never happen again."

"It wasn't your fault." She gave a shaky little laugh. "You can't be held responsible for all the criminals in the city. It's obvious he wasn't in his right mind. I mean—my God, he *jumped*. He killed himself." She shook her head, still unable to fathom it. "Did he say something before he jumped? It looked like he did."

She'd been too far away to hear it. " 'Twas gibberish. Made no sense. I'm sure you've the right of it. Like as not he was crazy or . . ." He shrugged.

"On drugs," she said, nodding. "His eyes were weird.

Like he was some kind of fanatic. I really thought he was going to kill me." A pause, then she said. "I fought back. I didn't just collapse."

She looked both shocked by and proud of that fact, and well she should be, he thought. How difficult it must have been for her, as wee as she was, to face a man so much larger than she, who'd been wielding a weapon with the intent to kill. It was one thing for a man of his size and girth, not to mention training, to enter battle, but her? The lass had courage.

"You did well, Chloe. You're an extraordinary woman." Dageus tucked a stray, damp curl behind her ear. He was beginning to lose the struggle to keep his gaze from hungrily roving her body, knowing she was nearly naked beneath the soft throw. A peculiar icy heat was flooding his veins. Dark and demanding. Need that cared not that she had been traumatized, need that endeavored to convince him that sex would make her feel better.

The tatters of his honor did not agree. But they were tatters and he needed to get her away from him. Fast.

"Are your feet better?"

She slid them from his lap to the floor, then stood, testing them.

He glanced out the window hastily, fisting his hands to keep from reaching for her. He knew if he touched her now, he would drop her, spread her and push himself inside her. His thought patterns were changing, the way they did when it had been too long. Becoming primitive, animal.

"Yes," she said, sounding surprised. "Whatever that salve is, it's amazing."

"Why doona you go up and finish packing your things?" His voice sounded thick and guttural, even to his own ears. He rose swiftly and moved toward the kitchen.

"But what about the police? Shouldn't we call the police?"

He paused, but kept his back to her. "They're already out there, lass." *Go*, he willed silently, desperately.

"But shouldn't we talk to them?"

"I'll take care of everything, Chloe." He used a brush of compulsion that time and told her to forget about the police. Just enough magic to ease her mind, to help her trust that he would handle things. To make her not wonder later why she'd not been questioned. So far as the police would be concerned, the man hadn't fallen from *his* terrace, but she need not know that.

He'd just entered the kitchen when she came up behind him and laid a hand on his shoulder. "Dageus?"

He stiffened and closed his eyes. He didn't turn around. *Christ, lass, please. I doona want to rape you.*

"Hey, turn around," she said, sounding mildly peeved.

Teeth clenched, he turned.

"Even though it's not like you did it on purpose, thank you for forgetting the key," she said, then cupped his face in her wee hands, stood on her tiptoes and pulled him down to plant a soft kiss on his lips. "You probably saved my life."

He could feel muscles leaping in his jaw. Leaping in his entire body. Had to unclench his teeth to manage a thick, "Probably?"

"I *was* putting up a good fight," she pointed out. "And I'd gotten to the claymore."

A wan but cheeky smile, then, blessedly, she moved toward the stairs.

At the foot of them, she glanced back. "I know you probably don't care, because we're leaving, but you should tell the building manager that this penthouse has some serious heating problems. Would you mind turning it up a bit?" She rubbed her arms through the coverlet and, without waiting for an answer, hurried up the steps.

Five minutes later, he was still leaning against the wall, shaking from the battle he'd almost lost when she'd so innocently touched her lips to his. She'd kissed him as if he were honorable, in control. Safe.

As if he weren't the man who'd been about to take her virginity by force. As if he weren't dark and dangerous. Once, he'd gone to Katherine when he'd been in nearly as bad a state. He'd seen the fear mixed with the excitement in her eyes when he'd taken her roughly, without speaking a word, in her kitchen where he'd found her. Had known she'd sensed it in him, the darkness. Had known it had turned her on.

But not Chloe. She'd kissed him gently. Beast and all.

Trevor watched Dageus MacKeltar and his companion from a distance as they exited the building onto Fifth Avenue. The police had been crawling all over the place for hours, removing Giles's body, and questioning witnesses, but by midafternoon, had moved on, leaving two grizzled and grouchy detectives in their wake.

He felt no grief for Giles; his death had been swift, and death was not a thing they feared, as the Druid sect of the Draghar believed in the transmigration of the soul. Giles would live again in some other body, some other time.

As the Draghar would live again in the Scotsman's body, once they'd taken full possession of him.

Trevor was awed that the man had managed thus far to fend off the transformation. As powerful as the Draghar were, Dageus MacKeltar must be uncommonly powerful in his own right.

But Trevor had no doubt the Prophecy would come to pass as had been promised. No man could contain such power and fail to use it. Day by day, it would seep into him until he no longer knew he was being transformed. They simply needed to provoke him, to goad and corner him. The use of dark magic for dark purposes would plunge him into an abyss from which there was no escape.

Then, the Draghar would walk the earth again. Then, all the power, all the knowledge the Tuatha Dé Danaan had stolen from them millennia ago would be restored. The Draghar would teach them the Voice of Power that brought death with a mere word, and the secret ways to move through time. When their numbers were many and strong, they would hunt the Tuatha Dé Danaan and take what should have been theirs long ago. That which the Tuatha Dé Danaan had ever denied the Draghar: the secret of immortality. Eternal life, no chancy rebirth necessary.

They would be gods.

Trevor studied the woman intently. Tiny little bit, she was, and he wondered how Giles had ended up going over that terrace. Had it been by choice? Had Dageus MacKeltar thrown him off? Surely the small female hadn't done it. She didn't amount to much. Barely topped five feet.

The Scot towered over her. The Draghar had been given a mighty vessel, his form strong, that of a warrior. Men would respond well to his innate authority. Even as Trevor thought that, he noted how the crowds parted for him, instinctively moving out of his way, and he strode as if he knew they would. No hesitation in the man, none whatsoever. Even from his safe distance, he could feel the power rolling off him.

When the Scot glanced down at the woman, Trevor's eyes narrowed.

Possessiveness in his gaze. Protectiveness in the way

he shielded her body from passersby, his intent gaze constantly scrutinizing his surroundings. Simon would not be pleased.

Before Trevor had found his calling in the Order, he'd run the con, quite successfully, and the cardinal rule of such business applied here: isolate the mark; the quarry falls faster alone.

He paced them, at a cautious distance.

They paused outside a bank and Trevor glided closer, dropped a few coins and bent to scoop them up. Listening, to see if he could overhear any conversation.

And finally he heard what he needed; they were planning to fly out to Scotland some time this evening.

He melted back into a small cluster of pedestrians and slipped out a cell phone. It would be a simple matter to have one of his computer-savvy brethren find out from which airport and when, and book him on the flight as well.

Speaking swiftly, he filled Simon in.

And Simon's instructions were precisely what he expected.

Hours later, Trevor slid into a seat a dozen rows behind them. He would have preferred to sit nearer, but the flight wasn't full, and he worried that the Scot might spot him.

He'd shadowed them all afternoon and not once gotten the chance to strike. Blades were his sect's weapon of choice, each spilling of blood a ritual in and of itself, yet he'd had to abandon his weapons before boarding. His tie would have served well to strangle her, if he'd only been able to get a moment with her alone.

He wished he knew what had transpired in the penthouse. Something had put Dageus MacKeltar on the alert for another attack. If caught, Giles was supposed to make it look like a robbery, or the work of a sociopath, whichever best fit the moment. Yet it was apparent that the Scot was anticipating another attempt. He'd not once left the woman's side. When twice she'd gone to the rest room in the airport, he'd trailed her there, waited in the doorway, and escorted her back. When too many people for his comfort had sat near them in the waiting area, he'd coaxed her off for a walk.

The bloody man was a walking shield.

Trevor massaged the back of his neck, sighing.

He would regroup in Scotland, acquire weapons, and eventually the man's guard would drop. If only for a few moments. A few moments were all he would need.

· 10 ·

The flight from JFK to London was only half full, the lights dimmed for the comfort of night travelers, the seats comfy (they had a whole row to themselves and had pushed all the armrests up), and Chloe fell asleep shortly after takeoff.

Now, stirring drowsily, she kept her eyes shut, mulling over the events of the day. It had whizzed by with incredible speed, from the attack, to the packing, to going to her place for her passport, to getting a box at the bank for her artifacts (*her* artifacts!), to a hasty late lunch/early dinner, and finally the trip to the airport.

No wonder she'd fallen asleep. She'd not slept much the night before, nervous and excited about the decision she'd made to accompany Dageus to Scotland. Then the day had been crammed full, and the shock of the attack, alone, had nearly drained her of energy. She still couldn't believe it had happened; it seemed surreal, as if she'd watched it on TV or it had happened to someone else. She'd been living in New York, in one of the less savory sections for almost a year, and nothing bad had ever happened to her. She'd never been mugged, never been harassed on the subway, in fact, hadn't encountered any adversity, so she supposed maybe her number had finally come up. Unless, of course, the police determined some other mot—

That thought was slippery and abruptly vanished from her mind.

Though it troubled her that her assailant had killed himself (and if that didn't demonstrate how crazy he'd been, she didn't know what would), she knew he'd intended to injure her severely, if not kill her. Pragmatism tempered her emotion. The simple fact was: She was grateful she'd survived. Sorry the man had been so crazy that he'd attacked her, then taken a leap off the terrace, but glad to be alive all the same. It was startling how having one's life placed in jeopardy reduced one to the basics.

Had Dageus not returned—that thought made her shudder—she would have fought to the death. She was discovering all kinds of parts of her personality she'd not known existed. She'd always worried that if someone attacked her, she might just crumple, or freeze helplessly. Had always wondered if she was a coward at heart.

Thank God she wasn't. And thank God Dageus had forgotten the key.

She'd been so gullible. Giles "Jones," indeed. What a tip-off that should have been. But she'd not given it a second thought because the man had looked and acted so darned normal, at first. Then again, she'd read somewhere that most serial killers looked like the guy next door.

When Dageus had walked in, the man had gotten the strangest look on his face. She couldn't quite pin it down. . . .

Mentally shrugging, she pushed the grim thoughts away. It had been awful; she'd never been so frightened in her life, but it was over, and she would look forward, not behind. Dwelling on it would make her feel terrified all over again. A freaky, awful thing had happened right before she'd left New York, but she would not let it characterize her time there, nor cast a pall over her future. He was dead; she would not grant the man the success of making her feel terrorized. In twenty-four years, she'd been the victim of an attack once. She could live with those odds. *Would* live with them, would not let it make her frightened in the future. More cautious? Absolutely. Afraid? Not a chance.

She was on her way to Scotland, with a man that made her feel more alive than anyone she'd ever known.

And she was determined to enjoy every last minute of it.

She wondered what Grandda would have made of Dageus.

Chloe Zanders. Chloe . . . MacKeltar.

Zanders, she chided herself instantly, *stop thinking like that!* She was not going to romanticize things. She'd promised herself that earlier, while sitting in the airport with him, waiting for their flight to leave. He'd been so attentive, walking her to the ladies' room, taking her for a snack, never leaving her side, yet with that eternal coolness. That infuriating reserve, that tight containment. It was no wonder women fell hard for him; such reserve challenged a woman, made her want to be the one who got inside Dageus MacKeltar. But Chloe wasn't going to make that mistake. So far as she could see, she was woman-of-the-hour, nothing more. She was determined to be smart about things, to view the trip as an adventure, to take things purely at face value and not read any more into them than there was.

Still, Grandda would've liked it. . . .

Her thoughts returned to touch briefly on the morning again, but on a less disturbing part. After the man had jumped, Dageus had stripped her fast and frantically, the look on his face enough to mute any protest. Scarcely bridled rage had emanated from him, making her think her assailant might just have been granted a more merciful death by jumping. His strong hands had been shaking when he'd begun tending her. She'd never seen someone so filled with fury behave so gently. He'd sponged the wine from her, cleansed and bandaged her wounds, all the while resolutely ignoring her state of undress.

It seemed the stronger his emotions, the more rigidly he controlled himself. That was a hypothesis she was curious to examine further. But why the fury? she wondered. Because someone had dared to trespass on his property? Messed up his home? A woman inclined to romanticizing things might have read some emotion for her into it, but Chloe wasn't going to be that fool.

With a soft sigh, she opened her eyes slowly to find him staring straight at her. He didn't speak, just looked at her. In the shadows, his chiseled face was breathtaking, savagely masculine.

His eyes.

She got lost in them for a long moment, wondering how she could have ever thought them tiger-gold. They were the color of dark whisky. And filled with some emotion. She stared. Something like . . .

Despair?

Deep beneath the coolness and mockery, well hidden beneath the relentless seduction, was it possible that Dageus MacKeltar hurt?

Don't read into things, she reminded herself. *Face value says the man looks like he wants to kiss you, not give you his babies, Zanders.*

God, he'd make beautiful babies though, a primordial, feminine part of her purred. That part of her that still bore the biological imprint from cavewoman days, and was drawn unerringly to the most able warrior and protector.

His eyes glittering, he bent his dark head to hers. *Oh, he definitely wanted to kiss her.* She knew she should turn away, called herself a fool in every language she knew, but it didn't help. The lights were down, most of the passengers were sleeping, the atmosphere was cozy and intimate, and she wanted to be kissed. What harm was there in a little kiss? Besides, they were on a plane, for heaven's sake—how far could it go?

Had she known the answer to that in advance, she would have scrambled across the aisle and sealed tape over her mouth. Duct tape. Several layers. Maybe taped her thighs together for good measure.

The moment his lips touched hers, a sultry storm whipped up inside her, and she sizzled with heat lightning. He rubbed his sensual lips over hers, taking it slow, making her feel needy and reckless.

Slow wasn't what she wanted. She'd allowed herself a kiss and, by God, she intended to have it. A real one, with all the trimmings. Lips and tongues and teeth and lots of soft sighs. With a little sound of impatience, she touched her tongue to his. His response was instant and electrifying, whipping her inner storm into a tempest of heat and desire. With a low growl deep in his throat, he fisted his hands in her hair, and yanked her head back against the seat, his tongue penetrating deep. She couldn't breathe around it.

The kiss he gave her was not meant to seduce, it was meant to mark a woman's soul, and it was working. Dominant like the man, hungry, demanding. Beckoning forth the secret Chloe that harbored hunger every bit as deep as his. He was a dark, seductive shadow, all around her, and she was drowning in him. In the spicy scent of leather-clad man, in the sleek wet glide of his tongue, the strong hands in her hair. And she dare not make all that sound that trembled inside her. It was unbearably erotic, being forced to take such a kiss in absolute silence.

His hot tongue thrust and withdrew in blatant mimicry of sex, and she felt herself getting hopelessly wet, just from his kiss. The man made a woman feel like she was being devoured, eaten up, lap by delicious lap.

When he stopped and traced the pad of his thumb over her swollen lips, she panted softly, staring, unable to say a word. He searched her face, clearly liking what he saw in her glazed eyes, the evidence of the mind-numbing effect his kisses had on her. With a low, satisfied laugh, he pressed his thumb against her bottom teeth and forced her mouth open wide, clamped his hands on the sides of her face, taking her in an open-mouthed, deep-tongued kiss. Stealing the breath from her lungs, then giving it back. Making love to her mouth, letting her know how he would make love to her in all kinds of other places.

When she was whimpering against his lips, he drew back, his gaze smoldering. Lifting her jean-clad legs, he pulled them across his own, positioning her so she leaned back against the window, giving him better access.

"If you wish me to stop, lass, say it now. I won't ask again."

Some other woman must have shaken her head "no," because Chloe *knew* she was supposed to say "yes."

And it certainly must have been some other woman who slipped her hands around the nape of his neck, beneath his soft black leather jacket and into his hair.

It was *definitely* some other woman who slid them hungrily down his rock-hard chest.

He caught them in one of his own and pushed them aside.

"Doona touch me, lass. No' now."

He shushed her protests by pushing one of his fingers between her lips. He touched her tongue, then traced the outline of her lips. Slowly, he trailed that damp finger down her neck, along the edge of her V-neck sweater, stopping in the valley between her breasts. She watched him, mesmerized. He was so incredibly beautiful, there in the shadows, his sensual lips parted, his eyes narrowed with desire. His breath was warm against the damp path he'd left, teasing nerve endings to fiery life.

When his dark gaze fixed on her breasts, her nipples puckered into hard peaks and her breasts felt swollen and heavy. God, the man was intoxicating! Even his gaze was potent, making her skin sizzle, making her frantic for more. The mere thought of his hot, wet mouth greedy on her nipples made her weak with desire.

With a glance so rife with sexual promise that it took her breath away, he tugged the blanket from her waist, back up to her neck. Then he slipped his hands beneath the blanket, and Chloe's head dropped limply back against the window, her eyes fluttering closed.

She should stop him. And she would. Soon. Really soon.

"Open your eyes, lass. I want to see you watching me when I touch you." A soft command, but command nonetheless.

Her lids lifted languorously. She felt as if he was sucking the will out of her with his touch, leaving her limp and utterly vulnerable to his demands.

He slipped his hands beneath her sweater, impatiently unhooked her bra, and bared her breasts, palming them roughly. *Oh, yes,* she thought. This was what she'd been wanting since the moment she'd seen him. To be naked with him, to feel his hot, big hands branding her bare skin. She was melting into a puddle of soft, feminine heat in the hands of a master, and she couldn't gather the will to care. He cupped her breasts, kneading and plumping, tugging her nipples between his fingers. His breath hot against her skin, he ran the tip of his tongue up her neck, then glided his mouth over her chin, to her lips, taking her in a bruising kiss, fingers closing on her nipples, pinching lightly. He continued the relentless barrage against her senses until she was helplessly arching her hips up from the seat.

Suddenly he broke the kiss, and pulled away, his eyes closed, his jaw tightly clenched. A breath hissed from between his gritted teeth. The sight of him fighting for self-control, the proof of the effect she had on him, sent a primitive, erotic thrill through her. The sight of him so aroused that he was in pain was beyond arousing. It had the same effect on her desire for him as gasoline splashed on an open flame.

She should stop him. She was helpless to stop him.

Then he opened his eyes, their gazes collided and she knew he knew exactly what she was feeling. Lost. On the edge. Hanging. In terrible need. He slanted his mouth over hers, sucking her tongue deep into his mouth.

A tiny convulsive spasm began to shiver inside her, and with it came the dim memory of where they were: On a plane, with nearly a hundred people around!

God, what if she came?

God, what if she screamed when she came?

"S-stop—" she panted against his lips.

"Too late, lass."

He cupped her intimately between her legs, through her jeans, pressing the heel of his palm hard against the vee between her thighs, and she nearly cried out from the exquisite pleasure of his touch *there*, where she was so empty and ached so desperately. His breathing harsh, he moved his hand in perfect rhythm, expertly finding her clitoris through the fabric of her jeans, using the bump of the inseam to create the perfect friction against it. Oh, the man knew how to touch a woman!

"Let go, lass. Give it to me *now*."

His husky growl pushed Chloe helplessly over the edge.

The noise that might have escaped her then, had he not crushed his mouth hard to hers, would have embarrassed her for perpetuity. Might have awakened the whole damned plane. She fancied it might have caused turbulence.

Her cries muffled, Chloe exploded. Helplessly, wantonly, lost, one of his big hands on her breasts, the other between her legs, she had a complete meltdown, shuddering against him, clamping her legs tight around his hand.

He took her cries with his tongue deep in her mouth, muting her, but for a tiny whimpering noise.

The pleasure was devastating, it crested and broke into a thousand shimmering pieces inside her. Her whole body shuddered and—had she been able to make a noise—she might well have done what she feared, and screamed.

But he took all that sound, his hot tongue devouring, thrusting deep, stealing her breath. He knew exactly how to touch her to keep the pleasure coming, his hand relentless between her legs, not letting up for a second and, as her first orgasm started to ease, it sort of stuttered and became a second one that sent her right back into a meltdown.

He kissed her while the aftershocks trembled through her, demanding kisses at first, tapering to soft, slow kisses as her tremors eased. She clung to him, unable to move. And though she'd just had a simply stupendous double climax, she ached, hot and wet. She'd been sated and yet—in no way sated—perhaps only finally, fully awakened.

Irrevocably awakened.

Oh, God, what have I done? He's addictive!

They stayed like that for a long moment, forehead to forehead, both breathing unevenly. Then, with a lingering caress, he withdrew his hand.

He was motionless a few moments, then she heard a sharp intake of breath and a pained groan when he reached down and adjusted himself.

She fisted her hands and squeezed her eyes shut, trying not to think about that part of him he'd just touched. That part she'd caught a glimpse of when he'd dropped his towel, just enough to feed her insatiable curiosity.

No wonder Katherine had said she was dying without him.

There was no way she could let such a thing happen again. If she permitted even one more kiss today, she'd be in his bed. He was too sexy; she was already far too infatuated with him, and once in his bed, her defenses would come crashing down and she'd lose herself.

Why not just toss your heart out the airplane window, Zanders? a small inner voice snapped. *You'd have about as much promise of a safe landing.*

Dageus MacKeltar was more man than she could handle. She was a little-leaguer, clutching a ratty, secondhand mitt, trying to play ball with the pros. Just one good ground ball would knock her on her ass. And the game would move on without her.

Neither of them said a word, just sat in the dim shadows of the plane, trying to regain control.

Chloe was suddenly afraid that she might *never* get it back around him.

She was dozing again, and Dageus was paging through the third Book of Manannán.

Or trying to.

He was concentrating as well as any man in acute sexual agony could be expected to.

Not at all.

He kept seeing Chloe's flushed face: her lips swollen from his kisses, the skin around her mouth chafed from whisker burn, her eyes sleepy-sexy with desire as she reached her woman's peak and shuddered against him. Twice. Clung to him—as if she'd *needed* him. He'd held her heavy breasts in his hands. He'd touched her between her thighs.

He'd needed her so desperately that he'd nearly cast a Druid spell to fog the minds of the passengers, and pushed as far as she would go. Had contemplated taking her to the bathroom with him. Only her maiden state had stopped him. He'd not spill Chloe's virgin blood like some barbarian, in a two-by-two room with cardboard walls.

She'd have gone farther, had he pressed. Might have permitted his hand inside her trews, but had he gone that far, there would have been no stopping. So he'd kept his hand safely outside her trews and settled for releasing one of them.

He'd never felt such lust before. Though tooping took the edge off, it was wont to leave him strangely wanting. Touching Chloe made him think there might be some eventual satisfaction he'd never before achieved.

In the meantime, he was rock-hard and in pain.

Still, he brooded, he supposed it was a fair trade-off, for though he was in an agony of sexual need, their intimacy had mellowed the fury within him. Where earlier in the penthouse he'd been afraid of what he might do, her kisses had given him back a measure of control. Not much, but enough to work with.

In the past, he'd always needed to complete the sexual act to gain respite, but not with Chloe. Merely kissing her, touching her, bringing her pleasure had calmed him, had cleared his mind a bit. He made no pretense to understand the how or why of it. It had worked.

He would accept that—that Chloe would tie him in knots, but preserve some measure of his sanity. What a boon her kisses would be on Scottish soil.

Och, the woman had something he needed. His instincts had been right when they'd said "mine."

And that started a whole new train of possessive thoughts. Thoughts he could do naught about at the moment, so he took slow deep breaths and forced his thoughts to the pressing issues at hand.

What was to come anon would require all his wits and will. Once he was in Scotland, he knew the changes would speed up again. Changes he had to find a way to stop.

And to do so, he had to face his brother.

Drustan, 'tis me, Dageus, and I'm sorry I lied, but I'm dark and I need to use the library.

Aye, that would go over well.

Drustan, I failed. I broke my oath and you should kill me.

Nay, not that, not yet.

Och, brother, help me.

Would he?

Bletherin' hell, you should have let him die! his da had shouted when, back in the sixteenth century, Dageus had summoned the courage to confide what he'd done.

How? How could I do that? Dageus had shouted back.

In saving him you destroyed yourself! Now I've lost both my sons—one to the future, the other to the black arts!

No' yet, he'd protested.

But the look in his da's eyes . . . it had said he'd believed there was no hope. Horrified, Dageus had fled through the stones, determined to find a way to save himself.

And now he'd come full circle, back to asking his clan for aid. He hated it. He'd not asked for help, not once in his life. 'Twas not his way.

Exhaling sharply, he accepted the scotch he'd requested from the flight attendant, and downed it in a single swallow. As the heat exploded inside him, the tightness in his chest first intensified, then eased. What could he say? How to begin? With Gwen, mayhap? She could work her feminine miracles with his brother. God knew, she'd been a miracle for Drustan.

He pondered various ways to approach him, but it was more than he could stand thinking on, so he forced his attention back to the text, needing something tangible to work with.

An hour later, just before landing, he paused, hand poised above his notebook. He'd finally found something worthwhile. The only mention he'd yet discovered about the fateful war that had occurred after the Tuatha Dé Danaan had left. Naught but a brief paragraph, it spoke of thirteen outcast Druids (so *that* was how many were inside him!) and of some heinous punishment they'd suffered. Though it did not elaborate further, beneath it was a notation that referred to the *fifth* Book of Manannán, as he'd suspected.

And if memory served him, the fifth volume was in the Keltar library.

Chloe mumbled softly in her sleep, drawing his gaze again. Reminding him that someone had tried to kill her—because of him.

He glanced at her bandaged hand and fierce protectiveness flooded him. He would let nothing harm her ever again.

He needed answers, and he needed them fast.

· 11 ·

For the second time in as many days, Chloe had the
strange and immensely irritating experience of walking
down a crowded street with Dageus MacKeltar. The first
time had been in Manhattan yesterday, and the same
thing had happened there.

Men got out of his way.

Not because he was impolite or barged rudely down
the sidewalk. On the contrary, he moved with the sleek
grace of a tiger. Sure-footed, perhaps a bit predatory. And
men instinctively circumvented him, going out of their
way to give him wide berth.

The women, now they were a different matter. They
were the irritating part. They'd reacted the same way in
New York, but yesterday it hadn't bothered her as much.
They moved aside, but *barely*, as if unable to resist brushing up against him, their heads turning twice, three

times. One woman had shamelessly pressed her breasts against his arm in passing. On several occasions, Chloe cast an indignant glance over her shoulder, only to catch several of them ogling his behind. She might be small but—blast it all—she wasn't *invisible,* walking along at his side, with his arm around her, his hand resting on her shoulder!

Not that he noticed the rubbernecking going on. He seemed oblivious to his effect on women. Probably so used to it that he no longer paid it any heed.

She longed for such oblivion, because watching so many women eye him hungrily was putting her in a bad mood. She cast more than a few pissed-off looks behind them.

The intense intimacy on the plane had stirred dangerously mushy feelings in her.

Face it, Zanders, you aren't the kind of girl who can be physically intimate with a man without getting emotionally involved. You're just not wired that way.

No kidding, she thought grumpily. She was having territorial feelings. Feelings she couldn't afford, for he'd certainly not evidenced any territorial feelings about her. Fortunately, as she watched women stare at him, irritation was making short work of softer emotions. She savored the anger, preferring it to waffling in uncertain emotions. Anger was refreshingly tangible.

The moment they'd stepped off the plane in Inverness he'd grown cool again. Preoccupied. Businesslike. Collecting their luggage, striding briskly to the rental car agency. She'd had to repeat three times her request that he stop in Inverness for a coffee she desperately needed after traveling for fifteen hours. She wasn't about to meet his family in the throes of caffeine withdrawal.

After so thoroughly losing control of herself on the plane, his detachment hurt. He'd kissed her into a stupor, given her her first-ever climax, then withdrawn in every possible way. She should have known, she brooded. *What did you expect, Zanders? A declaration of intimacy just because you let him touch you intimately?*

Damn it, she *knew* better than that. The two did not necessarily go together where men were concerned.

When they entered Gilly's Coffee House, she stood beside him at the counter as he ordered, peeking at his profile. She wondered what he was thinking about, what had changed his mood so completely. The man ran hot and cold. *That's a good comparison,* she thought, *he'll either scald me or freeze me; either way it'll hurt.*

Well, she wasn't about to make the first move. If he wanted to go all reserved and professional, she could too. After all, he hadn't said "Come with me to Scotland and let's get to know each other." He'd said, "Come with me to Scotland to help me translate texts. Oh, and I'll try to seduce you too."

How many times had Katherine called him? Had all nine of those messages been from her? That thought jarred her thoroughly back to reality She'd *hate* being that kind of woman. Pining after a man she couldn't have.

She folded her arms across her chest. Stared straight ahead at the menu behind the counter.

"I always want you, Chloe-lass," he murmured suddenly in a low voice, for her ears only. "There's no' a moment that I doona."

Chloe scowled. What was he—a mind reader? Damn him anyway! Arching a brow, she tipped her head back, narrowed her eyes and gave him a chilly look. "Who said I was thinking anything even remotely like that? Do you just think I sit around with nothing better to do than think about you?"

"Nay, of course not. I merely thought to assure you

that though my mind may seem far away, should you wish my attentions, you've only to say so."

"I'm fine. I just want some coffee."

"Mayhap you'd prefer to spend this eve with me at an inn, rather than going straight to my brother's," he suggested with a seductive smile.

Chloe scowl deepened.

"One eve is no' enough?" he teased, though his eyes were distant. "Greedy lass, would you be wishing a week?"

"Get over yourself, MacKeltar," she muttered. "Though the women out there"—she flung a hand toward the street—"seem to think so, I hate to break it to you, but the world does *not* revolve around you."

Dageus's nostrils flared and he inhaled sharply as he recognized her emotion. Jealousy. She'd been watching other women look at him (aye, he noticed, in a peripheral fashion) and it chafed her. That her desire for him was intense enough to make her feel jealousy, made him feel wildly possessive. His seduction was working. She was growing attached to him. Abruptly, he pulled her in front of him at the counter, and wrapped both arms around her waist. He held her while their order was filled, hungry for the feel of her wee body against his. She was stiff at first, but slowly the tension quit her small, lushly curved form.

When she leaned forward to take her latte and scone, he pressed against her from behind, deliberately brushing his hard arousal against her bottom, letting her know exactly how much she was always on his mind.

He smiled when she nearly dropped her coffee.

"I'd have bought you another," he said with a shrug, when she glanced sharply over her shoulder at him, blushing as furiously as she was scowling. Like as not, he'd buy her the café if she indicated the slightest desire for it.

"You're incorrigible," she hissed. "Just so you know, what happened on the plane is *not* going to happen again," she informed him, before turning and stalking off toward the rental car.

His eyes flared dangerously. Did the lass think to share such intimacies with him and then rescind them?

Och, nay, Dageus MacKeltar didn't go backward. She would find that out soon enough.

As they neared their destination, Dageus grew increasingly subdued. After lengthy deliberation, he'd decided it best to simply appear on Drustan's doorstep unannounced, hope Gwen answered the door, then hope for the best.

He glanced over at Chloe, acknowledging that he'd not have made this trip today alone. Even with her beside him, he'd considered turning around half a dozen times. Alone, he'd have tried the museums first, have put it off indefinitely, telling himself all manner of lies when the simple truth was that he didn't want to face Drustan. But somehow, with her at his side, it didn't seem nigh as impossible.

Her earlier irritation seemed to have passed or, as wee as she was, there simply wasn't enough room in her to contain irritation *and* excited curiosity. She was sipping her coffee, staring out the window, pointing, and asking endless questions. What was that ruin? When did summer begin? When did the heather bloom? Were there really pine martens, and could she see one? Could they be petted? Did they bite? Could they go to the museums while they were there? How about Glengarry? How much farther?

He'd been answering absently, but she was so enam-
ored by the vista that she hadn't seemed to notice his
inattention. He had no doubt that she would fall in love
with his country. Her enthusiasm made him remember a
time—what seemed a lifetime ago—when he, too, had
viewed the world with wonder.

He forced his gaze away from her, and his thoughts
back to the upcoming confrontation.

He hadn't seen Drustan—awake, that was—in four
years, one month and twelve days. Since the eve that
Drustan had been placed in an enchanted sleep, to slumber for five centuries. They'd spent that final day together, trying to wedge a lifetime into it.

Twin brothers and best friends since they'd drawn
breath, a mere three minutes apart, they'd said farewell
that night. Forever. Drustan had gone to sleep in the
tower, the tower that Dageus had to walk past a dozen
times a day. At first, he'd bid his brother a sardonic "good
morrow" each morn, but that had swift grown too
painful.

Before Drustan had gone into the tower, they'd labored together over plans for a new castle that was to be
Drustan and Gwen's home in the future. After Drustan
had gone to sleep, Dageus had immersed himself in over-
seeing the construction of it, directing hundreds of work-
ers, making certain all was perfect, working alongside
the men.

And while so involved with the building of it, he'd
become aware of an ever-growing, restless emptiness inside him.

The castle had begun to consume him. Impossible for
a man to labor daily for three long years and not lose a
part of himself to not merely the act of creating, but the
creation. The empty, waiting rooms were the promise of

family and love. The promise of a future he'd never been able to envision for himself.

When Drustan had died, he'd gone and stood outside the castle for hours uncounted, staring at its dark and silent silhouette in the gloaming.

He'd imagined Gwen in the future, waiting. And Drustan never arriving. She would live alone. Nell had told him Gwen was pregnant, though Gwen herself had not yet realized it, which meant Gwen would raise their babes alone.

He imagined no candles ever flickering beyond those windows. No children ever padding up and down those stairs.

All the empty places inside him had finally been filled—not with good things, but with anguish, fury, and defiance. He'd shaken his fist at the heavens, he'd raged and cursed. He'd questioned all he'd been raised to believe.

And by the misty, crimson-streaked dawn, he'd known but one thing: The castle he'd built *would* be filled with his brother and his family.

Aught else was simply unacceptable. And if the legends were true, if the cost was his own chance at life, he'd deemed it worthwhile. He'd little left to lose.

"Hey, are you okay?" Chloe asked.

Dageus started, realizing he must have been stopped at the stop sign for several minutes. He shook his head, scattering the grim memories. "Aye." He paused, weighing his next words. "Lass, I haven't seen Drustan in some time."

He had no idea how Drustan would react. He wondered if he would know, merely by looking at him, that he was dark. The bond of twins betwixt them was strong. *Aye, I used the stones, but the legends were wrong. There was no dark force in the in-between. I'm fine. 'Tis but that this century is a marvel and I've been exploring a wee. I'll come home anon.* 'Twas the lie he'd been telling his brother since the day he'd made the mistake of calling him, unable to resist hearing Drustan's voice, so he could assure himself that he was alive and well in the twenty-first century.

Dageus, you can tell me anything, Drustan had said.

There's naught to tell. 'Twas all a myth. Lie upon lie.

Then had begun the regular calls from Drustan, asking when he'd be home. He'd stopped picking up the phone months ago.

"So this is a reunion?"

"Of sorts." If Drustan turned him away, he'd take Chloe to the museums. He'd find another way. He was fair certain his brother wouldn't attack him. If he'd not come home, if he'd made Drustan hunt him, that might well have happened. But he hoped Drustan would understand his return for what it was: a request for aid.

She eyed him intently. He could feel her gaze, though he kept his profile to her.

"Did you and your brother have a falling out?" she said gently.

"Of sorts." He released the brake and resumed their journey, giving her a chilly look so she'd drop it.

A few moments later, she slipped her wee hand into his.

He tensed, startled by the gesture. He was accustomed to women reaching for many parts of him, none of them his hand.

He glanced at her, but she was staring straight ahead. Yet her hand was in his.

He closed his fingers around hers before she might snatch it away. Her wee hand was nearly swallowed by his. It meant more to him than kisses. More even than bedplay. When women sought him for sex, it was for their pleasure.

But Chloe's small hand had been given without taking.

❦

Adam Black watched the automobile wind up the roads into the Keltar mountains. Though his queen had long ago passed an edict forbidding any Tuatha Dé Danaan to go within a thousand leagues of a Keltar, Adam had decided that since The Compact had been violated on the Keltar side, old edicts didn't apply.

He knew why she'd passed the edict. The Keltar, having pledged their lives and all their future generations to upholding The Compact, were to be free of any Tuatha Dé Danaan interference, because his queen had known, even then, that there were those among their race that didn't like The Compact. Who'd not wanted to leave the mortal realm. Who'd argued to conquer the human race. Who might have tried to goad a Keltar into breaking it.

So since the day The Compact had been sealed, not one Keltar had so much as glimpsed one of their ancient benefactors.

Adam suspected that might have been a mistake. For, although the Keltar had faithfully performed their duties, over four thousand years they'd forgotten their purpose. They no longer even believed in the Tuatha Dé Danaan, nor did they recall the details of the fateful battle that had set them on their course. Their ancient history had become nothing more than vague myths to them.

While on Yule, Beltane, Samhain, and Lughnassadh, the Keltar still enacted the rites that kept the walls solid between their worlds, they no longer recalled that such was the purpose of those rites. Perhaps one generation had neglected to pass down the oral tradition in full to the next. Perhaps the elder had died before he'd been able to impart all the secrets. Perhaps old texts had not been faithfully recopied before time had disintegrated them, who knew? One thing Adam did know was that mortals ever seemed to forget their history. Those days that were so sacred to The Compact were now seen as feast days, little more.

He snorted, watching the car crest the hill. Humans couldn't even get their own religious history sorted out, from a mere two millennia past. It was no wonder that their history with his race had become so obscured by time's passage.

So, he thought, watching from his perch upon a high tor, *the darkest Druid has come home, bringing with him all the resurrected evil of the Draghar. Fascinating.* He wondered what his queen would make of it.

He had no plans to tell her.

After all, in Adam's opinion, it was her fault they'd been there to be resurrected in the first place.

Even now, she was ensconced with her council, where they were busy determining the mortal's fate.

Four thousand and some odd years ago, his people had withdrawn to their hidden places so that mortal and Fae would not destroy each other. Shortly thereafter, the Draghar, with their black arts, had nearly destroyed both their worlds.

His queen would *never* permit such a thing to happen.

He sighed. The mortal's time was finite.

· 12 ·

Gwen MacKeltar, former pre-eminent theoretical physicist, now wife and expectant mother, sighed dreamily, leaning back in the bathtub against her husband's hard chest. She was between his muscular thighs, with his strong arms around her, soaking in warm bubbly water and deliriously content.

Poor man, she thought, smiling. In her second trimester, she'd nearly punched him if he'd tried to touch her. Now, in her third, she was inclined to punch him if he *didn't* touch her. Frequently and exactly how she wanted. Her hormones were all over the place and the darned things just wouldn't function according to any equation she'd been able to compute.

But Drustan appeared to have forgiven her for the last few months, after the marathon sessions they'd been having. And not only didn't he seem to care that she was hopelessly fat, he'd happily devoted himself to finding new and unusual ways to make love that compensated for her physical changes. The tub was one of Gwen's favorites.

Hence, there she was at seven o'clock in the evening, with dozens of candles scattered about the bathroom, and her husband's strong arms around her, when the doorbell chimed downstairs.

Drustan dropped a kiss on the nape of her neck. "Are we expecting someone?" he asked, the small kiss turning into delicious nibbles.

"*Mmm.* Not that I know of."

Farley would get the door. Farley, properly christened Ian Llewelyn McFarley, was their butler and every time Gwen thought of him her heart went all soft. The man had to be eighty if a day, with bristly white hair and a tall, bowed frame. He lied about his age, and everything else, and she adored him.

What made her heart go *really* soft was that Drustan also had a tender spot for the old geezer. He had endless patience and invited his tall tales in the evening before a fire, as butler and laird shared a wee dram.

She knew that, regardless of how well her husband had adapted to her century, part of him would always be a sixteenth-century feudal laird. When they'd first moved into their new home—instead of doing what a normal twenty-first century person would have done, and taken an ad out in the paper for staff or contacted an employment agency—Drustan had gone to Alborath and dropped word in the local grocery and barber shop.

Within two hours, Farley had appeared on their doorstep claiming to have "buttled in some of the finest homes in England" (the man had never been out of Scotland), and further claimed he could arrange the entire staffing of their castle.

They'd since been overrun by McFarleys. There were McFarleys in the kitchen, McFarleys in the stables, McFarleys doing the ironing and the laundry and the dusting. As near as Gwen had been able to count, they'd employed the man's entire clan of nine children (and spouses), fourteen grandchildren, and she suspected there were a few "greats" floating about.

And though it had soon become clear that none of them had any experience in their respective positions, Drustan had pronounced them all satisfactory because he'd heard in the village that positions were hard to find.

In modern terms, the economy in Alborath was not good. Work *was* hard to find. And the feudal lord had surfaced, taking responsibility for the McFarleys.

She adored that about her husband.

A sharp knock at the bathroom door jarred her from her thoughts.

"Milord?" Farley inquired cautiously.

Gwen giggled and Drustan sighed. Farley refused to address him by any other title, no matter how persistently Drustan corrected him.

"Mister MacKeltar," Drustan muttered. "Why is that so difficult for him?" He was determined to adopt twenty-first century customs. Unfortunately, Farley was just as determined to preserve the old ones and had decided that since Drustan was the apparent heir of the castle, he was a lord. Period, the end.

"Aye?" Drustan replied more loudly.

"Sorry to be disturbing you and the lady, but there's a man here to see you, and I ken 'tis no' of my business, but I'm thinking I should have you know that he seems a bit the dangerous type, though he's polite enough as it is. Now the lass with him, och, in my opinion she's a sweet wee and proper lass, but him, well, 'tis more of an air about him, you ken? I'm thinking you mightn't hold well with me saying so, being as he looks so much like you, though no' like you at all. *Ahem.*"

Farley cleared his throat, and Gwen felt Drustan go rigid behind her. She'd gone rather tense herself.

"Milord, he's saying he's your brother, but being as you've no' mentioned a brother, despite the resemblance . . ."

Gwen didn't hear another word because Drustan shot from the bath so fast that she got a thorough dunking and her ears were filled with water. By the time she surfaced, Drustan was gone.

Dageus had neglected to mention that his brother lived in a castle. *Sheesh,* Chloe thought, shaking her head, *I should have expected it.* Where else would such a man have come from? Old World, indeed.

It was an elegant castle, with a great stone wall and authentic barbican, with round turrets and square towers and probably a hundred rooms or more.

Chloe pivoted, trying to look everywhere at once. She'd not uttered a word since they'd entered the tree-canopied drive and begun their approach. She'd been too stunned. She was in Scotland, and they were going to be staying in a castle!

The interior of the great hall was enormous, with corridors shooting off in all directions. An intricately carved balustrade encircled the hall on the second floor, and an elegant double staircase swept down from opposing sides, met in the middle, and descended in one wide train of steps. A lovely stained-glass window was inset above the double entry doors. Brilliant tapestries adorned the walls, and the floors were scattered with rugs. There were two fireplaces in the hall, both tall enough for people to walk around in, bigger than the bathroom in her efficiency had been! Her fingers curled as she wondered how many artifacts she might get to examine.

"Do you like it, lass?" Dageus asked, watching her intently.

"It's magnificent! It's—it's—" she broke off, sputtering. "Oh, thank you," she exclaimed. "Do you have any idea how thrilling it is to me to be standing in an authentic medieval castle? I've *dreamed* of this moment."

He smiled faintly. "Aye, the castle is magnificent, isn't it?"

He couldn't have sounded more proud if he'd built it himself, Chloe thought. "Did you grow up here?"

"Sort of."

"I could get tired of that answer in a hurry," she said, eyes narrowing. "I'm not exactly hard to talk to. You should try it." Since he'd told her that he and his brother had had some kind of falling out, she was better able to understand his withdrawn attitude. But if he thought it would keep her from asking questions, he was wrong.

"Ever the curious lass, aren't you?"

"If I waited for you to offer information, I'd never find out anything. Speaking of which, we need to talk about this curse-thing soon too. I can't help you if I don't know exactly what we're looking for."

Wariness flickered through his eyes. "Aye, I know. Anon, lass. For the now, let's see if I survive the wrath of my bro—"

He broke off abruptly, his gaze flying to the stairs.

Chloe's gaze followed, and she sucked in a sharp breath. A man who looked *exactly* like Dageus was standing there, halfway down the stairs, looking down at Dageus. She looked between them rapidly, disbelievingly.

"Oh, God, you're *twins*," she said faintly. Faintly, because the man at the top of the stairs wore only a towel around his waist.

"Stay right there!" the man on the stairs thundered. "I'll but get my trews. My apologies, lass. I had to see him with my own eyes." He turned around and loped up the stairs, three at a time.

Dageus mumbled something that sounded almost like, *if he drops his towel I'll kill him,* but Chloe decided she was imagining things.

The man skidded to a halt at the top and cast a sharp glance directly at Chloe. "Doona let him leave, lass," he roared at her.

"Wow," was all she could manage.

Beside her, she felt Dageus stiffen. For a moment, it seemed the hall grew markedly cooler.

"The lasses have oft said I am more handsome," he said icily. "And a better lover."

Chloe blinked up at him.

"So doona be ogling him. He's married, lass."

"I wasn't ogling," she protested, knowing full well she'd been ogling. "And if I was, it's only because you didn't warn me that you were twins."

He gave her a dark look.

"Besides, he only had a towel on," she justified.

"I doona care if he had naught but his skin on. 'Tisn't polite to ogle another woman's husband."

Chloe caught her breath. His expression was furious and he looked . . . jealous. About *her*? For looking at his brother? She peered at him, hardly daring to credit it.

Abruptly, his gaze was gone again, fixed at the top of the stairs, and hers followed. She glanced from Drustan to Dageus and back again.

And she wondered how Dageus might have worried for even a moment that Drustan wouldn't welcome him home. The expression on his brother's face took her breath away. Love blazed in his eyes and, though she couldn't tell from this distance, it looked as if they glistened with tears.

"Drustan," Dageus said with a cool nod.

Drustan's eyes dimmed and his mouth tightened.

"Drustan?" Drustan snapped. "That's it? A mere Drustan? No 'Good morrow, brother, 'tis sorry I am that I've been such an ass and no' come home'?" His voice was rising with each word and he began stalking down the stairs.

God, they even moved the same way, Chloe marveled, like great sinuous cats, all sleek strength and smoothly sculpted muscles. Though Drustan had pulled on "trews," he'd not bothered with a shirt and his hair was wet, dripping down his chest. The muscles in his glistening torso rippled with every movement. He must have been in the shower, she realized.

". . . is that how you'll greet me?" Drustan was still talking, but she'd missed part of his verbal barrage, apparently temporarily deafened by visual overload. "Get over here and greet me properly," he thundered.

Chloe tore her gaze away from Drustan and looked at Dageus. And stared. Though he looked as remote and impassive as ever, his eyes positively burned with emotion. He was as still as one of the many standing stones they'd passed, seeming every bit as ancient and obdurate. If one didn't notice the hands fisted at his sides. And those eyes.

Oh, there was more to Dageus MacKeltar than he let on! And her hypothesis was right. When he felt most deeply was when he exhibited the greatest reserve.

So *that* was how such a man wore love, she realized. Quietly. Not an expressive man. Not a man to laugh or cry or dance. A man who had hair to his waist, but never wore it down. Did he ever let himself go?

I'll bet he does in bed. She was utterly rattled by the

thought of all that disciplined muscle coming undone in bed. God, she could just taste it. . . .

She shivered, studying the two men.

They were twins, but they weren't completely identical, she realized. There were minute differences. Drustan's hair wasn't as long, a bit past his shoulders, his eyes silvery. Taller, and he probably weighed more. Drustan was packed with muscle, Dageus's body was leaner, more ripped. Same beautiful, chiseled features though. Even the same dark shadow beard on similar jaws. She peered intently. Dageus's mouth was more . . . full and sulky. The mouth of a born seducer.

She was so engrossed that she didn't even notice the woman's approach until she spoke softly.

"Gorgeous, aren't they?"

Chloe turned, startled. The woman who'd spoken was as short as she was, and extremely pregnant, with silvery-blond hair and wispy fringed bangs. Her hair was twisted up in a knot and slightly damp, and Chloe blushed a little, realizing they'd obviously *both* been in the shower, and she found it highly doubtful that they'd been in separate ones. She was beautiful, glowing with the unique radiance of a pregnant woman who was utterly thrilled by impending motherhood, or . . . the radiance of a woman who'd just been treated to a MacKeltar's special seductive talents in the shower, Chloe thought wistfully. The mere thought of taking a shower with Dageus made Chloe feel rather glowy herself.

"Very. I had no idea they were twins. Dageus didn't tell me."

"Drustan didn't tell me either. He regretted that later, when I kissed Dageus because I thought he was Drustan. Drustan didn't care for it one bit. They're possessive about their women, but I'm sure you know that. I'm Gwen, by the way, Drustan's wife."

"Hi. It's nice to meet you. I'm Chloe Zanders." Chloe nibbled her lip uncertainly, then felt it necessary to clarify, "But I'm not his . . . er, woman. We met only recently and I'm just here to help him with translations."

Gwen looked highly amused. "If you say so. How did the two of you meet?"

If you say so? Now just what did that mean? And how to answer the question about how they'd met? Chloe opened her mouth and shut it again. Surely not, *I snooped through his penthouse and he tied me to his bed. And then I started turning into a person I hardly recognize anymore.* "That's a long story," she said warily.

"Those are the best kind—I can't wait to hear it! I have a few of my own." Gwen looped her arm through Chloe's and steered her toward the staircase. "Farley," she called over her shoulder to the white-haired butler, "would you have tea and coffee sent up to the solar? And some snacks. I'm *starving*."

"Right away, milady." With a doting look at Gwen, the butler rushed off.

"Why don't we get to know each other while they catch up?" Gwen asked, turning back to Chloe. "They've not seen each other in quite some time."

Chloe glanced again at Dageus. He and Drustan were still standing in the middle of the great hall, talking intently. Just then, as if he felt her gaze on him, Dageus looked at her, tensed, and started to walk toward her.

Surprised by his concern for her at what was clearly a difficult moment for him, Chloe shook her head, assuring him wordlessly that she was fine.

After a moment's hesitation, he turned back to Drustan.

Chloe smiled at Gwen. "I'd like that."

· 13 ·

When the lasses hastened off to the solar, Drustan and
Dageus adjourned to the privacy of the library. A spacious, masculine room with cherry bookcases recessed
into paneled walls, comfortable chairs and ottomans, a
dusky-rose marble fireplace and tall, bay windows, the library was Drustan's retreat, much as the glass-faced solar
that overlooked the gardens was Gwen's.

Drustan couldn't take his eyes off his twin brother.
He'd nigh given up hope that Dageus would come home.
He'd been dreading what he might have to do if his
brother didn't. But he was here now, and the tight fist that
had been clutched around his heart since the day he'd
read and, in a fit of fury, burned the letter their da had left
him, finally, blessedly, eased a bit.

Dageus tossed himself into a chair near the fireplace,
stretched out his legs, and propped his feet on a stool.

"What think you of the castle, Drustan? It appears to have withstood the centuries well."

Aye, that it had. The castle had surpassed all of Drustan's expectations. If ever a man had received proof of his brother's love, it had been in the gift of their home. Then Dageus had topped even that gift by sacrificing himself to ensure Drustan would survive to live in it. But Dageus had always been like that: though not a man to whom soft words came readily, when he loved, he loved to a dangerous point. *'Tis both his greatest strength and weakness,* Silvan had oft remarked, and truer words had never been uttered. He had the wild, true heart of a child, in the body of a jaded man. Intensely guarded, unless he chose to give it, yet once given, it was given completely. Without thought to his own survival.

" 'Tis even more magnificent than I'd imagined when we worked on the plans," Drustan said. "I can't thank you enough, Dageus. Not for this. Not for anything." How did one thank a brother for sacrificing his soul for one's own happiness? *My life for yours,* his brother had chosen. Thanks weren't possible.

Dageus shrugged. "You drew the sketches."

Ah, so he will pretend I meant only the castle and evade deeper issues, Drustan thought. "You built it. Gwen loves it too. And we've nigh finished having electricity and plumbing installed."

There was so much they needed to talk about, and naught of it would be easy to address. After a moment's hesitation, Drustan decided to confront it directly, for he suspected Dageus would talk circles around it.

Crossing to the liquor cabinet, Drustan splashed Macallan into two glasses, and handed one to Dageus. Thirty-five-year-old single-malt scotch, only the finest for his brother's return. "So, how bad is it?" he asked matter-of-factly.

Dageus flinched, a small, hastily contained reaction, but there. Then he tossed back the drink in one swallow and handed him the glass for a refill. Drustan complied, waiting.

His brother sipped more slowly at the second one. "Worse now that I'm back on Scottish soil," he said finally.

"When did your eyes change?" It wasn't only his eyes that had changed, Dageus moved differently. His most minute gestures were carefully executed, as if he could contain what was in him only by constant vigilance.

A tiny muscle leapt in Dageus's jaw. "How dark are they?"

"They're not gold anymore. A strange color, nigh like your drink."

"They change when it starts to get bad. When I've used too much magic."

"What are you using magic for?" Drustan asked carefully.

Dageus tossed back the rest of his drink, rose, and went to stand before the fire. "I was using it to obtain the texts I needed to see if there was a way to . . . get rid of them."

"What is it like?"

Dageus rubbed his jaw, exhaling. " 'Tis as if I have a beast inside me, Drustan. 'Tis pure power and I find myself using it without even thinking. When did you know?" he asked, with a faint, bitter smile.

Cold eyes, Drustan thought. They hadn't always been cold. Once they'd been warm, sunny-gold, and full of easy laughter. "I've known since the first, brother."

A long silence. Then Dageus snorted and shook his head.

"You should have let me die, Dageus," Drustan said softly. "*Damn* you for not letting me die."

Thank you for not letting me die, he added silently, torn by emotion. It was a terrible mixture of grief and guilt and gratefulness. If not for his brother's sacrifice, he would never have seen his wife again. Gwen would have raised their babies in the twenty-first century, alone. The day he'd read Silvan's letter, and discovered the price his twin had paid to ensure his future, he'd nearly gone crazy, hating him for giving up his own life, loving him for doing it.

"Nay," Dageus said. "I should have watched over you more carefully and kept the fire from happening."

" 'Twas not your fault—"

"Och, aye, it was. Do you know where I was that eve? I was down in the lowlands in the bed of a lass whose name I can't even recall—" He broke off abruptly. *"How* did you know? Did Da warn you?"

"Aye. He left a letter for us explaining what had happened, advising that you'd disappeared. Our descendant, Christopher, and his wife, Maggie—whom you'll meet anon—gave it to me shortly after I'd awakened. You called not long after that."

"Yet you pretended to accept my lies. Why?"

Drustan shrugged. "Christopher went to Manhattan twice and watched you. You were doing naught I felt needed to be stopped."

His reasons for not going to America to retrieve his brother were complicated. Not only had he been loath to leave Gwen's side while she was pregnant, he'd been wary of forcing a confrontation. After talking with him on the phone, he'd known that Dageus was indeed dark, but was holding on somehow. He'd suspected that were Dageus a tenth as powerful as Silvan believed, trying to force Dageus to return would have accomplished naught. Had it come to force, one of them would have died. Now that Dageus was there in the room with him, Drustan knew 'twould have been himself who'd died. The power in Dageus was immense, and he wondered how he'd withstood it this long.

Cautiously, when Dageus turned his back to him and busied himself opening a new bottle of whisky, Drustan reached out with his Druid senses, curious to know more about what they were dealing with.

He nearly doubled over. The whisky he'd sipped, curdled in his gut and tried to claw its way back up.

He retracted instantly, frantically, violently. By Amergin, how did Dageus stand it? A monstrous, icy, rapacious beast pulsed beneath his skin, snaking through him, coiled, but barely. It had a fierce, gluttonous appetite. It was huge and twisted and suffocating. How could he *breathe*?

Dageus turned, one brow arched, his gaze icy. "Never do that again," he warned softly. Without bothering to ask, he poured Drustan a refill.

Drustan snatched it from his hand and tossed it back swiftly. Only after the heat of it had exploded in his chest, did he trust himself to speak. He'd not kept his senses open long enough to explore the thing. His throat constricted by whisky and shock, he said hoarsely, "How did you know I was doing it? I scarce even—"

"I felt you. So did they. You doona want them to. Leave them alone."

"Aye," Drustan rasped. He hadn't needed the warning; he had no intention of opening his senses around his brother again. "Are they different personalities, Dageus?" he forced out.

"Nay. They have no separateness, no voice." *As yet,* Dageus thought darkly. He suspected the day might well come when they found a voice. The moment Drustan had reached out, they'd stirred, sensing power, and for a moment he'd had the terrible suspicion that what was in him could drain Drustan, suck him dry somehow.

"So, it's not as if you can actually hear them?"

" 'Tis—och, how can I explain this?" Dageus fell silent a moment, then said, "I feel them inside me, their knowledge as my own, their hunger as my own. It intensifies my desire for even simple things such as food and drink, to say nothing of women. There's a constant temptation to use magic and the more I use it, the colder I feel. The colder I feel, the more reasonable it seems to use it, and the stronger my desires become. I suspect there's a line that, should I cross, I will no longer be myself. This thing inside me will take over. I doona know what would happen to me then. I think I would be gone."

Drustan inhaled sharply. He could see a man being devoured by such a thing.

"My thought patterns change. They become primitive. Naught matters but what I want."

"But you've controlled it this long." *How?* Drustan marveled. *How did a man survive with such a thing in him?*

" 'Tis more difficult here. 'Tis why I left in the first place. What did Da tell you to do, Drustan?"

"He told me to save you. And we will." He deliberately omitted the last line of their father's letter. *And if you cannot save him, you must kill him.* Now he knew why.

Dageus searched his gaze intently, as if not convinced that was the entirety of what Silvan had said. Drustan knew he was about to push, so he launched an offensive of his own.

"What of the lass you brought? How much does she know?" Though he was amazed that Dageus could still feel anything at all with *that* inside him, he'd not missed the possessiveness in Dageus's gaze, or the reluctance with which he'd left her in Gwen's care.

"Chloe knows me as naught more than a man."

"She doesn't feel it in you?" *Lucky lass,* Drustan thought.

"She senses something. She watches me strangely at times, as if perplexed."

"And how long do you think you'll be able to maintain the pretense?"

"Christ, Drustan, give a man a moment to catch his breath, will you?"

"Do you plan to tell her?"

"How?" Dageus asked flatly. "Och, lass, I'm a Druid from the sixteenth century and I broke an oath and now I'm possessed by the souls of four-thousand-year-old evil Druids and if I doona find a way to get rid of them I will turn into a scourge upon the earth and the only thing that keeps me sane is tooping?"

"What?" Drustan blinked. "What was that about tooping?"

"It makes the darkness ease. When I begin to feel cold and detached, for some reason bedding a wench makes me feel human again. Naught else seems to work."

"Ah, that's why you brought her."

Dageus gave him a dark look. "She resists."

Drustan choked on a swallow of whisky. Dageus needed tooping to keep that heinous beast at bay, yet he'd brought a woman with him who refused his bed? "Why haven't you seduced her?" he exclaimed.

"I'm working on it," Dageus snarled.

Drustan gaped at him. Dageus could seduce any woman. If not gently, then with a rough, wild wooing that never failed. He'd not missed the way the wee lass had looked at his brother. She needed no more than a firm nudge. So why the bletherin' hell hadn't Dageus nudged? A sudden thought occurred to him. "By Amergin, she's the one, isn't she?" he breathed.

"What one?" Dageus stalked to a tall window, pushed

the drapes aside and stared out at the night. He slid the window up and breathed deeply, greedily, of sweet, chilly Highland air.

"The moment I saw Gwen, a part of me simply said 'mine.' And from that moment, though I didn't understand it, I knew that I would do aught ever it took to keep her. 'Tis as if the Druid in us recognizes our mate instantly, the one we could exchange the binding vows with. Is Chloe that one?"

Dageus's head whipped around and the unguarded, startled look on his face was answer enough for Drustan. His brother had heard the same voice. Drustan suddenly felt a surge of hope, despite what he'd felt inside his brother. He knew from personal experience that oft love could accomplish miracles when all else seemed destined to fail. Dageus may be dark, but by some miracle, he wasn't lost to it yet.

And when one was dealing with evil, Drustan suspected love might be the most potent weapon of all.

⁂

When Gwen joined them in the library a short time later, without Chloe, Dageus tensed. He'd yet to speak to Drustan about the attempt on Chloe's life, and about the Draghar—whoever they were.

Is she the one? Drustan had asked.

Och, aye, she was the one for him. Now that Drustan had remarked upon it, Dageus understood it was what he'd sensed from the very first—the kind a man kept, indeed. 'Twas no wonder he'd refused to use a memory spell on her, and send her on her way. He was incapable of letting her go. 'Twas also no wonder he'd not been satisfied with merely trying to bed her.

In this, his darkest hour, fate had gifted him with his mate. The irony of it was rich. How was a man to woo a woman under such conditions? He knew naught of woo-ing. He knew only of seduction, of conquering. Tender-ness of the heart, soft words and pledges, had been burned out of him long ago. The youngest son of no no-ble consequence, pagan to boot, he'd caught too many of his youthful follies attempting to seduce his own brother.

One too many of them had coyly suggested a three-way bout of love-play—and *no'* with another woman. Nay, always with his own twin.

Four times he'd watched Drustan try to secure a wife—and fail.

He'd learned young and learned well that he possessed one thing a woman wanted, hence he'd perfected his skills and taken comfort from the knowledge that while women might eschew intimacy with him, they never turned him away from their beds. He was always wel-come there. Even when their husband was in the next room, a fact that had only deepened his cynicism involv-ing so-called matters of the heart.

Except Chloe. She was the one woman he'd tried to se-duce that had refused him.

Yet remained at his side.

Aye, but how long will she remain there when she discovers what you are?

He had no answer for that, only a relentless determi-nation to have all of her that he could. And if that deter-mination was more akin to the desperation of a drowning man than a courageous one, so be it. The night he'd tempted death and danced on the slippery terrace wall above the snow-covered city of Manhattan—and fallen on the safe side—he'd made a promise to himself: that he would not yield to despair again. He would fight it any way he could, with any weapon he could find, till the bitter end.

"Where is she?" he hissed, surging to his feet.

Gwen blinked. "It's wonderful to see you, too, Dageus," she said sweetly. "Nice of you to drop in. We've only been waiting forever."

"Where?"

"Relax. She's upstairs taking a long shower. The poor girl traveled for an entire day and, though she said she slept a bit on the plane, she's clearly exhausted. What on earth have you been doing to her? I adore her, by the way," Gwen added, smiling. "She's a brainy geek like me. Now, can I have a hug?"

His tension ebbed slowly, aided by the knowledge that if Chloe was safe anywhere, it was within these walls. He'd personally chiseled the protection spells into the cornerstones when the castle had been built. So long as she remained within them, no harm would find her.

He skirted the sofa and opened his arms to Gwen, the woman who'd once saved his life. The woman he'd pledged his own to protect. " 'Tis good to see you again, lass, and you're looking lovely as ever." He bent his head to kiss her.

"No lips," Drustan warned. "Unless you wish me to be kissing Chloe."

Dageus averted his face swiftly. "How are the wee bairn, lass?" he asked, with a glance at her rounded belly.

Gwen beamed and prattled on about her most recent doctor's visit. When she paused finally for a breath, she peered at him intently. "Has Drustan told you our idea yet?"

Dageus shook his head. He was still having a hard time fathoming that Drustan had known he was dark all this time. A hard time believing he was home, that his brother had welcomed him. Had, in fact, been waiting for him.

"You're my brother," Drustan said quietly, and Dageus knew that he'd read his feelings in that uncanny way his twin had. "I would never turn my back on you. It wounds me that you thought I would."

"I but thought to fix it myself, Drustan."

"You hate to ask for help. You always have. You've ever shouldered more than your share of the burden. You had no right to sacrifice yourself for me—"

"Doona even start with me—"

"I didn't ask you to—"

"Och, you rather be *dead*?"

"Enough!" Gwen snapped. "Stop it, both of you. We could sit here for hours arguing about who should or should not have done what. And what would that accomplish? Nothing. We have a problem. We'll fix it."

Dageus hooked a ladder-back chair with his foot, turned it about and dropped into it backward, stretching his legs around the frame, resting his forearms on the top of the back. He took a perverse pleasure in seeing his elder brother chastened. Drustan was well met by his wee, brilliant wife. The bond betwixt them was a precious thing.

"We've given this a lot of thought," Gwen said, "and we think we can send someone back to warn you before the tower burns, that it's going to burn. That way you can prevent the fire, which would save Drustan, and keep you from ever turning dark."

Dageus shook his head. "Nay, lass. It wouldn't work."

"What mean you? 'Tis a brilliant solution," Drustan protested.

"Not only doona we have someone we could send, because that person might be forever stuck in the past, but I doona believe it would change me now."

"No, Drustan and I thought of that," Gwen insisted. "If the person was one you met as a result of turning dark, like—oh, say, gee, Chloe—the same thing that happened to me should happen to her. She'd be sent back to her own time the moment she succeeded in changing your future."

"Chloe goes nowhere without me. And she doesn't know. You didn't tell her, did you?" The tension was back again. He'd been so caught up in seeing his brother again, so relieved to be accepted, that he'd forgotten to warn Gwen to say naught to Chloe of his plight.

"I didn't say anything," Gwen hastened to assure him. "It was apparent she knew very little, so I kept the conversation light. We talked about college and jobs mostly. Who else have you met in this century that we might send?"

"No one. It wouldn't work anyway. There are things you doona know."

"Such as?" Drustan probed.

"I'm no' the same man anymore. I suspect that even if someone went back and warned the past me, and the past me didn't break his oath, what I've become would still exist in the here and now."

"That's impossible," Gwen declared, with the firm conviction of a physicist having weighted her proofs both valid and true.

"Nay 'tis not. I tried something very similar. Shortly after I broke my oath, I went back to a time before the fire, hoping to cancel myself out. To see if the past me might cause the dark me to cease to exist."

"The way things occurred when I took Gwen back into the past," Drustan said thoughtfully. "The future me ceased to exist because two identical selves couldn't coexist in the same moment in time."

"Aye. I even managed to carry a note to myself through the stones, so the past me would know to move you from the tower. But the canceling hinges on two *identical* selves."

"What are you saying?" Drustan demanded, hands clenching on the arms of his chair.

"When I went back, not only didn't the future me cease to exist, *neither* me did. I watched myself through a window for hours before fleeing again. He never disappeared. I might have strolled in and introduced myself."

" 'Tis wise you didn't. We must be ever wary of creating paradoxes," Drustan said uneasily.

Gwen gaped. "That's not possible. According to the laws of physics, one of you would *have* to cease to exist"

"You'd think after all she experienced with me, she wouldn't be so hasty labeling things possible or impossible," Drustan said dryly.

"*How* could it be possible?" Gwen demanded.

"Because I am no longer the same man I was. I'm different enough now with these ancient beings inside me, on some elemental level, that my past self did not conflict with who or what I've become."

"Oh, God," Gwen breathed. "So even if we sent someone back, and they changed the past . . ."

"I doubt it would have any effect on me at all. What I am now, seems to exist beyond the natural order of things. 'Tis possible it may cause some negative effect we can't even imagine. There's too much we doona understand here. I fear creating multiple moments in time for no good purpose. Nay, my only hope is the old lore."

Drustan and Gwen exchanged an uneasy look.

" 'Twas a clever idea," Dageus reassured them. "I can see why you considered it. But I've given this matter endless thought and my only hope is to discover how they were imprisoned in the first place, and reimprison them. 'Tis why I came. I need to use the Keltar library. I need to examine the ancient texts that deal with the Tuatha Dé Danaan."

Drustan sighed gustily and raked a hand through his hair.

"What?" Dageus's eyes narrowed.

"It's just that we were so certain our idea would work," Gwen said miserably.

"And?" Dageus pressed warily.

Drustan rose and began pacing. "Dageus, we no longer have those texts," he said in a low voice.

Dageus lunged to his feet so swiftly that the chair clattered to the floor. Nay—it couldn't be so! "What? What say you? How can we not have them?" he thundered.

"We doona know. But they're not here. After reading Da's letter, I decided to research the Tuatha Dé Danaan to discover aught I could about the mythic race, in hopes of discovering a way to cast them out. That's when Christopher and I found that we're missing a great many tomes."

"But surely *some* of the volumes I need are here." He began naming the ones he was specifically seeking, but at each title, Drustan shook his head.

"That's inconceivable, Drustan!"

"Aye, and it nigh seems deliberate. Christopher and I suspect someone intentionally removed them, though we cannot discern how it might have been done."

"I need those texts, damn it!" He slammed his fist against the paneled wall.

There was a moment of silence, then Drustan said slowly, "There is a place—or should I say a time—they can be found. A time both you and I know our clan's library was fully extant."

Dageus smiled bitterly. Right. And just how was he going to explain *that* to Chloe? *Ahem, lass, the tomes I needed aren't here, so we're going to have to go back in time and get them?* He snorted. Would nothing be simple? It seemed she'd be learning more about him, whether he was ready to tell her or not.

"I could go for you," Drustan offered. "Just long enough to get what we need."

"Then I'm going too," Gwen said instantly.

"Nay!" Drustan and Dageus both snapped at the same time.

Gwen glared. "I will *not* be left behind."

"*Neither* of you will be going." Dageus halted that argument before it built steam. "We have no guarantee that the Tuatha Dé Danaan didn't plant other dangers in the in-between. Any Keltar who opens a bridge for personal reasons is at risk. No Keltar but I will be opening any bridges to another time. I'm already dark. Besides, what one brings into the stones at one end doesn't always show up on the other end. I lost several heirlooms when I came through last time."

Gwen nodded slowly. "That's true. I lost my backpack. It went spiraling off into the quantum foam somewhere. We can't risk trying to bring the books through."

"Can you open the stones safely? What will the use of magic do to you?" Drustan asked cautiously. To Gwen, who hadn't been privy to their earlier conversation, he explained, "When he uses magic, it makes the . . . er, ancient ones stronger."

"Then maybe you shouldn't go," Gwen worried.

Dageus exhaled dismally. All his hopes were pinned on those Keltar texts, and he'd wasted as much time as he dare. "If what you say is true, and the tomes aren't here, I doona have a choice. As for the magic, I'm more concerned about what Da might do to me. I'll deal with the darkness somehow."

"We're clan, Dageus," Drustan said softly. "Da would never turn his back on you. And the timing couldn't be more fortuitous. The spring equinox is but a few days hence—"

" 'Tis no' necessary," Dageus cut him off. "I can open the stones any day, at any hour."

"What?" Drustan and Gwen exclaimed together.

" 'Twould seem our esteemed benefactors withheld significant portions of knowledge from us. The stones can be opened any time. It but requires a different set of formulas."

"And you know these formulas?" Drustan pressed.

"Aye. Because those within me do. Their knowledge is mine."

"Why would such knowledge have been withheld from us?"

"I suspect they intended it as a deterrent to keep a Keltar from opening a bridge through time rashly. One might entertain the notion—say, if one's brother died— to go through the stones that very day and undo it. But if one was forced to wait until the next solstice or equinox, one might have endured the worst of the grief by that time, and decide against it." Dageus's voice dripped self-mockery.

"How long did you wait?" Drustan asked quietly.

"Three moons, four days and eleven hours."

No one said anything for a time after that. Finally, Gwen shook herself, and rose. "While you two discuss this, I'll go prepare a room for Chloe."

"She sleeps with me," Dageus said in a low growl.

"She said you weren't sleeping together," Gwen said evenly.

"Christ, Gwen, what did you do? *Ask* her?"

"Of course I did," Gwen replied, as if she couldn't believe he'd even ask such a silly question. "But aside from admitting that much, she wasn't exactly forthcoming. So, what is she to you?"

"His mate," Drustan said softly.

"Really?" Gwen beamed. "Oh!" She clapped her hands delightedly. "I'm so happy for you, Dageus!"

Dageus pinned her with a forbidding stare. "Och, lass, are you witless? 'Tis no' a time for celebration. Chloe doesn't ken what I am and—"

"Don't underestimate her, Dageus. We women are *not* as fragile as you men like to believe."

"Then put her in my room," he said evenly.

"No," Gwen said just as evenly.

"You will put her in my room."

Gwen tipped her chin up and fisted her hands at her waist, staring him down. For a moment, Dageus was reminded of Chloe brandishing one of his own blades at him, and wondered how such wee women could be so unafraid of men such as he and his brother. Remarkable, but they were.

"No, I won't, Mr. Big Bad and Dark," she said. "You don't scare me. And you're not bullying me, or her, into anything we don't want."

"You shouldn't just go about asking people if they're sleeping with each other," he hissed.

"How else was I going to know where to put her?"

"By asking *me*." He glowered but she showed no signs of budging, so he turned to Drustan for support.

Drustan shrugged. "My wife is lady of the castle. Doona be looking to me."

"She's safe here, Dageus," Gwen said gently. "I'll put the two of you across the hall from each other. She can share your room if she *chooses* to."

As Gwen slipped from the library, she cast a last glance over her shoulder at the two magnificent Highlanders. She was both elated and deeply troubled, elated that Dageus had come home, troubled by what was yet to come. She and Drustan had been so certain their idea would work, they'd not thought beyond it.

Now Dageus was going to have to go back into the past. Open a bridge through time and search the old lore. She didn't want to let him go, and knew Drustan didn't either. But there wasn't much choice. She intended to try to cajole him into waiting a few days, but harbored little hope on that score.

Even without the benefit of her husband's Druid senses, she could feel that Dageus was different. There was something violent in him. Something barely contained, on the verge of exploding.

She arched a brow, thinking that, though she would *never* tell her husband so, Dageus was even sexier dark than he'd been before. He was raw and primal and something about him made a woman's every nerve stand up on end.

Her thoughts went to the woman upstairs. If Chloe had any sense at all, she mused, she'd be sharing his room tonight, and for however many future nights they might have.

Not only was refusing a Keltar male's bed a difficult thing to do, but it was a criminal waste of a woman's time, in Gwen's opinion. Drustan was an extraordinary lover, and with all that raw sexual heat Dageus was giving off, she had no doubt he would be too.

Long ago, in another century, she'd watched Dageus sit on the front steps of the MacKeltar castle in the gloaming, staring at the night sky. She'd recognized his loneliness—she'd been lonely once too—and had made a vow to help find him a mate. It seemed he'd found her himself. The least she could do was help him win her. The debt she owed Dageus MacKeltar was enormous.

She tucked her bangs behind her ear, smiling faintly.

She would have to let slip a few comments to Chloe about Keltar expertise and stamina. As well as imparting a few other bits of hard-earned wisdom when the time was right.

Hours later, Dageus followed Drustan abovestairs. They'd talked long into the night and soon it would be dawn.

After Gwen had left, he'd told Drustan about the attack on Chloe's life, and the words her strange assailant had said, then filled him in on the few references he'd found about the Draghar. Unfortunately, Drustan had been as baffled as he. They'd bandied about possibilities, but Dageus was getting blethering weary of possibilities. He needed answers.

"When will you be leaving?" Drustan said, as they reached the end of the north corridor and prepared to part for their respective chambers.

Dageus looked at Drustan, savoring the sight of his brother alive, awake, and happy. Though he'd like to spend more time with Drustan and Gwen, now that he was on Scottish soil again, he couldn't afford further delays. Chloe was in danger, and his time was growing short. He could feel it. He suffered no doubt that another attack would come, and didn't know if the Draghar, whoever they were, could follow them through time. If they were part of the Tuatha Dé Danaan, they could follow them anywhere.

"On the morrow."

"Must you go so soon?"

"Aye. I doona ken how much time I have."

"And the lass?" Drustan asked carefully.

Dageus's smile was icy. "She goes where I go."

"Dageus—"

"Say no more. If she doesn't go, I doona go."

"I would protect her for you."

"She goes where I go."

"And if she doesn't wish to?"

"She will."

· 14 ·

" 'Tis time, Chloe-lass," Dageus said.

"Wh-what do you mean?" Chloe asked warily. "Time for what?"

"It occurs to me that mayhap I've no' made my intentions clear," Dageus said with soft menace, stalking toward her.

"What intentions?" Though Chloe was determined to hold her ground, her cowardly feet had other plans. Traitorous little ninnies, they took a step backward for each step he took forward.

"My intentions about you."

"Oh, yes, you have," Chloe assured him hastily. "You want to seduce me. You've made that crystal clear. Any clearer would require an X rating. I'm not going to be just another one of your women. I'm not made like that. I can't leave my panties beneath a man's bed to be swept out with the trash. That's why I'm still a virgin, because it means something to me and I'm not going to toss my virginity at your charming feet just because you're the most gorgeous, fascinating man I've ever met and I happen to like your last name. Those are not good enough reasons." She nodded her head to punctuate the rush of words, then looked horrified by what she'd admitted at the last.

"The most gorgeous, fascinating man you've ever met?" he said, his dark eyes glittering.

"There are oodles of gorgeous men around. And dusty, boring ancient texts are fascinating too," she muttered. "Stay away from me. I'm not going to fall for your seduction."

"Doona you even wish to know my intentions?" he purred.

"No. Absolutely not. Go away." Her back struck the wall and she stumbled a little, then folded her arms across her chest and scowled up at him.

"I'm not going away. And I am going to tell you." He rested his palms against the wall on either side of her head, walling her in with his powerful body.

"I'm waiting with bated breath." She faked a delicate yawn and examined her cuticles.

"Chloe-lass, I'm going to keep you."

"Keep me, my ass," she snapped. "I don't agree to being kept."

"Forever," he said, with a chilling smile. "And you will."

❧

"Argh! Can't I just not dream about that man one freaking night?" Chloe cried, rolling over in bed and pulling the pillow over her head.

He was on her mind incessantly when she was awake. She didn't think it was so much to ask to be able to escape him in her dreams. She'd even dreamed about him when she'd dozed on the airplane! And all the dreams had been so intensely detailed that they'd seemed almost real. In this one, she'd been able to smell the spicy man-scent of him, to feel his warm breath fanning her face when he'd informed her he was going to keep her.

As if!

What did her dream Dageus think? she brooded irritably. That such a barbaric, utterly Teutonic declaration would melt her to her toes?

Wait a minute, she thought, backtracking mentally—it had been *her* dream, which meant that it wasn't what he thought, but apparently what *she* was subconsciously thinking about.

Oh, Zanders, you are so not politically correct, she thought dismally.

It *had* melted her. She'd love to hear such words from him. One teeny declaration of that sort and she'd be stuck on him like superglue.

She sat up and flung the pillow across the room in frustration. The Gaulish Ghost in New York had been fascinating enough, but the glimpse of emotion she'd seen last night when he'd been reunited with his brother had made him even more dangerously intriguing.

It had been one thing to think of him as a womanizer, a man not capable of love.

But she couldn't think that anymore, because she'd seen love in his eyes. Love that she wanted to know more about. She'd glimpsed depths to him that she'd convinced herself he didn't have. What had happened between the two brothers to make them so estranged? What had happened to Dageus MacKeltar to make him so tightly guard his emotions?

She was doing it—wanting to be the woman who got inside him. Dangerous want, that.

She hugged her knees and rested her chin atop them, brooding.

A significant part of the blame for her dream, she thought peevishly, could be attributed to Gwen. Last night, after Chloe had finished showering, Gwen had brought a dinner tray to her room. She'd stayed while Chloe had eaten, and the talk had turned, as it was wont to do when women got together, to men.

Specifically to Keltar men.

Facts that Chloe had known about Dageus prior to Gwen's little visit: He was irresistibly seductive; he had a fantastic body—she'd seen it when he'd dropped his towel; he wore condoms for the "Extra-Large Man."

And now—thank you Gwen MacKeltar—she knew that he was a man of both immense appetites and stamina, and had been known to spend, not a few hours, but *days* in bed with a woman. Oh, Gwen hadn't actually come out and said those things, but she'd made her point clear enough in bits and pieces that she'd dropped.

Days in bed? She couldn't even begin to imagine what that would be like.

Oh, yes, you can, a snide little voice poked, *you dreamt about it a few nights ago, in shocking detail for a virgin.*

Scowling, she pushed her curls out of her face and swung her legs over the side of the massive, antique bed piled with down ticks. Her toes dangled a foot above the floor and she had to hop to get out of it.

Shaking her head, she grabbed her clothes and headed for the shower. She didn't really need to, having showered late last night, but this morning she suspected she might benefit from a cold one.

When she stepped out into the corridor a half an hour later, she stopped abruptly, bristling. She'd taken a chilly shower, forcing herself to think about the artifacts she might get to see, and what she'd like to explore first. It had taken her nearly the entire half an hour to get him off her mind, and now he was right back on it.

"What are you doing?" she asked grumpily, feeling that dratted, instant surge of attraction that demanded plaintively (and incessantly!), *Would you just jump on him and to hell with the consequences?* The man of her dreams— literally—was sitting on the floor, leaning against the door across the corridor from hers, his long legs outstretched, his arms folded over his chest. He wore black trousers and a charcoal crew-neck wool sweater stretched over his powerful torso, showcasing his perfect physique. He'd shaved, and the skin on his face looked smooth and soft as velvet. Coppery eyes met hers.

He rose, towering over her, his sheer masculinity making her feel small and feminine.

"I was waiting for you. Good morrow, lass. Did you have pleasant dreams?" he inquired silkily.

Chloe kept her expression bland. He looked immensely pleased with himself this morning, and there was no way she was letting him know she'd had even one nocturnal thought about him. "I can't remember," she said, blinking guilelessly. "In fact, I slept so deeply I don't think I dreamt at all."

"Indeed," he murmured. When he moved forward, she nearly jumped out of her skin, but he simply reached behind her and pulled the door to her bedchamber shut.

Then backed her against it.

"Hey," she snapped.

"I sought but to give you a good morrow kiss, lass. 'Tis a Scots custom."

She craned her neck, scowling up at him, and gave him a look that said *Yeah, right, nice try.*

"A wee one. No tongue. I promise," he said, his lips curving faintly.

"You never give up, do you?"

"I never will, sweet. Doona you know that by now?"

Oooh, that was beginning to take on shades of her

dream. And he'd called her "sweet," a little endearment. She clamped her mouth shut and shook her head.

He lifted his hand to her face and lightly traced his fingers down the curve of her cheek. A soft touch, nothing overtly seductive about it. The gentleness of it startled her, stilled her. He moved his hand from her face to her soft curls, threading them through his fingers.

"Have I told you, Chloe-lass, that you're beautiful?" he said softly.

She narrowed her eyes. If he thought a generic compliment would buy him a kiss, he was sadly mistaken.

"Och, aye, lovely as can be." He smudged her cheek with the back of his knuckles. "And without a trace of artifice. I sat in my cab and stared at you the day I first saw you. I watched other men looking at you and wished them blind. You bent back into the car to say something to your driver. You were wearing a black skirt and jacket with a sweater the color of heather, and your hair was falling into your eyes and you kept pushing it back. It was misting a bit, and the hose on your legs glistened with droplets of rain. You didn't mind the rain, though. For a moment, you tipped your head back, turning your face up to it. It took my breath away."

The caustic comment coiled on the tip of her tongue died.

He looked at her a long moment, then dropped his hands.

"Come, lass." He offered her his hand. "Let's fetch some breakfast, then I'd like to take you somewhere."

Chloe struggled for composure. The man had a way of throwing her off-kilter like no one else she'd ever known. Just when she thought she knew him, he threw something unexpected at her. Where had that just come from? He remembered exactly what she'd been wearing the day they'd met, and it *had* been misting that morning. And she had briefly turned her face up into the mist; she'd always liked rain. She cleared her throat. "So when do I get to see the texts?" she hastily forced the conversation to less uncertain terrain.

"Soon. Very soon."

Other men were watching you and I wished them blind. She shook her head, trying to scatter his words from her mind. Unable to determine what "face value" to place upon them. "Does your brother have other artifacts too?" she pressed brightly.

"Aye. You'll see many things before the day is through."

"Really? Like what?"

He smiled faintly at her eagerness and caught her hands in his. "Do you know how I know when you're excited about something?"

Chloe shook her head.

"Your fingers start to curl, as if you're imagining touching whatever it is you're thinking about."

She blushed. She hadn't known she was so transparent.

"Och, lass, 'tis charming. Do you recall that I said I could show you a Scotland no other man ever could?"

She nodded.

"Well, this afternoon, lass," he said with a strangely wry note in his voice, "I'll be making good on that promise."

❦

Some distance from the castle in which Chloe and Dageus were currently breakfasting, a man leaned back against the side of a nondescript rental car, talking quietly on the phone.

"I haven't had the opportunity to get close," Trevor was telling Simon. "But it's only a matter of time."

"You were supposed to take care of her before they left London," Simon's voice was faint on the cell phone, yet still rang with implacable authority.

"I couldn't get near her. The man is constantly on guard."

"What makes you think you can get close on Keltar ground?"

"He'll drop his guard eventually, if only for a few minutes. Just give me a few more days."

"It's too risky."

"It's too risky *not* to. He has an emotional bond with her. We need his ties gone. You said so yourself, Simon."

"Forty-eight hours. Ring me every six. Then I want you out of there. I'm not willing to run the risk that one of our Order is taken alive. He must know nothing about the Prophecy."

With a soft murmur of assent, Trevor hung up.

· 15 ·

The day had been sunny and surprisingly temperate for March in the Highlands: mid-forties, a light breeze, the sky dotted by a few fat, fluffy white clouds.

It had been one of the most exhilarating days of Chloe's life.

After breakfast, she, Dageus, Drustan, and Gwen had driven to the north, taking the winding roads to the top of a small mountain, above the colorful, bustling city of Alborath, where'd she'd met Dageus's cousins, Christopher and Maggie MacKeltar, and their many children.

She'd spent the day with Gwen and Maggie, touring the *second* MacKeltar castle (this one quite a bit older than Gwen's). She'd seen artifacts that Tom would have blithely committed felonies to acquire: ancient texts sealed in protective cases, weapons and armor from too many different centuries to count, rune stones scattered casually about the gardens. She'd toured the portrait gallery lining the great hall, a painted history of centuries of the MacKeltar clan—what a wonder to know such roots! She'd brushed her fingertips to tapestries that should be in museums, furniture that belonged under much tighter security than she'd been able to see on the grounds. Though she'd inquired repeatedly and rather anxiously about their anti-theft system (which seemed criminally nonexistent), she'd gotten nothing but reassuring smiles, forcing her to conclude that none of the Keltars bothered to lock things up.

The castle itself was an artifact, meticulously preserved and protected from time's gentle erosion. She'd wandered through the day in a dreamy kind of stupefaction.

Now she stood on the front steps of the castle with Gwen in the rosy, early evening light. The sun was resting on the horizon and tendrils of mist were wisping up from the ground. She could see for miles from her perch on the wide stone stairs, past a sparkling many-tiered fountain, out over the valley where the lights of Alborath were nudging back the encroaching twilight. She could imagine how glorious the Highlands would be in spring, or better yet, the full bloom of late summer. She wondered if she might find some way to still be there by then. Maybe after her month with Dageus, she mused, she would stay in Scotland, indefinitely.

Her gaze skimmed the front lawn, coming to rest on the gorgeous, dark man who'd turned her world so completely upside down in just under a week. He was standing, some distance from the castle, inside a circle of massive, ancient stones, talking with Drustan. Gwen had told her the brothers hadn't seen each other in years, though she'd offered no explanation for their estrangement. Inquisitive as Chloe usually was, for a change, she'd resisted prying. It just hadn't seemed right.

"It's so beautiful here," she said, sighing wistfully. To live here, to belong in such a place. The rowdy enthusiasm of Maggie and Christopher's six children, from teens down to tots, was unlike anything Chloe had ever experienced. The castle was stuffed to overflowing with family and roots, the air rang with the sounds of children playing and occasional bickering. As an only child, raised by an elderly grandparent, Chloe had never seen anything like it before.

"That it is," Gwen agreed. "They call those stones the *Ban Drochaid*," she told Chloe, gesturing at the circle. "It means 'the white bridge.' "

" 'The white bridge,' " Chloe echoed. "That's an odd name for a group of stones."

Gwen shrugged, a mysterious smile playing about her lips. "There are lots of legends in Scotland about such stones." She paused. "Some people say they're portals to another time."

"I read a romance novel like that once."

"You read romance novels?" Gwen exclaimed, delighted.

The next few moments were filled with a hasty comparison of favorite titles, female bonding, and recommendations.

"I *knew* I liked you." Gwen beamed. "When you were talking earlier about the history of all those artifacts, I was afraid you might be the stuffy literary type. Nothing against literary novels," she added hastily, "but if I want to get all existential and depressed, I'll pick a fight with my husband or watch CNN." She was silent a moment, her hand resting lightly on her rounded belly. "Scotland isn't like any other country in the world, Chloe. You can almost feel the magic in the air, can't you?"

Chloe cocked her head and studied the towering megaliths. The stones were thousands of years old and their purpose had long been heatedly debated by scholars, archeoastronomers, anthropologists, even mathematicians. They were a mystery modern man had never been able to unravel.

And yes, she did feel a brush of magic about them, a sense of ancient secrets, and was struck suddenly by how right Dageus looked standing in the middle of them. Like a primitive sorcerer, wild and forbidding, a keeper of secrets, arcane and profane. She rolled her eyes at her absurd fancy.

"What is he doing, Gwen?" she asked, squinting.

Gwen shrugged but didn't reply.

It looked as if he was writing something on the inner face of each stone. There were thirteen, towering around a center slab that was fashioned of two stone supports, and one large flat stone placed atop it in the shape of a squat dolmen.

As Chloe watched, Dageus moved to the next stone, his hand moving with brisk surety across its inner face. He *was* writing on it, she realized. How odd. She narrowed her eyes. God, the man was beautiful. He'd changed after breakfast. Soft, faded jeans hugged his powerful thighs and muscled butt. A thick wool sweater and hiking boots completed his rugged outdoorsman look. His hair fell in a single braid to his waist.

I'm going to keep you forever, her dream Dageus had said.

You've got it bad, Zanders, she reluctantly acknowledged with a little sigh.

"You have feelings for him," Gwen murmured, jarring her.

Chloe paled. "Is it that obvious?"

"To someone who knows what to look for. I've never seen him look at a woman the way he looks at you, Chloe."

"If he looks at me any differently than others, it's only

because most women fall into bed with him the minute they meet him," Chloe said, puffing a curly strand of hair from her face. "I'm just the one who got away." *So far,* was the dry thought accompanying that.

"Yes, and that's *all* they ever do."

That got her attention. "Isn't that all he wants?"

"No. But most women never get past that beautiful face and body, his strength and his reserve. They never, never trust him with their hearts."

Chloe pulled her long hair back, twisting it into a loose knot, and held her silence, hoping Gwen might continue to volunteer information. She was in no hurry to admit to her pathetic romanticizing, which had only worsened throughout the day. All day long she'd been treated to glimpses of the incredible relationship between Gwen and her husband. She'd watched, with shameless longing, the way Drustan treated his wife. They were so unabashedly in love with each other.

Because he looked so much like Dageus, comparisons had been inevitable. Drustan had popped up oodles of times, toting a light jacket for Gwen, or a cup of tea, or an inquiry if her back ached, if she needed a rub, if she needed to rest, if she'd like him to leap into the sky and pull down the blasted sun.

Making Chloe think ridiculous thoughts about his brother.

Oh, yes, she had feelings. Treacherous, deceitful little feelings.

"Chloe, Dageus doesn't look for love from a woman, because he's never been given any reason to."

Chloe's eyes widened and she shook her head disbelievingly. "That's impossible, Gwen. A man like him—"

"Terrifies most women. So they take what he offers, but they find some other man to love. A safer man. A man they feel more in control with. Is he doing the same thing to you? I thought you were smarter than that."

Chloe jerked, wondering how the conversation had gotten so personal so fast.

But Gwen wasn't done yet. "Sometimes—and trust me, I know this from personal experience—a girl has to take a leap of faith. If you don't try, you'll never know what might have been. Is that how you want to live?"

Chloe fumbled for a reply, but came up empty-handed, because deep inside her that nagging voice that had so persistently begun asking recently "is this all there is?" was nodding sagely, agreeing with Gwen's words.

Naught risked, naught gained, Grandda had always said.

When had she forgotten that? Chloe wondered, staring at the ancient stones. When she was nineteen, and Grandda died, leaving her alone in the world?

As she stood there, atop the MacKeltar's mountain in the falling twilight, Chloe was suddenly back in Kansas again, in the silent cemetery, after all their friends had gone, weeping at the foot of his grave. Uncertain, poised on the brink of adulthood, with no one to help her make decisions and choose her way. She'd suffered the comforting delusion that he would live forever, not die at a mere seventy-three from a stroke. She'd gone away to college, never imagining that he wouldn't always be there, at home, puttering around his garden, waiting for her.

The phone call came during finals week her sophomore year. She'd just talked to him on the phone a few days before. One day he was there, the next day he was gone. She hadn't even gotten to say good-bye. Same as her parents. Couldn't anyone die a slow death from some disease, she'd felt like wailing (painlessly, of course, she'd not wish a painful death on anyone), and give her a damned sense of closure? Did they have to just go away? One moment, smiling and alive, the next, still and silent and forever lost. There were so many things she hadn't gotten to say to him before he left. He'd seemed so fragile in his coffin; her robust, temperamental Scot, who'd always seemed invincible to her.

Was that when she'd begun playing things safe? Because she'd felt like a turtle without a shell, fragile and exposed, unwilling to love and lose again? Oh, she'd not decided such a thing consciously, but she'd gone back to college and buried herself in a double major, then a master's. Without even thinking, she'd kept herself too busy to get involved.

She blinked. The grief was still raw, as if she'd never faced it, only pushed it into a dark corner, blocking it. It occurred to her that maybe a person couldn't shut out one emotion, such as grief, without losing touch with all of them. By shutting out pain, refusing to face it, had she missed innumerable chances to love?

Chloe glanced at Gwen searchingly. "It sounds like you're encouraging me."

"I am. He's going to ask something of you. The mere fact that he's going to ask it speaks more than any words could, of how he feels about you."

"What is he going to ask me?"

"You'll know soon enough." Gwen paused and sighed heavily, as if she were having a heated internal debate with herself. Then she said, "Chloe, Drustan and Dageus come from a world that's hard for girls like us to understand. A world that—though it may initially seem impossible—is firmly grounded in reality. Just because science can't explain something, doesn't make it any less real. I'm a scientist and I know what I'm talking about. I've seen things that defy my understanding of physics. They're good men. The best. Keep an open mind and heart, because I can tell you one thing for sure: when these Keltars love, they love completely and forever."

"You're freaking me out," Chloe said uneasily.

"You haven't *begun* to be freaked out. One question, just between you and me, and don't lie to me: Do you want him?"

She stared at Gwen in silence for a long moment. "Is this *really* just between you and me?"

Gwen nodded.

"I have since the moment I met him," she admitted simply. "And it doesn't make a bit of sense to me. I'm all possessive about him, and I have no right to be. It's crazy. I've never felt anything like this before. I can't even reason with it," she said, frustration underscoring her words.

Gwen's smile was radiant. "Oh, Chloe, the only time reason fails is when we're trying to convince our minds of something our heart knows isn't true. Stop trying. Listen with your heart."

"I doona like this," Drustan growled at Dageus.

"Did you give Gwen a choice?" Dageus countered, as he finished etching the second-to-last formula on the central slab. He need but etch the final one to open the bridge through time. He and Drustan had agreed that he should return to six months after last he'd been there, to avoid his past self, and in hopes that Silvan may have discovered something useful in the interim. "Chloe's a strong lass, Drustan. She held the point of my own sword at my chest. She fought off her attacker valiantly. She *chose* to come to Scotland with me. Though sometimes she hesitates, she fears nothing. And she's smart, she speaks many languages, she knows the old myths, and she loves artifacts. I'm about to take her to them. If for naught else, she'll forgive me for that," he added, dryly.

Och, aye, she would. He could put texts in her hands that would make her weep with the joy of a true bibliophile and guardian of relics. They shared that: Her chosen profession was to preserve the old things, and she hadn't been satisfied with merely preserving, she'd studied it all, much as he had in his role as Keltar Druid.

"Gwen knew what I was."

"But she didn't believe you," Dageus reminded. "She thought you were mad."

"Yes, but—"

"No buts. If you'd haud yer wheesht a moment, you'd hear that I intend to give her a choice."

"You *do?*"

"I'm no' entirely without scruples," was his mocking reply.

"You're going to tell her?"

Dageus shrugged. "I said I'd give her a choice."

"The honorable thing would be to tell her—"

Dageus's head whipped up and his eyes sparked dangerously. "I doona have time to tell her!" he hissed. "I doona have time to try to convince her, or help her understand!"

Silvery gaze warred with copper.

"You do realize that once you take her through, she's going to know that you're a Druid, Dageus. You'll no longer be able to pretend you're naught but a man."

"I'll deal with that. She knows there's something no' quite right with me."

"But what if she . . ." Drustan trailed off, but Dageus knew he'd been about to voice the fear that he'd been forced to face when he'd sent Gwen back.

"What if she runs screaming from me? Cries 'pagan sorcerer' and hates me?" Dageus said with a chilly smile. " 'Tis my worry, no' yours."

"Dageus—"

"Drustan, I need her. I *need* her."

Drustan stared at the scarce-concealed despair in his

brother's eyes, and had a sudden flash of insight: Dageus was walking a razor's edge, and he knew it. He knew he had no right to take Chloe, verily, he knew he had no right to have brought her this far. But were Dageus to give up on those things he wanted—to accept that, because he was dark, he had no promise of a future, no true rights to anything—he would have nothing left to live for. There would be nothing to keep him fighting another day.

And which would win then? Honor? Or the seduction of absolute power?

Christ, Drustan thought, a chill seeping through his veins, the day his brother stopped wanting, the day he stopped believing there was hope, he would have to face the fact that his only choices were to become utterly evil . . . or . . .

Drustan couldn't make himself finish that thought. And in Dageus's tortured gaze, he could see that his twin had figured this all out long ago, and was fighting the only way he could. If Dageus's desire for Chloe was the thing standing most firmly betwixt he and the gates of hell itself, Drustan would chain the wee lass to his brother himself.

A bitter smile curved Dageus's lips, as if he sensed Drustan's thoughts. "Besides," Dageus said with light mockery, "at least I know I can return her. Gwen had no such assurance, yet you took her. If aught goes awry with me, I promise to send Chloe back, one way or another."

It would mean he was dying, for that was the only way he'd let her go. Even then, she might have to be pried from his fingers as the life fled his body.

"All right." Drustan nodded slowly. "When will you return?"

"Look for us three days hence. 'Tis as close as I care to pass myself."

They regarded each other in silence, much unsaid between them. Then there was no further opportunity, for Chloe and Gwen joined them in the circle.

"What are you doing?" Chloe asked curiously, peering at them. "Why are you writing on those stones, Dageus?"

Dageus looked at her a long moment, drinking her in greedily. Och, she was beautiful, so unselfconscious, standing there in her slim blue trews, sweater, and hiking boots, her hair a riot of curls tucked into a loose knot that was already falling out. Huge eyes, wide and full of innocent joy. She wore Scotland well. With a flush in her cheeks and a sparkle in her eyes.

Eyes that, in a short time, might regard him with fear and loathing, as the lasses in his century would have, had he ever revealed the extent of his Druid power.

And if such comes to pass? his honor prodded.

I'll do aught I can to seduce her back out of it, he thought, shrugging, *using every underhanded trick I've got.* He'd give up when he was dead.

If anyone could accept it, she could. Modern women were different from the lasses of his time. While sixteenth-century lasses were quick to see "magycks" in the inexplicable, twenty-first-century women sought scientific explanations, were better able to abide the thought of natural laws and physics beyond their understanding. He suspected 'twas because so much progress had been made into scientific inquiry in the past century, explaining previously inexplicable things and exposing a whole new realm of mystery.

Chloe was a strong, curious, resilient lass. Though not a physicist like Gwen, she was clever and had knowledge of both the Old World and the new. An added boon was her insatiable curiosity, which had already led her into places most would not have ventured. She had all the right ingredients to be able to accept what she was soon going to experience.

And he would be there to help her understand. If he knew Chloe half as well as he thought he did, once she recovered from shock, she would be positively giddy with excitement.

Averting his gaze from Chloe's inquisitive look, he glanced at Gwen. "Be well, lass," he said. He hugged her, then Drustan, and stepped away.

"What's going on?" Chloe asked. "Why are you saying good-bye to Gwen and Drustan? Aren't we staying here to work on his books?" When Dageus didn't answer, she looked at Gwen, but Gwen and Drustan had turned and were walking out of the circle.

She looked back at Dageus.

He extended his hand to her. "I have to leave, Chloe-lass."

"What? What on earth are you talking about?" There was no car nearby. Leave how? For where? Without her? He'd said "*I* have to leave" not "we." Her chest felt suddenly tight.

"Will you come with me?"

The tightness eased a bit, but confusion still reigned. "I d-don't understand," Chloe sputtered. "Where?"

"I can't tell you where. I have to show you."

"That's the most ridiculous thing I've ever heard," she protested.

"Och, nay, lass. Give me a bit more time and you'll not think it so," he said lightly. But his eyes weren't light. They were intense and . . .

Listen with your heart, Gwen had said. Chloe drew a deep breath and exhaled slowly. She forced herself to push her preconceptions aside, and tried *looking* with her heart. . . .

. . . and she saw it. There in his eyes. The pain she'd

glimpsed on the plane, but had told herself wasn't really there.

More than pain. A brutal, unceasing despair.

He was waiting, one strong hand outstretched. She had no idea what he was doing, or where he thought he was going. He was asking her to say "yes" without knowing. He was asking for that leap of faith Gwen had warned her about. For the second time in less than forty-eight hours, the man was asking her to throw all caution to the wind and leap with him, trusting that he wouldn't let her fall.

Do it, Evan MacGregor's voice suddenly said in her heart. *You may not have nine lives, Chloe-cat, but you mustn't be afraid to live the one you've got.*

Chills shivered up her spine, raising the fine hair on her skin. She glanced around at the thirteen stones encircling them, with funny symbols that looked like formulas etched on their inner faces. More symbols on the central slab.

Was she about to find out what those standing stones had been used for? The concept was too fantastic for her to wrap her brain around.

What on earth did he think was going to happen?

Logic insisted *nothing* was going to happen in those stones. Curiosity was proposing, quite persuasively, that if something did, she'd have to be a fool to miss it.

She blew out a gusty sigh. What was one more plunge, anyway? she thought with a mental shrug. She'd already been so completely derailed from the normal track of her life that she couldn't get too worked up at the prospect of another loopy turn. And frankly, the ride had never been so fascinating. Drawing herself up to her full height, squaring both her shoulders and her resolve, she turned back to Dageus and slipped her hand into his. Notching her chin up, she met his gaze and said, "Fine. Let's go, then." She was proud of herself for how firm and nonchalant it had come out.

His eyes flared. "You'll come? Without knowing where I'm taking you?"

"If you think I've come this far to be dumped along the wayside, you don't know me very well, MacKeltar," she said lightly, seeking strength in levity. The moment was simply too tense. "I'm the woman who snooped beneath your bed, remember? I'm slave to my curiosity. If you're going somewhere, I am too. You're not getting away from me yet." *God, had she really said that?*

"That sounds as if you're telling me you plan to keep me, lass." His eyes narrowed and he went very still.

Chloe caught her breath. It was so similar to her dream!

He smiled then, a slow smile that caused tiny lines about his eyes to crinkle, and for a moment something danced within the coppery depths. Something younger and . . . free and breathtakingly beautiful. "I'm yours for the asking, sweet."

She forgot how to breathe for a moment.

Then his eyes went cool again and abruptly, he turned back toward the center slab and wrote a series of symbols. "Hold my hand and doona let go."

"Keep him safe, Chloe," Gwen shouted, as a sudden, fierce wind kicked up through the stones, scattering dried leaves in swirling eddies of mist.

Safe from what? Chloe wondered.

And then she wondered no more, because suddenly the stones began spinning in a circle around her—but that wasn't possible! And even while she was arguing with herself over what was and was not possible, she lost the ground and was upside down, or something, and then she lost the sky too. Grass and twilight swirled together, speckled by a mad rush of stars. The wind soared to a deafening howl, and suddenly she was . . . *different* somehow. She glanced wildly about for Drustan and Gwen, but they were gone, and she could see nothing at all, not even Dageus. A terrible gravity seemed to be pulling at her, sucking her in and stretching her out, bending her in impossible ways. She thought she heard a sonic boom, and then suddenly there was a flash of white so blinding that she lost all sense of sight and sound.

She could no longer feel Dageus's hand.

She could no longer feel her *own* hand!

She tried to open her mouth and scream, but she had no mouth to open. The white grew ever more intense and, though there was no longer any sense of motion, she felt a nauseating vertigo. There was no sound, but the silence itself seemed to have crushing substance.

Just when she was certain she couldn't endure it one more instant, the white was gone so abruptly that the blackness slammed into her with all the force of a Mack truck.

Then there was feeling in her body again, and she wasn't thrilled to have it back. Her mouth was dry as a desert, her head felt swollen and oversized, and she was pretty sure she was about to throw up.

Oh, Zanders, she chided herself weakly, *I think this was a little more than just another loopy turn.*

Chloe stumbled and collapsed to the ice-covered ground.

"Those who do not remember the past are condemned to relive it."

—THE PROPHETESS EIRU, sixth century B.C.E.

"Those who do not remember the past are condemned to relive it."

—MIDHE CODEX, seventh century C.E.

"Those who do not remember the past are condemned to relive it."

—GEORGE SANTAYANA, twentieth century C.E.

· 16 ·

There were voices inside his head. Thirteen distinct ones: twelve men and the jewel-bright tones of a sultry-voiced woman, talking in a language he couldn't understand.

The voices were but a susurrus, a sibilant murmuring. No more than a stiff wind rustling through oaks, yet like a wind, it blew darkly through him, stripping away his humanity like a fragile autumn leaf no longer firmly anchored to its branch. It was the wind of winter and of death and it accepted no censure and would abide no moral judgment.

There was only hunger. The hunger of thirteen souls confined for four thousand years in a place that was not a place, in a time that was not a time. Locked away for four thousand years. Locked away for one-hundred-and-forty-six *million* days, for three-and-a-half *billion* hours——and if that was not eternity, what was?

Imprisoned.

Adrift in nothing.

Alive in that heinous dark oblivion. Eternally aware. Hungry, with no mouth to feed. Lusting, with no body to ease. Itching, with no fingers to scratch.

Hating, hating, hating.

A seething mass of raw power, unsated for millennia.

And as they felt, so Dageus felt, too, lost in darkness.

The storm was nature at her height of savagery. Chloe had never seen such a squall before. Rain mixed with jagged chunks of hail pelted from the sky, bruising her, stinging her skin, even through the thickness of her jacket and sweater.

"Ow!" Chloe cried *"Ow!"* A large chunk of ice struck her in the temple, another in the small of her back. Cursing, she tucked into a protective ball on the hail-covered ground and wrapped her arms around her head.

The wind soared to a deafening pitch, keening and howling. She screamed into it, calling Dageus's name, but couldn't even hear her own voice above the din. The ground trembled and tree limbs crashed to the earth. Lightning flashed and thunder boomed. The shrieking wind whipped her hair into a sodden tangle. She hunched in a ball with no hope but to endure it and pray it didn't get worse.

Then suddenly—as abruptly as the fierce storm had arisen—it was gone.

Simply gone. The hail stopped. The deluge ceased. The wind died. The night fell still and silent but for a soft hissing sound.

For a few moments Chloe mentally tallied her bruises,

refusing to move. Moving would mean acknowledging she was alive. Acknowledging she was alive would mean she'd have to look around. And frankly, she wasn't sure she wanted to.

Ever. Thoughts were colliding in her head, all of them impossible.

Come on, Zanders, get a grip, the voice of reason endeavored valiantly to assert itself. *You're going to feel downright silly when you look up and see Gwen and Drustan standing there. When they say "Gee, don't you hate it when a storm comes up so fast? But that's how they are in the Highlands."*

She wasn't buying it. She wasn't certain of much at the moment, but she was pretty darned certain storms like that didn't happen, in the Highlands or anywhere else, and furthermore, she didn't hold out much hope that Gwen and Drustan were anywhere nearby. Something had happened in those stones. Just what, she couldn't say, but something . . . epic. Something that reeked of a kernel of truth secreted in ancient myths.

After a few more moments, she drew her arms back and peeped cautiously out. Rain poured from her hair, dripping down her face. She braced her palms on the ground and suddenly understood what the hissing noise was.

The earth was warm, as if it had been sun-heated all day, and the pellets of hail were steaming on it. How could the ground be warm? she wondered, baffled. It was March, for heaven's sake, and forty-degree weather didn't heat the soil. Even as she thought that, she realized the *air* was warm, now that the heavens had stopped dumping a small icy flood on her. Humid and positively summery.

Gingerly, she raised herself up a few inches and glanced about, only to discover she was swathed in a cloud. While she'd huddled, a thick soupy fog had surrounded her. She was completely walled in by white. It made the already eerie situation even spookier.

"D-Dageus?" Her voice quavered a little. She cleared her throat and tried again.

If she was still in the circle of stones—and she was beginning to think that might be A Very Big If—she could no longer see them. The fog consumed everything. It was like being blind. She shivered, feeling horribly alone. The past few minutes had been so bizarre that she was beginning to wonder if she'd not . . . well, she wasn't sure what she was beginning to wonder, and would rather not wonder it.

Some people say they're portals . . .

She scooped at the fog with her hand. Condensation beaded on her palm. It was thick, dense stuff. She blew at the white air in front of her. It didn't puff away.

"H-hello?" she called, feeling frantic.

A dark swirl of movement flickered in the whiteness. There. No, she thought, turning, there. Inexplicably, the temperature dropped again and her teeth began to chatter. The hail stopped steaming on the ground.

She sat back on her knees, drenched to the bone, shivering and waiting nervously, half-expecting something awful to leap out at her.

Just when her frayed nerves were about to snap, Dageus glided out of the fog, or rather, one moment he wasn't there and then he materialized in front of her.

"Oh, thank *God*," Chloe breathed, relief flooding her. "Wh-what—" *just happened* was what she was trying to say, but the words died in her throat as he moved nearer.

He was Dageus, but somehow . . . not Dageus. As he moved, the fog swirled away from him like something out of a creepy sci-fi movie. Against the whiteness, he was a great, hulking dark shape. The expression on his chiseled features was as cold as the ice upon which she knelt.

She shook her head, once, twice, trying to scatter the idiotic illusion. Blinked several times.

He's almost inhumanly beautiful, she thought, staring. The storm had ripped his hair free from his thong and it fell to his waist in a wet, wind-tossed tangle. He looked wild and untamed. Animal. Predatory.

He even moved like an animal, fluid strength and surety.

And all the devil ever wants in exchange, a small voice said warningly, *is a soul.*

Oh, puh-lease, Chloe rebuked herself sternly. *He's a man, nothing more. A big, beautiful, sometimes scary man, but that's all.*

Graceful as a stalking tiger, the big, beautiful, scary man dropped into a crouch on the ground before her, his dark eyes glinting in the shadowy night. They knelt mere inches apart. When he spoke, his words were painstakingly articulated, as if speaking was an immense effort. His words were carefully spaced, tight, coming in rushes, with pauses between.

"I will give you. Every. Artifact I own. If you kiss. Me and ask no. Questions."

"Huh?" Chloe gaped.

"No questions," he hissed. He shook his head violently, as if trying to scatter something from it.

Chloe's mouth snapped shut.

It was too dark to see his eyes clearly, the sharp planes of his face shadowed. In the misty gloom, his exotic coppery eyes looked black as midnight.

She peered at him. He was perfectly still, motionless as a tiger before the killing lunge. She reached for his hands and found them, in tight fists. *Most reserved when he feels most strongly,* she reminded herself. She closed her hands over his.

His body was racked with sudden shudders. He closed his eyes briefly and when he opened them again, she could have sworn she saw shadowy . . . *things* moving behind them, and she had that strange feeling she'd had once before in his penthouse, as if there was another presence with them, ancient and cold.

Then his eyes cleared, revealing such utter desolation that her chest tightened and she almost couldn't draw a breath.

He hurt. And she wanted to take it away. Nothing else really mattered. She didn't even want his stupid artifacts in exchange; she only wanted to wipe that horrid, awful look from his eyes however she could.

She wet her lips and that was all the encouragement he seemed to need.

He crushed her in his arms, swept her up and, in a few powerful strides, backed her hard against one of the standing stones.

Ah, so the stones are still here, she thought dimly. *Or I'm still here. Or something.*

Then his mouth was hot and hungry on hers and she couldn't have cared less where she was or wasn't. She might have been leaning up against a great big nasty, winter-starved bear for all she cared, because Dageus was kissing her as if his life depended upon their tangle of tongues and the heat between them.

He sealed his mouth tightly over hers, his velvety tongue seeking, claiming. He thrust his hands into her wet curls, wrapping handfuls of it around his fists, holding her head cradled in his big, powerful hands, his hot tongue plunging deep into her mouth.

He kissed like no man she'd ever known. There was something about him, a rawness, an earthy sensuality that bordered on barbaric, something she'd never be able to explain to someone else. A woman had to be kissed by Dageus MacKeltar to fully understand how devastating it was. How it could bring a woman to her knees.

For a moment she couldn't even move. Could only take his kiss, not manage the strength to return it. She felt like she was being consumed, and knew that sex with him would be a little bit dirty and a whole lot raw. No inhibitions. She'd been tied to his bed with silken scarves; she knew what kind of man he was. Dizzy, light-headed, she clung to him, arching against him, reveling in the sensation of his big hands gliding over her body, one burrowing impatiently beneath her bra to close roughly over her breasts, teasing her nipples, the other cupping her bottom and lifting her against him. Feverishly, she wrapped her legs around his powerful hips.

She was so aroused that she throbbed, aching and empty. She whimpered into his mouth when he shifted that last bit, fitting them together so the hard ridge of him was cradled in her yielding heat. *Oh, finally!* After denying herself, refusing to even let herself *think* about it, he was there, trapped snugly in the vee of her thighs, huge, hot man. He braced her back against the stone again, grinding himself against her, driving her to an erotic frenzy.

Tangling her fingers in his thick silky hair, she strained against him, arching forward each time he thrust, meeting him. His lips were locked to hers, his tongue deep in her mouth. She was delirious with need. Her defenses had not merely dropped, they'd toppled, and she wanted shamelessly, everything, all that he'd been teasing her with for so long now.

As if he'd read her thoughts, he captured one of her hands in his and guided it between them, pressing her palm to the hard ridge in his jeans, and she gasped when she realized how big he was. She'd only caught a glimpse of him when he'd dropped his towel, but she'd been wondering about him ever since she'd found those incriminating condoms. It wasn't going to be easy to take him, she thought, with a dark erotic shiver. *Everything* about him was too much man, and it exhilarated her, seduced her into finally acknowledging her most private fantasies. By his sheer nature, he was the answer to them all. Dark, dominant, dangerous man.

She touched him frantically, trying to shape her fingers over him through his jeans, but the damn things were too constricting, strained by his heavy bulge. She gave a small whimper of frustration and, growling savagely, he shifted her in his arms, braced her against the stones, holding her with one arm, while roughly unfastening his jeans.

Chloe panted, her eyes wide, watching his beautiful dark face, taut with lust while he freed himself. She wanted, needed, was beyond thinking about it anymore. The intensity of the attraction between them was mind-numbing. Then he was pushing the hot, thick hardness of himself into her hand.

She couldn't close her hand around it. Her breath hitched in her throat and she dropped her head forward against his chest. There was no way.

"You can take me, lass." He cradled her jaw with his palm and forced her face back up for more urgent, heated kisses. He closed his hand over hers, moving it along his thick erection. She whimpered, wishing her jeans would just melt away so she could take him inside her.

"Do you need me, Chloe?" he demanded.

"I'd say she does, but I doona think 'tis either the time or the place," a dry voice cut through the night briskly.

Dageus stiffened against her with a savage oath.

Chloe made a sound that was half-startlement, half-sob. *No, no, no!* she wanted to scream. *I can't stop now!*

Never in her life had she wanted so desperately. She wished that whoever had spoken would simply disappear. She didn't want to come back to reality, didn't want to think about the consequences of what she was about to do. Didn't want to return to the myriad questions that she would have to face: about Dageus, about her whereabouts, about herself.

They froze in that intimate moment for what felt like a miserable eternity, then Dageus shuddered and with a hand beneath her bottom, leaned her against the stone and dislodged her hand. She had a hard time making herself let go and they waged a short, silent, silly little battle that he won, which she reluctantly conceded was probably only fair since it was part of his body. He stood still, inhaling measured breaths, then lowered her to the ground.

It took him several minutes to refasten his jeans. Dropping his dark head forward, lips to her ear, he said in a burr thickened by desire, "There will be no takin' this back, lass. Doona even think to be tellin' me later that you willna hae me. You *will* hae me." Then abruptly, wrapping one strong arm around her waist, he turned them both to greet the intruder.

Still dizzy and breathless with desire, it took Chloe a few moments to focus. When she did, she was startled to discover that the fog had vanished as utterly as the storm, leaving the night bathed in pearly luminance by a fat moon hovering just beyond the mighty oaks that towered around the circle of stones. She refused to dwell on the fact that a short time ago there had been no oaks around the circle of stones, only a vast expanse of manicured lawn. If she thought about that too long, she might start to feel sick to her stomach again.

So she concentrated instead on the tall, elderly man, with shoulder-length, snowy-white hair, clad in long blue robes, who stood about a dozen paces away, his narrow back to them.

"You can turn around now," Dageus barked at him.

"I was but ceding you what privacy I could," the man muttered defensively, his posture rigid.

"Had you wished to cede me privacy, you would have steered yourself right back into the castle, old man."

"Aye," the man snapped right back, "so you could off and disappear again? I think not. I lost you once. I'll no' be losing you again."

With that, the elderly man turned around to face them and Chloe's eyes widened in astonishment. She'd seen him somewhere before! But where?

Oh, no. As quickly as it occurred to her, she denied it, shaking her head. Earlier in the day, in the portrait gallery at Maggie MacKeltar's castle. She'd seen several portraits of him displayed in a section where half a dozen other paintings around them had been removed, leaving great dark spots on the wall. That was part of what had drawn her eye to them. Maggie had told her that the others from that particular century—the fifteen hundreds—had been taken down and sent out to be restored.

This man's face had lingered in her mind because she'd been captivated by his uncanny resemblance to Einstein. With his snowy hair, rich brown eyes feathered by fine lines, and deep grooves bracketing his mouth, the man looked unnervingly like the great theoretical physicist. Albeit with a slightly wizardish cast. Even Gwen had agreed with a sunny smile when Chloe had remarked upon it.

"Wh-who is th-that?" Chloe stammered to Dageus.

When Dageus didn't reply, the elderly man raked both hands through tufts of white hair and scowled. "I'm his da, m'dear. Silvan. 'Tis thinking, I am, that he told you no more than Drustan told Gwen afore he brought her here.

Is that so? Or did you even tell her that much?" He shot an accusing glance at Dageus.

Dageus was as still as stone beside her. Chloe looked up at him, but he wouldn't look at her.

"You said your father was dead," she said uneasily.

"I am," Silvan agreed, "in the twenty-first century. But not in the sixteenth century, m'dear."

"Huh?" Chloe blinked.

"Rather odd when one ponders it," he allowed with a pensive expression. "As if I'm immortal in my own slice of time. Gives a thinking man the shivers."

"The s-sixteenth c-century?" She tugged on Dageus's sleeve in a plea for him to jump right in and clear things up anytime now. He didn't.

"Aye, m'dear," Silvan replied.

"As in, you mean that since I'm seeing you—which means either you're alive or I'm dreaming or I've lost my mind—that if I'm not dreaming and haven't lost my mind, I must be, er . . . where it is that you aren't dead?" Chloe asked gingerly, making certain she didn't spell it out too clearly because then she'd have to entertain it as a valid thought.

"A brilliant deduction, m'dear," Silvan said approvingly. "Though a bit roundabout. Still, you've the look of a clever lass about you."

"Oh, no," Chloe said firmly, shaking her head. "This isn't happening. I'm *not* in the sixteenth century. That's not possible." She looked up at Dageus again, but he was still refusing to look at her.

Disjointed bits of conversation flashed through her mind: talk of portals and ancient curses and mythical races.

Chloe stared at Dageus's chiseled profile, sorting through facts that were suddenly imbued with a terrible significance: He knew more languages than anyone she'd ever met, languages long dead; he had artifacts in mint condition; he was searching books that centered on the history of ancient Ireland and Scotland. He'd stood her in the center of a circle of ancient stones and asked to her to go somewhere with him that he couldn't tell her about, but had to show her, as if only seeing was believing. And in that circle of stones a powerful storm had risen and she'd felt as if she were being torn apart. There'd been a sudden climate change, the scenery currently included full-grown, century-old trees that hadn't been there before, and there was an elderly man claiming to be his father—in the sixteenth century.

And while they were on that topic—if any part of her current circumstances was actually real—what was his father doing in the *sixteenth century*, for heaven's sake? She latched onto that lovely little bit of blatant illogic as proof that she must be dreaming.

Unless . . .

What if I told you, lass, that I'm a Druid from long past?

"What?" she snapped, glaring up at him. "Am I supposed to believe that *you're* from the sixteenth century too?"

He finally looked at her then, and said stiffly, "I was born in fourteen hundred and eighty-two, Chloe."

She jerked as if he'd struck her. Then she started laughing, and even she heard the note of hysteria in her voice. "Right," she said gaily. "And I'm the Tooth Fairy."

"You know you felt something about me," he pressed ruthlessly. "I know you did. I could see it in the way you watched me sometimes."

God, she had. Repeatedly. Felt that he was strangely anachronistic, felt a bizarre sense of ancientness.

"You're strong, Chloe-lass. You can accept this. I know you can. I'll help you. I can explain it to you, and you'll see that 'tis no' . . . magic, but a sort of physics modern men doona—"

"Oh, no," she cut him off, shaking her head vehemently. A hiccup terminated her laughter abruptly. "It's impossible," she insisted, rejecting it all in one grand unilateral sweep. "This is all impossible." Hiccup. "I'm dreaming, or . . . something. I don't know what, but I'm not going to"—*hiccup*—"think about it anymore. So don't even bother trying to convince—"

She broke off, suddenly too light-headed to continue. The trauma of the storm, the absurdity of the conversation was all too much. Her knees felt as if they might buckle beneath her. *Really,* she thought dimly, *there was only so much a girl could be expected to handle, and time-travelling Druids just weren't part of it.* More of that helpless laughter bubbled inside her.

As if from a far distance, she heard Silvan say gruffly, " 'Tis good to be seeing you again, lad. Nellie and I have been sore fashed o'er you. Och, the wee lass is going, son. You might catch her now."

When Dageus's strong arms slipped around her, Chloe tuned out the voices and embraced the mercy of oblivion, because she just knew that when she woke up again, everything would be all right. She'd be in bed, in Gwen and Drustan's castle, having had one of those strangely intense dreams about Dageus.

I like the sex dreams better was her final peevish thought, as her knees gave way and her mind went blank.

Adam Black was dozing—not sleeping, for the Tuatha Dé Danaan did not sleep—but drifting in memory and time when the nine members of the council appeared behind his queen's dais.

He sat up abruptly.

One of them spoke into the queen's ear. She nodded and dismissed them back to wherever it was the elusive council made their home.

Then Aoibheal, queen of the Tuatha Dé Danaan, raised her hands to the sky and said, "The council has spoken. It shall be trial by blood."

Adam tensed to rise, but caught himself, and forced himself to sink back down on his cushioned chaise. He waited, measuring the reactions of the others gathered in the forest bower on the isle of Morar where the queen was wont to hold her court. Drowsing beneath silken canopies, the others stirred languidly, their melodic voices humming softly.

He heard no protests. *Fools,* he thought, *it's a wonder we've survived this long.* Though immortal, they could be destroyed.

When Adam spoke, his voice was dispassionate, bordering on bored, as befitted his kind. "My queen, I would speak, if you will it."

Aoibheal glanced his way. There was a glimmer of appreciation in her gaze as it raked over him. He wore her favored glamour—that of a tall, dark-haired smith, rippling with muscle. An otherworldly beautiful man who was wont to waylay human travelers, particularly women. A smith who took them to places and did things to them they later recalled as dark dreams of unending pleasure.

"You have my ear." She inclined her head regally.

And on rare occasions, Adam thought, other parts of her when she so graced him. Aoibheal had a certain fondness for him, and he was counting on it now. He was unlike any other of their race in small ways that baffled both he and them. But the queen seemed to enjoy those differences. Of all her subjects, Adam suspected he was the only one who still managed to surprise her. And surprise was nectar of the gods to those who lived forever, to those who'd lost wonder and awe an eternity ago. To those who spied on mortal's dreams because they possessed no dreams of their own.

"My queen," he said, sinking to one knee before her, "I know the Keltar broke his oath. But if one examines these Keltar, one finds that they have, for thousands of years, comported themselves in exemplary fashion."

The queen regarded him a long cool moment, then shrugged a delicate shoulder. "So?"

"Consider the man's brother, my queen. When Drustan was enchanted by a seer and forced to slumber for five centuries, the Keltar line was destroyed. When he was awakened in the twenty-first century by a woman, he went to extraordinary lengths to return to his time and prevent the catastrophe from happening so their line would remain intact, always protecting the lore."

"I am aware of that. Unfortunate his brother wasn't more like him."

"I believe he is. Dageus broke his oath solely to save Drustan's life."

"That's personal motive. The line was not threatened. They were expressly forbidden to use the stones for personal gain."

"How was it personal gain?" Adam countered. "What did Dageus gain by so doing? Though he saved Drustan's life, Drustan continued to slumber. He didn't get his brother back. He didn't get anything."

"Then more fool he."

"He is as honorable as his brother. There's no evil in what he did."

"The question is not if he is evil, it's if he broke his oath, and he did. The terms of The Compact were clearly defined."

Adam drew a careful breath. "We are the ones who

gave them the power to travel through time. If we hadn't, the temptation would never have existed."

"Ah, now it's our fault?"

"I'm merely saying that he didn't use the stones to gain wealth or political power. He did it for love."

"You sound like a human."

It was the lowest insult among his kind.

Adam remained wisely silent. He'd had his proverbial wings clipped before by his queen.

"Regardless of why he did it, Adam, he now harbors our ancient enemy within him."

"But he still isn't dark, my queen. It's been many mortal months since they took him. How many mortals do you know that could withstand those thirteen Druids by will alone? You knew them well. You know their power. Yet you would subject him to the trial by blood the council has called for? You would kill every person this man cares for to test him? If you destroy his entire line for this, who then will renegotiate The Compact?"

"Perhaps we shall live without it," she said lightly, but he saw the merest hint of unease in her lovely, inhuman eyes.

"You would risk that? Our worlds colliding? Shall human and Tuatha Dé Danaan live together again? The Keltar have broken their oath, but we have not yet violated our end of it. The moment we do, The Compact will be void and the walls between our realms will crumble. Trial by blood will force us to share the earth, my queen. Is that what you want?"

"He's right," her consort stirred himself to speak. "Did the council consider that?"

If Adam knew the council half as well as he thought he did, yes. There were those on the high council who missed the old ways. Those who thrived on chaos and petty machinations. Fortunately, they did not include his queen. With the exception of whimsical entertainment, she disdained humans and had little desire to see them walking in her world again.

Silence shrouded the court.

Aoibheal templed slender fingers and rested her dainty chin upon them. "Interest me. Are you suggesting an alternative?"

"An order of Druids in Britain, descendants of those you scattered millennia past, has been awaiting the return of the Draghar; they have plans to force the Keltar's transformation. If they succeed, do what you wish with him. Let that be his test."

"Are you presenting a formal plea for his life, Amadan?" Aoibheal purred, her iridescent gaze shimmering with sudden intensity.

She'd spoken part of his true name. A subtle warning. Adam stared off into the distance for time uncounted. Dageus MacKeltar meant nothing to him. Yet he had a relentless fascination with mortals, indeed, spent most of his time among them in some form, to some degree. Yes, his race had power, but mortals had another kind of power, an entirely unpredictable one: Love. And once, long ago—almost unheard of among his kind—with a mortal woman, he'd felt it.

Had sired a half-mortal son.

Though he'd long endeavored to, he'd not forgotten those brief years with Morganna. Morganna who'd refused his offer of immortality.

He glanced at his queen. She would exact a price should he lodge a formal plea for a mortal's life.

It would be a heinous price.

Then again, he thought, with a shrug of immortal ennui, eternity had been placid of late. "Yes, my queen," he said, tossing his hair back and smiling coolly when the court gasped collectively. "I am."

The queen's smile was as terrifying as it was beautiful. "I shall name your price when the Keltar's test has been met."

"And I shall bide your law, given this boon: Should the Keltar best the sect of the Draghar, the thirteen will be reclaimed and destroyed."

"You would barter with me?" A faint note of incredulity laced her voice.

"I barter for the peace of both our races. Lay them to rest. Four thousand years was long enough."

What could only be called a very human smirk crossed the queen's delicate features. "They wanted immortality. I merely gave it to them." She cocked her head. "Shall we wager upon the outcome?"

"Yes, I wager he'll lose," Adam said rapid-fire. There it was, what he'd been waiting for. The queen was the most powerful creature of their race.

And hated to lose. Though she would not raise a hand to help him, at least now, she would not raise her hand to harm him.

"Oh, you'll pay, Amadan. For that, you'll pay dearly."

Of that, he had no doubt.

· 17 ·

"Stop *peering* at me like that," Dageus hissed.

"What?" Silvan bristled. "I'm not allowed to look at my own son?"

"You're looking at me as if you're expecting me to sprout wings, a forked tail, and cloven hooves." No matter that he was feeling as if he might. Since the moment he'd come through the stones, since the moment the thirteen had found their voices, he'd known that the battle betwixt them had moved into a new and much more dangerous arena. The ancients within him had been fed pure power when he'd opened the bridge through time.

With an immense effort of will, he shuttered, closed, tightened himself and projected pretense that all was well and fine. Using magic to conceal his darkness was an egregious error and he knew it, feeding precisely that which he endeavored to hide, but he had to do it. He dare not let Silvan see him clearly at the moment. He needed to search the Keltar library and if Silvan felt him now, God only knew what he'd do. Certainly not wave him into the inner sanctum of Keltar lore.

Silvan looked startled. "Is shape-shifting one of their arts?" he inquired, evincing utter fascination.

Typical Silvan, Dageus thought darkly, curiosity exceeding caution. He'd worried a time or two that Silvan might one day be tempted to dabble in black arts himself, out of naught more than driving curiosity. His father and Chloe shared that, an insatiable need to know.

"Nay. And you're still doing it," Dageus said coldly.

"I'm merely curious about the extent of your power." Silvan sniffed, affecting an unassuming expression. With such piercing intellect in his gaze, it was far from convincing.

"Well doona be. And doona be poking at it." Och, aye, the ancients inside him were growing more aggressive. Sensing Silvan's power, they were trying to reach for it. For *him*. Silvan was far richer fodder than Drustan; he'd always had a stronger center than his sons.

His father was also adept at the art of deep-listening that Dageus had never managed to perfect, a meditative regard that peeled away lies, exposing the bare bones of truth. 'Twas why the hopelessness he'd glimpsed in his da's gaze the eve he'd fled had fashed him so. He'd been afraid Silvan had seen something he himself couldn't see, and wouldn't want to.

And it was why, now, he was using all his will both to keep them in, and his father out.

"I ken it, lad," Silvan said, sounding suddenly weary. "You've changed since last I saw you."

Dageus said nothing. He'd managed to avoid looking directly into his father's gaze since the moment Chloe had fainted, taking only cursory glances. Betwixt the heightened awareness of the thirteen and the sexual storm that was raging hot and unsated inside him, he wasn't about to look him in the eyes.

When he'd carried Chloe abovestairs to his bedchamber, tucked her into bed, and whispered a soft sleep spell over her so she would rest easy through the night, Silvan had followed him and Dageus had felt his measuring regard hammering at the back of his skull.

He'd nearly not been able to let go of her. And though he'd not look at his father, he'd been grateful for his presence, for it had made short work of the dark thoughts he'd been having about bringing her only partially awake and—

"Look at me, son," Silvan said, his low voice implacable.

Dageus turned slowly, careful not to meet his gaze. He took measured breaths, one after another.

His father was standing in front of the hearth, his hands buried in the folds of his cobalt robe. In the soft light of dozens of tapers and oil globes, his white hair was a halo about his wrinkled face. Dageus knew the origin of each line. The grooves in his cheeks had appeared shortly after their mother had died, when he and Drustan had been lads of fifteen. The wide creases on his forehead had been worn into his skin by a constant raising of his brows as he pondered the mysteries of the world and the stars beyond it. The lines bracketing his mouth were from smiling or frowning, never weeping. Stoic bastard, Dageus thought suddenly. No one wept in Castle Keltar. No one knew how. Except mayhap Silvan's second wife and Dageus's next-mother, Nell.

The lines feathering Silvan's deep brown eyes, winging upward at the outer edges, were from squinting in low light as he labored over his work. Silvan was a fine scribe, possessing an enviably steady hand, and had devoted himself to recopying, with exquisitely embellished carpet pages, the older tomes whose ink had faded o'er time.

When he'd been a lad, Dageus had thought his da had the wisest eyes he'd ever seen, full of special, secret knowledge. He realized he still thought that. His da had never been toppled from his pedestal.

His gut clenched. Mayhap Silvan had never fallen, but *he* certainly had. "Go ahead, Da," he said tightly. "Roar at me. Tell me how I failed you. Tell me how I've been naught but a disappointment. Remind me of my oaths. Throw me out if you're of a mind to, for I've no time to waste."

Silvan's head jerked in sharp negation.

"Tell me, Da. Tell me how Drustan never would have done such a thing. Tell me how—"

"You truly wish me to be telling you that your brother is less of a man than you?" Silvan cut him off, his voice low and carefully measured. "You need to be hearing me say that?"

Dageus stopped speaking, his mouth ajar. "What?" he hissed. "My brother is no' less of a—"

"You gave your life for your brother, Dageus. And you ask your father to condemn you for that?" Silvan's voice broke on the words.

Much to Dageus's horror, his da crumpled. His shoulders bowed and his lean frame jerked. Suddenly his eyes were glistening with tears.

Och, Christ. Dageus cursed silently, bearing down hard on himself. He dare not weep. No cracks. Cracks could become crevices and crevices canyons. Canyons a man could get lost in.

"I thought I'd never see you again." Silvan's words echoed starkly in the stone hall.

"Da," he said roughly, "yell at me. Berate me. For the love of Christ, *scream* at me."

"I can't." Silvan's wrinkled cheeks were wet with tears. He skirted the table and grabbed him, hugging him fiercely, pounding him on the back.

And weeping.

If Dageus lived to be a hundred, he never wanted to see his father weep again.

It was some time later, after Nell had appeared and the whole awful matter of tears had been repeated, after she'd bustled about preparing a light repast, after she'd retired again to check on his wee brothers, that the conversation turned to the grim purpose of why he'd returned.

Speaking in brisk, detached tones, Dageus updated Silvan on all that had transpired since last he'd seen him. He told him how he'd gone to America, and searched the texts, only to finally admit that he was going to have to ask Drustan for help. He told him of the strange attack on Chloe, and of the Draghar. He told him they'd discovered the texts about the Tuatha Dé Danaan had disappeared, and that it seemed intentional.

Silvan frowned at that. "Tell me, lad, did Drustan check beneath the slab?"

"Beneath the slab in the tower? The one on which he slumbered?"

"Aye," Silvan said. "Though to date I've put but two texts there, I've been planning to find aught I could that may be of help and seal them away beneath it. In anticipation of that, I left clear instructions for Drustan to look there."

Dageus closed his eyes and shook his head. Had this trip been unnecessary? Might he have avoided all of it? Probably. In a few more years, it was quite likely that Silvan would have gathered up every tome he'd been searching for and tucked them beneath the slab. They'd been there in the twenty-first century the whole time.

"Where were the instructions? In the letter you left for him?"

"Aye."

"The same letter in which you told him what I'd done?"

Silvan nodded again.

"Did you spell it out, or say something cryptic, Da?" Knowing his father, it had been cryptic.

Silvan scowled. "I said, 'I left some things for you beneath the slab,'" he replied peevishly. "How much clearer must a man be?"

"Much more, because apparently Drustan never looked. 'Tis my guess he was so distraught by the news your missive contained, that he crumpled the letter and threw it away. From the way you worded it, like as not, he thought you'd left mementos or some such trifles."

Silvan looked sheepish. "I hadn't thought of that."

"You said you've been searching the tomes. Have you discovered anything yet?"

A wary expression flickered across his father's features. "Aye, I've been looking, but 'tis slow work. The older texts are much more difficult to read. There was no uniformity of spelling, and ofttimes they had little grasp of the alphabet."

"What about—"

"Enough about the texts for now," Silvan cut him off. "There'll be time enough on the morrow. Tell me of your lass, son. I must confess, I was surprised to see you'd brought a wee woman with you."

Dageus's heartbeat quickened and his veins were filled with that peculiar icy heat. His lass. *His.*

"Though she seemed to be having a hard time fathoming your use of the stones as a bridge betwixt the centuries, I sensed a strong will and fiery mind. I suspect she'll come around without too much fuss," Silvan mused.

" 'Tis my belief as well."

"You haven't told her what's wrong with you, have you?"

"Nay. And doona be telling her. I'll tell her when the time is right." As if there would ever be a "right" time. Time was his enemy now as never before.

A silence fell then. An awkward, ponderous silence filled with questions but too few answers, rife with unspoken worries.

"Och, son," Silvan said finally, "it was killing me, not knowing what had become of you. 'Tis glad I am you've returned. We'll find a way. I promise."

Later, Silvan pondered that promise ruefully. He paced, he grumbled, he cursed.

Only after Dageus had retired abovestairs and the wee hours of the morn had filled his weary bones with disenchantment—by Amergin, he was three score and five, too old for such doings—did he admit that by now, he should have *something* to show for his work. He'd not been entirely forthright with Dageus.

He'd been devouring the old texts since the night Dageus had confessed and fled. Oddly, though he'd damn near torn the castle apart, he couldn't find any documents predating the first century. And he *knew* they'd once had many. They were referenced in many of his texts in the tower library.

Yet he couldn't find the bletherin' things, and granted the castle was enormous, but one would think one could keep track of one's own library!

According to the legends, they even had the original Compact that had been sealed betwixt the race of man and fairy. Somewhere. God only knew where. How could they not know?

Because, he answered himself wryly, *when so much time passes that a tale becomes far removed from its origination, it loses much of its reality.*

Though he'd dutifully told his sons the Keltar legends, he'd privately thought that the tales from millennia past were *surely* embellished a bit, possibly a fabricated creation-myth of sorts, to explain away the Keltar's unusual abilities. Though he'd obeyed his oaths, a part of his mind had never fully believed. His daily purposes had been purpose enough: the Druid rituals marking the seasons, the care of the villagers in Balanoch, the education of his sons and his own studies. He hadn't needed to believe all the rest of it.

The sad truth was, not even *he'd* really believed there was some ancient evil in the in-between.

How much we've forgotten and lost, he brooded. He'd scarce given thought to the legendary race that had allegedly set the Keltar on their course. Not until his son had gone and broken his oath, thus violating an alleged Compact whose existence had become far more myth than reality.

Well, he brooded darkly, *now at least we know the old legends are true.*

Little comfort, that.

Nay, his search had failed to unearth even an iota of useful information. Indeed, he'd begun to fear that the Keltar had been unforgivably careless in their guardianship of the old lore, that Dageus's broken oath was merely one more failing in a long list of failings.

He suspected they'd quit believing centuries ago, pushing away the mantle of a power that exacted too high a price. For generations, the Keltar men had been growing increasingly morose, weary of protecting the secret of the stones, weary of hiding away in the hills and being regarded with fear. Weary of being so damned different.

As the dark ages gave way to lighter ones, so, too, did the Keltar seem to wish to lay down the burden of their past.

His son thought he had failed, but Silvan knew better. They'd *all* failed.

On the morrow they would sit down with the ancient writings and search anew. Silvan hadn't the heart to tell his son that he'd nearly finished searching, and if there was some answer to be found in them, he was too dense to discern it.

His eyes narrowed and his thoughts turned to the wee lass his son had brought with him. When the storm had wakened him—a storm the likes of which he'd heard but a few times before—he'd rushed outside, praying 'twas Dageus returning.

It had taken some time for the fog to clear, and though he'd called out, Dageus had not replied.

When the fog had lifted, Silvan had understood why.

In Silvan's estimation, 'twas the lass that might yet prove to be their finest hope. For so long as his son loved her—and he did, though he knew it not himself—well, evil didn't love. Evil tried to seduce and possess and conquer, but it didn't *feel* for the object of its desire. So long as love was alive in Dageus, they had a toehold, however small.

Och, he and the lass were going to become close, Silvan decided. She was going to learn about the young Dageus who'd once strolled these heathery hills, nurturing the earth and healing the wee beasties, the gentle Dageus with the wild heart. He and Nellie would see to it. Dageus's gifts had always leaned toward the healing arts, and now he was in need of healing himself.

If the lass didn't already love his son—he'd not had sufficient chance to probe her—he would do all in his power to win her for him.

Doona poke at them, Dageus had warned him bitterly, meaning the ancient evil within him.

But Silvan had poked. Silvan *always* poked. And despite the barriers his son had erected, buffering it a bit, it had poked back and Silvan was, quite simply, horrified by what was growing inside Dageus.

· 18 ·

"I know I'm dreaming," Chloe announced conversationally the next morning as she descended the stairs to the great hall. She slipped into a chair, joining Silvan, Dageus, and a woman she'd not yet met—er, dreamed about—for breakfast.

Three pairs of eyes regarded her expectantly and, heartened by the attention, she continued.

"I know I didn't just use the equivalent of a little outhouse upstairs in a closet." With straw for toilet paper, no less. "And I know I'm not really wearing a gown, and I'm certainly not wearing"—she peered down at her toes—"beribboned little satin slippers." Straightening in her chair, she scooped a spoon of jam from a dish. "And I know this strawberry jam is just a figment of—*eww*—what *is* this?" Her lips puckered.

"Tomato preserves, m'dear," the man who'd been

identified to her earlier in the dream as Silvan replied mildly, with a smile he tried to hide.

Not good, Chloe thought. In a dream, the dreamer controlled how things tasted. She'd been thinking sweet strawberry jam and gotten a nasty, unsweetened vegetable. More proof, she thought dismally, as if she'd needed it. She glanced about the table for something to drink.

Dageus slid a mug of creamy milk across the table to her.

She drank deeply, peeking at him over the rim. She'd had erotic dreams about him all night. Frighteningly intense dreams in which he took her in every way it was possible for a man to take a woman. And she'd loved every minute of it, had awakened feeling all soft and kittenish, nearly purring. His black hair was pulled back from his sculpted face in a loose braid. He wore an unlaced linen shirt that revealed a sinful expanse of golden, muscled chest. Big, beautiful man. Sexy, scary man.

Chloe wasn't stupid. She knew she wasn't dreaming. A part of her had acknowledged it last night or she wouldn't have fainted. That, in a strange way, seemed proof itself: a dreaming mind fainting from the "reality" of its own dream? An already unconscious mind slipping into unconsciousness? She could get tangled up in that thought if she pondered it too long.

Upon awakening this morning, she'd wandered the upper floor, scurrying down corridors, peeking into chambers and out windows, piecing together bits of information. She'd touched, peered, shaken, even broken a few minor things that she'd deemed replaceable as part of her examination.

All of it, the textures and scents and tastes were simply too tangible to be a figment of her unconscious mind. Furthermore, dreams had narrow focuses; they didn't come complete with periphery guards and servants going about duties she'd never conceived of, beyond the windows.

She was in Maggie MacKeltar's castle . . . but not quite that castle. There were additions missing, an entire wing not yet constructed. Furniture that hadn't been there yesterday, more furniture that was missing today, to say nothing of all the new people! To all appearances—impossible though it was to fathom—it was Maggie's castle nearly five centuries ago.

"Aren't you going to introduce me?" She slid Dageus's mug back and glanced curiously at the older, fortyish woman. She couldn't be his mother, she mused, unless she'd had him incredibly young, even for medieval times. Dressed in a lapis gown similar to her own, the lovely woman had a gently faded but timeless beauty. Her ash-blond hair was swept up in an intricate plait, with fringy bangs wisping about her face, rather like Gwen's, Chloe thought.

" 'Tis your dream, lass. Make up her name yourself," Dageus said, watching her with a mocking expression.

He knew she knew. Damn the man.

"Oh, Dageus," Chloe sighed, slumping in her chair, "*what* did you do to me? I thought you were just a wealthy, eccentric womanizer. Well, I also thought you were a thief for a while," she muttered, "and a kidnapper, but I didn't think—"

"Would you like to see the library, lass?" he offered, his dark eyes glittering.

Chloe narrowed her eyes. "You think it's going to be that easy? Show the girl a few impressive books and she'll think it's all right that you somehow yanked her back in time?" Sadly, she mused, he might be onto something, because the instant he'd said "library" her heart rate had quickened. A zillion questions perched on the tip of her tongue, but she couldn't yet bring herself to talk about reality as if it were real.

"All right, then. Let's go to the stones. I'll send you back this very moment." He pushed himself to his feet and she got her first look at him from the waist down. Snug black leather trews encased his powerful hips and thighs. Holy cow. Her mouth went dry. There was an impossible-to-ignore bulge in them.

"Wait just a—" Silvan began, but stopped abruptly at Dageus's warning look.

"You know you're not dreaming," Dageus said flatly.

Chloe forced herself to tear her gaze away from his lower body and pursed her lips.

"Then come. I'll send you back." Dageus gestured impatiently at her.

Chloe remained seated. She wasn't going anywhere. "Are you saying that you could send me back any time?"

"Aye, lass. 'Tis naught more than a bit of physics your century hasn't yet stumbled upon for themselves." His tone was detached, as if discussing nothing of any more significance than a new bit of twenty-first century technology. "Though from what I read while in your time," he continued, "I'd wager it won't be much longer." When she made no reply, he said, "Chloe, Druids have long possessed more knowledge of archeoastronomy and sacred mathematics than anyone. Did you truly believe yours was the most advanced civilization ever to have existed? That none came before? Consider the Romans and the subsequent Dark Ages. Think you Rome was the first great civilization to rise and fall? Knowledge has repeatedly been gained and lost, to be one day regained again. Druids have merely managed to hold onto their lore through the dark times."

A plausible, albeit mind-boggling possibility, she conceded silently. It certainly explained the purpose of all those mysterious stone monuments that stumped modern man, many of them constructed as early as 3500 B.C.E. Historians couldn't even agree on *how* the ancient monuments had been built. Was it conceivable that thousands of years ago a race or tribe had lived that had achieved an advanced understanding of physics, necessary to both construct those "devices" and use them?

Yes, she acknowledged, awed. It was conceivable.

He'd said "Druids," as in *he* was a Druid. So, she mused wryly, the tricky man had actually told her the truth back in his Manhattan penthouse. She'd simply not believed it.

She'd studied Druids as part of her course work in the master's program. She'd waded through the scant facts and stranger fictions. What was it Caesar had written in the first century C.E. during the Gallic War? *Druids have much knowledge of the stars and their motion, of the size of the world and of the earth, of natural philosophy, and of the powers and spheres of action of the immortal gods.*

Caesar himself had said it. Who was she to argue?

Pliny, Tacitus, Lucan, and many other classical writers had also written about the Druids. The Romans had persecuted the Druids for centuries (while their emperors privately availed themselves of their prophetesses), forcing them into hiding. Christianity had further forced them to adapt or disappear. Had it been because they'd feared the power the Druids possessed? Were Druids perhaps like the Templars? Hiding throughout the centuries, protecting fabulous secrets?

She was starting to feel light-headed again, dizzied by the possibility that all those myths and legends carefully scribed in Ireland thousands of years ago were true. When the truth was so fantastical—why bother hiding it? Who would ever believe it? Nobody but a girl who'd gotten herself all wrapped up in it. A girl who'd stood in an

ancient circle of stones and felt a gate or portal or whatever it was, open around her.

"Come, lass," Dageus interrupted her thoughts. "I'll
return you and you can forget all about me. You may
keep your artifacts. I release you from your obligations.
Go home to New York. Have a nice life," he added coolly.

"Oh!" Chloe snapped, leaping to her feet. "You are *so*
cold. And you certainly managed to pick up your share of
modern colloquialisms, didn't you? Have a nice life, my
ass. Do you really think I'm not in this up to my ears
now? Do you really think that if I'm in sixteenth-century
Scotland I'm letting you send me away?"

His smile was chillingly predatory, carnal and possessive. "Do you really think I brought you this far to be letting you go, Chloe-lass?"

Chloe had a sudden urge to fan herself. He *knew* her,
she realized. He'd learned a bit about what made her tick.
If, when she'd come downstairs pretending it was a
dream, he'd coddled her, she might have trundled back
upstairs and tried to convince herself that if she went
back to sleep everything would be okay.

Instead, he'd pushed her, threatened to send her away,
knowing she had a mile-wide stubborn streak and would
fight to remain.

"I'm *really* in the sixteenth century?"

Three people said "aye" with calm assurance.

"And I haven't gone crazy?"

Three firm "nays."

"And you could really send me back that easily? Any
time I wish?"

"Aye, lass. 'Tis that easy. Though I would endeavor to
talk you out of it."

She'd come to know him a little, too, what made him
tick. And from the deceptive gentleness of his voice and
the look on his face, she knew he'd tie her to the bed

again if she tried to leave, not attempt reason. She peered at him intently. He was still. Implacable. Hands fisted at his sides.

He *cared* about her. She had no idea how much of it was just that mind-boggling attraction between them, but it was a start. And he obviously had a high opinion of her, if he'd thought she could handle this. She felt a little flush of pride. No, she wasn't going anywhere.

However, he owed her some *serious* explanations.

Oh, for heaven's sake, she thought with droll exasperation, *this certainly explains a lot. It's no wonder I haven't been able to keep my hands off the blasted man since the day I met him. He's an artifact! A Celtic one at that!*

"Well, that's one way of thinking of me, lass," Dageus purred, his dark eyes gleaming with satisfaction.

"Tell me I didn't just say that aloud!" Chloe was horrified.

Silvan cleared his throat. "You did. He's an artifact."

Chloe groaned, wishing she could just sink into the floor and be swallowed up.

"I'm Silvan's wife, Nell, by the bye," the pretty fortyish woman said. "Dageus's next-mother. Would ye be liking some kippers and tatties, lass?"

She decided next-mother must be the medieval equivalent of second wife. "It's, er, very nice t-to meet you. And yes, I would," Chloe stammered, sinking limply down into her chair.

Only then did Dageus reclaim his seat. He was staring at her intensely, his gaze full of sensual promise. She shivered. His expression couldn't have said any more clearly that Chloe Zanders had kept her virginity quite long enough.

"You look lovely this morn, lass," he said silkily, as he passed her first a platter of potatoes and eggs, then one of fat wedges of ham and kippers. "I fancy you in a gown."

His eyes added that he knew there'd been nothing to put beneath it when she'd gotten dressed, intimating that he was the one who'd chosen her gown and brought it to her room while she'd slept.

Her erotic awareness of the man—an eleven on a scale of one to ten—rocketed to a twenty. Chloe took a deep breath, managed a "thank-you" and turned her attention toward something tangible to tackle: food.

Simon Barton-Drew's face was grim as he replaced the phone in the cradle.

Trevor hadn't phoned in for fourteen hours. Simon had been trying to reach him on his cell since early that morning, with no success.

And that could mean only one thing.

Scowling, he kicked a chair across the room. Trevor had better be dead, he brooded.

Stalking to the outer door of his office, he swiftly locked it. Before closing the blinds, he glanced out at the rain-slicked street. With the exception of a mangy alley cat noisily wrestling a bit of trash from a nearby Dumpster, the area was deserted, the street lamps buzzing as they flickered on. As much time as he spent in the dilapidated Belthew Building on Morgan Street in a seedy section on London's outskirts, Simon felt more at home there than in the elegant brownstone where his wife had stopped waiting dinner for him twenty years ago.

The land on which The Belthew Building stood had been owned by the Druid sect of the Draghar for centuries. Constructed above ancient labyrinthine crypts, it had served as their headquarters for nearly a millennia, in various incarnations. Once an apothecary, then a bookstore specializing in rare books, then a butcher's shop, once even a brothel, it now housed a small printing business that drew little notice, and there was no paper trail connecting it to the powerful Triton Corporation.

Their members were the elite, well-placed in society, many in government, more still in the upper echelons of large holding companies. They were wealthy, learned men with impeccable pedigrees.

And they would be furious to know that he'd lost contact with Trevor. Though Simon was Master of the Order, he was nonetheless accountable. Highly accountable, in this sensitive time. His followers had not funneled so much money and time into the sect for anything less than the promise of absolute power. They all possessed a certain degree of ruthlessness that would come to the fore should they think him incapable of controlling his minions.

Flipping off the lights, he moved through his darkened office by rote. He removed a painting mounted on one of the many recessed wood panels of the wall and typed in a sequence of numbers. He replaced the painting and, as the paneling slid up behind his desk, he opened a second door and strode down a narrow hallway.

Several minutes and several additional complex passkeys later, he entered a passageway that sloped sharply downward, where it met a precipitous fall of worn stone stairs. When he reached the bottom, he turned and took the next flight, then a third, then hurried through a maze of dimly lit, damp tunnels.

He had to send someone to Inverness to discover if Trevor had been taken alive. And if so—to tidy up. It would require the most loyal and committed men he had. Men who would never let themselves be taken alive. Men who would die for him without hesitation. The best men he had.

His sons were where they could nearly always be

found, in the electronic heart of their operation, monitoring innumerable facets of their business.

And they were, as always, eager to serve.

After breakfast, Dageus asked Nell to take Chloe to find a light cloak suitable for her to ride in. Chloe, her inquisitive gaze darting everywhere, allowed herself to be led from the great hall.

After the women departed, Silvan arched an inquiring brow. "Doona you wish to be starting with the texts, lad?"

Dageus shook his head. "I need this day. I need to show Chloe my world, Da. What it was like. What *I* was like. If only for a day." That wasn't exactly the truth. The truth was the night had been hellish and the morn wasn't getting any better. He'd not been able to sleep, strung tight as a corded bow. He'd passed the time till dawn fantasizing about Chloe and all the ways he would seduce her. He'd scarce maintained his tight façade of calm through breakfast. And when Chloe had admitted what a battle she'd been fighting to keep her hands off him, it had been all he could do not to toss her over his shoulder and drag her off to his bed.

He'd studied himself in a small mirror this morn, while shaving with a hand that shook more than was safe when a man had an open blade at his own neck. He'd seen eyes a darker shade of brown. He'd been nigh a sennight without a woman. Too long. Far too long.

How long, he wondered almost idly, till his eyes would turn full black? Another day, mayhap two? And what would happen then? he mused, a part of him afraid, another part of him aware that he wasn't as afraid as he ought to be.

The voices yestreen in the stones had caught him by surprise. 'Twas the first time he'd ever heard the beings inside him speak, the first time he'd ever perceived them as individual entities. And though feeling them so intensely had been horrifying, had made him feel as if he were choking on some dead thing in the back of his throat that he couldn't scrape out, it had also been . . . intriguing.

Part of him was curious to know their language, to hear what they might say. He had thirteen ancient beings inside him! What might they tell him of ancient history? Of the Tuatha Dé Danaan, and what the world had been like four thousand years ago? Of what it was like to hold so much power. . . .

Inviting a dialogue with them would be your first step through the gates of hell, his honor hissed.

Aye, he knew that.

You can't trust a thing they might say!

Still . . .

No "still" about it, his honor seethed. *I doona care who you fuck today, just do it.*

That jarred him a bit.

It would be Chloe. If he went to another woman—even if only out of deference to her, to spare her his brutal need—and she found out, she would never have him. Things could get very bad, very fast, then. He was afraid that if he went to her and she denied him, he might force her. He didn't want to do that to Chloe. He didn't want to hurt Chloe.

The antithesis of his honor scoffed: *So what? If she doesn't care for something you do, use the Voice of Power on her. Tell her to forget what she may not like. Tell her she adores you, worships you. You need but tell her she loves you to make it so. 'Tis so easy. The world can be anything you want it—*

"Dageus!" Silvan shouted, slamming his fists down on the table in front of him.

Dageus jerked and stared at his father.

"Where were you?" Silvan exclaimed, looking both frightened and furious.

"Right here," Dageus said, shaking his head. A soft whisper, a rustle stirred inside him. Faint voices murmured.

"I shouted your name three times, and you dinna so much as blink a lash," Silvan snapped. "What were you doing?"

"I . . . I was merely thinking."

Silvan regarded him intensely for a strained moment. "You had the strangest look on your face, son," he said finally.

Dageus didn't want to know what kind of look. "I'm fine, Da," he said, pushing himself from the table. "I doona know how late we'll be. Doona wait a meal for us."

Silvan's piercing gaze followed him as he walked away.

⁂

Nell placed two mugs of cocoa (one specially supplemented with herbs for an absent-minded man who too oft forgot to eat) on a tray and went in search of her husband.

Her husband. The words never failed to bring a smile to her lips. When Silvan had found her lying on the road nearly fifteen years ago, on the brink of death, he'd brought her back to Castle Keltar and sat at her bedside, demanding she fight for her life at a time when she'd wanted naught more than to die.

Before Silvan had found her, she'd been mistress to a married laird whom she'd loved unwisely and deeply, incurring the wrath and jealousy of his barren wife. While he'd lived, he'd been there to protect her, but when he'd been killed in a hunting accident, his wife had stolen Nell's babies, had her driven out, beaten and left for dead.

Upon recovering, for the next twelve years she'd been Silvan's housekeeper, caring for him and mothering his young sons in lieu of her own. Despite her firm resolve to never again get involved with a laird—wed or no'—she'd fallen in love with the eccentric, gentle, brilliant man. Verily, the day she'd opened her mud- and blood-caked eyes to find him bending over her in the roadway, something inexplicable had quickened inside her. She'd contented herself with loving him from a distance, hiding it behind a caustic demeanor and sparring words. Then three and a half years ago, events with Gwen and Drustan had thrown them together, stirring a passion that she'd been elated to discover Silvan had been hiding as well, and life had been sweeter than aught she'd ever known. Though nothing could replace the babies she'd lost so long ago, fate had blessed her in her late years with a second chance, and their twins were currently sleeping in the nursery under careful watch of their nanny, Maeve.

She loved Silvan more than life itself, though she rarely let him know that. There was something stuck in her craw, a thing she'd never make peace with. Silvan hadn't given his first wife the binding Druid vows of mating. That had heartened her when he'd asked her to wed him, but in three and a half long years, he'd not offered them to her either. And so long as that distance was betwixt them, she would never be able to make completely free with her heart. She would always wonder why, always wonder how come he didn't love her enough. A woman hated knowing she loved her man more deeply than he loved her.

Silvan was, as she'd expected, in his tower library, one hundred and three steps above the castle proper.

He was also, as she'd expected, downright broody.

"I brought ye cocoa," she announced, placing the tray on a small table.

He glanced up and smiled at her, though with an utterly distracted air. For a change, there was no book on his lap. Nor was he seated at his desk, scribing away. Nay, he was in a chair near the open window and had been staring sightlessly out it.

" 'Tis Dageus, is it no?" Nell drew a chair close to his and sipped at her cocoa. Silvan had long had a fondness for the costly chocolate drink, and during her pregnancy she'd developed a taste for it herself. "Why dinna ye tell me all about it, Silvan," she encouraged gently. She knew what he was thinking, for she was worrying the same things. Dageus had always been her favorite of the Keltar lads, with his wild passionate heart and private pains. As she'd watched him grow, watched the world harden him, she'd prayed a special lass might someday come along for him, as Gwen had for Drustan. (Gwen who'd gotten the blethering binding vows from *her* husband!)

Silvan's brown eyes sobered and he raked a hand through his snowy mane. "Och, Nellie, what am I to do? What I felt in him six moons past, before he left, is naught compared to what I now sense."

"And there's naught in the tomes ye've been searching that tells how to reimprison them?"

Silvan shook his head and exhaled dismally. "Not a blethering thing."

"Have ye checked all the tomes?" she pressed. Since the day Dageus had left, Silvan had been a man fair obsessed, laboring from dawn till dusk on his studies, determined to find something to pass on to Drustan, where they'd both suspected Dageus had gone.

Silvan replied that he'd thoroughly searched both his tower library and the study belowstairs.

"Did ye check the chamber library?" Nell asked, frowning.

"I told you I checked the study."

"I dinna say the study. I said the chamber library."

"What are you talking about, Nellie?"

"The one beneath the study."

Silvan went very still. "What one beneath the study?"

"The one behind the hearth," she said impatiently.

"*What* one behind the hearth?" Silvan snapped, surging to his feet.

Nell's eyes flew wide. "Och, for heaven's sake, Silvan, dinna ye know about it?"

Silvan grabbed her hand, his brown eyes flashing. "*Show me.*"

· 19 ·

Chloe clutched the stallion's mane as they sped across heather-covered fields toward a lush, overgrown forest.

When she and Dageus had ridden out from the castle half an hour ago, she'd seen more evidence that she was truly in the past. A towering wall that hadn't been there yesterday, patrolled by guards, encircled the perimeter of the estate. Clad in authentic medieval garb and armor, the guards had been toting weapons that made her fingers curl. She'd barely resisted the temptation to pluck them from their hands and lock them up somewhere safe.

When they'd exited the gates she'd peered curiously down into the valley, not really expecting to see the city of Alborath. Still, seeing the vast vale, that twenty-four hours earlier had been filled with thousands of homes and shops, currently occupied by contentedly grazing, fat sheep, had left her feeling utterly discombobulated.

Face it, Zanders, however he did it—physics, Druidry, archeoastronomy—he took you back.

Which meant that the man behind her on the horse, who'd not spoken a word since they'd ridden out, guiding them at a dizzying speed across wide-open fields, was a man who possessed the knowledge to command time itself.

Wow. Not exactly what she'd expected the day she'd stood in his penthouse fantasizing about what kind of man Dageus MacKeltar might be. Nope, not once had she thought "time-travelling Druid." It was making her reevaluate her entire concept of history—how little historians really knew! She felt as if she'd been sucked into one of Joss Whedon's scripts, into a world where nothing was what it seemed. Where girls discovered they were vampire-slayers and fell for men who didn't have souls. A *Buffy* addict to the bone, she wondered who Dageus was more like, Spike or Angel?

The answer came with swift certainty: There was something about him that was far more Spike than Angel, a tortured duality, a driving, underlying darkness.

His grip was tight on her waist, almost painful, his body rigid behind hers. The sheer size of him was daunting, being clutched between his powerful thighs, held tightly to his broad chest, made her feel delicate and overwhelmed. He seemed different in his own century, and she wondered how he'd ever passed as a twenty-first century man. He was all warrior and imperious command. His was regal Celtic blood, hot and passionate. He was man enough to swing the massive claymores that decorated the walls in The Cloisters. Man enough to survive, even thrive in such a rugged, untamed land.

She'd hardly noticed his silence when they'd first rode out, too fascinated by the vista, but now it was a chill wind behind her making her skin prickle.

"Why are we stopping here?" she asked nervously when he slowed the horse to a trot near a copse of rowan trees.

His reply was a soft, biting laugh as he shifted in the saddle so the hard thickness of him rubbed briefly against her bottom. Despite how nervous he was making her, lust filled her to a dizzying degree. There were questions, zillions of questions she should ask, and suddenly she couldn't recall a single one. Her mind had blanked alarmingly when he'd rubbed against her.

He reined in the stallion, dropped to the ground, and dragged her from its back. Off balance, she fell into his arms and he crushed her mouth with a hot, savage kiss.

Then he shoved her away, leaving her gasping for breath and clutching at air. She stood, watching with wide eyes as he grabbed a folded length of plaid from behind the saddle. Without a word he dropped it to the ground, spreading it with the toe of his boot. He slapped the stallion lightly on the rump, driving it away.

"I thought you told Silvan you were taking me to see a medieval village. What are you doing, Dageus?" she managed. She knew what he was doing. She could practically smell it on him—sex and lust and ruthless determination.

No matter that she was ready for him, she backed away a few steps. Couldn't help it. Then a few more. Tiny breaths slammed into each other, clotting in her throat. That danger she'd sensed in him so many times before had escalated to an extreme pitch.

His gaze was mocking. A strange flash of temper and impatience whipped through his eyes. "You had your hand wrapped around my cock last eve, Chloe, and you want to know what I'm doing? What do you think I'm doing?" he purred with a baring of teeth that only a fool would term a smile.

Nostrils flaring, he stalked toward her and paced a

slow circle around her. Stripping the thong from his hair, he raked his hands through the braid, freeing it. It spilled in waves of midnight around his body. *The beast is loose*, Chloe thought with a bone-melting surge of excitement. She pivoted slowly to keep pace with him. She was too nervous to allow him at her back.

He fisted a hand in his shirt behind his neck, yanked it over his head and flung it to the ground.

The air left her lungs in a great *whoosh* of breath. Dressed in nothing but black leather trews, hair falling about his savage face, he was forbiddingly beautiful. When he bent and stripped off his boots, the muscles in his powerful back and wide shoulders rippled, reminding her that he was twice her size, his arms were bands of steel, his body a meticulously honed machine.

Something about him is different. . . .

It took her a few moments to understand what it was. For the first time, she was seeing him without his eternal reserve and icy control. His gestures were no longer smoothly executed. Standing there, legs splayed, he was pure male aggression, insolent and unleashed.

She was startled to realize she was panting softly. That big, rock-hard aggressive man who was coming unraveled was going to make love to her.

He paced two more silent circles around her—*oh, yes, there was a reckless masculine swagger in his walk*—then closed in on her, his hand working at the laces of his trews. He was regarding her with mocking, possessive amusement as if he sensed she verged on fleeing, knew he could outrun her, and rather hoped she'd try.

As his big hand undid the laces, her gaze was drawn there, down his rippling stomach to the bulge in his pants that was . . . quite large. And soon to be inside her.

"M-maybe we should do this really slow," she stammered. "Dageus, I think—"

"Hush," he snapped, as he freed himself from his trews.

Chloe closed her mouth, staring. The sight of him in leather pants half-undone, legs spread, hard body glistening gold in the sunlight, with his thick erection pushing hungrily up would be engraved in her memory until the end of time. She couldn't breathe, she couldn't even swallow. She sure as hell wasn't going to blink and miss a minute of it. Nearly six and a half feet of raw, pulsing man was standing there, his hot gaze raking her, as if he were contemplating which part of her to taste first. She simply stared, her heart hammering.

"You know I'm no' a good man," he said, his voice deceptively gentle, belying the steel beneath it. "I've made no excuses. I've given you no pretty lies. You came with me anyway. Doona pretend you doona know what I want and doona think to deny me. Twice now you've tried to go back. *There is no going back with me, Chloe-lass.*" He hissed the last words, his lips drawing away from his teeth. "You know what I want and you want it too. You want it just the way I'm about to give it to you."

Chloe's knees nearly buckled. Anticipation shivered through her. He was right. On all counts.

He stalked. "Hard, fast, deep. When I'm done, you'll know you're mine. And you'll never think of naysaying me again."

Another predatory step toward her.

She didn't even think about it, she just yielded to the instinct: her feet spun her about and she broke into a run. As if she *could* outrun him. As if she could outrun what she'd been trying to outrun since she'd met him—the reckless, terrifying intensity of her desire for him. As if she even wanted to. She wanted him more than was wise, more than was rational, more than was controllable.

Still, she ran, a final symbolic resistance and—a part of

her knew—she ran because she *wanted* him to chase her. Thrilled with the knowledge that Dageus MacKeltar was running after her and when he caught her he was going to teach her all those things his eyes had been promising. All those things she wanted so desperately to know. She sped through the tall, thick grass and he actually let her run for a time, as if he, too, were enjoying the chase. Then he was on her, taking her down to the ground on her stomach beneath him. *Laughing* as he took her down.

His laughter turned into a rough growl as he stretched his big hard body the full length of hers, his erection an iron bar prodding her behind through the fabric of her gown. She wriggled, panicked by the feel of how large he was, yet he gave no quarter, wrapping his arms tightly around her, pinning hers to her sides. He rubbed himself back and forth between the cleft of her bottom, growling in a language she couldn't understand.

Banding her arms with one of his, he slid a hand between her body and the ground and cupped the vee of her thighs. She cried out at the shatteringly intimate touch. Every nerve in her body awakened brutally to a sharp, hungry emptiness. Muscles deep inside her bore down on nothing, aching to be filled and soothed. His strange temper, his roughness, fed a desire in her she'd not known she had. To be taken, consumed by the man. Hard and fast and without words. Every bit as animal as she'd known he was the day she'd met him.

She *liked* the danger in him, she realized then. It stirred a reckless part of her she'd long denied, been a little afraid of it. The part of her that sometimes dreamed she was in The Cloisters at night and the alarm systems had failed, leaving all those glorious artifacts unprotected.

His weight was so heavy atop her she could scarcely breathe. When his lips grazed the back of her neck, she whimpered. When his teeth closed on it in a little love-bite, she practically screamed. She was dizzyingly aroused, hot, achy, and needy. Then his big hand was on her face, a finger slipping between her lips and she sucked on it, willing to take and taste any part of him she could get. With his other hand he shoved the skirts of her gown up, his fingers ruthlessly probing her exposed soft folds, spreading the dampness, slipping and sliding. As the hard maleness of him prodded her bottom, he worked a finger inside her and thrust deeply.

Chloe cried out and pushed back against his hand. *Yes, oh, yes—that was what she needed!* Small broken sounds escaped her lips as he deftly slid a second finger in till she reached her virgin barrier. Gently, but relentlessly, he thrust through it, covering her bare neck and shoulders with searing, open-mouthed kisses interspersed with tiny bites. The pain was fleeting, a small tearing, swiftly surpassed by the pleasure of his fingers moving inside her, his mouth hot on her skin, his powerful body rippling against hers. He was her most private fantasy come to life. She'd dreamed of this, him taking her as if there were no force on earth that could prevent it.

None could, she thought dimly. Since the moment she'd seen him she'd known it would come to this. It had never been a question of "if," it had always only been a question of where and when.

Then he was nudging, thick and hard as steel, against those soft, delicate folds and she made a small helpless sound of distress. She'd *seen* him. She knew what was coming, and didn't think she could take it.

"Shh," he crooned against her ear, thrusting forward.

"I can't," she half-sobbed, as he began to push inside her. The pressure of him trying to enter was too intense.

"Aye, you can."

"No!"

"Easy lass," he purred. He drew back out the small

inch he'd gained, wrapped a hand around himself and tried again, slowly. Though she wanted desperately to have him inside her, her body resisted the intrusion. He was too big and she was simply too small. With a barely smothered oath he stopped again, then he was roughly bunching the thick folds of her gown into a wad beneath her pelvis, raising her bottom higher for him, at just such an angle.

Then his full weight was on her again. He curled one powerful arm around her shoulders, the other around her hips.

He rubbed himself back and forth between her legs until she was pushing wildly back against him. At this new angle she felt exposed and vulnerable, but knew it would make it easier for him to enter. When she was crying out incoherently, he pushed himself in slowly, easing inside, his breath hissing from between his teeth. She panted, struggling to accommodate the impaling thickness of him. Minutes inched by as he pushed deeper, taking every tiny bit her body yielded. Just when she was certain he'd seated himself to the hilt, that she had all of him, he pushed a final time with a rough sound, deeper still, and she made helpless mewling noises.

"I'm in you, lass," his voice was a deep burr against her ear. "I'm part of you now."

God, he'd been in her since the moment she'd seen him. A larcenous thief, he'd broken and entered *her*, claiming residence just beneath her skin. How had she lived without this? she wondered. Without this fierce, savage intimacy, without this big intense man inside her?

"I'm going to love you now, slow and sweet, but when you come, I'm going to fuck you the way I need to. The way I've been dreaming about since the moment I saw you."

She whimpered in reply, burning inside, desperate for

him to move, to do as he promised. She wanted both: tenderness and wildness, man and animal.

"When you bent back inside your friend's car that day, Chloe, I wanted to be behind you, just like this. I wanted to slip your skirt up and fill you up with me. I wanted to carry you up to my penthouse and keep you in my bed and never let you go." He groaned, a soft rough, purring sound. "And, och, when I saw your legs sticking out from beneath my bed—" He broke off, abruptly switching to a language she couldn't understand, but the exotic dialect in his husky voice wove an erotic spell around her.

He withdrew slowly, filled her again, thrusting in long, slow strokes, nudging deep. The largeness of him stirred nerve endings in places she'd not known existed. She could feel her climax building with each sure thrust, yet the moment she was about to reach it, he withdrew, leaving her aching and nearly sobbing with frustrated desire.

He filled her almost lazily, purring in that strange language. He withdrew, inch by inch, with excruciating slowness, until she was gripping the grass in thick handfuls and ripping it from the ground. Till with each thrust she struggled to arch against him and take more of him, keep him inside her so she could gain her release. For a short time she thought it must be her fault it kept eluding her, or perhaps he was just too big, then she realized he was deliberately withholding it. His big hands on her hips, he was pressing her down when she tried to arch up, preventing her from controlling the pace or taking what she needed.

"Dageus . . . please!"

"Please what?" he purred against her ear.

"Let me come," she wailed.

He laughed huskily, his hand sliding between her pelvis and the bunched fabric beneath it, prodding at her folds, exposing her taut nub. He flicked a finger over it and she almost screamed. A heartbeat passed, then two. He flicked lightly again. "Is this what you want?" he said silkily. His touch was expert, tantalizing, torturing, not quite enough, meted out with the sure skill of a man who knew a woman's body as well as she did.

"Yes," she gasped.

"Do you need me, Chloe?" Another light pass of his finger.

"Yes!"

"Soon," he purred, "I'm going to taste you here." He brushed the pad of his thumb over the hard nub.

Chloe slammed the ground with her palms and squeezed her eyes shut. Those simple words had nearly— but not quite, damn it!—pushed her over the sweet edge.

He pressed his lips to her ear and whispered in a sultry, erotic voice, "Do you feel like you can't breathe without me inside you?"

"*Yes*," she sobbed, dimly aware that there was something déjà vu-ish about his words.

"Ah, lass, that's what I needed to hear. 'Tis yours, then, aught you want from me." Cupping her face with his large palm he turned her head to the side and slanted his mouth over hers at the same moment he thrust deep and held, grinding his hips in circles against her bottom, pumping into her. As she arched back against him he tightened his arm around her waist and deepened the kiss, his tongue plunging in tempo with his lower body, both driving into her. The tension gripping her body suddenly exploded, flooding her with the most exquisite sensation she'd ever felt. It was different than what had happened on the plane; this was a deeper quake at the very core of her, immensely more intense, and she screamed his name as she came.

He continued the steady thrusting until she went limp beneath him, then he drew her hips up and back, raising her to her knees and drove into her, the heavy weight of his testicles slapping against her hot, aching skin. With each thrust she whimpered, unable to prevent the broken sounds spilling from her lips.

"Och, Christ, lass," he hissed. Rolling her with him onto his side, he wrapped his arms around her so tightly she could scarcely breathe, and thrust. And thrust, his hips flexing powerfully behind her.

He breathed her name when he came and the broken note in his voice, coupled with his hand moving so intimately between her legs brought her to another swift climax. When she peaked again it was so intense that the edges of darkness folded gently around her.

When she roused from the dreamy half-doze, he was still inside her. And still hard.

He took her to the village of Balanoch much later, which was actually a bustling little city. They ate in the central square, far from the shops on the outer perimeter that housed the smellier, noisier trades such as the tanneries, the smiths, and the butchers. Chloe was famished and ate with gusto strips of salted beef and fresh-baked bread, cheese, some kind of fruit tart, and spiced wine that went straight to her head, making her just tipsy enough that she couldn't keep her hands off him.

She saw things in the busy village that sealed beyond a shadow of a doubt—not that she'd really had any left—that she was in the past. The houses were wattle and daub, with tiny yards in which barefoot children played. The shops were constructed of stone with thatched roofs, their wide faces sporting shutters that opened horizontally, the bottom one displaying their wares. Beside the tanner's vats, she'd watched young lads shaving skins with currier's knives. At the blacksmith's forge, she'd stared in fascination at a strangely compelling smith while he pounded a long length of red-hot steel, sparks flying.

She'd peered in the single window of the goldsmith's abode and glimpsed books therein, at which point Dageus had threatened to toss her over his shoulder if she tarried overlong. When she'd started up the stairs, he'd backed her against the door and kissed her until she lost not only her breath, but all memory of where she'd been trying to go.

There were chandlers, weavers, potters, even an armorer and several kirks.

She couldn't help herself, she gaped, and a dozen times or more Dageus had gently closed her mouth with a finger beneath her chin. She lost count of how many times she muttered something inane like *Ohmigod, I'm really here!*

They didn't stay in Balanoch long, however, nowhere near long enough for Chloe to thoroughly explore; but frankly, she was more obsessed with exploring the big beautiful man who'd done things to her that made her feel as if she were coming apart at the seams.

They stopped several "leagues" as he called them, from the village, near a copse of oak trees, beside a tumbling stream that widened into a shimmering pool.

When he slid her from the stallion this time, his gaze was tender, his every touch a languid caress, as if wordlessly apologizing for his earlier roughness (which she hadn't minded a bit!). And when he took her again it was in the sun-warmed pool, after he'd gently washed those parts of her he'd battered. He went slow this time, giving her dozens of hot, wet, lazy kisses, lavishing her breasts with tiny nibbles and caresses. Lying her back at the edge of the pool, slipping between her legs and hooking her calves over his shoulders so he could taste her as he'd told her earlier he would. Lapping sweetly until she was wild for him, then dragging her back into the pool and lifting her astride him. She clung to him, staring into his eyes while he filled her and became part of her again.

And just before she drifted off in his arms, beyond replete, exhausted and sore in places that had never been sore before, she knew that she'd gone and done what she'd been determined not to do: She'd fallen head over heels for the strange, dark Highlander.

The moon was silvering the heather when Dageus finally stirred from his doze. He was sprawled on the plaid with Chloe in his arms, the lush curves of her plump backside pressed to his front, their legs twined together. Had he been a weeping man, he might have wept then from simple pleasure.

She'd taken him as he was. *All* of him. He'd been wild with the darkness goading him, beyond kindness, his humanity slipping, and she'd brought him back to himself. He'd tried to make it up to her with tender loving, slower and gentler than he'd ever taken a woman.

However he'd taken her, she'd met him and matched him. He'd been right, Chloe was wanton, had a wildness of her own. She'd been ready to lose her innocence, eager to be awakened, to be taught, and he'd relished every moment of it. Relished knowing he was her first lover. Her last, too, he thought possessively. She was a daring wee lass, loving every part of sex just as he'd known she would.

After they'd gone to Balanoch (which he'd scarce even seen, too consumed by the wee woman between his thighs on the horse), they'd lazily sunned themselves naked beside the tumbling brook that fed the pool. They'd run their hands over each other's body, learning every plane and curve. Tasting all the hollows and crevices. They'd shared more spiced wine and talked.

They'd *talked*.

She'd told him about her childhood, what it was like to grow up without parents. She'd made him laugh with stories of her elderly grandda warily taking her shopping for her first bra, (making him picture Silvan trying to choose female undergarments—och, that would be a sight!) and having The Talk with her about what she called "the birds and the bees." Try as he might, Dageus couldn't grasp that colloquialism. What birds and bees had to do with tooping, was beyond him. Horses he could understand. But bees? Unfathomable.

He'd spoken a bit about his childhood—the finer parts, growing up with Drustan, before he'd been old enough to know that the Keltars were feared, during those years he'd still harbored a young lad's dreams and fancies. He'd sung her bawdy, outrageous Scottish ditties as the sun had raced across the sky, and she'd laughed until tears filled her eyes. He was astonished by her every expression, so open and unguarded. Amazed by her resilience. Amazed by the emotions she stirred in him, feelings he'd long forgotten.

She'd asked him questions about Druidry and he'd told her of the myriad Keltar duties: performing the seasonal rituals on Yule, Beltane, Samhain, and Lughnassadh, tending the earth and the wee creatures, preserving and guarding the sacred lore, using the stones on certain necessary occasions. He'd also explained, as best he could, how the stones worked. The physics of it had flummoxed her, and when her eyes had begun to glaze over, he'd spared her further edification. He'd told her what little they knew about the Tuatha Dé, and how the Keltar had formed an alliance with them many thousands of years ago—though he wisely avoided the subject of oaths.

So the Tuatha Dé really existed? she'd exclaimed. *An actual race of technologically advanced people? Where did they come from? Do you know?*

Nay, lass, we doona ken. There is very little we know about them for a certainty.

He'd known the precise moment she'd truly accepted it; her eyes had sparkled, her cheeks had flushed, and he'd half-feared she was going to rush right back to the stones to examine them further. He'd swift given her something else to examine.

Och, aye, his mate was wanton. . . .

Strangely, she'd not brought up "the curse," nor had she pressed to know what he was searching for, and for that he was endlessly grateful. He had no doubt it was only a temporary reprieve and that she'd hammer him with questions before long, but he'd take what he could get. He sensed that she'd been as determined as he to steal a day with no worry for the morrow. 'Twas a gift he'd never expected her to give him, a gift that humbled him. If he had naught ever again, he'd had this day.

She knew he was a Druid, knew how ancient and strange his bloodline, and hadn't feared him. He'd shamelessly milked it for all it was worth and basked in her acceptance.

Now, as she slumbered in his arms, he nudged her a bit so the palm of his right hand slipped between her breasts, coming to rest above her heart. He shifted himself so the palm of his left rested above his own.

There were words he'd waited his entire life to say and he would not be denied them. Silvan had ever accused him of loving too much. If he did, he couldn't help it. Once his heart made the decision, there was no arguing with it. She was his mate and, for however long the gods granted, he would belong to his woman completely.

He kissed her till she stirred drowsily and murmured

his name. 'Twould do him no good to say the vows whilst she slept; his mate must actually hear the words. Then he began speaking reverently, pledging himself to her forever, though the bond wouldn't take on its full life unless she one day gave the words back.

"If aught must be lost, 'twill be my honor for yours. If one must be forsaken, 'twill be my soul for yours. Should death come anon, 'twill be my life for yours."

He tightened his arm around her and drew a deep breath, knowing that what he was about to complete was irrevocable. She'd said no words of love to him (though she'd used it in a sentence once in Balanoch—she'd said she *loved* the way he made *love*—and had nearly caused his heart to stop beating). Completing the vow would seal him to loving her for all eternity, and if there were lives beyond this one, he would be bound to love her in those as well. In eternal torment, aching endlessly for her, if she never loved him back.

"*I am Given*," he murmured, holding her close. The moment he uttered the final words of the oath, a wave of intense emotion crashed over him. He couldn't begin to imagine what it might be like were she ever to give the vow back. Completion, he suspected. Two hearts made as one.

Deep inside him the ancient ones hissed furiously and recoiled. They hadn't liked that at all, he brooded darkly. Good.

"That was beautiful," Chloe murmured. "What was it?" She poked her head up and peered over her shoulder at him. In the pearly moonlight her skin shimmered translucent, her aquamarine eyes were sleepy and sexy, sparkling. Her lips were still swollen from his kisses, achingly lush. Her tousled curls fell in a tumble about her face and he could feel himself growing hard again, yet knew it would be the morrow at least before he could have her again. Were he a patient man, he should give her a sennight to recover. He'd be lucky if he made it a few more hours. Now that he'd tasted her, tasted how sweet it was to make love to a woman he loved, he was starved for more.

"Och, lass, you are so lovely. You fair take my breath away." Trite words, he scorned himself, such weak words compared to what he felt.

She flushed with pleasure. "Was that some kind of poem you recited?"

"Aye, something like that," he purred, rolling her over in his arms so she was facing him.

"I liked it. It sounded . . . romantic." She peered at him curiously, nibbling her lower lip. "What was it again?"

When he didn't repeat it, she mused a moment then said, "Oh! I think I've got it! You said 'if aught must be lost—' "

"Nay, lass," he shouted, going rigid. Och, Christ, what had he done? He dare not let her give the vows back. If aught happened to him, she would be bound to him *forever*. And if something terrible happened, if—God forbid—he actually turned dark, would she then be bound to him, a beast from hell? She might be tied for all eternity to the rage and fury that was the Draghar! Nay. Never.

Chloe blinked, looking wounded. "I just wanted to repeat it so I could remember it." The little poem had made her feel funny, strangely compelled to say it back for some reason. They were the sweetest words he'd ever spoken, even if only a bit of a poem, and she'd like it safely tucked away in her memory. He wasn't a man who bandied idle words about. He'd meant something by it. Was that how Dageus MacKeltar spoke of his feelings? By reciting a few lines of a poem?

Though she'd been drowsy when he'd spoken, she

was pretty certain he'd said something like "my life for yours." If only he might love her like that! She no longer wanted merely to be the woman who got inside Dageus MacKeltar, she wanted to be the one who *stayed* inside him. Forever. The last woman he ever made love to. She wanted it so fiercely that the mere wanting was a kind of pain.

And by God, she wanted to hear those words again.

She opened her mouth to press, but the moment she did, he slanted his mouth hard over her parted lips and—damn the man for being able to kiss a woman into a swarm of hormones buzzing about like drunken little bees!—in a few moments the only thing she was thinking about was the way he was touching her.

❦

Silvan wasn't a man given to lurking. Well, he hadn't been until his sons had gone and taken mates, then it seemed he'd begun doing all sorts of things he'd not done before. Like eavesdropping on an embarrassingly personal and sizzling conversation between Drustan and Gwen that had ended with Silvan dragging Nellie off to bed. And wed to her a short time later.

He grinned. A damn fine woman she was too. Knew more about the Keltar than the Keltar knew themselves. In her twelve years as his housekeeper, she'd learned nearly every secret in their castle, including one not even he had known: a secret place that had been forgotten for nearly eight centuries, according to the last entry he'd read in the journal he'd found therein.

She said she'd discovered the underground chamber during a fit of spring cleaning a score of years ago. She'd not mentioned it because she thought he'd known—*and besides*, she'd added acerbically, *that was when ye weren't speaking to me.* Silvan snorted softly. What a fool he'd been, denying his desire for her. So many wasted years.

Are you wasting yet more time, old man? a caustic inner voice inquired. *Aren't there still things you refuse to say?*

He shoved that thought brusquely away. Now was not the time to brood on himself. Now was the time to focus on finding a way to save his son.

The contents of the chamber were the reason he currently lurked in the shadows of the great hall awaiting Dageus's return. There were texts and artifacts, relics Dageus needed to see. The sheer volume of material in the underground chamber was overwhelming. It could take them weeks simply to catalog it all.

Silvan sensed his son before he entered the great hall, and began to rise, but at the last moment before the door opened, he heard a soft rush of throaty female laughter. Then silence that could only be filled with kisses. Then more laughter.

Soft, faint, but *Dageus's* laughter.

He went motionless in a half-crouch above the chair. How long since he'd heard such a sound?

Och, the darkness was still there beneath it, but whatever had transpired this day had granted Dageus a merciful reprieve. He didn't need to see his son to know that his eyes would be—if not golden—at least lighter.

When his son swung the door open, Silvan slipped back into the chair, gathering the gloom around him with a few soft words.

His news would keep till the morn.

· 20 ·

There's something I haven't told you, Chloe-lass, Dageus
said, stepping forward from the shadowy circle of stones.
His eyes said he wanted to tell her. His eyes said he was
afraid to tell her. What might such a man fear? That he
feared it, frightened her as well, and diminished her need
to know substantially. For a novel change, her curiosity
curled up and played dead.

You don't have to tell me if you don't want to, she prevari-
cated, wanting the dreamy pleasure of their newfound
intimacy to remain unspoiled by difficult truths. From
the look on his face, difficult was a mild word for whatever he was withholding.

The tendons in his strong neck worked and he opened
and closed his mouth several times. He took a deep
breath. *Mayhap you should know—*

A sudden pounding at the door jarred Chloe instantly

awake. Her dream shattered into tiny particles of sand-man's dust.

When she jerked, Dageus's arms tightened around her.

"Are ye awake in there?" Nell was calling through the door. "Silvan's nigh beside himself with impatience. He's requestin' ye both belowstairs."

"We're awake, Nell," Dageus replied. "Would you mind having a bath sent up?"

"Dageus, yer da will get himself in a fankle. He's been waiting to show ye what he's found since early yester-morn and ye know he's ne'er been the most patient man."

Dageus exhaled loudly. "A quarter hour, Nell," he said, sounding resigned, "then we'll be down."

"I wouldn't be disturbin' ye, were it left to me." A soft laugh, and her footsteps faded down the corridor.

Dageus rolled Chloe over on her side to face him, cap-turing one of her legs between his, cupping her full breasts possessively.

"G'morning," she said drowsily, flushing from the memory of what he'd done to her through the night. What she'd encouraged him, even begged him to do. She smiled. She was achy and sore and felt scrumptious. She'd spent the entire night in his arms. Funny, she mused, of all the things that were so difficult to believe, the past twenty-four hours with him seemed the most astonish-ing. Since she'd given herself to him, he'd been a com-pletely different man. Warm, sexy, playful. Oh, still every inch dominant, basely sexual man, but infinitely more ap-proachable. Where, previously, sometimes it had seemed he was there but not quite there—a part of him some-where else entirely—in bed he was one hundred percent *there*. One hundred percent focused and involved.

It was devastating to be the focal point of such raw, re-lentless eroticism. He was everything she'd fantasized

Dageus MacKeltar might be in bed and more. Wild and demanding, battering past all her inhibitions.

Just as she was thinking how nice it was to see him at ease, his body as relaxed as a lion lazily sunning himself, he smiled back, but it didn't reach his eyes.

"Oooh! Stop that. When you smile at me I want all of it."

"What?" He looked confused.

Chloe slid her hands to his ribs, wondering if such a strong, disciplined man might be ticklish. He was, and it delighted her to discover that in some small way he was as helpless and as human as the rest of the world. She tickled mercilessly until, laughing, he captured her hands in his.

"I punish wenches who tickle me," he purred, stretching her arms above her head.

"How?" she asked breathlessly.

He ducked his dark head and caught one nipple in his mouth, suckling gently before releasing it and dragging his tongue over her breasts to capture the other. "You have perfect breasts, lass," he growled huskily. "As to the punishing, I'll need to think on that," he purred against her skin. "None has e'er tickled me before."

"Gee, I wonder why?" she managed. When he circled a budded nipple with his tongue, her back arched and she inhaled sharply. Her breasts felt swollen, chafed by his shadow beard, and exquisitely sensitive. "Could it be because you're always so reserved and in control? They were probably afraid to," she said, gasping.

He released her nipple and looked up at her, startled. "But you're not, are you, Chloe?"

"Smile," she panted, not wanting to answer that. Not wanting to admit that some part of her was afraid of the intimidating man who danced between centuries. Not exactly *of* him, more afraid of the power he had over her because she had such intense feelings for him. With all the scorching, incredibly intimate things he'd done to her, he'd not said any of those words lovers were wont to say, words hinting at a future together. As he'd told her yesterday, he made no excuses and offered no pretty lies. No promises either.

She wouldn't mind one or two. Or ten.

Taking her cue from him, she'd kept her feelings silent, resolved to be patient; wait and watch, try to catch some of those subtle little signs that were all Dageus ever revealed.

He arched a brow and smiled as she'd requested.

"Oh, that one was much better," she said, smiling back. It was impossible not to smile back when he truly smiled. When he slid his hands down her arms, over her breasts, then to her hips, she shook her head warily. "Huh-uh. I can't. Not now." She deliberately teased him with, "It could be a week before I can again." She topped it with a demure batting of her lashes.

Growling, he tossed his head, his black mane spilling like dark silk over her skin. "Och, nay, lass, I doona think so. A bath will hasten your recovery." He prodded her in the thigh, hard and ready. Did the man never tire? she wondered blissfully.

Despite her extreme soreness, desire flared, hot and greedy, stirring all those battered nerve endings to life. He made her feel insatiable. Having sex with him made a woman feel like she was doing something forbidden somehow, and she could get downright obsessed with it. Though she felt bruised and tender, if they had the time, she'd be all over him, or rather, he'd be all over her, for he certainly liked the dominant position. "You heard Nell. We're not getting a bath. Silvan wants us." Chloe felt a sudden flush of embarrassment. She'd slept with Silvan's son in Silvan's castle. Though she hadn't felt awkward about it with Nell at the door, for some reason she felt uneasy about it when she thought about Silvan, perhaps because he was of her grandda's age.

"Doona worry, lass," he reassured her, guessing at her thoughts from her expression. "Silvan saw us come in last eve. He'll no' think less of you. Verily, he'll be delighted. I've no' had a lass in my chamber before."

"Really?" she asked a bit breathlessly. When he nodded, Chloe smiled radiantly: At least here in his bedroom, she was the only one. Though not what she'd prefer (like a declaration of undying love or a request that she have his babies), it was something. Then her eyes narrowed. The sun was spilling in the window behind her and Dageus's eyes were golden, dappled with darker flecks. Smoky and sensual, fringed by thick dark lashes, but gold nonetheless. "What is *with* your eyes?" she exclaimed. "Is it part of being a Druid?"

"What color are they?" he asked warily.

"Gold."

He flashed her another unguarded smile. It was like basking in the sun, she thought, tracing her fingers over his beard-shadowed jaw, smiling helplessly back.

He prodded her again. "You're good for me, lass. Now get off your back woman, lest I start something you refuse to let me finish." He sat up, bringing her with him, kissing her, nipping at her lower lip. The kiss turned heated and fierce while he was trying to stand and they fell out of bed, so she landed on the floor atop him. He promptly rolled her beneath him and kissed her till she was gasping for breath.

He gave her a cocky smile a few moments later as he helped her to her feet. "I'll wager you won't be sore long," he purred.

Definitely not, she thought, *damn the teasing, torturing man!* Muscles in the inner parts of her thighs she'd not known she had, protested when she tried to walk. And still, she wanted more.

Only much later did she realize that he hadn't answered her question.

⬧❧

" 'Tis nigh time," Silvan grumbled when they entered the great hall.

"Da, where's the fifth Book of Manannán?" Dageus asked without preamble.

"There *is* no fifth Book of Manannán," Chloe said matter-of-factly. "There are only three. Everyone knows that."

Dageus gave her a cool smirk. "Ah, the nefarious everyone. I've long wondered who comprises that group."

Silvan looked amused, cocked his head and glanced inquiringly at Dageus. "Think you she needs a distraction? I thought you'd been distracting her quite thoroughly."

Chloe blushed.

" 'Tis in the tower library," Silvan added. "But hurry back, we've much to discuss and Nellie has shown me a most amazing thing."

When Dageus loped out of the hall, Silvan patted the seat beside him. "Come, m'dear," he said with a warm smile. "Bide a wee with me and tell me of yourself. How did you meet my son?"

When was she ever going to come up with a suitable answer for that? Chloe wondered wryly. She glanced away from his penetrating gaze, blushing a bit.

"The truth, m'dear," Silvan said softly.

Chloe glanced back at him, startled. "Am I that transparent?"

He smiled reassuringly. "Knowing my son as I do, I doona believe 'twas an ordinary meeting."

THE DARK HIGHLANDER • 271

"No," she agreed with a gusty little sigh. "We didn't exactly meet. We . . . er, well, it was more like we collided. . . ."

Her story made him laugh aloud and Silvan couldn't wait to repeat it to Nellie, who would savor every word of the outrageous tale. The lass was a fine storyteller, melodramatic enough to keep things lively and exploit the good parts for all they were worth. Funny, too, with a self-effacing sense of humor that was most appealing. The lass had no idea how bonny and unusual she was. She considered herself "a bit of a nerd." After she'd defined the word, Silvan decided a nerd was a fine thing to be. (That he himself fell into the "brainy, not particularly graceful, and a little bit backward" category might have influenced his opinion a wee.) Aye, the telling of the tale was a lovely bit of word-weaving, and the tale itself reeked of the fated meeting of a Keltar and his mate.

While she spoke, he deep-listened. He sensed a pure heart in her, a heart like Dageus's, more sensitive than most, wildly emotional, hence carefully guarded. He heard her love for his son in the slightly husky timbre of her voice. A love so strong that it fashed her a wee, and she was not yet ready to speak of it.

That it was there was enough for Silvan. His son had indeed found his mate. He pondered the irony of the timing, even as he blessed it.

One thing gave him pause, however: She still didn't know what was wrong with Dageus, and there was a newly blossomed bit of fear in her heart.

He understood that well. When a heart realized it loved was also, paradoxically, when a heart learned to fear most deeply. She wanted to know what was wrong with Dageus, yet she didn't want to hear aught that might spoil their joy, and Silvan suspected she'd have a bit of a battle with herself before she finally got around to asking.

When Dageus handed Chloe the fifth Book of Manannán, the senior MacKeltar decided he was besotted with her. She handled the tome with utter reverence, touching naught but the barest tips of the edges of the thick pages, staring with huge wondering eyes.

And sputtering. "B-b-but this isn't s-supposed to even exist and—oh, God, it was written using the early L-Latin alphabet! Do you think I could trade one of my relics for this?" she breathed, turning a gaze on Dageus that Silvan himself would have been hard-pressed to deny.

Och, aye, the lass could happily pass hours as he himself was wont to do, puzzling over the ancient texts, delighting in the stories therein. Nerd, indeed. And Dageus, well, Dageus seemed fair frozen by the prospect of denying her aught. He rescued his son swiftly. "I'm afraid it has to stay here, m'dear. There are reasons certain tomes have ne'er been made available to the world."

"Oh, but you must at least let me read it!" she exclaimed.

Silvan assured her she could, then focused his attention on Dageus. The discovery of the chamber library had invigorated him, made him feel a score of years younger and given him a whole new sense of what it meant to be a Keltar. And in that chamber, surely there were answers to their problems. He could scarce wait to show it to his son. Enjoying the moment, he said with studied nonchalance, "I'm assuming I'm no' the only one that wasn't aware of the chamber library beneath the study?"

Dageus made a choking noise and his startled gaze flew to Silvan's. "*Beneath* the study?"

"Aye."

Dageus grabbed Chloe's hand, tugged her from the chair, fought a little battle with her as she tried to hang onto the text, plucked it from her hands and firmly deposited it on the table, then dragged her along as they hastened after Silvan.

When Silvan applied pressure to the left brace beneath the mantel on the hearth, the entire side of the hearth swung out, revealing a passageway behind it. He explained how Nellie had, one day in a fit of energetic cleaning, stumbled upon it whilst sweeping cobwebs from beneath the mantel and scrubbing black soot from the stone face of the hearth. She'd grasped the brace while scrubbing and the next thing she'd known the fireplace was moving, with her clinging to it.

"And *why* didn't she tell us?" Dageus said, incredulous.

Silvan snorted. "She thought we knew and believed she wasn't supposed to know."

Dageus shook his head. "And 'tis another library?"

"Och, son, it looks to be our entire history, undisturbed for centuries."

Stunned, and she suspected a bit forgotten by the two Keltar men for the moment, Chloe followed Dageus and Silvan into the dark void, down steep stone steps into a cavernlike chamber that was roughly fifteen feet across and twice that long. The chamber was lit by dozens of candles in wall sconces. It was lined from floor to ceiling with shelves, dotted with tables, chairs, and trunks.

Chloe's head whipped left and right, back and forth at a dizzying speed.

Focus, Zanders. You're going to make yourself sick from excitement.

No archaeologist entering a heretofore sealed and forgotten tomb could have felt any giddier. Her heart was racing, her palms sweaty, and she was not managing deep breaths very well. She strode forward, pushing past the two men, determined to see all she could before they remembered her and perhaps thought twice about letting her see it. She was in an ancient underground chamber, surrounded by her most favorite things: dusty relics from ages long past. Relics that would send the scholars in her century into paroxysms of joy, giving them topics to gnaw on and argue contentedly about for the rest of their lives.

There were stone tablets chiseled with Irish oghamic inscriptions. More stones with what looked like Pictish ogham script, a script modern scholars had never succeeded in translating, as Picts had adopted Irish ogham but hadn't been able adapt it to their own language since Pictish and Gaelic were phonetically incompatible. Maybe they could teach her how to read it! she thought, dizzied by the possibility.

There were cloth-bound volumes, secured and tied in faded fabric, leather-bound volumes and scrolls, enameled plates, hand-stitched codices, bits of armor and weaponry, and—heavens—even that long-forgotten flagon was a relic!

After a few moments of breathless perusal, she glanced over her shoulder at Dageus and Silvan who'd paused just inside the chamber, their heads bent above a squat stone column upon which lay a sheet of gold.

"Da, is this what I think it is?" Dageus's voice sounded strangled.

"Aye, 'tis The Compact, as legend told, etched upon a sheet of pure gold."

"That's not very sensible," Chloe pointed out faintly. "It's too malleable. Pure gold is too soft, too easily damaged. That's why so many of the ancient torcs had cores of iron beneath the gold. Well, that and to help deflect a potential sword. What Compact, anyway?"

"Precisely their purpose," Silvan murmured, lightly tracing the edge of the gold sheet. " 'Twas said they did it to symbolize how fragile The Compact was. To underscore that it must be handled gently."

"What Compact?" Chloe asked again, stepping gingerly between a pile of leather-bound tomes and a heartbreakingly rusted shield, peering deeper into the shadowy corners of the chamber. She wondered if they'd let her live down here for a while. Another glance at Dageus made her recant that thought. Unless he lived down there with her.

"The Compact betwixt the Tuatha Dé Danaan and man."

Chloe sat down heavily on her bottom.

"Not on the tomes!" Silvan gasped.

Chloe, startled, toppled sideways and sprawled on the dusty stone floor, appalled that she'd just planted her rump on a pile of priceless texts. "Sorry," she mumbled. "I'm just a little over-excited. How old is it supposed to be? What language is it in? Can you translate it? What does it say?"

Silvan busied himself sorting through an urn of scrolls.

Dageus shrugged. "No idea what language it's in."

"You can't read it?"

"Nay," Dageus muttered.

Silvan harrumphed.

Chloe's eyes narrowed but she decided to leave it alone for the moment. She was feeling light-headed again and didn't want to push it. She needed to slowly absorb her new perspective of history, one that included both Druids with the power to manipulate time itself, and the existence of an ancient civilization that had possessed knowledge and technology advanced far beyond anything man had ever achieved.

Grandda had been right—the Tuatha Dé Danaan had once lived, and not just in myth!

Breathe, Zanders, she told herself, dropping to her knees on the floor and reaching for the nearest tome.

Many hours later, Chloe rested her head back against the cool stone wall and closed her eyes, listening to Silvan and Dageus talk. Languages she couldn't translate, scribed in long-unused alphabets, danced on the insides of her eyelids.

There was dust in her hair, on her face and in her nose, she was wearing a dust-covered medieval gown in a castle that had no showers or indoor plumbing, and she couldn't have been happier. Well, unless she'd been sent back in time to the Alexandrian Library right after Anthony had given Cleopatra the Pergamum Library, bringing the estimated total of volumes housed therein to nearly a million, if anything historians claimed was to be trusted.

"So, according to the journal you found, our ancestors rarely used this chamber, passing the knowledge of the place only from laird to eldest son?" Dageus was saying. His deep burr sent little shivers of sexual awareness through her.

"Aye," Silvan replied. "I spent a bit of time paging through it yestreen. The most recent entry was made in eight hundred and seventy-two. 'Tis my guess the laird died unexpectedly and, like as not, quite young, and the chamber was forgotten."

"All this history," Dageus said, shaking his head. "All this lore, and we never even knew about it."

"Aye. Had we, things might have been very different. Mayhap some of us would have made different choices."

Chloe opened her eyes a slit. There'd been a strange, pointed note in Silvan's voice when he'd made the last comment. She studied Dageus's chiseled profile, bronzed by the flickering candlelight, wondering what he wasn't telling her. She'd not forgotten about the curse or his unceasing searching of the old tomes. Though she'd had ample opportunity to ask him yesterday, she'd not wanted anything to mar the wonder of their day together.

Truth was, she didn't want anything to mar the wonder of this day, either. She would zealously defend it from the merest hint of gloom. She'd never felt so bubbly, so elated, and she didn't want it to end. She—who always pushed inquisitively, who never took "I don't know" for an answer—abruptly had no desire to make even the smallest inquiry.

Tomorrow, she promised herself. *I'll ask him tomorrow.*

For now, between suddenly finding herself in the past, experiencing passion with such an intense man, and discovering so many treasures, she had enough to contend with. She was having a hard time just keeping pace. Merely pondering the fact that she was in the sixteenth century was overwhelming enough.

As if he felt her gaze on him, Dageus turned his head suddenly and looked straight into her eyes.

His nostrils flared and his eyes narrowed, his gaze hot and possessive. "Da, Chloe needs a bath," he said, without taking his gaze from hers. He caught his lower lip with his teeth and all the muscles in her lower body clenched. *"Now."*

"I'm a bit dusty myself," Silvan agreed after a brief, awkward pause. "I suspect we could all use a bit of a break and a bite to eat."

Dageus rose, seeming larger than usual in the confines

of the low-ceilinged chamber. He held out his hand. "Come, lass."

Chloe went.

* * *

"Must we chain him like that?" Gwen asked, frowning.

"Aye, love," Drustan replied. "He'll kill himself before he'll talk, if I'm fool enough to give him the opportunity."

They stepped back, staring through the bars of the dungeon where a lean man with close-cropped brown hair was chained to the wall, his arms and legs outspread. He snarled at them through the bars, but the sound was muffled by his gag.

"And you have to gag him?"

"He was muttering something that sounded suspiciously like a chant before I did. Unless I'm questioning him, he stays gagged. Doona venture down here without me, lass."

"It just seems so . . . barbaric, Drustan. What if he's not even involved in this?"

Drustan collected the assortment of personal possessions he'd removed from the man's pockets before restraining him. He'd divested him of two lethally sharp daggers, a cell phone, a length of cord, a large amount of cash, and a few pieces of hard candy. The man carried no wallet, no identification, no papers of any sort. He tucked the phone, cord, and candy in his pocket, palmed the blades and wrapped an arm around Gwen's shoulders, guiding her away from the cell toward the stairs.

"He is. I caught him lurking outside the study doors. When he saw me, he looked as if he recognized me. Then he looked puzzled and finally shocked. I'm fair certain he thought I was Dageus and didn't know Dageus had a twin. Further, Dageus told me that Chloe told him her assailant had a tattoo on his neck. Though Dageus

His hot gaze raked her from head to toe and he swallowed a little growl of ever-present desire. Dressed in a thin, clinging lilac gown—one of several Nell had altered for her, and he suspected Nellie was deliberately choosing ones to drive him to distraction—with a deeply scooped neckline and snug bodice, she was a vision. Her tousled curls spilled about her face and she was pinching her luscious lower lip, deep in thought. She got as lost as his da did in the old tales, becoming absorbed to the point of deafness.

When she shifted position, curling on her side on the soft cushions, her breasts pushed together above the neckline of her gown and lust quickened within him. Though he'd loved her upon awakening, as he did each morn, he ached anew to bury his face in that lush valley, kiss and lick and nibble till she was panting and crying his name.

The past ten days had passed swiftly, far too swiftly for Dageus's taste. He wanted to halt time, to elongate each day, stretch it to the length of a year. To cram a lifetime into the now, suck it dry of the bittersweet joy of being mated.

Sweet because he had his woman.

Bitter because he had to stay his tongue, and not make promises he burned to speak. Promises that weren't his to give because his future was uncertain. To his immense frustration, he couldn't offer what small truths he possessed either, because Chloe still hadn't asked him about the "curse."

He wanted to tell her. He *needed* to tell her. Needed to know that she knew what he was and could accept it. Thrice he'd tested the waters, once in her dream, once later, while strolling the gardens with her beneath a silvery half-full moon. In her dream, she'd flinched and evaded. In her waking, she'd done the same.

The third time he'd begun speaking of it, she'd tugged his head down and used one of his tactics: She'd silenced him with a kiss and made him forget not only what he was about to say but what century he was in.

It wasn't like him to fail to confront a difficult situation, but he'd reluctantly ceded to her resistance and let it go for the time being.

He had no doubt that, eventually, she would ask. Chloe was nothing if not tenaciously curious. He knew he'd burdened her with a great many new things in a very short time: time-travel, Druids, legendary races, new relics, the demands of his insatiable lusty appetites. She'd proven remarkably resilient. If she needed a bit of time to work her way around to beginning to ask questions again, he certainly couldn't begrudge her the respite.

So for the past ten days, he'd focused instead on the sweet half of bittersweet, drawing succor from her sunny optimism and endless enthusiasm. Each day that passed, he grew ever more fascinated by her. He'd known she was intelligent, strong, and had a true heart, but it was the small things about her that truly enchanted him. The way her eyes went wide and excited whenever Silvan read a choice bit from one of the texts. The way she'd stood hovering above The Compact for half an hour, hands curling, but refusing to touch because she wouldn't risk marring the soft gold with so much as a fingerprint. The way she chased his young half brothers around the hall in the evenings after supper, pretending she was "a wee fierce beastie," until they were shrieking with excitement and mock-fear. The way she teased his cantankerous da, flirting with him in a winsome way, until she succeeded in bringing a blush to his wrinkled cheeks and a smile to his lips, chasing some of the worry from his somber brown eyes.

He was proud of the woman she was, and savagely

possessive of her. He was fiercely glad that he'd been the one to awaken her to intimacy, that he was the one to whom she'd entrusted a small part of her heart.

Aye, he knew he'd touched her heart. She was not a lass who could hide her feelings, she simply didn't possess such guards. Though she'd not said the words, he could see it in her eyes, and feel it in her caress. No woman had ever touched him quite the way she did. At times, it seemed she was touching him with near reverence, as if she was as awed as he was that they meshed so perfectly, two interlocking pieces of wood carved from the same tree.

She had no idea what it did to him to see her dressed in the colors of his clan, strolling through his childhood home. It made him feel all elemental warrior and lover, a man of fierce needs and primitive laws. The only thing that could make it sweeter would be if he, too, could don the Keltar colors again.

But that was a bearable loss. At a time when he'd expected little from life, she'd given him everything, including a reawakening of the wonder and hope he'd so long ago lost. The heathery fields seemed again fertile with burgeoning life. Everywhere he looked, he saw something of beauty: a wee pine marten questing the breeze, a golden eagle soaring overhead, tawny-crowned and majestic, mayhap simply a stately oak he'd walked past a hundred times but not truly seen. The night sky ablaze with stars seemed again full of secrets and miracles.

Chloe was a shaft of sunlight that had lanced through the storm clouds he'd lived beneath for so long, illuming his world.

She'd flung herself wholly and without reservation into their intimacy. She loved to touch, indeed, she seemed to crave it. She was constantly slipping her wee hand into his, or burying them in his hair, grazing his scalp with her nails. Like a wild tomcat who'd had absolute freedom, but known no place to call home, he savored the gentle constancy of the familiar touch of familiar hands.

He'd been right in thinking that with her, lovemaking might yield some indefinable result he'd not before experienced. Sex had always calmed and soothed him, easing his muscles, relaxing his mental tension, but now, when he fell sated, holding Chloe close, his heart was also at ease.

But if his present was a vast and sunny blue sky, his future was filled with the ominous roll of crashing thunderheads.

And he dare not forget that.

He dragged his gaze away from Chloe and inhaled deeply, forcing his thoughts back to less savory matters.

In the past ten days, though he and Silvan had discovered a wealth of long-forgotten information about their clan in the chamber library, and learned more about their purpose as Druids than they'd ever known, they'd still found no mention of the thirteen and scant information concerning their benefactors. Silvan was hoping they might find some way to contact the Tuatha Dé in the old records, but Dageus didn't share his da's optimism on that score. He wasn't convinced the ancient race was even still about. And if they were, why would they bother to appear to a Keltar who'd fallen from grace when they'd not bothered to appear to any other Keltar? He wouldn't be surprised to learn they'd planted their traps in the in-between and gone away thousands of years ago, never to return.

The search was taking too long. In the twenty-first century there'd been a dearth of information, now there was too much, and sifting through it was an epic undertaking.

That wouldn't have fashed him, except he'd recently noticed something that had made him realize time was critical: His eyes were no longer returning to gold, not even with their constant lovemaking. Nay, his eyes were now burnished copper, and darkening further each day.

Though he was using no magic, though he was tooping incessantly, though the ancient ones had not spoken again, the darkness inside him was changing him anyway, in the same manner that wine inevitably soaked into and permeated the cask that held it.

He could feel the thirteen growing stronger, and himself growing more comfortable with them. They'd been a part of him for so long that they were beginning to feel like another appendage—and why wouldn't he use an extra hand? Now, instead of catching himself only a few times a day about to use magic for something simple like filling the bath, he was catching himself a score of times or more.

At least he was still catching himself. He knew that anon he wouldn't. And in even yet more time, he wouldn't care. That fine line he mustn't cross was getting increasingly difficult for him to see clearly.

Rubbing his unshaven jaw, he wondered if it might be possible to strike some kind of deal with the thirteen.

Strike a deal with the devil? his honor hissed. *Like what? They get to use your body part of the time? The devil cheats, you fool!*

Aye, there was that worry. The beings in him were not honorable, could not be trusted. The mere fact that he was considering trying to barter with them proved how critical time had become.

And proved how desperate he was to find a way to secure some kind of future with Chloe.

Sighing, he turned his attention back to the text. Now more than ever, 'twas imperative he exercise utmost discipline. Though he'd far prefer to sweep Chloe into his arms, carry her from the chamber and show her more of his world, live only in the moment, he knew he had to revert to the schedule he'd kept in Manhattan.

Work from dawn till dusk, love Chloe only in the night, then work again whilst she slumbered.

He had his eye on much more than a few moons with his mate. He was determined that he would have his full measure of life with her.

When she got up and slipped from the chamber, he kept his gaze firmly fixed on the tome in his lap.

Chloe strolled blissfully through the gardens, marveling that already a week and a half had sped by. They'd been the finest days of her life.

Her time had been divided primarily between exploring the contents of the chamber library and exploring the newfound pleasure of passion. The explosive heat between her and Dageus was evidently palpable enough that on several occasions Silvan had ordered them to leave the chamber library, telling them dryly "to go . . . walk a wee or . . . some such activity. The two of you are like a pair of tea kettles, steaming up my tomes."

The first time he'd said such a thing, Chloe had blushed furiously, but then Dageus had given her what she'd come to think of as The Look and she'd swiftly forgotten her embarrassment. He had a way of canting his head low and looking up at her, his dark gaze heated and intense, that never failed to make her weak-kneed with desire, thinking about all the things he was going to do to her.

Because she was unable to read a lot of the stuff in the chamber and was insatiably curious about the sixteenth century, while the men had worked, she'd stolen away frequently. She'd thoroughly explored the castle, leaving no part untouched: the buttery, the larders, the kitchens, the chapel, the armory, the garderobes (though scrupulously cleaned daily, those she could have done without), even Silvan's tower library—where she was grateful to discover she could translate some of the more recent works. The elderly man had copies of every philosophical, ethical, mathematical, and cosmological treatise of historical significance on his meticulously organized shelves.

Also during those hours away from Dageus, she'd gotten to know Nell and had met his young half brothers, Ian and Robert, precious dark-haired two-and-a-half-year-old boys with sunny dispositions. She could hardly look at them without thinking what beautiful babies Dageus would make.

And that she'd like to be the one he made them with.

A delicious little shiver raced over her skin at the thought of making a family with him, building a future.

For the past ten days she'd watched him carefully and had concluded that he definitely cared about her. He treated her the same way Drustan had treated Gwen that day at Maggie's castle, anticipating her desires: slipping from the chamber library to fetch her a cup of tea or a snack, or a damp cloth to wipe dust from her cheek. Disappearing into the gardens and returning with an armful of fresh flowers, leading her to bed and covering her naked body with them. Lazily, tenderly bathing her in the evenings before a peat fire, helping her plait her hair like Nell's. She felt treasured, cosseted, and though he didn't say it, loved.

She'd realized, while watching him and reflecting upon all she knew of him, that Dageus MacKeltar would probably never speak of love, unless someone spoke to him about it first. Gwen had essentially told her that much back in the stones.

Dageus doesn't look for love from a woman because he's never been given any reason to.

Well, Chloe Zanders was going to give him the reason to. Tonight. Over a romantic dinner in their bedchamber, which she'd already filled with urns of fresh-cut heather and dozens of oil globes that she'd pilfered from other rooms in the castle.

She'd set the scene, embellishing it with romantic touches, Nell had arranged the menu, and all she had to do was speak her heart.

And if he doesn't say it back? a niggling little doubt tried to surface.

She thrust it firmly away. She would entertain no doubts, no fears. A few days ago, over mugs of cocoa in the kitchens, she and Nell had had a long talk. Nell had openly shared her own experience with Silvan, and had told her about the twelve years they'd wasted. Chloe couldn't imagine loving in silence for so long.

Twelve years! Sheesh, she wasn't going to be able to wait twelve more *hours.*

⁂

When Chloe had been a teenager, not knowing anything about kissing, she'd practiced on a pillow, feeling inordinately silly, but how else was a girl supposed to get a feel for it? She'd read books, and avidly watched movies to see how lips met and where noses went, but it wasn't the same as actually trying to press her lips to something. (Personally, she harbored the firm conviction that there wasn't a person alive anywhere in the world that hadn't practiced kissing on *something.* A mirror, a pillow, the back of their hand.)

Since her first kiss had been reasonably successful, she

decided that practicing saying "I love you," wasn't a completely idiotic idea.

As there weren't exactly a plethora of mirrors around the castle, when she left the gardens, strolled into the great hall and spied the shiny shield hanging on the wall near the hearth, she yielded to impulse, dragged a chair over to it and hopped up, peering at her reflection.

She wanted the moment tonight to be just right. She didn't want to stutter or stammer around.

"I love you," she told the shield softly.

It hadn't come out quite right. It was a good thing she'd decided to practice.

She wet her lips and tried it again. "I love you," she said tenderly.

"I love you," she said firmly.

"I love you," she tried a sexy voice. Reflecting a moment, she decided it was probably better that she just speak normally. She didn't do throaty well.

Saying it felt *good*, she thought, staring at her reflection. She'd been holding it so tightly inside her that she had begun to feel like a pressure-cooker about to blow her lid off. She'd never been able to keep her feelings to herself. It wasn't part of her make-up, any more than casual sex was.

She smiled radiantly at the shield, pretending it was Dageus. The three simple words just didn't seem like enough. Love was so much larger than words.

"I love you, I love you, I love you. I love you more than chocolate. I love you more than the whole world is big." She paused, thinking, searching for a way to explain what she felt. "I love you more than artifacts. I love you so much it makes my toes curl just *thinking* about it."

Pushing her hair back from her face, she donned her most sincere expression. "I *love* you."

"You can have the confounded shield if you love it that much, lass," Dageus said, sounding utterly bewildered.

Chloe felt all the blood drain from her face.

She swallowed hard. Several times. *Oh, God*, she thought dismally, *was it humanly possible to feel any more stupid?*

She shifted awkwardly on the chair, cleared her throat and stared down at the floor, thinking frantically, trying to come up with some excuse for what she'd just been doing. Back rigidly to him, she began to babble. "It's . . . er, not the shield, um, you know. I wasn't really talking to the shield, I just couldn't find a mirror and this is just a little positive reinforcement thingie I do sometimes. I read it in a book somewhere that it boosted self-confidence and . . . er, engendered a general sense of well-being, and it really does work, you should try it sometime," she said brightly.

She realized she was talking with her hands, gesturing a bit wildly, so she clasped them firmly behind her back.

He remained silent behind her, stressing her out completely, and she began babbling again. "What I'm saying is that I really don't want the shield. I mean, I think you've given me more than enough artifacts already, and I couldn't ask for anything else, so if you'll just go away now I'll resume my exercises. It's important that one does them alone."

More silence.

What on *earth* was he thinking? Was he going to burst into laughter? Was he smiling? She peered in the shield, but since she was up on the chair, he was several feet lower than she was and she couldn't see him.

"Dageus?" she said warily, refusing to turn. If she looked at him now, she might start crying. She'd *so* wanted the moment tonight to be tender and romantic, and damn it all, now if she said it to him tonight, he'd *know* she'd been practicing and he'd think she was a total dweeb!

"Aye, lass?" he said finally, slowly.

"Why aren't you going away?" she asked tightly.

A long pause, then a cautious, "If you doona mind, lass, I'd like to watch."

She closed her eyes. Was he making fun of her? "Absolutely not."

"With all the things we've done together, there's something you wouldn't let me watch? I think 'tis a bit late to be getting self-conscious around me," he said. She couldn't decide if she was picking up a hint of lazy amusement in his voice or not.

"Go. A. Way," she gritted.

He didn't. She could *feel* him standing there, his regard an intense pressure on the back of her skull.

"Chloe-lass," he said then, softly. Tenderly. "Turn around, sweet."

He *knew*, she thought, absolutely mortified. Nobody would fall for that pathetic excuse she'd made up.

But this wasn't the moment she'd picked. She'd had it all planned out and he was ruining it for her!

"Chloe," he repeated softly.

"*Oh!*" Something in her suddenly, simply snapped, and she spun about to face him. Plunking her fists at her waist, she shouted, "I love you! Okay? But I didn't want to say it that way, I wanted to say it just *right* and you *ruined* it."

Scowling, she leaped from the chair and stormed from the hall.

· 22 ·

Dageus stood motionless in the great hall.

That had been singularly the most unforgettable moment of his life.

When he was his da's age—in the event he had the luxury of living that long—he had no doubt he'd still be replaying the vision of Chloe perched on that chair before the shield, practicing how to say she loved him, just right.

At first when he'd come abovestairs to fetch fresh candles for the chamber library, and he'd walked into the great hall, what she'd been doing hadn't made sense to him. He'd genuinely thought she was gushing over the artifact.

He teased her, and only then had he noticed the tension and misery emanating from her. She'd begun to babble, which was always a dead giveaway that she was upset. When she'd given him her absurd spiel about positive reinforcement or some such nonsense, he'd realized what she'd really been doing.

Practicing how to tell him she loved him.

How utterly adorable she was.

She loved him. She'd said it. Of course she'd shouted it at him, but a man could deal with that when the woman loved him more than the whole world was big.

He laughed exultantly, turned sharply on his heel, and hurried off to catch her. And to tell her that, since he was bigger, he was fair certain he loved her more.

But it didn't work out quite that way, for he didn't catch her until she was almost to the bedchamber.

And when he caught her, grasping at the billowing skirt of her gown, he tugged harder than he'd meant to and the thin silky fabric ripped. Clear up the back. And she had nothing on beneath it. Only those luscious shapely legs and the round curves of her beautiful behind. The fabric ripped clean to her nape and his thoughts turned instantly primitive and wild.

She glanced back at him, looking shocked, and though he suspected he should assure her he hadn't meant to do that, he couldn't seem to manage a word. Her declaration of love coupled with all that naked rosy skin had rendered him witless.

Growling low in his throat, he scooped her into his arms and planted his mouth firmly over hers.

She was stiff at first, but in a few moments she was kissing him back passionately.

"You didn't have to rip my dress," she said plaintively when he let her breathe. "I love this one. Nellie worked on it for days."

"I'm sorry, lass," he said somberly. " 'Twas an accident,

lass. Sometimes I forget my strength. I mean to be gentle but it doesn't come out that way. Can you forgive me?"

She sighed, but nodded and kissed him again, locking her arms behind his neck as he carried her toward the door of their bedchamber.

"You have, without a doubt, Chloe, the most lovely behind I've ever seen," he purred, shifting her in his arms to splay his big palm over the twin curves of it.

"Oh!" She squirmed in his arms. "I tell you I love you and *that's* what you say?"

He silenced her with another kiss, and kicked open the bedchamber door.

"And I'd love you even if you didn't," he said softly.

She melted in his arms.

"And I think that no man has ever been told he was loved in such a memorable fashion, and I shall always treasure the memory."

She smiled beatifically. "Really? You don't think I'm the biggest geek in the world?"

He tossed her to the bed and slipped a dirk from his boot. "I think," he said silkily, as he gripped the bodice of her ruined gown in his hand and slit it down the front, laying the gown neatly in two halves, "that you are perfect exactly as you are and I wouldn't change one thing about you."

He tossed the torn dress from the bed and tugged his shirt over his head.

She watched him with wide eyes, then laughed. "Nell is *really* going to wonder what happened to my dress."

"I'm fair certain Nellie will never ask," he said huskily, as he stretched his body atop hers. "I've seen a gown or two of hers in the rag heap."

"Really?" Chloe blinked, pondering Silvan in a new light. He was a handsome man, and it *was* from his genes that Dageus and Drustan had come. Behind his scholarly mien, she suddenly realized, Silvan MacKeltar probably concealed a lot of things.

"Aye. Truly."

"You have too many clothes on," Chloe complained breathlessly a few moments later.

He offered her his dirk to cut them off, but she took one look at those snug leather trews and decided there was no way she was letting a sharp blade get near what she knew was inside them.

So she borrowed another of his delicious tactics and undressed him mostly with her mouth.

Chloe was deliriously content. Curled with her backside to Dageus's front, his strong arms wrapped around her, she was blissfully sated.

He loved her. He'd not only told her, he'd shown her with his body. It was there in the way he stroked her cheek or brushed her curls from her eyes. It was there in his long, slow kisses. It was there in the way he held her in the aftermath.

With that resolved, she was impatient to lay all her concerns to rest. With such love between them, she knew they could face anything together.

She squirmed in his embrace, slipping around in his arms to face him. He smiled at her, one of those lazy, melting smiles he gave so rarely, and kissed her.

Sighing with pleasure, and before he could distract her again, she drew her head back, breaking the kiss. "Dageus, I'm ready to know about the curse now. Tell me what it is, and tell me what you're looking for."

He kissed her again, lazily, sucking her lower lip.

"Please," she persisted. "I need to know."

He smiled faintly, then sighed. "I ken it. I've wanted to tell you, but it seemed you needed a bit more time."

"I did. So many things happened so quickly, that I felt like I needed to catch my breath or something. But I'm ready now," she assured him.

He stared at her a long moment, his eyes narrowed. "Lass," he said softly, "if you tried to leave me, I fear I wouldn't let you. I fear I would do whatever I had to do, no matter how ruthless, to keep you."

"I consider myself warned," she said pertly. "Trust me, I'm not going anywhere. Now tell me."

He held her gaze a bit longer, silently assessing her. Then, capturing her hands in his, he twined their fingers together and began.

⁂

"So let me get this straight," a wide-eyed Chloe clarified some time later, "you used the stones to go back in time and—oh! *That's* what that quote in the Midhe Codex meant about the man who takes the bridge that cheats death! The bridge is the *Ban Drochaid*, 'the white bridge,' because you can take it backward in time and undo a person's death. That quote *was* about you."

"Aye, lass."

"So you saved Drustan's life, but because you broke a sacred oath that you'd sworn to the Tuatha Dé, you ended up setting an ancient evil free?"

He nodded warily.

"Well, where is this ancient evil?" she asked, bewildered. "Are you chasing it through the centuries or something?"

He made a sound of dry, dark amusement. "Something like that," he muttered.

"Well?" she prodded.

"Rather, 'tis chasing me," he said, nearly inaudibly.

"I don't understand," Chloe pressed, blinking.

"Why doona you just leave it for now, Chloe? You

know enough to help us search. If, while reading, you find aught about the Tuatha Dé or the Draghar, bring it to my or Silvan's attention."

"Where is this ancient evil, Dageus?" she repeated evenly.

When he tried to turn his face away, she cupped it in her hands and refused to let him look away.

"Tell me. You *promised* to tell me it all. Now tell me where the damned thing is and, more important, how do we destroy it?"

Dark gaze boring into hers, he wet his lips and said softly, " 'Tis inside me."

· 23 ·

Chloe delicately turned a thick vellum page of the tome on her lap, though she was not really reading it, too lost in thought.

'Tis inside me, he'd said, and so many things finally made sense to her. Bits and pieces slid neatly into place, giving her her first real glimpse of the whole man.

He'd told her everything that night, several days ago, as they lay in bed, faces close, fingers laced. About Drustan and Gwen (no wonder Gwen had been trying to brace her!), and about how Drustan had been enchanted and put in the tower. He told her how he'd immersed himself working on Drustan's future home (and now she knew why he'd sounded so proud of the castle), and about the fire in which Drustan had died. He told her about the night he'd warred with himself, then gone into the stones and broken his oath. He told her that he'd not truly believed in the old legends till the ancient evil had descended upon him in the in-between, and it had been too late.

He told her what the use of magic did to him, and how making love helped him. How he'd gone through the stones to the future, to make certain Drustan had indeed been reunited with Gwen, needing to know that his sacrifice hadn't been for naught. And how he'd stayed, unwilling to face his clan as he was, hoping to find a way to save himself.

He told her he'd not worn the plaid of the Keltar since, though he'd not mentioned the scrap she'd found beneath his pillow, so she'd not brought it up either. She knew what it meant. She could picture him lying alone in his bed in his museum of a penthouse, in a world that must have seemed so strange to him, staring at it. It had symbolized all his hopes, that worn piece of cloth.

She'd thought him an idle womanizer when she'd met him, this man who was so much more than that!

Now she understood the sensation she'd had on several occasions of an ancient, evil presence: It had always been when Dageus had recently used magic. She understood how he'd breached such impenetrable security systems: with a bit of supernatural help. She understood the quixotic nature of his eyes: They darkened as he darkened. She had an entirely new appreciation for his discipline and control. She suspected that she'd only glimpsed the tip of the iceberg, and couldn't begin to fathom the battle he was waging every waking moment.

Although he condemned himself for carrying such evil within him, for having freed it to begin with, Chloe couldn't quite see it that way.

Dageus had done what he'd done out of love for his brother. Should he have cheated death in such a fashion? Maybe not. It did seem to go against the natural order of things; still, if the power to do so existed, well . . . was that not then part of the natural order of things? It was an ethically explosive issue, not because of the act itself but because of the potential for a man to abuse such power, to cheat at every turn.

Yet Dageus hadn't cheated again. Since he'd broken his oath he'd become the repository for absolute power, and not once abused it. Instead, he'd devoted every moment of his existence to trying to find a way to lay that power to rest.

What was his actual transgression? Loving so much that he'd risked it all. And heaven help her—she loved him all the more for it.

Surely his intent mitigated his action to some extent? Even in man's court of law, punishment for a crime was meted out in degrees respective of intent.

"It wasn't as if any of you asked for such power," she said irritably.

Silvan and Dageus both glanced up from their texts. Since Dageus had confessed everything two nights ago, they'd spent nearly every waking minute in the dusty chamber, determined to find answers.

"Well you didn't," she seethed. She'd been quietly fuming about for days, and like every other emotion she felt, she could only hold it in so long.

"Verily, m'dear, I doona think man *should* possess the power of the stones," Silvan said softly. "I canna tell you how many times I've wanted to topple them, to destroy the tablets and the formulas."

"Do it," Dageus said intensely. "After we've gone again, do it, Da."

"It would be outright defiance of them, you ken," Silvan pointed out. "And what if the world—"

"The world should have the right to either prosper or destroy itself, by itself," Dageus said quietly.

"I agree with Dageus," Chloe said, reaching for her cup of cooling tea. "I don't think man should have power he's not capable of understanding and discovering himself. I can't help but think that by the time we're evolved enough to fathom how to manipulate time, we'd be wise enough not to do it. Besides, who can really say that any of the times the stones were used, the outcome was better?"

Dageus had explained to her the only conditions under which they were permitted to use the stones: were their line in danger of extinction, or were the world in great peril. He'd told her of the few occasions they'd opened a gate through time: once to relocate sacred, powerful objects belonging to the Templars, in order to whisk them from the grasp of the power-hungry king who'd destroyed their Order. Yet, who could say that, had man been left to his own devices, he wouldn't have found another way that would have served as well?

Dageus met her gaze and they shared a long intimate look. There was such heat in his eyes that she felt it like a sultry caress against her skin. *I doona ken how this may end, Chloe,* he'd said to her that night.

When *it ends,* she'd replied firmly, *it will end with me at your side and we will have freed you.*

I love you, he mouthed to her across the chamber.

Chloe smiled radiantly. She knew that. Knew it more completely than she'd ever thought a woman could know. Since discovering what his "curse" truly was, she'd not wavered in her feelings for him, not for even a moment. What was inside him was *not* him, and she refused to believe it ever would be. A man who could withstand such a thing for so long was a man who was good to the very core. *I love you too,* she shaped the words soundlessly.

They fell silent again, returning to their work with quiet urgency. Though Dageus had not admitted his condition was worsening, both she and Silvan had noticed that his eyes no longer returned to their natural color. They'd discussed it earlier, when Dageus had slipped out to fetch Chloe some tea, and knew what it meant.

They took a brief break when Nell brought the midday meal down into the chamber. Shortly after Nell had cleared the dishes away, Dageus straightened abruptly in his chair. "Och, 'tis about blethering time!"

Chloe's heart began to pound. "What? What did you find?"

"Aye, speak, lad, what is it?" Silvan pressed.

Dageus scanned the page for a moment, translating silently. " 'Tis about the Tuatha Dé. It tells what happened when the thirteen were . . ." He trailed off, reading to himself.

"Read aloud," Silvan growled.

Dageus raised his gaze from the fifth Book of Manannán. "Aye, but give me a moment."

Chloe and Silvan waited breathlessly.

Dageus scanned the page and flipped to the next. "All right," he said finally. "The scribe tells that in the early days of Ireland, the Tuatha Dé Danaan came to the isle 'descending in a mist so thick it dimmed the rising of three suns.' They were possessed of many and great powers. They were not of man's tribe, though they had a similar form. Tall, slender, entrancing to gaze upon—the scribe describes them as 'shining with empyreal radiance'—they were graceful, artistic people who claimed to be seeking no more than a place to live in peace. Mankind proclaimed them gods and tried to worship them as such, but the rulers of the Tuatha Dé forbade such practice. They settled among man, sharing their knowledge and artistry, and so ensued a golden age unlike any before. Learning attained new heights, language became a thing of power and beauty, song and poetry developed the power to heal."

"That much is similar to the myths," Chloe remarked when he paused.

"Aye," Dageus agreed. "As both races seemed to prosper by the union, in time, the Tuatha Dé selected and trained mortals as Druids: as lawgivers, lorekeepers, bards, seers, and advisors to mortal kings. They gifted those Druids with knowledge of the stars and of the universe, of the sacred mathematics and laws that governed nature, even inducting them into certain mysteries of time itself.

"But as time passed, and the Druids watched their otherworldly companions never sickening or aging, envy took root within their mortal hearts. It festered and grew, until one day thirteen of the most powerful Druids presented a list of demands to the Tuatha Dé, including among them, the secret of their longevity.

"They were told man was not yet ready to possess such things."

Rubbing his jaw, Dageus fell silent, translating ahead. Just when Chloe felt like screaming, he began again.

"The Tuatha Dé decided they could no longer remain among mankind. That very eve, they vanished. 'Tis said that for three days after they left, the sun was eclipsed by dark clouds, the oceans lay still upon the shores, and all the fruit in the land withered on the limb.

"In their fury, the thirteen Druids turned to the teachings of an ancient, forbidden god, 'one whose name is best forgotten, hence not scribed herein.' The god to whom the Druids supplicated themselves was a primitive god, spawned in the earliest mists of Gaea. Calling upon those darkest of powers, armed with the knowledge the Tuatha Dé had given them, the Druids attempted to follow the immortal ones, to seize their lore, and steal the secret of eternal life."

"So they really were . . . er, are immortal?" Chloe breathed.

" 'Twould seem so, lass," Dageus said. He skimmed the text again. "Give me a moment, there are no comparable words for some of this." Another long pause. "I think this is the gist of it: What the thirteen did not know is that the realms—I can't think of a better word—within realms are impenetrable by force. Such travel therein is a delicate process of . . . er, sifting or straining time and place. In their attempt to brutalize or coerce a path between the realms, the thirteen Druids nearly tore them all asunder. The Tuatha Dé, sensing the distress in the . . . weaving of the world, returned to avert catastrophe.

"The Tuatha Dé's fury was immense. They scattered their once-friends, now bitter enemies, to the far corners of the earth. They punished the evil ones, the Druids who'd chosen greed over honor, who'd loved power more than they'd valued the sanctity of life—not by killing them—but by locking them into a place between realms, giving them the immortality for which they'd lusted. Eternity in nothingness, without form, without cease."

"By Amergin, would that not be hell?" Silvan breathed.

Chloe nodded with wide eyes.

Dageus made a choking noise. "Och, so *that's* who the Draghar are!"

"Who?" Chloe and Silvan said as one.

He frowned. "The scribe tells that even before the disagreement with the Tuatha Dé, the thirteen Druids had formed a separate, secret sect within the larger numbers of their brethren, with their own talisman and name.

Their symbol was a winged serpent, and they called themselves the Draghar."

It was Chloe's turn to make a strangled sound. "A w-winged serpent?"

Dageus glanced at her. "Aye. Does that mean something to you, lass?" he asked swiftly.

"Dageus, that man who attacked me in your penthouse—didn't you see his tattoo?"

He shook his head. "I saw it, but I didn't get a good look at it. I doona ken what it was."

"It was a winged serpent! I saw it up close when he was on top of me in the kitchen."

"Bletherin' hell," Dageus exploded. "It begins to make sense." He leapt to his feet so abruptly that the Book of Manannán tumbled to the floor. "But . . ." he trailed off. "How could that be?" he muttered, looking baffled.

Chloe was about to ask what made sense and how what could be, when Silvan rose and retrieved the fallen tome. While Dageus paced, muttering beneath his breath, Silvan continued reading where Dageus had left off.

" 'Tis said that some time after the Druids were scattered, and the thirteen locked away in their prison, a small band of those who survived regrouped in an effort to reclaim their lost lore. Och, listen to this: An Order arose, founded upon the divination of a seer who claimed the Draghar would one day, far in the future, return and reclaim the powers the Tuatha Dé had stolen from them. Apparently this seer wrote a detailed prophecy, describing the circumstances under which the ancient ones would return, and the Druid sect of the Draghar was formed to watch and await such events that would signify the prophecy's fruition—" He broke off abruptly, read a few moments in silence, then flipped the page. Then he scanned through the final few remaining sheaves. "That's it. 'Tis all that was written about it." He cursed, skimming and reskimming the subsequent pages. Then he snapped the tome shut and placed it aside.

Chloe's mind was whirling as she watched Dageus pace. She and Silvan exchanged uneasy glances.

Finally Dageus stopped pacing and looked at his father. "Well, that seals it. Chloe and I must return to her century."

"Doona be hasty, lad," Silvan protested. "We need to reflect on this—"

"Nay, Da," he said, his features taut, his gaze dark. " 'Tis evident that the man who attacked Chloe was a member of this Draghar sect. Their prophecy must have guided them to me. From what we just read, 'tis apparent they doona have the power of the stones, so they can't come through time after me. I doona know how to find the sect in this century, but in hers, they know where I am."

"You *want* them to find you?" Silvan exclaimed. "Why?"

"Who else might possess the most detailed information on these beings that inhabit me, than the Druid Order that has preserved their Prophecy all these millennia?" He cast a sweeping glance around the contents of the chamber. "We could waste many moons searching here, to no avail, and I . . . well, let's just say I've a feeling my time is swift being exhausted."

Chloe drew a deep, fortifying breath. "I think he's right, Silvan," she said. "The Keltar have all this lore about the Keltar, it's logical to assume that the Draghar have an equally large collection of works about the Draghar. Besides, you can continue searching here, and pass it forward to us, if you find something. If I understand this time-travel stuff correctly, anything you find would be waiting for us when we get back."

"I doona like this," Silvan said stiffly.

"Da, even if we'd not uncovered this information today, I wouldn't have been able to remain much longer and you know it. In case you've no' noticed, my eyes—"

"We've noticed," Chloe and Silvan said together.

"Then," Dageus said firmly, "you know I've the right of it. If naught else, I must get Chloe back to her time before 'tis too risky for me to use the magic to open the white bridge again. We must go back and best we do so without delay."

They spent their final night in the sixteenth century over a leisurely dinner in the great hall, then passed the remainder of the gloaming on the terrace. Chloe sat on the cobbled stones with Silvan and Nell and watched Dageus playing with his young half brothers, chasing them about the lawn beneath the crimson-streaked sunset.

It was hard to believe they were going back again, Chloe thought, savoring the soft hooting of owls and hum of crickets. She'd missed such peaceful sounds since she'd left Kansas and had thoroughly been enjoying falling asleep each night to such sweet music in the strong arms of her Highlander. It occurred to her that though she'd been in the past for weeks, she'd scarcely gotten to see much of it, other than the castle and one dusty chamber. She'd so wanted to return to the village of Balanoch and explore more, and if she'd had enough time would have begged to go to Edinburgh to really get a good look at the medieval life. She especially rued having to leave Silvan and Nell, knowing she'd never see them again, except in portraits on Maggie's castle walls.

But she understood his insistence that they return immediately, and knew that, even if he'd been willing to stay, she wouldn't have been able to enjoy it. Until they found what they needed to save him, she doubted she'd enjoy much of anything.

"Ye will take care of him, won't ye?" Nell said softly.

Chloe glanced over to find both she and Silvan watching her intently.

She smiled. "I love him. I'll be at his side every step of the way," she vowed firmly. "Doona be getting yerself all in a fankle, Silvan," she added in a teasing lilt, hoping to lighten his somber expression. "I'll take care of your son. I promise." Her gaze skimmed back to Dageus. He was carrying Robert while chasing Ian, and both were squealing with delighted laughter. His dark hair was loose, and his chiseled face fairly blazed with love.

"Believe me, if I have anything to do with it," she added fervently, "I'll be putting my *own* babies in that man's arms."

Nell laughed delightedly. "Now there's a fine lass," she clucked approvingly. Silvan heartily concurred.

· 24 ·

Dageus finished etching the second to last of the for-mulas necessary to open the white bridge. Though they'd spent weeks in the sixteenth century, they would return to a time in the twenty-first century, a mere three days after the day they'd departed. He would etch the final complex series of symbols when they were ready to go.

Outside the circle of towering megaliths, his da and Nell stood with his wee brothers in their arms. He'd long since said his good-byes. Now Chloe was hugging and kissing them, and both her and Nell's eyes were suspiciously bright. How easily, he marveled, women faced those canyons of grief men were wont to venture far and wide in hopes of circumventing. He wondered if women were, in some intangible way, stronger for it.

While Silvan and Nell gave Chloe messages for Drustan and Gwen, Dageus pondered what he'd discovered last eve, after Chloe had fallen asleep. In the wee hours of the morn, he'd crept back down to the chamber library. He was no fool; he knew his canny father had broken off too abruptly when reading the final passage in the fifth Book of Manannán.

And indeed, there it had been. One crucial bit of information Silvan had opted to keep to himself. Dageus didn't need to ask him, to understand why he'd omitted the telling words. Silvan would argue that a prophecy was no more than a foretelling of a "possible" future. However, Dageus knew (and hadn't Drustan's experience with the seer Besseta proved it?) that the future foretold was the most *likely* future, which meant it was going to be damned difficult to avert.

Inscribed in the fifth Book of Manannán, in a slanted majuscule script, had been his most likely future:

> *The thirteen shall be made one, and the world will descend into an epoch of darkness more brutal than mankind has ever known. Unspeakable atrocities will be committed in the Draghar's name. Civilization will fall and ancient evils rise, as the Draghar pursue their unceasing quest for vengeance.*

He would never permit such a future to become reality. Chloe's love had strengthened him and hope burned like a beacon in his heart. Though the darkness was ever growing in him, his resolve and determination had never been stronger.

He glanced at her, drinking her in. For their return, they'd donned the clothing they'd worn in the twenty-first century, and she stood in her slim blue trews and creamy sweater, her tousled curls spilling down her back. Desire quickened in his veins. Anon he would be loving her, and every minute betwixt now and then was a minute too long.

He'd warned her how opening the bridge would affect him.

I won't be . . . quite myself, Chloe. You remember how I was when we came through the first time?

I know, she'd said firmly. *I know what you'll need.*

He'd gritted his teeth. *I may be . . . rough, love.*

I'm tougher than you think. A pause, then those words he would never tire of hearing: *I love you, Dageus. Nothing will change that.*

She was so wee, yet so strong and determined. She was, quite simply, everything he'd ever wanted.

"Son," Silvan's voice shattered his thoughts, "I'd have a word with you before you go."

Dageus nodded and made his way toward Silvan, who led him toward the castle. He'd already said his good-byes to his da, Nell, and his brothers, and was impatient to go, lest someone weep again and tear at his heart.

"When you return, son, you must tell Drustan about the chamber library."

Dageus blinked, perplexed. "But he'll know. We opened it again, and you'll be passing the knowledge to Ian and—"

"I'll be doing no such thing." Silvan said calmly.

"But why?"

"I spent some time last eve pondering the possibilities. If the chamber library is made known to the Keltar, it may affect too many things over the next centuries. It must be forgotten. 'Tis too risky for us to restore such a wealth of knowledge to successive generations and think naught else might change. I plan to seal it this very eve and will no' enter it again."

Dageus nodded, instantly seeing the wisdom of it. "Ever clever, you are, Da. I hadn't thought of it, but you're right. It could indeed cause inestimable changes."

'Twas good, he realized then, that he and Chloe weren't remaining in the past any longer. He could trust his father to tidy up any loose ends, if aught were to be found.

Unable to endure a prolonged leave-taking, he turned back toward Chloe and the stones.

"Son," Silvan said, his voice low and urgent.

Dageus kept his back to him. "Aye?" he said tightly.

There was a long pause. "If I could be there with you, I would. A father should be with his son at such times." He swallowed audibly. "Lad," he said softly, "Give my love to Drustan and Gwen, but know you carry the bulk of it with you." Another pause. "I ken a da shouldn't have favorites, but—och, Dageus, my son, you were always mine."

When, a few moments later, Dageus returned to the center slab and began to etch the final symbols, he noticed Chloe staring at him strangely. Her eyes got misty again and her lower lip quivered a bit.

He didn't understand until she pulled his head down to hers and kissed the tear from his cheek.

Then, as the white bridge opened, she flung herself into his arms, clasped her hands behind his neck and kissed him passionately. He pulled her legs around his waist and held her tightly. It became a battle of wills for him then: It was him against the devastating, shifting, dimensional storm. He felt as if—if he could only make it through the chaos of the white bridge without losing hold of her—he could make it through anything.

He held onto her for all he was worth.

"Oomph!" Chloe gasped as they hit the icy ground, still in each other's arms. A fierce little smile curved her lips—they'd made it without letting go of each other! She didn't know why it seemed so important to her, but it did, as if it somehow proved that *nothing* could ever tear them apart.

A low growl, a rough rumble more animal than human, was the only sound Dageus made as he rolled her beneath him and slanted his mouth hard over hers. His body was rock-hard against the softness of hers, his hips grinding into the cradle of her thighs, and in a heartbeat she was breathless with lust. The man had only to look at her to make her feel weak with desire, but when the hot, thick hardness of him rode between her legs, she became mindless with need. Every single time, her mouth went dry, and she felt shaky from head to toe, anticipating all those delicious things he would do to her. All those ways of touching and tasting, all those very specific demands he made of her that she so loved filling.

She yielded, greedily taking all of him, locking her arms around his strong neck, burying her fingers in his wet hair. They rolled and tumbled across the hail-covered ground as the rain poured down and the wind shrieked deafeningly, numb to all around them but the searing intensity of their passion.

Mouth sealed tightly to hers, his kiss was both dominating and yet utterly seductive, demanding yet coaxing. When he slipped his hands beneath her wet sweater, popped the clasp of her bra and cupped her breasts, she panted against his lips. *There*, she thought dimly, *oh, yes*. He played with her nipples, rolling them between his fingers, tugging lightly, and she could feel her breasts swelling beneath his hands, growing excruciatingly sensitive.

When he drew abruptly away, she cried out, reaching for him, trying to pull him back down on her, but he moved out of her grasp, leaning back on his heels at her feet. Her back arched as she stared up at him, his gaze black in the shimmering moonlight. "Please," she gasped.

He gave her a feral smile. "Please what?"

She told him. In detail.

His black eyes glittering, he laughed as she listed her many and varied requests, and she could see that her boldness was making him recklessly aroused. A month ago, Chloe would never have been able to say such things, but what the hell, she thought, *he'd* made her this way.

His laughter was of short duration. As he listened, desire narrowed his eyes and lust drew his chiseled features taut. He peeled away her jeans and sweater, and stripped off her panties and bra, baring her to his hungry gaze. Then he picked her up and tossed her naked over his shoulder, his big palm possessively roaming over her bare behind. He stalked from the circle of stones, walking with her through the night, deep into the gardens. He stopped at a low stone bench where he deposited her on her feet, ripped open the fly of his jeans and shed them. In a matter of seconds he was gloriously naked.

Then the big, fierce Highlander with wild black eyes who was clearly seething with impatience to be inside her, surprised her by dropping to his knees before her. He planted lazy, open-mouthed kisses on the thin, sensitive skin of her hips, and across her thighs. Gripping her bottom with both hands, he pulled her hips forward, his velvety tongue sliding deep, slipping over her taut bud and deeper still.

Her legs buckled and she cried out his name. He didn't let her go down, but caught her weight, and forced her to remain standing, his dark head between her thighs, his long hair like silk against her skin. Slowly, he turned her in his arms, scattering scorching kisses over every inch of her behind, licking and teasing, his fingers slipping to the wetness between her thighs. Desperate to have him inside her, the minute his grip loosened a bit, she dropped forward to the ground on her hands and knees, and looked invitingly back over her shoulder at him, wetting her lips.

He made a strangled sound, his breath hissing between his teeth. "Och, lass," he chided, "I tried to be gentle."

Then he was on her, covering her with his big, hard body, pushing into her.

"Gentle later," she panted. "Hard and fast now."

As ever, her sexy Highlander was only too willing to oblige.

🙚🙠

Much later, heads close together, hands entwined, they borrowed Maggie's Jeep, and drove back to Drustan and Gwen's castle. There they crept into the back entrance, quiet as mice so as not to wake anyone, where they fell into bed and began the loving all over again.

🙚🙠

It was nearly noon by the time Dageus and Chloe ventured belowstairs, and when they did—much to Drustan's irritation—they went straight to the kitchens, evidently famished. He could hear a passel of McFarleys banging about in there, putting together a late brunch.

Drustan shook his head and resumed pacing in the library, scarcely able to contain his impatience. The elderly McFarley butled in, trying to find something he might bring "his lordship," but the only thing his lordship wanted was his damned brother's attention.

He'd been up since dawn, and already a dozen times this morn he'd stalked toward the stairs, yet each time

Gwen had met him at the bottom and firmly turned him back toward the library.

He'd heard them slip in last eve (as if he'd be able to fall asleep on the night Dageus was to return!) and had begun to rise from bed to go to them then, but Gwen had placed her hand on his arm. *Let them have tonight, love,* she'd said. He'd growled, frustrated, eager to share his news and discover what they'd learned, but then she'd begun kissing him and his mind had stuttered the way it always did when she used that luscious mouth of hers on any part of him. Och, and the parts she'd used it on last eve!

He glanced at her. She was curled on the window seat beneath one of the library's bay windows. Rain pattered lightly against the glass. She'd been reading for the past hour, but now she was staring dreamily out the window. Her skin had the unique translucent radiance of a pregnant woman, her breasts were full and tight, her belly heavily rounded with his—*their*—children. Fierce elation and protectiveness flooded him, accompanied by that never-ending need to be holding her, touching her. As if sensing his gaze on her, she turned from the window and smiled at him. He dropped into an armchair near the fireplace and patted his thigh. "Bring your bonny self over here, wee English."

Her smiled deepened and her eyes sparkled. As she slipped from the window seat, she warned him, "I might squish you."

He snorted. "I doona think there's any danger of that, lass." At but a few inches over five feet, even heavily pregnant, his wife would ne'er be aught but a wee lass in his mind. He pulled her onto his lap and clasped his hands around her, holding her close.

The day was overcast, rainy and chill, a perfect day for a cozy peat fire, and in time, lulled by the combination of the woman in his arms and the comforts of home, he relaxed. He was nearly dozing when Dageus and Chloe finally finished eating and joined them.

Gwen rose from his lap and greetings and hugs were exchanged.

"Silvan and Nell said to give you their love," Chloe told them.

Drustan grinned, noting that Chloe's hair was still slightly damp from her shower. So was his brother's. 'Twas no wonder they'd not come down. Keltar men had a decided penchant for making love in the shower or bath. Indoor plumbing was one of the many luxuries of the twenty-first century that he wasn't sure how he'd lived without. A shower? Delicious. Sex in the shower? Och, life didn't get any better.

Gwen beamed. "Didn't you just love Silvan and Nell? I was so envious that I couldn't go along and see them again."

"Nell gave me a letter for you, Gwen," Chloe said. "It's upstairs. Do you want me to get it now?"

Gwen shook her head. "Drustan might die of impatience if I let you leave the room. We have news—"

"But first," Drustan interjected firmly, "let's hear yours." He studied Dageus carefully. Though his eyes were the color of deeply burnished copper, the outer edges of his irises rimmed with black, there was a sense of peace about him that hadn't been there before. *Och, aye,* Drustan thought, *love could indeed work miracles.* He had no idea how long they'd spent in the past, but it was long enough that they'd fallen head over heels in love. Long enough that they were united as one against the uncertain future.

While Dageus filled them in on what they'd discovered, he listened patiently. When Dageus told him of the chamber library beneath the study in Maggie and

Christopher's castle, he had to grip the arms of his chair to prevent himself from leaping up and racing off to explore it. To touch and read the legendary Compact, to rediscover their lost history.

Finally, it was his turn to tell the news.

"These members of the Druid sect of the Draghar you spoke of," Drustan began.

"Aye?" Dageus encouraged when he paused.

"We have one of them in our dungeon."

Dageus shot to his feet. "How did this come about? Have you questioned him? What did he tell you?" he demanded.

"Easy, brother. He told me all. The base of their Order's operation is in London, in a place called The Belthew Building, on the lower West Side. 'Twas he and his companion that were after Chloe in Manhattan. 'Twas his companion who leaped from your terrace. He followed you here, hoping to get another chance at Chloe. They were trying to provoke you to use magic and force the transformation."

"I'll kill the son of a bitch!" Dageus snarled and began to move toward the door of the library.

"Sit," Chloe said, dashing after him and tugging firmly at his sleeve. "Let's hear the rest of it. You can kill him later."

Bristling with unbridled fury, Dageus refused to move for a moment, then he snorted and followed her back to the sofa. *You can kill him later*, she'd said, almost absently. When he sank back down on the sofa beside her, she snuggled into his arms and patted him like one might soothe a rabid wolf. He shook his head, nonplussed. Sometimes, he mused, it might be nice if she were a *wee* bit intimidated by him.

But not his mate: She feared nothing.

"He admitted"—Drustan smiled with grim satisfaction—"under a bit of duress—"

"Good," Dageus snapped. "I hope 'twas excruciating."

"—that the building is constructed atop a labyrinth of catacombs, and in those crypts is where all their records are kept. So far as he knows, the building is commonly occupied by no more than three or four men, and at night, 'tis most oft but two, deep in the heart of it. The building has a security system, yet I believe 'tis naught to present a challenge to someone with your unique skills, brother," he added dryly. "There are complex passkeys, and much to his dismay, he described to me precisely what we must do to pass them. To the best of his knowledge, they still believe you have no idea they exist, and that you do not know of the Prophecy."

"Perfect. It should be a simple matter to break in late at night and search their records and histories. Did you ask if he knew of a way to get rid of the thirteen?"

Drustan frowned. "Aye. Of a certain, I did. 'Twas one of the first things I asked. He indicated there was a way, but he didn't know what it was. He overheard the Master of their Order, a man called Simon Barton-Drew, express concern that you might discover it. I assure you, I probed him thoroughly, but the man has no idea what the method is."

"Then we need to find this Simon Barton-Drew, and I doona give a damn what harm we must do to him to discover what he knows."

Chloe and Gwen nodded their agreement.

"So, when do we leave?" Gwen asked matter-of-factly.

Dageus and Drustan both skewered her with a glare.

"*We* doona," Dageus said firmly.

"Oh, yes, *we* do," Chloe rebutted immediately.

Dageus scowled. "There is no way we're taking the two of you in there—"

"Then just take us to London with you," Gwen said, managing to sound both soothing yet obdurate. "We'll stay in a hotel nearby, but we will *not* remain here while you two go traipsing off into danger. This is not negotiable."

Drustan shook his head. "Gwen, I willna have you takin' risks with either yourself or our bairn, lass," he said, his burr thickened by tension.

"And you should trust that I wouldn't either," Gwen said levelly. "I'm not going to let anything happen to our babies. Chloe and I will stay in the hotel, Drustan. We're not stupid. I know there's not much a woman as pregnant as I am could do when it comes to stealthily breaking in and searching. But you can't leave us here. If you tried to, we'd only follow you. Take us with you, settle us safely in the hotel. You can't shut us out. We're part of it too. It would drive us both crazy sitting here and waiting."

The debate went on for well over half an hour. But in the end, the women prevailed and the men reluctantly agreed to take them to London the following day.

*

"He's back, Father, as is the woman," Hugh Barton-Drew informed Simon, as he spoke softly into his cell phone. "We saw them return late last night."

"Any idea where they were?" Simon asked.

"None."

"And there's still been no sighting of Trevor?"

"No. But we can't get in the castle. Even if it weren't warded, I'm not certain it would be safe to try," he said quietly. Hushed tones were unnecessary, as far from the castle as he and his brother were, watching through binoculars, but Dageus MacKeltar made him uneasy. This Keltar castle, unlike the other one atop the mountain, was in a vast vale, and the surrounding forest-covered hills provided excellent cover. Still, he felt exposed. His brother had complained of the same sensation.

"Report in to me every two hours. I want to be kept apprised of every move they make," Simon said.

· 25 ·

It was late at night, long after everyone was asleep, that Dageus slipped stealthily from the castle.

The day had seemed to drag on endlessly, while he'd struggled to conceal from those he loved what he was planning. To keep his gaze mild, his impatience in check. It had worn him down, comporting himself as if he were in complete agreement, betraying no telltale sign, however minute, to the brother who knew him too well, that he had no intention of going along with the plan they'd spent the rainy afternoon meticulously formulating.

The plan wherein they would all go to London and *all* be in jeopardy.

During the latter part of the afternoon, while Chloe and Gwen had packed for their trip to London—the trip that was never going to happen—he'd gone down to the dungeon and interrogated the man from the sect of the

Draghar himself. He'd used magic to ruthlessly strip the information from his mind, but as Drustan had assured him, although the man knew there was *some* way to re-imprison the thirteen and prevent the transformation, he did not know the specifics of it.

That a way definitely existed was enough to fill Dageus with a heady exhilaration, and a seething impatience to see it done *now*.

The four of them gathered for dinner in the great hall, and shortly thereafter, he swept Chloe back up to bed, where he made love to her until she collapsed, replete in his arms.

He'd held her then, savoring the feel of her in his arms for nearly another hour before he'd finally left their bed.

And now, as he stepped out into the night, he was ready. It was time to face the enemy and finish things for once and for all.

Alone.

He would never permit any of the people he loved to take this risk with him. 'Twas he who'd created the mess and 'twould be he who fixed it. He was at his best solitary, unencumbered—the Gaulish Ghost again, a sleek, dark wraith, scarce visible to the human eye—with no need to watch over his shoulder to protect someone else.

He hadn't saved Drustan for Gwen once, only to lose one or both of them now. And he would *never* lose Chloe.

He knew they would be furious, but with luck, it would be over before they even awakened, or at worst, shortly thereafter. He needed it this way, needed to know they were safe in the castle, so he could keep his mind focused on his goal with no distractions.

He would penetrate the Draghar sect's headquarters, search their records, locate Simon Barton-Drew's address, hunt him down, and peel from his mind the information he needed. The thought that he might, in a short time, be free of the exhausting battle he'd been waging for so long was hard for him to comprehend. The idea that, by morning, he might be able to return to Chloe, naught more than a Druid and a man, seemed a dream too good to be true.

But it wasn't. According to Trevor—and a mind so ruthlessly violated was incapable of lying—Simon Barton-Drew knew how to return the ancient ones to that prison from whence they'd come.

The flight to London was short, though it took him several frustrating hours to locate The Belthew Building. He'd not been in London before, with the exception of the airport, and it was confusing to him. He stood outside the unlit building for some time, studying it from back, front, and all sides. It was a large warehouse constructed of stone and steel, with four floors, but from what Trevor had confessed, that which he sought would be found belowground.

He took slow, even breaths of the chill, foggy night air. Moving briskly, silently, he approached the building and worked the lock with a softly murmured phrase. That made twice today that he'd used magic, and he dare use it only sparingly henceforth.

Even now the beings within him were stirring. He could sense them reaching out, as if trying to fathom their surroundings.

He opened the door and slipped partly in, punching the code into the keypad. He was prepared; he had lifted all the knowledge he needed from Trevor's mind and committed it to memory. He knew every sequence of numbers, every alarm to circumvent, every passkey.

Stepping across the threshold, he felt a sudden pinching pain in his chest, deep in a ridge of muscle. He shrugged his shoulder, trying to work the kink out, but it didn't go away and, bemused, he glanced down.

For a moment the sight of the silver dart quivering in his chest simply baffled him. Then his vision swam alarmingly and narrowed to a dim tunnel. Blinking, he stared into the dark room.

"A tranquilizer," a cultured voice informed him politely.

A few moments later, cursing viciously, Dageus crashed to the floor.

He roused—he had no idea how long later—to the sensation of cool stone against his back. As his drug-induced stupor receded slowly, he became aware that he was securely restrained.

He felt strange, but was unable to pinpoint exactly what it was. Something was different inside him. Mayhap the lingering effects of the tranquilizer, he decided.

Without opening his eyes, he flexed minutely, testing his bonds. He was chained to a stone column several feet in diameter. Thick-linked chains bound his arms behind him, around the column's circumference. His ankles were chained together as well, bound again to the base of the column. Without calling upon magic, he could move naught but his head.

Keeping his eyes closed, he listened, noting the different voices that spoke over the next few moments, tallying the numbers of his enemy. Half a dozen, no more. Had they not drugged him, they would never have taken him, and if he could get free, he would have no problem escaping. He reached out with his Druid senses, testing the strength of the chains.

Bletherin' hell, he thought darkly. There was a binding spell on them. He poked at it lightly, testing its strength with magic, not wishing to use more than was necessary. But instead of a subtle, directed probing, a sudden, uncontrolled rush of power ripped through him, far more than he'd meant to use, more than he'd ever used at a single time before. He felt the instant response of the thirteen; they began murmuring in their incomprehensible language, their voices buzzing like insects inside his skull. He was bombarded with sensations. . . .

Icy darkness. Endless stretches of bickering amongst themselves. Enforced eternal togetherness with no escape. Periods of lucidity, longer periods of madness, until finally there was nothing left but rage and hatred and an all-consuming thirst for vengeance.

His whole body shuddered. 'Twas the strongest taste of them he'd gotten yet and it was so revolting that, had his hands been free, he suspected he would have clawed at his head in a futile effort to gouge them out of his skull.

He realized two things then: the sect of the Draghar was more advanced in Druidry than he'd thought, to weave such a powerful spell into cold iron, and they'd given him something besides a mere tranquilizer. They'd given him some kind of drug that was impairing his ability to control the power within him. He was like a man who'd consumed too much whisky, who could, intending a gentle caress, lash out with a killing blow, out of sheer sloppiness.

And he had no doubt that such a blow would turn him fully dark.

He inhaled shallowly, forcing his senses outward, away from the chaotic buzzing in his mind. He tasted the air, trying to envision the shape of the room from the echo of conversation. It seemed to be low-ceilinged, and long, and there was a faint odor of moss on stone. He had no idea how long he'd been unconscious. He was fair certain he was in the catacombs beneath the building.

What a fool he'd been, barging in, underestimating his foe! He'd acted rashly, driven by impatience and a desper-

ate need to protect those he loved. Not once had it occurred to him that the sect of the Draghar might have
people watching him, reporting his every move. Apparently they had, for they'd certainly been ready for him.
What was their plan? To use this deadly drug to force his
transformation?

"He's coming around," someone said.

He would have preferred they continue to think him
unconscious, buying precious time for the effects of the
drug to diminish, but evidently, though he'd remained
motionless, he'd given himself away somehow. Mayhap
his chest was rising and falling more deeply. He opened
his eyes.

"Ah, there you are," a tall, lean man with salt-and-
pepper hair said, moving to stand before him. The man
looked at him for a long moment. "I'm Simon Barton-
Drew, master of the sect. This isn't quite how I'd hoped
to meet you. My apologies for the restraints but, for the
time being, they are necessary. I assume Trevor is dead?"
he inquired politely.

"Trevor lives," Dageus said, modulating his voice carefully. He would betray no sign of his inner conflict to the
man. "Unlike your Order, the Keltar do not take life without cause." No matter how much he would have liked to.

Simon circled the stone column. "Nor do we. All
we've done was necessary to serve the purpose of restor-
ing our rightful powers. To fulfill our destiny."

"They were never your rightful powers. They were
given by the Tuatha Dé and they were the Tuatha Dé's to
reclaim when it became evident man would abuse
them."

Simon gave a short bark of laughter. "Thus speaks the
man who broke his own oaths. See it as you wish. No
matter, you will lead us."

"I will never fulfill the Prophecy."

"Ah, so you know of it. I wondered if you did. When did you find out? Did Trevor tell you? Not that I blame him, for I know what you're capable of. It's all here." He swept an arm behind him, at piles of manuscripts and texts stacked carefully on dozens of shelves. "All that the Draghar can do. All they will teach us. The power to move through space and time, the power to open the realms."

"The Draghar you worship nearly destroyed the world once, trying to open the realms. What makes you think that once they're free, they won't again?"

"Why destroy the world when they can rule it?" Simon countered. "I believe we can determine what went wrong the last time they tried to go after the Tuatha Dé. Our world is far more advanced now than it was then. And there are so many faithful followers waiting to welcome them."

"What makes you think they have any intention of becoming part of your little Order? Why would they remain with *you*?" Dageus goaded.

"What do you mean?" The briefest flicker of unease flashed across the man's lean face.

"If they can travel through time, what is there to prevent them from returning to their own century? What do you think they want more than anything?"

"To reclaim their power. A chance to live again, to rule again. To take their rightful place in the world."

Dageus *tsk*ed mockingly. Though he couldn't understand their language and didn't know what the Draghar's intentions were, Simon didn't know that. Sowing doubts could be a useful weapon. If he could keep him talking long enough, mayhap enough of the drug's effects would pass that he could risk probing Simon's mind. "They want *bodies*, Simon, and they will have the power to return to their own. Once you release them, how will you stop them from going back? You won't be able to control them. They may destroy your Order the moment I change. What use have they for you? They'll return to their century, keep the war from happening, and utterly rewrite the past four thousand years of history." Dageus laughed. "Like as not, none of us will ever even be born by the time they're done changing things."

Och, aye, the men in the room looked decidedly uneasy. Uneasy was good. Violent dissension would be even better.

"You'll be releasing a power that you can't possibly begin to understand and have no hope of mastering." Dageus gave him a chilling smile.

After a tense silence, Simon waved a dismissive hand. "Enough. I am not going to fall for your ruse. The Draghar would not try to return because they would run the risk of being imprisoned again. They will never risk that."

"So you say, when in truth, you know nothing about them. *I* do."

Simon's jaw set and he motioned to two of the men standing nearby. "I will not be swayed from the course of the Prophecy. It is my sworn duty to fulfill it. And I may not know as much about the Draghar as I'd like, but I do know much about you." He glanced at the men. "Bring her," he ordered.

The men hastened from the chamber.

Dageus went rigid. Her—*who*? he nearly roared. There was no way, he told himself. Chloe was safe and sleeping within the castle's warded walls.

He was so very wrong.

When they returned a few moments later, his gut clenched. "Nay," he whispered, lips scarce moving. "Och, nay, lass."

"Och, aye, Keltar," Simon mocked. "A lovely woman,

isn't she? We tried to get to her in Manhattan. But fear not, you may have all of her you want once you've yielded to the inevitable. I suspect the Draghar will be hungry for a woman after four thousand years."

The men roughly half-dragged, half-carried Chloe forward. Her hands and feet were bound and her face ashen, streaked with tears.

"I'm so sorry, Dageus," she gasped. "I woke up when I heard the car door slam and ran outside, trying to catch you—"

One of the men cuffed her into silence, and every muscle in Dageus's body screamed. He closed his eyes, fighting the dark storm rising in him. *I am a man and a Keltar. I will not lash out blindly*, he told himself over and again. It was several moments before he managed to open them again and when he did, their gazes locked.

I love you, she mouthed. *I'm so sorry!*

He shook his head, rejecting her apology, hoping she understood that he was saying no apology was necessary. It was his fault, not hers. *I love you too, lass*, he shaped the words silently.

"How touching," Simon said dryly. He motioned the men holding Chloe to bring her forward, stopping them half a dozen paces from the column to which Dageus was bound. "Having a private plane has its uses," he said, smiling. "She was here before you'd even landed in London. And now my men will kill her unless you'd care to prevent it. Being bound should present no obstacle for a man with such power."

"You son of a bitch." Dageus strained violently against the chains, but to no avail. Without magic, he wasn't going anywhere.

Rage consumed him, accompanied by the fierce temptation to use the most horrific power at his disposal. He could taste the potency of the ancient ones, piling up in the back of his throat, begging to be freed. The words that brought death coiled on the tip of his tongue. He wanted blood, and the beings inside him were lusting to spill it.

Simon had planned his strategy well. He'd drugged Dageus so he wouldn't be able to control the amount of magic he used, taken captive the woman Dageus loved more than life itself, and was now going to kill her, unless Dageus used magic to prevent it.

And if he used magic to save her, he would transform.

It was inevitable, he realized with a peculiar detachment. This was it. He was backed into a corner with no way out. There was no way he would permit Chloe to be harmed. Ever. She was his mate, she held his *Selvar*. His life was her shield.

For a split second, a curiously suspended instant in time, it was as if he were there in the catacombs, yet not there. His mind slipped to a quiet place where memories flashed in swift conjunction.

He was seeing Chloe for the first time, standing in the misting rain on a bustling street in Manhattan. He was discovering her beneath his bed. He was feeling the lushness of her lips when he'd stolen that first kiss.

He was feeding her bites of salmon. Listening to her haver incessantly away about some obscure tome, her eyes sparkling. Watching her puff on a fat cigar.

He was seeing her sleepy-sexy eyes when he'd brought her to her first peak on the airplane. Making love to her in a sparkling pool beneath an endless blue sky in his beloved Highlands. Spilling inside her, becoming part of her. Watching, as she perched on a chair and practiced saying that she loved him to a shield, then turning to shout it at him. Saying it again, after he'd told her his darkest secret. Remaining steadfastly at his side.

And in that strange quiet moment, he realized that had he not broken his oath, had he not gone through the stones to save Drustan, he would never have met Chloe. Ironic, he mused, that his fate had required his own fall to lead him to the woman who'd been his salvation in so many ways. Had he been given the choice, to go back in time and choose not to break his oath and never meet Chloe Zanders, he would have resolutely walked into the stones and done it all over again, with full awareness that it would lead to this moment.

Simply to have the joy of loving Chloe for what time he'd had.

From that quiet place, his mind glided swiftly to another: to the bitterly cold night he'd danced upon his ice-slicked terrace wall. He'd done it because he'd always known that he could end it all by dying. Simple solution, really. No vessel—no resurrection. Mate, endgame, and match.

A part of him had been so weary of fighting.

But he'd resolved that eve to continue fighting, and relegated thoughts of suicide to his arsenal of the last resort, loathing the notion of it.

Then he'd met Chloe, who'd given him a thousand reasons to live.

He smiled bitterly. He couldn't call forth the magic necessary to free her and see her safe without also releasing the Draghar, which put him in an impossible position.

He would never usher in that "epoch of darkness more brutal than mankind has ever known," of which the Prophecy foretold. There was no telling how many millions might die. What if those words he'd taunted Simon with truly were what the thirteen planned to do? What if they *did* intend to go back in time? Mayhap fight the war all over again? Mayhap win this time?

It would utterly change four thousand years of mankind's history. Man might no longer even exist in present times by the time they were done.

Nay. His choices, his chances, had all been exhausted. *Och, love,* he grieved, *it wasn't supposed to end this way.*

When he opened his eyes, it was to discover that they'd stuffed a gag in Chloe's mouth. Her aquamarine eyes sparkled with tears.

"Cut her," Simon said softly. "Show him her blood."

Dageus bit down on his tongue, filling his mouth with a bitter metallic taste. He knew he had to time it to perfection. He had to make certain he inflicted a sufficiently mortal wound on himself that he would die before the transformation was complete, but not before the sect members were dead and Chloe was free. He steeled himself to act with flawless resolution. A single moment of hesitation could undo him. He had to be one hundred percent committed to dying.

And that was a damned hard thing to be when looking at Chloe.

One of the men drew a blade over the skin of her neck, and crimson droplets welled. Chloe writhed in their arms, bucking and struggling.

Now, he told himself, even as he whispered a soft "good-bye" to his mate. Grief flooded him so acutely, so intensely, that he tossed his head back and howled from the very depths of his soul.

Then, for the first time since the eve they'd claimed possession of him, he dropped his guard and stopped resisting the thirteen.

He opened himself up to them. He invited them. He embraced them.

The response was instantaneous. Power, cunning, and madness flooded him. He was suddenly bombarded with bits and pieces of thirteen lives, filled with the phenomenal force of twelve men and one woman whose lust for life had been so intense that they'd wanted to live forever. But far surpassing any sense of them as individuals was

their united rage and hatred of their gaolers, a driving incessant determination to see the Tuatha Dé destroyed,
even if they had to destroy *all* the realms in the process.

As they swarmed into him, he ripped into Simon's
mind, brutally probing. Though the answer would be of
no use to him now, he still wanted to know. He wanted to
know how things might have played out differently, had
he acted less rashly, been wiser.

The answer he discovered made him laugh. The irony
of it was rich: he'd come tonight with so much hope, yet
now knew that, even had Chloe not been taken, this had
always been his only alternative.

Simon indeed knew the way to reimprison the thirteen.
Dageus had to die.

⬥

Chloe struggled in her assailants' arms, blinking back
tears. She'd been such an idiot, running out of the castle,
but damn him for trying to do it alone! How was she to
know men would jump on her the moment she walked
outside? She'd not even gotten the opportunity to scream
and warn Drustan and Gwen that she was being taken.

She chewed desperately on her gag, but it was no use,
she couldn't make so much as a whimper. *Oh, Dageus*, she
thought helplessly, watching him. He looked at her and
his lips moved, but she couldn't make out what he'd said.

Then suddenly he made a sound of raw agony, and his
dark head slammed back into the stone column with
such force that Chloe nearly stopped breathing, screaming silently inside. His neck arched, and his body strained
as if he were being pulled on a rack.

The man called Simon cried out and collapsed to the
floor, clutching his head.

Dageus laughed, and the sound chilled Chloe's blood.
Dageus had never—*would* never—make such a twisted

dark sound. Shaking violently, she watched as his head tipped slowly down. When she saw his eyes, she choked on the gag.

They were almost full black.

A tiny sliver of white rimmed them, hardly there at all. She ceased struggling, frozen by horror.

An icy gale rushed into the chamber, scattering books from the shelves, toppling tables and chairs, whipping sheets of paper and parchment through the air.

Suddenly the two men holding her were gone. The knife at her neck shot away through the air, and she lost sight of it amid the flying debris. The ropes at her wrists and ankles snapped, and the gag was abruptly torn from her mouth.

As if from a far distance, she heard Dageus's voice—but not quite his voice, it was more like dozens of voices layered upon each other—telling her to close her eyes, telling her that she would see and hear *nothing* till he commanded otherwise. And she knew that he'd done something to her, used some magic on her, because suddenly she was blind and deaf. Panicked by the loss of her senses, she dropped to the floor and held very still.

That time of sightless silence seemed to go on for an eternity. The only sensation left to her was feeling the chilling caress of that bitter, dark wind.

She huddled on the floor, refusing to contemplate what might be going on. Refusing to believe what she thought she'd seen before all hell had broken loose. She knew Dageus; he would never do such a thing. Not even for her. He was too honorable at the core. He would *never* choose her life over the fate of the world.

Then why had it looked like he was becoming the Draghar?

· 26 ·

Silence was all Chloe heard when she could hear again, though it wasn't exactly silence, for, in contrast to the utter vacuum of deafness, silence was a mishmash of white noise: the faint hum of fluorescent lighting, the soft push of air from dehumidifiers installed to protect the ancient texts. She'd never been so grateful for such simple, comforting sounds in her life. It had been terrifying to be stripped of the ability to both see and hear.

But she still couldn't see, and she suffered another moment of absolute panic before realizing that her eyes were closed. Opening them, she pushed herself shakily up from the floor into a sitting position. Her gaze flew to the stone column, but Dageus was no longer chained to it. Frantically, she skimmed the room.

Once, twice, three times she looked through the wreckage.

And jerked her head in abject denial.

There was blood all over the place. Puddles of it. Still more sprayed across the tables and chairs, and the chaos of books and papers on the floor.

Yet more blood on the stone column.

And there wasn't a single other person—not even a body—in the room with her.

Time is a companion that goes with us
on a journey.
It reminds us to cherish each moment,
because it will never come again.
What we leave behind is not as important as
how we have lived.

—JEAN LUC PICARD, captain of the *Enterprise*

· 27 ·

"I don't want you to go," Gwen said for what Chloe was certain must be the hundredth time. "*Please*, stay with us, Chloe."

Chloe shook her head wearily. Over the past two weeks, she and Gwen had grown close, which both soothed and chafed, for it made Chloe think about how incredible her life could have been if things had worked out differently. She had no doubt that she and Dageus would have gotten married, remained in Scotland, and bought a house near Gwen and Drustan. She and Gwen were similar in many ways, and in time Gwen would have become the sister she'd never had.

What a perfect, blissful dream that would have been! Living in the Highlands, surrounded by family, married to the man she loved.

But everything had gone so *damn* wrong and those

things would never be, and her growing affection for the brilliant, nurturing woman who'd stayed tirelessly at her side since that terrible night, had begun to hurt more than it helped.

"I've stayed as long as I can, Gwen," Chloe said, continuing her grimly determined march toward the security gate. They were in the airport, and she was desperate to be in the air, to escape so many painful reminders. If she didn't get out of there soon, she was afraid she might start screaming and just never stop. She couldn't look at Drustan one more time. Couldn't bear being in the castle Dageus had built.

Couldn't bear being in Scotland without him even one more second.

It had been two weeks since the horrible night that she'd been awakened by the sound of a car door slamming. Two weeks since she'd run outside after him, only to be taken hostage by sect members who'd been waiting for just such an opportunity.

Two weeks since she'd fled, sobbing, from the heart of the catacombs, and stumbled out of The Belthew Building to call Gwen and Drustan from a pay phone.

Two weeks since they'd joined her in London and searched every inch of the damned building.

At first, when Gwen and Drustan had taken her back to Castle Keltar, she'd been in shock, incapable of talking. She'd huddled in a darkened bedchamber, dimly aware that they were hovering nearby. Eventually, she'd managed to tell them what had happened—the part of it she'd seen—then she'd curled in bed, replaying it over and over in her mind, trying to fathom what had *really* transpired.

Realizing that they would never know for sure.

All they knew for certain was that Dageus was gone.

For two weeks, Chloe lived in a kind of excruciating suspension, a bundle of tension and grief . . . and treacherous hope. It wasn't as if she'd actually *seen* his dead body. So, maybe . . .

So, nothing.

Two weeks of waiting, praying, hoping against hope.

And each day of watching Gwen and Drustan together had been the purest kind of hell. Drustan touched Gwen with Dageus's hands. He lowered Dageus's face to kiss her. He spoke with Dageus's deep, sexy voice.

And he wasn't Dageus. He wasn't hers to hold, though he looked like he should be. He was Gwen's, and Gwen was pregnant, and Chloe wasn't. She knew, because Gwen had persuaded her to take an EPT a few days ago, arguing that if she tested positive it would give her something to hold onto. Unfortunately, she hadn't gotten the cheery news Gwen had gotten seven months ago.

Her test result had been negative.

Like her life. A great big fat negative.

"I don't think you should be alone," Gwen protested.

She tried to smile reassuringly, but from the look on Gwen's face, she suspected she'd managed only a frightening baring of teeth. "I'll be okay, Gwen. I can't stay here any longer. I can't stand seeing . . ." She trailed off, not wanting to hurt Gwen's feelings.

"I understand," Gwen said, wincing. She'd felt much the same when she'd thought Drustan was forever lost to her, and had met his descendants. She could only imagine what Chloe must feel each time she looked at Dageus's twin. And Chloe didn't have the promise of his babies to cling to as she'd had.

The worst of it was, there were no answers. Dageus was simply gone. Gwen had clung to hope too, in those first few days, until Drustan had confided that since the night his brother had disappeared he'd not been able to feel the unique twin-bond he and Dageus had always shared.

They'd decided not to tell Chloe that just yet. Gwen still wasn't sure they'd made the right decision. She knew a part of Chloe was still hoping.

"We'll be coming to Manhattan in a few weeks, Chloe," Gwen told her, hugging her tightly. They clung to each other for a time, then Chloe tore herself away and practically ran to the security gate, as if she couldn't get out of Scotland fast enough.

Gwen wept for her as she watched her go.

⁂

The Maybe Game, Chloe swiftly came to realize, was the cruelest game of all, far worse than the What-Might-Have-Been Game.

The Maybe Game was parents who left for dinner and a movie and never came home again. The Maybe Game was a closed-casket funeral and a four-year old's imagination when confronted with sleek, glossy boxes and the attendant, bewildering rituals of death.

The Maybe Game was an empty *freaking* room full of blood and no answers.

Maybe Dageus had used the power of the Draghar to free her, to kill the sect members, and magically transport their bodies elsewhere so she wouldn't be confronted with the horror, where he'd then killed himself to make certain the Prophecy would never be fulfilled.

That was what Drustan believed. And deep down inside her heart, that was what Chloe believed as well. In her heart, she knew Dageus would never risk freeing the ancient evil to walk the earth again. Not even for her. It had nothing to do with love. It had everything to do with the fate and future of the entire world.

She'd endlessly replayed in her mind that moment when the knife had whipped away from her neck and gone hurtling through the air.

It had gone in his direction.

But *maybe*, another insidious little voice kept insisting, he and the sect of the Draghar had vanished one another . . . er, inadvertently, and . . . they would all come back. Eventually. Stranger things could happen. Stranger things happened on *Buffy* all the time. Maybe they were locked somewhere in mortal combat or something.

Maybe, her mind tortured her, *he's still alive somewhere, somehow*. That was the most excruciating maybe of all.

How many years had she believed that her parents would one day walk through the front door again? When Grandda had come to take her to Kansas, she'd been terrified to go. She still remembered shrieking at him that she couldn't leave because *when Mommy and Daddy come home they won't know where to find me!*

For years she'd clung to that agonizing hope, until she'd finally been old enough to understand what death was.

"Oh, Zanders," she whispered. "You can't play the Maybe Game. You know what it does to you."

❧

She had no idea how many days she huddled in her tiny apartment, completely withdrawing from the world. She didn't answer the phone, she didn't check her E-mail or mail, she rarely even stirred from bed. She passed her time mentally reliving every precious moment she and Dageus had spent together.

She'd had the most incredible month of her life, she'd met the man of her dreams and fallen head over heels in love. She'd had the promise of a blissful future. She'd held everything that she'd ever wanted right there in the palms of her hands, and now she had nothing.

How was she supposed to go on? How was she supposed to face the world? To get dressed, to maybe brush her hair, to go out on the sidewalk and see lovers talking and laughing with each other?

Impossible.

And so the days crept by in a bleak fog until one morning she woke up obsessed with wanting the artifacts he'd given her, in her apartment. Needing to hold the *skean dhu*, to wrap her fingers around it in the same places his had once rested.

Which meant leaving her apartment. She tried to think of some other way to get them, but there was none. Only she could access the safety deposit box.

Numbly, she dragged herself to the shower, got sort of wet, then sort of dry, then stumbled to the suitcase she still hadn't unpacked. She tugged on rumpled clothes that may or may not have matched—frankly, she didn't care, at least she wasn't naked and wouldn't get arrested, which would have forced her to speak to people, something she had no desire to do—and took a cab to the bank.

Within a short time she was ushered into a private room with her safety deposit box. She looked at it for a long while, just standing and staring, trying to summon the immense energy necessary to root around in her purse for her wallet. Eventually, she rummaged about for the key and unlocked the long metal box.

She opened it, and froze, staring. Atop her short sword, *skean dhu*, Keltar brooch, and intricately etched first-century arm band, lay an envelope with her name on it.

In Dageus's handwriting.

She closed her eyes, frantically shutting the sight of it out. She hadn't been prepared for that! Merely seeing his handwriting made her heart feel as if it were breaking all over again.

She took several slow, deep breaths, trying to calm herself.

Opening her eyes, she reached for the envelope with trembling hands. What on earth might he have written to her so many weeks ago? They'd only known each other five days before she'd left for Scotland with him!

She untucked the flap and withdrew a single sheet of paper.

Chloe-lass:

If I'm not here with you now, I'm beyond this life, for 'tis the only way I'll ever let you go.

She flinched, her whole body jerking. Several long moments passed before she managed to force herself to keep reading.

I hoped I loved you well, sweet, for I know even now that you are my brightest shining star. I knew it the moment I saw you.

Ah, lass, you so adore your artifacts.
This thief covets but one priceless treasure: You.

Dageus

She squeezed her eyes shut as fresh pain lanced through her. The knot in her throat swelled, the burning behind her eyes grew excruciating—yet, still, she refused to cry. There was a perfectly good reason that she hadn't cried since the night he'd disappeared. She knew that if she cried, it would mean he was really gone.

Which also seemed to imply, in perhaps a less than logical way, that as long as she didn't cry, there was hope.

Oh, God, she could picture him! She could see them both, standing in the bank that day. He was tall, dark, and too gorgeous for words. She was so excited, so thrilled and nervous. So fascinated by him.

So distrustful, too, of the dastardly, impossibly sexy Gaulish Ghost. She'd watched every move he made, to be certain he *really* put her precious artifacts in the box before he locked it and gave her the key.

Still, he'd managed to slip the letter in at the last moment without her seeing it.

Even then. He'd wanted her even then. He'd said, even then, that he would never let her go.

"Ma'am?" a brisk voice interrupted. "My apologies for disturbing you, but they just informed me that you'd arrived. Is Mr. MacKeltar with you?"

Chloe opened her eyes slowly. The bank manager was standing in the doorway. She wasn't ready to talk to anyone yet, so she shook her head.

"Well, then, he asked me to give you this, should you come to collect the contents of the box without him." He handed her a set of keys. "He said he wanted you to have"—he shrugged, regarding her with open curiosity—"whatever it is these keys open. He said it was paid for, and if you didn't wish to retain ownership, you could sell it. He expressed his conviction that it would keep you quite comfortably for the rest of your life." He scrutinized her intently. "Mr. MacKeltar has fairly sizeable accounts in our bank. Might I inquire as to his intentions about those?"

Chloe took the keys with a trembling hand. They were the keys to his penthouse. She shrugged, to indicate that she had no idea.

"Are you all right, ma'am? You look pale. Are you feeling sick? Could I get you a glass of water or a soft drink or something?"

Chloe shook her head again. She tucked the letter in her pocket and slipped the carefully wrapped *skean dhu* in her purse. The rest of the artifacts she would leave in the bank until she had what she felt was a safe place to keep them.

They would *never* be sold. She would not part with so much as one precious memory.

She eyed the keys, feeling strangely numb. How carefully he'd planned, how far ahead he'd been looking, even then. Leaving her his penthouse, as if she could ever bear to live there. Or sell it. Or even think about it.

"Ma'am, I've noticed that we have no next of kin listed in Mr. MacKeltar's files—"

"Oh, hush, just hush, would you?" Chloe finally managed, pushing past him. She was dying inside, and all he cared about was whether his bank might lose Dageus's money. It was more than she could stand. She left both box and bank manager without a backward glance.

She wandered the city for a time, pushing blindly through the masses of people, with no concept of where she was walking. Head down, she walked while the sun passed the noon hour, descended behind the skyscrapers, and slipped to the horizon.

She walked until she was too exhausted to take another step, then she slumped down on a bench. She couldn't bear the thought of going back to her apartment, she couldn't bear the thought of going to Dageus's penthouse. She couldn't bear the thought of being anywhere, or even *being* for that matter.

Yet . . . she mused, perhaps it would help. Perhaps

merely being surrounded by his things, smelling him on his pillows again, touching his clothes—

Would be agonizing.

At complete odds with herself, she got up and began walking aimlessly again.

Night had fallen and a full moon graced the sky by the time Chloe found herself entering the elegant foyer of Dageus's building. She hadn't exactly made the decision to go there, she'd simply walked until her feet had taken her someplace.

So, she thought dismally, *here I am. Ready or not.*

She trudged past the security desk, numbly waving the keys at them. They shrugged—they really *should* be fired—she thought as she keyed the elevator to the forty-third floor.

When she stepped into the anteroom, her legs got shaky and, in her mind, she was reliving it all over again. The first day she'd stood at his door, clutching the third Book of Manannán, calling the man she was to deliver it to every nasty name she could think of. Worrying that some bimbo might damage the tome. Scoffing over the gold hinges. Entering his home and seeing the claymore hanging above the fireplace—the artifact that had lured her to her destiny.

Getting caught beneath his bed. Pretending to be a French maid.

Being kissed by him that first time.

Oh, what she wouldn't give to be able to go back in time and live it all over again! She'd settle for any *one* of those days. And if she had it to do all over again, she'd never resist his seduction. She'd drink greedily of each moment.

But such a wish was futile. Neither she nor anyone else was ever going back in time again.

Drustan had told her that the night Dageus had disappeared, he'd felt the bridge in the circle of stones go dead. He'd said it was as if an energy he'd sensed all his life was simply gone. The next day, he and Christopher had discovered that the tablets that held the sacred formulas were also gone, as was their recall of the ones they'd committed to memory as part of their training.

Whatever Dageus had done that night, he'd accomplished one thing he'd wanted. The Keltar no longer bore the duty of guarding the secret of time travel. They were finally free of the immense responsibility and the temptation. Able, at last, to live simpler lives.

How Dageus would have loved that, she thought with a sad smile. He'd wanted nothing more than to be a simple man. To wear his clan colors again. And though he'd never said it, she known he'd wanted children. Wanted his own family as much as she had.

How could life have cheated me like this? she wanted to scream.

Steeling herself for the onslaught of yet more painful memories, she unlocked the door (wonder of wonders, he'd actually locked it when they'd left) and pushed it open. She went straight to the fireplace and ran her fingers over the cool metal of the claymore.

She had no idea how long she stood there in the dark, bathed only by the faint light of the full moon spilling in the wall of windows, but eventually, she tossed her purse to the floor, and dropped down on the sofa.

Later, she would brave the rest of his penthouse. Later, she would drag herself up to his magnificent bed and fall asleep, wrapped up in the scent of him.

Chloe-lass: If I'm not here with you now, I'm beyond this life, for 'tis the only way I'll ever let you go.

And there it was. He'd said it himself in the letter he'd left her.

Chloe made a small, helpless choking sound.

And finally the tears came in a hot rush. He was dead. He was really, truly gone.

She curled into a tight knot on the sofa and wept.

· 28 ·

Chloe was awakened some time later by an unfamiliar, persistent noise. It took her several moments to pinpoint the source, to understand that the scrabbling sound was coming from the door of the penthouse.

Rubbing her eyes, she pushed herself into a sitting position on the sofa. She'd cried herself to sleep and her eyes were swollen, her face crusty with tears. She peered into the darkness toward the door and listened intently.

Oh, God, she thought, horrified, it sounded like someone was trying to break in!

She listened a few more moments. Yes, that *was* it. She could hear the metallic grating as someone tried to pick the lock. She counted her blessings that she'd bestirred herself from grief enough to flip the inner lock when she'd come in.

Oh, for heaven's sake, she thought, suddenly exasperated,

what is this? My year of misery? Is every bad thing that could possibly happen to me, going to?

She was not going to be victimized again. Period. Chloe Zanders had had entirely enough. There was only so much a girl could tolerate. She was suddenly dangerously furious at whoever was outside that door, daring to mess up her life even further.

How dare anyone give her more grief?

Dimly aware that she might not be acting quite rationally, but beyond caring, she slipped from the sofa, snatched the claymore from the prongs above the hearth and crept toward the door.

She briefly contemplated pounding on it, in hopes of scaring the intruder away, but swiftly decided that as isolated as the penthouse level was, the intruder might break in anyway and she would have sacrificed her advantage of surprise.

So she stood quietly behind the door and waited. It wasn't long before she heard clicks as the tumblers slipped and the lock turned. Sucking in a shallow breath, she balanced on the balls of her feet, crouching low for a solid stance, and raised the heavy sword with both hands.

The door opened slowly and a dark shape slipped in.

Swiftly, and perhaps harder than she'd intended, Chloe whipped the blade of the sword to his throat. She heard a swift intake of air, and suspected, as sharp as the blade was, she'd cut him.

Good, she thought.

"Och, Chloe-lass, please put the blade down," Dageus said softly.

Chloe screamed.

❧

Keltar mates ne'er come easily to their men. Some travel distances too vast and strange to fathom, others travel

but a short path, though a far distance in their hearts.
Most resist every step of the way, yet for each Keltar, one
woman will make that journey. 'Tis up to the Keltar to
claim her.

Silvan lay the tiny tome he'd found in the chamber library upon his lap. It was the only tome he'd risked removing from the chamber before sealing it. Now, ensconced in what had once been his bedchamber and private sanctuary—the tower library one hundred and three steps above the castle proper—he'd finished reading it. The book did not name its scribe, as did most in a request for a blessing upon he who'd scribed the words therein, and was comprised of only a few dozen tiny sheets of parchment. Yet those few sheets, a compendium on the mating of the Keltar males, had been fascinating.

And why haven't you claimed your mate, old man?

The answer to that was complicated, he brooded, glancing about the tower chamber.

Fat pillars of candles scattered across several small tables burned brightly, flickering in the warm night breeze, and he smiled, looking around his peaceful haven. As a lad, he'd delighted in everything about the tower, the spiraling stairs, the stones walls with their myriad cracks and crevices covered with thick tapestries, the breathtaking beauty of the view from the tall window in the spacious circular room. As an old man, he found it no less enchanting.

He'd sat in this same deep chair gazing out into the night as a man of a mere score of years, then two, and now three plus a few odd ones. He knew every wrinkle and rise of the land beyond his window. As much as he loved it, however, the solitude he'd sought as his salvation had in time become his prison, and he'd been more than ready to leave it a few years ago when he'd wed Nell and moved down into the castle proper.

Still, there were evenings, like this one, when he craved the lofty heights and a quiet place to think. Dageus and Chloe had left nearly a moon before, and he wondered how much time would have to pass before he finally accepted that he would ne'er know what had become of his son. Though he believed Dageus would do aught that must be done, not knowing the final outcome would plague him to the end of his days.

And Nellie too. The atmosphere in the castle had been somber indeed since they'd gone.

Nellie. How she'd blessed his life. Without her, he'd have lost both his sons and been living alone high atop the Keltar mountain.

Anon, he would blow out the candles and make his way down the winding stairs. He would go first to the nursery where their sons would be slumbering by now. He would sit beside them as he did every eve, and marvel over them. Marvel over the second chance at life he'd gotten when he'd least expected it.

He flipped open the tome to the page where his finger held the place.

The exchange of the binding vows will seal their hearts together for all eternity, and once mated, they can never love another.

And that was the crux of his problem. He'd not fully claimed his mate because of the age difference betwixt them. He knew he would die before her. Possibly long before her.

And then what? She wouldn't remarry because he was gone? She would spend the next score or two of years alone? The thought of her lying with another man made him nigh crazed, yet the thought of her lying alone in bed for so many years made him equally crazed. Nellie should be loved, cherished, petted, and caressed. She should be savored and . . . and . . . and—och! 'Twas an impossible conundrum!

It should be her choice, his conscience prodded.

"I'll think on it," he grumbled.

And if you die before you finish thinking on it?

Scowling, he slipped the tome into one of the clever pouches Nellie had stitched for him inside the blue robes he favored and was about to rise when he became aware of a presence in the room, standing just behind his shoulder.

He went motionless, reaching out with his Druid senses to identify the intruder, but whoever or whatever it was that stood behind him, defied his comprehension.

"Sit, Keltar," a silvery, lilting voice said.

He sat. He wasn't certain if he'd chosen to comply, or if her voice had robbed him of will.

As he sat tensely waiting, a woman stepped forward from the shadows behind him. Nay, a . . . och, a being. Wonderingly, he cocked his head, staring up at her. The creature was so brilliant, so lovely that he could scarce gaze upon her. She had eyes of iridescent hues, colors impossible to name. Hair of spun silver, a delicate, elfin, inhumanly beautiful face. He suddenly wondered if he'd gotten a bit of bad beef for dinner and was suffering some instability of the mind induced by poisoned digestion. Then a worse fear gripped him, one that made his head feel alarmingly light and his blood pound too fast inside his chest: mayhap 'twas his time, and this was Death, for she was certainly beautiful enough to lure any man to that great unknown that lay beyond. He could hear his own breath coming too fast and harsh, could feel his hands going curiously tingly, as if they were about to go numb. A cold sweat broke out on his skin.

I canna die now, he thought dimly. *I haven't claimed Nellie.* He wouldn't be able to bear it, he thought, blinking enormously heavy eyelids. They might never find each other again. He might be forced to suffer a hundred lives without her. 'Twould be the purest hell!

"Aoibheal, queen of the Tuatha Dé Danaan, bids you greeting, Keltar."

His vision blurred alarmingly, and his last thought before . . . er, before the stress of the moment temporarily leeched him of his wits, was relief that he wasn't dying, and fury at himself for missing even a second of what was surely the most thrilling event in his entire life.

The legendary Tuatha Dé Danaan had come! And what did the grand Keltar laird do?

Fainted like a willy-nilly peahen.

⨐

A few minutes later, Chloe was sitting on the sofa with her head between her knees, trying desperately to breathe.

Dageus was at her feet, his hands wrapped around her calves. "Lass, let me get a paper bag, you're hyperventilating."

"Don't you"—*pant-pant*—"DARE"—*pant-pant*—"leave me!" She clutched at his shoulders.

"I doona plan to leave you ever again, love," he said soothingly, stroking her hair. "I'm but going to the kitchen for a bag. Try to relax, sweet."

Chloe nearly screamed again out of sheer frustration. Relax. *As if.* She needed to hold him, to kiss him, to demand to be told what in the world was going on, but she couldn't get a deep enough breath to manage anything.

Standing there at the door, when she'd heard his voice

slicing through the darkness, she'd nearly fainted. The sword had clattered from her suddenly lifeless hands, her knees had turned to butter, and her lungs had simply stopped functioning properly. She'd thought hiccups were awful, but she'd take them over hyperventilating *any* day.

And she'd cut him! There was a thin line of blood on his neck. She tried to dab at it, but he caught both her hands in one of his, pressed them gently to her lap, then began moving toward the kitchen. She craned her head sideways and watched him go. How could this be? How was he alive? Oh, God, he was *alive*!

She couldn't take her eyes off him, and twisted around, following his progress, not letting him out of her sight for a minute. He was here. He was really here. He was real. She'd touched him.

She knew, from how ashen his face was, that her inability to get a deep breath was scaring him. It was scaring her too, so she forced herself to concentrate on unknotting inside.

By the time he returned with the paper bag, although she was still trembling visibly, she was managing complete breaths. She stared up at him, tears of joy spilling down her cheeks.

"How? How is this possible?" she cried, flinging herself into his arms.

"Och, lass," he purred, catching her in his embrace. He ducked his head and brushed his lips to hers. Once, twice, a dozen times. "I thought I'd lost you forever, Chloe," he groaned.

"*You*? So did I!"

More frantic kisses, deep and hungry. She locked her hands behind his neck, savoring the solidity of him, the warm press of his body against hers—a thing she'd thought she would never get to feel again.

Finally, Dageus murmured against her lips, "How did you get here, lass? How did you get back from Scotland so quickly?"

"Quickly?" Chloe drew back and gaped at him. "Dageus, it's been three and a half *weeks* since you disappeared." Just thinking about those awful weeks was enough to make her start crying again.

He gazed down at her, stunned. "Three and a half—ah! So that's what the queen meant," he exclaimed.

"The queen? What queen? What happened? Where have you been? And why were you picking the lock? Why didn't you just—oh!" She broke off and gazed deep into his exotic, sensual golden eyes.

Golden.

"Oh, Dageus," she breathed. "They're gone, aren't they? You're not just alive—you're *free*, aren't you?"

He flashed her a dazzling smile and laughed exultantly. "Aye, lass. They're gone. Forever. And as for picking the lock, since they're gone, I no longer know their spells. I'm afraid my thieving days are over, lass. Will you still be having me as little more than a man? A simple Keltar Druid, naught more?"

"Oh, I'll have you, Dageus MacKeltar," Chloe said fervently. "I'll have you any way I can get you."

It took dozens of kisses before she was finally calm enough—and convinced enough that he was real—that she let him pull her down onto his lap on the sofa and tell her what had happened.

When Silvan regained consciousness and stirred in his chair, the queen was sitting across from him, watching him intently.

"You're real," he managed to say.

She looked mildly amused. "It was recently drawn to my attention that perhaps we should not have left you so completely unguided. That perhaps you'd begun to think we weren't real. I wasn't convinced. I am now."

"What are you, precisely?" Silvan asked, abjectly fascinated.

"That would be difficult to explain in your language. I could show you, but you didn't fare so well with this form, so I think not."

Silvan stared at her, trying to commit every detail of her to memory.

"Your son is free, Keltar."

Silvan's heart leapt. "Dageus triumphed over the Draghar? Did he succeed in reimprisoning them?"

"In a manner of speaking. Suffice to say, he proved himself."

"And he lives?" Silvan pressed. "Is he with Chloe?"

"I gave him back to the woman who chose him as her consort. He can never return to this century. Already time has been altered more than is wise."

Silvan's mouth opened and closed several times as he tried to decide what to say. Nothing remotely intelligent occurred to him, so finally he settled for a simple, "Thank you for coming to tell me this." He was utterly flummoxed that the queen of the legendary race had bothered to come tell him.

"I didn't come to tell you this. You appeared weak upon awakening. I thought to increase your strength with glad tidings. We have work to do."

"We do?" His eyes widened.

"There is the small matter of a broken Compact. Broken in this century on the Keltar side. It must be resealed, here and now."

"Ah," he said.

"So you *did* take the knife from my neck," Chloe said, sniffling and wiping her eyes with a tissue. He'd told her everything: how the sect of the Draghar had drugged him with a potion that had made it impossible for him to control the use of magic, how he'd realized when they'd brought her in that he had only one choice left.

As she and Drustan had both suspected, Dageus had been honorable to the last—he'd tried to kill himself. "You were going to die and *leave* me," she hissed, thumping his chest with her fist. "I could almost hate you for that." She sighed gustily, knowing she loved him for it too. His honor was an integral part of him, and she wouldn't have him any other way.

"Believe me, lass, 'twas the most difficult thing I've ever forced myself to do. Bidding you farewell nigh ripped my heart to pieces. But the alternative was releasing something that might ultimately destroy—not only the world—but you as well. Think you I didn't suffer a thousand deaths fearing what the Draghar might do to you if I failed to die before they took me over? Verily, I never want to endure such fears again." He ran his hands up her arms, swept them into her hair and kissed her hard and demanding, his tongue gliding deep.

When they were both breathless, she said, "So what happened then?" She traced her fingers over his face, savoring the feel of his rough, unshaven jaw, the softness of his sinfully sensual lips. And oh—the sight of those clear, golden tiger-eyes with no shadows!

He told her that he'd used magic to rob her of vision and hearing so she wouldn't be forced to watch him change and die. A mere moment after he drove the knife into his heart, a man and a woman—of sorts—had appeared. The Tuatha Dé Danaan themselves.

"The Tuatha Dé came? You actually *met* them?" Chloe nearly shouted.

"Aye." Dageus smiled at the expression of insatiable curiosity on her face. He suspected he'd be forced to repeat this portion of his story dozens of times over the next fortnight, so she could be certain she hadn't missed a single detail. "They did something to the fallen sect members that made them disappear. I've no idea where they went. My chains fell away and the next thing I knew, they'd taken me somewhere . . . else. I was dimly aware that I was lying on a beach near an ocean in a place that was . . . unlike any other place I've ever been. The colors around me were so brilliant—"

"What about *them*?" Chloe exclaimed impatiently. "What were the Tuatha Dé like?"

"Not human, for a certainty. I suspect they truly doona look like us at all, though they choose to appear in a similar fashion. They are much as the legends describe them: tall, willowy, mesmerizing to behold. Verily, they are difficult to look at directly. Had I not been bleeding and so weak, like as not, their appearance would have fashed me far more than it did. They were immensely powerful. I could feel it in the air around them. I'd thought the ancient Druids possessed of great power, but they were mere dust motes compared to the Tuatha Dé."

"And? What happened?"

"They healed me." Dageus then explained what they'd done and why.

The woman had identified herself as the queen of the Tuatha Dé. She'd said that, though he'd broken his oath and used the stones for personal motive, he'd absolved himself by being willing to take his own life to prevent the Prophecy from being fulfilled. She'd said that by his actions, he'd proved himself worthy of the Keltar name, and hence was being given a second chance.

Dageus smiled wryly. "You should have seen me, Chloe-lass, lying there, believing that I was dying and never going to see you again, then realizing not only was she going to free me, but she planned to heal me and return me to you." He paused, pondering what else had transpired, but he couldn't think of a way to explain it because it hadn't made full sense to him.

He suspected it never would. There'd been a thick tension between the queen and the other Tuatha Dé, whom she'd called Adam. As he'd lain there, the queen had instructed Adam to heal him, but Adam had protested that Dageus was too near death. Adam had argued that it would cost him too much to save the mortal's life.

The queen replied that such was the price she was claiming due for the formal plea Adam had lodged—whatever that had meant.

The male Tuatha Dé had not been pleased. Verily, for such an otherworldly being, he'd seemed mortally horrified by her decree.

"What? What aren't you telling me?" Chloe said impatiently, cupping his face with her hands.

"Och, 'tis naught, lass. I was just thinking there were undercurrents betwixt the two Tuatha Dé that I didn't fathom. At any rate, Adam healed me and the queen lifted the souls of the Draghar from my body and destroyed them."

Chloe sighed happily. "Is that when she closed the stones?"

"Aye. She said she'd reconsidered and decided the power to move through time was not one man should yet possess."

"So why did it take you so long to get back here?"

"Chloe-love, for me, but a few hours have passed since that moment in the catacombs. Only when you told me that it's been nearly a month, did I understand what the queen meant when she said that time didn't pass the same way in our realms."

"So that part of the legend is true too!" Chloe exclaimed. "The ancient tales claim that a single year in the Tuatha Dé's realm is roughly a century in the mortal world."

"Aye. Theirs is a different dimension." He paused, staring down at her with a troubled gaze. He took in the sight of her swollen eyes, her reddened nose. "Och, lass, you've been grieving me for a long time," he said sadly. "I wouldn't have had such a thing happen. What did you do?"

"I waited with Gwen and Drustan and—oh! We have to call them!" She tried to squirm from his lap for the phone, but he tightened his arms around her, refusing to let her go.

"Anon, love. I'm so sorry you suffered. If I'd known—"

"If you'd known, what? If this is what had to happen so I could have you back, I don't have a single regret. It's okay. You're *here* now, and that's all that matters. I couldn't ask for anything more."

"I could," Dageus said quietly.

Chloe blinked, looking confused and a bit wounded.

Dageus kissed her tenderly. "I've been wanting to ask you this for so long, but I feared I may not have a future to promise you. I do now. Will you marry me, Chloe-lass? Here, at this moment, in the Druid way?"

And so commenced one of the most thrilling hours of Silvan MacKeltar's life. He sat across from the queen of the Tuatha Dé Danaan and renegotiated terms. It was fascinating; it was frustrating because she would tell him nothing of herself; it was exhilarating. She was clever, and immensely powerful, tenfold what he'd sensed in the Draghar.

There was no need to ask that the power of the stones be removed from their duties, for he'd felt them close shortly after Dageus had left. The ancient circle of stones had felt abruptly dead. Void of energy, left with a mere brush of presence that made them seem slightly more *there* than the surrounding landscape. When he inquired about it, she merely said that she'd reconsidered the Keltar's duties.

They squabbled a bit—he squabbled with the queen!—over a few minor points. Mostly because it was rather like a game of chess and finessing for the advantage was as much a part of her nature as it was his.

Gold was required, the amount unimportant, the queen told him, as it was simply a token, to be melted and added to the original Compact. Naught else was at hand, so he pledged the ring Nellie had given him on their wedding day.

Though she'd steadfastly refused to answer any of his questions about their race, she advised him that henceforth she would personally attend one Keltar in every generation so they would never lose sight of their place in things again.

And so The Compact was pledged anew and the responsibility of the stones was bid a grateful farewell, to be suffered again only on the day—and Silvan hoped it would not come for a very, very long time—that man discovered such dangerous secrets on his own.

When all was done and the queen had vanished, Silvan went in search of Nellie.

He had so much to tell her, yet first, there was an entirely different matter weighing heavily on his mind. In that moment he'd thought he was dying, he'd realized what a fool he'd been. He had to try. He had to at least offer, and let Nellie choose whether or not she wanted him forever.

He found her in their bedchamber, fluffing the pillows, preparing for bed. In his eyes, there was no woman more beautiful. In his heart, there was none more perfect.

"Nellie," he said softly.

She glanced up and smiled. It was a smile that said she loved him, a smile that beckoned him to join her in their bed.

Hurrying to her side, he plucked the pillow from her hand and tossed aside. He wanted her full attention.

And now that he had it, he found himself unaccountably nervous. He cleared his throat. He'd prepared, he'd rehearsed a dozen times what he was going to say, but now that the moment had come, now that he was gazing into her lovely eyes, it all seemed to have fled his mind. He ended up beginning rather badly.

"I'm going to die before you," he said flatly.

Nell gave a little snort of laughter and patted him reassuringly. "Och, Silvan, where do ye come up with yer—"

"Hush." He laid a gentle finger against her lips and kept it there.

Her eyes widened and she gazed at him inquiringly.

"The odds that I will die before you, Nellie, are significant. I would not have you grieve me. I ne'er offered my first wife the binding vows because she was not my mate, and I knew it. I ne'er offered them to you because you are my mate, and I knew it." He paused, searching for the right words. Her eyes were huge and round and she'd gone very still.

"That is without a doubt the most discombobulated bit of logic ye've e'er spouted, Silvan," she finally whispered against his finger.

"I couldn't bear the thought of leaving you alone, bound to me."

She took his finger from her lips and slipped her hand

into his. "I could bear any number of years, Silvan, if I know we'll meet again."

"Do you mean that? Truly?"

"How could ye doubt it? Have I not shown ye my love?"

Och, in so many ways, he thought, exhilarated. And it was nigh time he show her his. Gently, Silvan placed his hand between her breasts, above her heart, and rested his other above his own. "Place your hands atop mine."

She glanced down at his hand and her eyes narrowed. "What happened to yer ring?"

" 'Tis no band of simple metal that holds us together, Nellie. 'Tis something far greater than that. As to what happened to my ring, I gave it to the queen of the Tuatha Dé Danaan when she came and told me Dageus was alive and well, and free at last."

"What?" Nellie gasped.

"I'll tell you all anon." Silvan said impatiently. Now that he'd made up his mind to take the binding vows, he was desperate for her answer. He didn't want to waste another moment. He was frantic to claim her, lest something awful happen, like his heart give out before he could complete the vows. "Will you be saying the words after me, lass?"

"Och, life with ye is ne'er simple, is it?" she exclaimed. Then she smiled radiantly. "Aye, Silvan. I'll be saying the words."

Silvan's voice was firm and deep. "If aught must be lost . . ."

"So, how does one marry a Druid?" Chloe asked breathlessly. She couldn't stop touching him, couldn't believe that he was alive, that she had him back and everything had worked out.

With a finger beneath her chin, he tipped her face up for a soft kiss. "It's fairly simple, really. You nearly did it once," he said, flashing her a smile. A smile that fully reached his golden eyes, filling them with warmth. A smile that promised heated lovemaking the moment they completed his Druid rites. And she was definitely in need of some heated lovemaking. She felt as if she might burst from happiness.

His words penetrated a bit belatedly. She frowned, perplexed. "I did?"

"Aye." He placed one hand over her heart, the other over his own. "Place your hands atop mine, lass."

When she complied, he kissed her again, this time slow and sweet, holding her lower lip hostage for a long, delicious moment. Then he said, "Repeat after me, love."

She nodded, her eyes sparkling.

"If aught must be lost, 'twill be my honor for yours . . ."

❧

"I am Given," Nellie said, blinking back tears. Emotion swelled inside her, crashing through her like an ocean wave, and she might have fallen to her knees had Silvan not caught her in his arms.

"Aye, lass, now you're truly mine," he said fiercely. "Forever."

❧

"You *married* me that day in the heather?" Chloe shouted. "And you didn't tell me? *Ooh*! We are going to have to have a *serious* talk about how we communicate!" She scowled up at him. "And while we're on that subject, we still haven't discussed you leaving that night without telling me!"

"After the loving, lass," Dageus purred, lowering his

dark head to hers. "There will be plenty of time to speak of such things then."

And the loving, he vowed, as he slipped her sweater over her head, was going to take a very, *very* long time.

He was no longer dark; time was no longer his enemy. He'd claimed his mate, and the future loomed ahead of them, resplendent with promise.

SOURCES

The Celts, Juliette Wood, Duncan Baird Publishers

Heroes of the Dawn, Fleming, Husain, Littleton and Malcor, Duncan Baird Publishers

The Book Before Printing, David Diringer, Dover Publications

The Alphabet, David Diringer, The Philosophical Library, Inc.

Illuminated Manuscripts, Christopher De Hamel, Phaidon Press Ltd.

The World of the Druids, Miranda J. Green, Thames and Hudson, Ltd. London

Caesar Against the Celts, Ramon Jiménez, Castle Books

Dictionary of Celtic Mythology, James MacKillop, Oxford University Press

How the Irish Saved Civilization, Thomas Cahill, Doubleday

Irish Legends, Iain Zaczek, Collins & Brown, Ltd.

Dear Reader:

Many of you have written to ask me if there is a particular order in which one should read my Highlander novels, and how they are connected. I've written each of them to stand alone, yet I suspect the reading experience is richer if they are read in the following order: *Beyond the Highland Mist, To Tame A Highland Warrior, The Highlander's Touch, Kiss of the Highlander,* and *Dark Highlander.*

The novels are all connected to varying degrees. Adam Black, of the Tuatha Dé Danaan (pronounced "tua day dhanna"*), appears in *Beyond the Highland Mist, The Highlander's Touch,* and *The Dark Highlander.* Dageus's twin brother, Drustan, is the hero of *Kiss of the Highlander.*

The hero of *To Tame A Highland Warrior,* Grimm (Gavrael Roderick), is the best friend of the hero in *Beyond the Highland Mist,* Hawk Douglas. Adam Black knows there's more of a connection than that, but Adam's not talking.

I'd originally intended to write Adam Black's story next, however, I've found myself temporarily detoured by another story. I do plan to return and tackle the millennia-old, fascinatingly complex antihero Adam.

*Irish Legends, Iain Zaczek, Collins & Brown, Ltd.

So what's next for 2003? Here are a few key ingredients of the work in progress: a stubborn, intelligent heroine who gets drawn into a quest against her will when she comes into possession of a most unusual artifact; a powerful, mysterious, darkly sexual Highlander who is trying to help her . . . or kill her . . . ; and a fascinating mystery, the key to which has been hidden for centuries in an ancient Scottish chapel.

If you're itching for a hint about what's in store for Adam, Dageus's thoughts about the undercurrents between the two Tuatha Dé Danaan, when the queen told Adam to heal Dageus and Adam protested that it would "cost him too much" because the mortal was so close to death, were most apt:

The male Tuatha Dé had not been pleased. Verily, for such an otherworldly being, he'd seemed mortally horrified by her decree.

Mortally being the key word there.

All my best,
Karen

ABOUT THE AUTHOR

Karen Marie Moning graduated from Purdue University with a bachelor's degree in Society & Law. Her novels have appeared on both the *New York Times* and *USA Today*'s extended bestseller lists, and won numerous awards, including the prestigious RITA award.

You can visit Karen at: www.kmoning.bizland.com/tartan.